STORM WARNING
NIGHT OF THE FOX

Jack Higgins

STORM
WARNING

NIGHT OF
THE FOX

WHSMITH
EXCLUSIVE
· BOOKS ·

Storm Warning first published in Great Britain
in 1976 by William Collins Sons & Co. Ltd
Copyright © Jack Higgins 1976

Night of the Fox first published in Great Britain
in 1986 by William Collins Sons & Co. Ltd
Copyright © Jack Higgins 1986

This edition first produced exclusively
for WH Smith in 1990 by Grafton Books,
a division of Harper Collins, Publishers

ISBN 0 00 223716 4

Printed and bound in Great Britain by
The Bath Press, Avon

CONTENTS

STORM
WARNING

From the Journal of Rear Admiral Carey Reeve, USN
. . . and this I find the greatest mystery of all – the instinct in man to sacrifice himself that others might live. But then, courage never goes out of fashion, and at no other time im my life have I seen it better displayed than in the affair of the *Deutschland*. In the midst of the greatest war history has known, people on opposite sides in that conflict were able to come together for a time, take every risk, lay themselves on the line, in an attempt to save a handful of human beings from man's oldest and most implacable foe – the sea. I have never seen the tragic futility of war better demonstrated nor felt prouder of my fellow men than at that time . . .

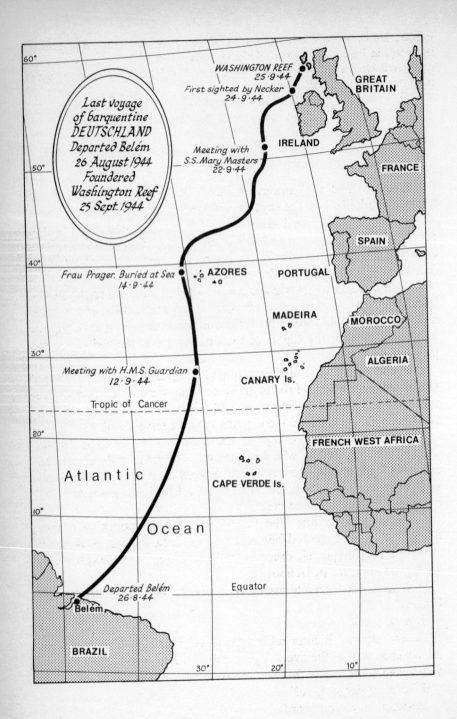

Last voyage
of barquentine
DEUTSCHLAND
Departed Belém
26 August 1944
Foundered
Washington Reef
25 Sept. 1944

WASHINGTON REEF
25·9·44
First sighted by Necker
24·9·44

GREAT BRITAIN

IRELAND

FRANCE

Meeting with
S.S. Mary Masters
22·9·44

SPAIN

Frau Prager. Buried at Sea
14·9·44

AZORES

PORTUGAL

MADEIRA

MOROCCO

ALGERIA

Meeting with H.M.S. Guardian
12·9·44

CANARY Is.

Tropic of Cancer

FRENCH WEST AFRICA

Atlantic

CAPE VERDE Is.

Ocean

Equator

Departed Belém
26·8·44

Belém

BRAZIL

Barquentine *Deutschland* 26 August 1944. Eleven days out of Rio de Janeiro. At anchorage in Belém. Begins hot. Moderate trades. Last of the coal unloaded. No cargo available. In ballast with sand for run to Rio. Hatches battened down and ready to sail. Rain towards evening.

One

As Prager turned the corner, thunder rumbled far out to sea and lightning flashed across the sky, giving for one brief moment a clear view of the harbour. The usual assortment of small craft and three or four coastal steamers were moored at the main jetty. The *Deutschland* was anchored in midstream, distinctive if only for the fact that she was the one sailing ship in the harbour.

Rain came suddenly, warm and heavy, redolent with rotting vegetation from the jungle across the river. Prager turned up the collar of his jacket and, holding his old leather briefcase under one arm, hurried along the waterfront towards the Lights of Lisbon, the bar at the end of the fish pier.

There was the sound of music, muted yet plain enough, a slow, sad samba with something of the night in it. As he went up the steps to the verandah he took off his spectacles and wiped rain from them with his handkerchief. He replaced them carefully and peered inside.

The place was empty, except for the bartender and Helmut Richter, the *Deutschland*'s bosun, who sat at the end of the bar with a bottle and a glass in front of him. He was a large, heavily-built man in reefer jacket and denim cap, with long, blond hair and a beard that made him look older than his twenty-eight years.

Prager stepped inside. The bartender, who was polishing a glass, looked up. Prager ignored him and moved along the bar, shaking the rain from his panama. He dropped the briefcase on the floor at his feet.

'A good night for it, Helmut.'

Richter nodded gravely and picked up the bottle. 'A drink, Herr Prager?'

'I think not.'

'A wise choice.' Richter refilled his glass. 'Cachaca. They say it rots the brain as well as the liver. A poor substitute for good Schnapps, but they haven't seen any of that since thirty-nine.'

'Is Captain Berger here?'

'Waiting for you on board.'

Prager picked up his briefcase again. 'Then I suggest we get moving. There isn't much time. Has anyone been asking for me?'

Before Richter could reply a voice said in Portuguese, 'Ah, Senhor Prager, a pleasant surprise.'

Prager turned quickly as the curtain of one of the small booths behind him was pulled back. The man who sat there, a bottle of wine in front of him, was immensely fat, his crumpled khaki uniform stained with sweat and bursting at the seams.

Prager managed a smile. 'Captain Mendoza. Don't you ever sleep?'

'Not very often. What is it this time, business or pleasure?'

'A little of both. As you know, the position of German nationals is a difficult one these days. Your government is more than ever insistent on a regular report.'

'So, it is necessary that Berger and his men are seen by you personally?'

'On the first day of the last week in each month. Your people in Rio are most strict in this respect.'

'And the good Senhora Prager? I am given to understand she was on the plane with you.'

'I have a few days' leave due and she has never seen this part of the country. It seemed the ideal opportunity.'

Richter slipped out without a word. Mendoza watched him go. 'A nice lad,' he said. 'What was it he used to be? Chief helmsman on a U-boat. Obersteuermann, isn't that the word?'

'I believe so.'

'You'll have a drink with me?'

Prager hesitated. 'Just a quick one, if you don't mind. I have an appointment.'

'With Berger?' Mendoza nodded to the barman who poured brandy into two glasses without a word. 'When does he leave to go back to Rio? In the morning?'

'I believe so.' Prager sipped the brandy, on dangerous ground now. He was sixty-five, an assistant consul at the German embassy in Rio until August 1942, when the Brazilians, enraged by the torpedoing of several of their merchant ships by U-boats, had declared war. Little more than a gesture, but it had presented the problem of what to do about German nationals – in particular the increasing number of sailors of the Kriegsmarine who found themselves washed up on her shores.

Prager, having spent twenty years in the country, and being acceptable in high places, had been left behind to cope with that. There were, after all, five thousand miles of ocean between Brazil and Germany so no need to set up expensive internment camps. The Brazilian government was content with the monthly reports he presented on his fellow citizens. As long as they were gainfully employed and not a charge on the state, everyone was happy.

Mendoza said, 'I've been harbourmaster here for two years now and for most of that time the *Deutschland* has been coming in regularly. Say every couple of months.'

'So?'

'A boat of that size usually manages with a master, mate, bosun, probably six foremast hands and a cook.'

'That is correct.'

Mendoza sipped a little of his wine thoughtfully. 'According to my information, Berger has a crew of something like twenty this trip.'

He smiled genially, but the eyes in the fat face were sharp. Prager said carefully, 'There are many German seamen in Rio.'

'And more each day. The war, my friend, does not go well for you.'

'Berger is probably trying to employ as many as possible.'

Mendoza smiled beautifully. 'But of course. That explanation had not occurred to me. But I mustn't keep you. Perhaps we'll have time for another drink tomorrow?'

'I hope so.'

Prager went out quickly. Richter was waiting on the verandah by the steps. Beyond, the rain hammered relentlessly into the ground. 'Everything all right?' he asked.

'Not really,' Prager told him. 'He knows something's going on. But how could he possibly suspect the truth? No one in his right mind would believe it.' He clapped Richter on the shoulder. 'Now let's get moving.'

The bosun said, 'I didn't get a chance to tell you inside, but there was someone asking for you.'

There was a movement behind and, as Prager turned, a nun in tropical-white habit stepped into the light. She was a small woman, not much over five feet tall, with clear, untroubled eyes and a calm, unlined face.

'Sister Angela,' Richter said.

'. . . of the Sisters of Mercy from the mission station on the Rio Negro. Introductions are not necessary, Helmut. Sister Angela and I are old acquaintances.'

He took off his panama and held out his hand which she clasped briefly in a grasp of surprising strength.

'It's good to see you again, Sister.'

'And you, Herr Prager. I think you know why I'm here.'

'Why, yes, Sister.' Otto Prager smiled warmly. 'I believe I do.'

* * *

An anchor light hung from the *Deutschland*'s forestay, as required by marine regulations, and this they saw first as Richter worked the dinghy across the harbour. Then suddenly she was very close, her masts and spars dark against the sky.

Prager looked up with conscious pleasure as he climbed the Jacob's ladder. She was a three-masted barquentine built by Hamish Campbell on the Clyde in 1881 and built with love and understanding and grace, with an elegant clipper bow to her and an extended jib-boom.

She had spent a lifetime in trade; Newcastle-on-Tyne with steam coal for Valparaiso; Chilean nitrates for America's west coast; lumber for Australia; wool for Britain . . . an endless circle, as sail died in a doomed attempt to combat steam, one owner after another through three changes of name until, finally, she had been bought by the Brazilian firm of Mayer Brothers, a family of German extraction, who had rechristened her *Deutschland* and put her to the coastal trade. Rio to Belém and the mouth of the Amazon – just the craft for such waters, having a draught of only eight feet fully loaded.

Prager went over the bulwark and extended his hand to Sister Angela. Richter was close behind on the ladder. Three seamen by the main mast gazed in astonishment as the little nun came over the side, and one of them hurried forward to take her other hand.

She thanked him, and Prager said to her, 'I think it would be better if I spoke to Captain Berger alone to start with.'

'Whatever you think best, Herr Prager,' she said tranquilly.

He turned to Richter. 'Take the good sister down to the saloon, then wait for me outside the Captain's cabin.'

Richter and Sister Angela descended the companionway and Prager went aft towards the quarterdeck. Berger's cabin was underneath. He hesitated, then braced himself, knocked on the door and went in.

The cabin was small, spartan in its furnishings – narrow bunk and three cupboards and not much else except for the desk behind which Berger sat, making a measurement with parallel rulers on the chart spread before him.

He glanced up, and there was relief in his eyes. 'I was beginning to get worried.'

He was at that time forty-eight years old, of medium height with good shoulders, his wiry, dark hair and beard flecked with grey, and his face weathered by sea and sun.

'I'm sorry,' Prager said. 'We ran into a bad electric storm on the flight from Rio. The pilot insisted on touching down at Carolina until the weather cleared. We were there for four hours.'

Berger opened a sandalwood box and offered him a cheroot. 'What's the latest war news?'

'All bad.' Prager sat in the chair opposite and accepted a light. 'On the fifteenth of this month American and French forces landed on the Mediterranean coast. Two days ago French tanks entered Paris.'

Berger whistled softly. 'Next stop the Rhine.'

'I should imagine so.'

'And then Germany.' He stood up, crossed to one of the cupboards, opened it and took out a bottle of rum and two glasses. 'What about the Russians?'

'The Red Army is on the borders of East Prussia.'

Berger poured rum into the glasses and pushed one across. 'You know, Otto, we Germans haven't had to defend the soil of the Fatherland since Napoleon. It should prove an interesting experience.'

'Brazil might be the best place to be for the next year or two,' Prager said. 'A hell of a time to go home.'

'Or the only time,' Berger said. 'It depends on your point of view. Have you got the papers?'

Prager put his briefcase on the desk. 'Everything needed and I've checked again on the barquentine you mentioned when you first spoke of this crazy affair, the *Gudrid Andersen*. She's still in Gothenburg harbour. Hasn't been to sea since the first year of the war.'

'Excellent,' Berger said. 'Plain sailing from here on, then.'

'You are fully prepared?'

Berger opened a cupboard and took out a lifejacket which he dropped on the desk. The legend *Gudrid Andersen – Gothenburg* was stencilled on the back.

'And this, of course.' He produced next a Swedish ensign. 'A most important item as I'm sure you'll agree.' He smiled. 'Everything is ready, believe me. The official change of name we'll make once clear of the coastal shipping lanes.'

'And the log?'

'I've already prepared a false one in the name of the *Gudrid Andersen* for use with our friends from the other side if we should be so unlucky as to run into them. The true log of the *Deutschland* I shall continue to keep privately. It would not be correct to do otherwise.' He put the lifejacket and ensign back in the cupboard. 'As for you, old friend, what can I say? Without your hard work during these past few months, the information you have obtained, the forged papers, we could not have ever begun to contemplate such an enterprise.'

Prager said carefully, 'There is just one more thing to discuss, Erich.'

'What's that?'

Prager hesitated, then said, 'Seven passengers.'

Berger laughed harshly. 'You must be joking.'

'No, I'm perfectly serious. You've carried them before, haven't you?'

'You know damned well I have.' There was something close to anger in Berger's voice. 'I have accommodation for eight passengers. Two cabins on either side of the saloon, two bunks to each. I should also point out that this ship is amply crewed by ten men including myself. At the moment, we are twenty-two, as you very well know. Seven passengers would mean that the additional crew would have to bunk elsewhere. An impossible situation.'

'But you'll be in ballast,' Prager said. 'No cargo, and surely genuine passengers would only strengthen your cover story?'

'Who are these passengers?'

'Germans, like you and your men, who want to go home.' Prager took a deep breath and carried on. 'All right, you might as well know the worst. They're nuns. Sisters of Mercy from a mission station on the Negro. I've been visiting them regularly for the past two years, just like all the other Germans on my list. Every three months; a special dispensation from the authorities as the place is so difficult to get to.'

Berger stared at him in astonishment. 'For God's sake, Otto, am I going out of my mind or are you?'

Prager got up without a word and opened the cabin door. Richter was standing outside smoking a cigarillo. Prager nodded and the bosun hurried away.

'Now what?' Berger demanded.

'I brought one of them on board with me. The others are waiting on shore. At least hear what she has to say.'

'You must be out of your head. It's the only conceivable explanation.'

There was a knock at the door. Prager opened it and Sister Angela stepped inside. He said, 'Sister, I'd like you to meet Fregattenkapitän Erich Berger. Erich, this is Sister Angela of the Little Sisters of Mercy.'

'Good evening Captain,' she said.

Berger looked down at the tiny nun for a moment, an expression of astonishment on his face, then he grabbed Prager by the arm and pushed him outside into the rain, pulling the cabin door behind him.

'What in the hell am I going to do? What am I supposed to say?'

'You're the captain,' Prager told him. 'You make the decisions and no one else, or so I've always been given to understand. I'll wait for you here.'

He walked to the mizzen shrouds on the port side. Berger cursed softly, hesitated, then went back in.

She was standing behind the desk, leaning over the chronometer in its box under a glass plate. She glanced up. 'Beautiful, Captain. Quite beautiful. What is it?'

'The seaman's measure of the heavens, Sister, along with a sextant. If I can check the position of the sun, moon and stars then I can discover my own exact position on the earth's surface – with the help of tables as well of course.'

She turned to the desk. 'A British Admiralty chart. Why is that?'

'Because they're the best,' Berger told her, feeling for some reason incredibly helpless.

'I see.' She carried on in the same calm voice. 'Are you going to take us with you?'

'Look, Sister,' he said. 'Sit down and let me explain.' He pulled another chart forward. 'Here we are at the mouth of the Amazon and this is the route home.' He traced a finger up past the Azores and west of Ireland. 'And if we get that far, there could be even greater hazards to face.' He tapped at the chart. 'We must pass close to the Outer Hebrides in Scotland, a graveyard for sailing ships, especially in bad weather – which is usually six days out of seven up there. And if we survive that, we only have the Orkneys passage, the run to Norway, then down through the Kattegat to Kiel,' he added with heavy irony. 'Five thousand miles, that's all.'

'And how long will it take us?'

He actually found himself answering, 'Impossible to say. Forty, maybe fifty days. So much depends on the weather.'

'That seems very reasonable, under the circumstances.'

Berger said, 'Tell me something. When you first came out here, how did you make the trip?'

'A passenger liner. The *Bremen*. That was just before the war, of course.'

'A fine ship. Comfortable cabins, hot and cold running water. Food that wouldn't disgrace a first-class hotel. Stewards to fetch and carry.'

'What exactly are you trying to say, Captain?'

'That on this ship, life would be very different. Bad food, cramped quarters. A lavatory bucket to empty daily. Salt water only to wash in. And a blow – a real blow under sail – can be a frightening experience. In bad weather we can spend a fortnight at a time without a dry spot in her from stem to stern. Have you ever strapped yourself into a bunk in wet blankets with a full gale trying to tear the sticks out of the deck above your head?' He rolled up the chart and said firmly, 'I'm sorry. I can't see any point in prolonging this discussion.'

She nodded thoughtfully. 'Tell me something. How does a German naval officer come to command a Brazilian trading vessel?'

'I was captain of a submarine supply ship, the *Essen*, camouflaged as the US fuel ship *George Grant*. We were torpedoed in the South Atlantic on our third trip by a British submarine, which wasn't taken in by the disguise. You may consider that ironic in view of the fact that I intend to try and pass the *Deutschland* off as a similar ship of Swedish registration.'

'And how did you manage to reach Brazil?'

'Picked up by a Portuguese cargo boat and handed over to the Brazilian authorities when we reached Rio. The Brazilians have been operating a kind of parole system for any of us who can find work. The Mayer Brothers, who own the *Deutschland*, are coastal traders, Brazilian citizens but German by origin. They've helped a great many of us. We make the run from Rio to Belém and back once a month with general cargo.'

'And you repay them now by stealing their boat?'

'A point of view; for which I can only hope they'll forgive me when they know the facts. But we don't really have any choice.'

'Why not?'

'The Brazilians are starting to play a more active part in the war. Last month they sent troops to Italy. I think things could get much more difficult for us here.'

'And the other reason?'

'You think I have one?'

She waited, hands folded, saying nothing. Berger shrugged, opened the drawer of his desk and took out a wallet. He extracted a snapshot and passed it across. It was badly creased and discoloured by salt water, but the smiles on the faces of the three small girls were still clear enough.

'Your children?'

'Taken in forty-one. Heidi, on the left, will be ten now. Eva is eight and Else will be six in October.'

'And their mother?'

'Killed in a bombing raid on Hamburg three months ago.'

She crossed herself automatically. 'What happened to the children?'

'Herr Prager got word about them for me through our embassy in the Argentine. My mother has them in Bavaria.'

'Thank God in his infinite mercy.'

'Should I?' Berger's face was pale, jaw set. 'Germany is going under, Sister, a matter of months only. Can you imagine how bad it's going to be? And my mother's an old woman. If anything happens to her . . .' A kind of shudder seemed to pass through his body and he leaned heavily on the desk. 'I want to be with them because that's where I'm needed, not here on the edge of the world, so far off that the war has ceased to exist.'

'And for that you'll dare anything?'

'Including five thousand miles of ocean dominated completely by the British and American navies, in a patched-up sailing ship that hasn't been out of sight of land in twenty years or more. An old tub, that hasn't had a refit for longer than I care to remember. An impossible voyage.'

'Which Herr Richter, your bosun, is apparently willing to make.'

'Helmut is a special case. The finest sailor I've ever known. He has invaluable experience under sail. Served his time as a boy on Finnish windjammers on the Chilean nitrate run. That may not mean a lot to you, but to seamen anywhere . . .'

'But according to Herr Prager there are another twenty men in your crew who are also willing to make this so-called impossible voyage.'

'Most of them with a reason roughly similar to mine. I can think of at least seventy men in Rio who would gladly stand in their shoes. They held a lottery for the last ten places in a German bar on the Rio waterfront two weeks ago.' He shook his head. 'They want to go home, Sister, don't you see? And for that, to use your own words, they'll dare anything.'

'And my friends and I are different, is that it? We too, have families, Captain, as dear to us as yours. More than that, because of what lies ahead, home is where we are needed now.'

Berger stood staring at her for a moment, then shook his head. 'No. In any case, it's too late. You'd need Swedish papers, that's an essential part of the plan. Prager's arranged them for all of us.'

She got to her feet, opened the cabin door and called, 'Herr Prager!'

He moved in out of the rain. 'What is it?'

'My papers, please. May I have them now?'

Prager opened his briefcase. He searched inside, then took out a passport which he dropped on the desk in front of Berger.

Berger frowned. 'But this is Swedish.' He opened it and Sister Angela stared out at him from the photo. He looked up. 'I wonder if you'd be so kind as to step outside for a moment, Sister. I'd like a few words with my good friend here.'

She hesitated, glanced briefly at Prager, then went out.

Prager said, 'Look, Erich, let me explain.'

Berger held up the passport. 'Not something you can pick up at twenty-four hours' notice, so you must have known about this for quite some time. Why in the hell didn't you tell me?'

'Because I knew you'd react exactly as you are doing.'

'So you thought you'd leave it until it was too late for me to say no?

Well, you made a mistake. I won't play. And what about this mission station they've been operating? Is it suddenly so unimportant?'

'The Brazilian Department of the Interior has changed its policy on the Indians in that area; moving them out and white settlers in. The mission was due to close anyway.'

'They're a nursing order, aren't they? Surely there must be some other outlet for their talents up there.'

'They are also Germans, Erich. What do you think it's going to be like when those first Brazilian casualty figures start filtering through from Italy?'

There was a long pause. Berger picked up the Swedish passport, opened it and examined the photo again. 'She looks like trouble to me. She's been used to getting her own way for too long.'

'Nonsense,' Prager said. 'I knew her family from the old days. Good Prussian stock. Her father was an infantry general. She was a nurse on the Western Front in nineteen-eighteen.'

Berger's astonishment showed. 'A hell of a background for a Little Sister of Mercy. What went wrong? Was there some sort of scandal?'

'Not at all. There *was* a young man, I believe. A flier.'

'. . . who didn't come back one fine morning so she sought refuge in a life of good works.' Berger shook his head. 'It's beginning to sound like a very bad play.'

'But you've got it all wrong, Erich. The way I heard it, he simply let her think he was dead. She had a breakdown that almost cost her life and was just coming out of it nicely when she met him walking along the Unter den Linden one day with another girl on his arm.'

Berger held up both hands. 'No more. I know when I'm beaten. Bring her back in.'

Prager went to the door quickly and opened it. She was standing outside talking to the bosun.

Berger said, 'You win, Sister. Tell Richter to have you taken ashore to collect the rest of your friends. Be back here by two a.m. because that's when we leave, and if you aren't here, we go without you.'

'God bless you, Captain.'

'I think he's got enough on his plate at the moment without me.' As she moved to the door, he added, 'Just one thing. Try not to let the crew know before they have to.'

'Are they likely to be disturbed by our presence?'

'Very much so. Sailors are superstitious by nature. Amongst other things, sailing on a Friday is asking for trouble. Taking any kind of a minister along as a passenger, the same. We should certainly pick up all the bad luck in the world with seven nuns sailing with us.'

'Five, Captain. Only five,' she said and went out.

Berger frowned and turned to Prager. 'You said seven passengers.'

'So I did.' Prager rummaged in the briefcase and produced two more Swedish passports which he pushed across the desk. 'One for Gertrude and one for me. She, too, is waiting on shore with our baggage which includes, I might add, that wireless transmitter you asked me to try and get you.'

Berger gazed at him in stupefaction. 'You and your wife?' he said hoarsely. 'Good God, Otto, you're sixty-five if you're a day. And what will your masters in Berlin say?'

'From what I hear, the Russians are far more likely to get there before I do, so it doesn't really matter.' Prager smiled gently. 'You see, Erich, we want to go home, too.'

When Berger went up to the quarterdeck just before two it was raining harder than ever. The entire crew was assembled on the deck below, faces pale, oilskins glistening in the dim glow of the deck lights.

He gripped the rail, leaned forward and spoke in a low voice. 'I won't say much. You all know the score. It's one hell of a trip, I'm not going to pretend any different, but if you do as I tell you, we'll make it, you and I and the old *Deutschland* together.'

There was a stirring amongst them, no more than that, and he carried on, a touch of iron in his voice now. 'One more thing. As most of you will have observed, we're carrying passengers. Herr Prager, once assistant consul at our embassy in Rio and his wife, and five nuns from a mission station on the Negro.'

He paused. There was only the hissing of the rain as they all waited. 'Nuns,' he said, 'but still women and it's a long journey home, so let me make myself plain. I'll personally shoot the first man to step over the line, and so enter it in the log.' He straightened. 'Now everyone to his station.'

As he turned from the rail his second-in-command moved out of the darkness to join him. Leutnant zur See Johann Sturm, a tall, fair youth from Minden in Westphalia, had celebrated his twentieth birthday only three days earlier. Like Richter, he was a submariner and had served in a U-boat as second watch officer.

'Everything under control, Mr Sturm?' Berger enquired in a low voice.

'I think so, Captain.' Sturm's voice was surprisingly calm. 'I've stowed the wireless transmitter Herr Prager brought with him from Rio in my cabin, as you ordered. It's not much, I'm afraid, sir. A limited range at the best.'

'Better than nothing,' Berger told him. 'And the passengers? Are they safely stowed away also?'

'Oh yes, sir.' There was a hint of laughter in the boy's voice. 'I think you could say that.'

A white figure appeared out of the darkness and materialized as Sister Angela. Berger swallowed hard and said in a low, dangerous voice, 'Could you now, Mr Sturm?'

Sister Angela said brightly, 'Are we leaving, Captain? Is it all right if I watch?'

Berger glared at her helplessly, rain dripping from the peak of his cap, then turned to Sturm and said, 'Haul up the spanker and outer jib only, Mr Sturm, and let the anchor chain go.'

Sturm repeated the order and there was a sudden flurry of activity. One seaman dropped down the forepeak hatch. Four others hauled briskly on the halliard and the spanker rose slowly. A moment later there was a rattle as the anchor chain slithered across the deck, then a heavy splash.

Richter was at the wheel but, for the moment, nothing seemed to happen. Then Sister Angela, glancing up, saw through a gap in the curtain of rain, stars pass across the jib.

'We're moving, Captain! We're moving!' she cried, as excitedly as any child.

'So I've observed,' Berger told her. 'Now will you kindly oblige me by going below.'

She went reluctantly and he sighed and turned to the bosun. 'Steady as she goes, Richter. She's all yours.'

And Richter took her out through the harbour entrance, drifting along like some pale ghost, barely moving, leaving a slight swirl of phosphorescence in her wake.

Fifteen minutes later, as Captain Mendoza sat playing whist in his booth at the Lights of Lisbon with a young lady from the establishment next door, the man he had assigned to keep watch on the fish pier burst in on him.

'What is it?' Mendoza demanded mildly.

'The *Deutschland*, Senhor Capitan,' the watchman whispered. 'She is gone.'

'Indeed.' Mendoza laid his cards face down on the table and stood up. 'Watch her, José,' he called to the barman. He picked up his cap and oilskin coat and went out.

When he reached the end of the fish pier, the rain was falling harder than ever in a dark impenetrable curtain. He lit a cigar in cupped hands and stared into the night.

'Will you notify the authorities, senhor?' the watchman enquired.

Mendoza shrugged. 'What is there to notify? Undoubtedly Captain Berger wished an early start for the return trip to Rio, where he is due in eight days from now, although it would not be uncommon for him to be perhaps one week overdue, the weather at this time of the year being so unpredictable. Time enough for any official enquiry needed to be made then.'

The watchman glanced at him uncertainly, then bobbed his head. 'As you say, Senhor Capitan.'

He moved away and Mendoza looked out over the river towards the mouth of the Amazon and the sea. How far to Germany? Nearly five thousand miles, across an ocean that was now hopelessly in the grip of the American and British navies. And in what? A three-masted barquentine long past her prime.

'Fools,' he said softly. 'Poor, stupid, magnificent fools.' And he turned and went back along the fish pier through the rain.

Barquentine *Deutschland*. 9 September 1944. Lat. 25°.01N., long. 30°.46W. Fourteen days out of Belém. Wind NW 6–8. Hove the log and found we were going twelve knots. In the past twenty-four hours we have run two hundred and twenty-eight miles. Frau Prager still confined to her bunk with the sea-sickness which has plagued her since leaving Belém. Her increasing weakness gives us all cause for concern. Heavy rain towards evening.

Two

The morning weather forecast for sea area Hebrides had been far from promising: winds 5 to 6 with rain squalls. Off the north-west coast of Skye, things were about as dirty as they could be – heavy, dark clouds swollen with rain, merging with the horizon.

Except for the occasional seabird, the only living thing in that desolation was the motor gunboat making south-west for Barra, her Stars and Stripes ensign the one splash of colour in the grey morning.

Dawn was at six-fifteen, but at nine-thirty visibility was still bad enough to keep the RAF grounded. No one on board the gunboat could have been blamed for failing to spot the lone Junkers 88S coming in low off the sea astern. The first burst of cannon shell kicked fountains of water high into the air ten or fifteen yards to port. As the plane banked for a second run, the 13mm machine-gun firing from the rear of the cockpit canopy loosed off a long burst that ripped into the deck aft of the wheelhouse.

Harry Jago, in his bunk below trying to snatch an hour's sleep, was awake in an instant, and making for the companionway. As he reached the deck, the gun crew were already running for the twin 20mm anti-aircraft cannon. Jago beat them into the bucket seat, hands clamping around the trigger handles.

Suddenly, as the Junkers came in off the water for the second time, heavy, black smoke swirled across the deck. Jago started to fire as its cannon punched holes in the deck beside him.

The Junkers was making its pass at close to four hundred miles an hour. He swung to follow it, aware of Jansen on the bridge above him working the Browning. But it was all to no purpose, and the Junkers curved away to port through puff-balls of black smoke and fled into the morning.

Jago stayed where he was for a moment, hands still gripping the handles. Then he got out of the seat and turned to Leading Seaman Harvey Gould, who was in charge of the anti-aircraft cannon.

'You were five seconds too late, you and your boys.'

The men of the gun crew shuffled uneasily. 'It won't happen again, Lieutenant,' Gould said.

'See that it doesn't.' Jago produced a crumpled pack of cigarettes from his shirt pocket and stuck one in his mouth. 'Having survived the Solomons, D-Day and the worst those E-boat flotillas in the English Channel could offer, it would look kind of silly to die in the Hebrides.'

The pilot of the Junkers, Captain Horst Necker, logged his attack as having taken place at 09.35 hours precisely. A hit-and-run affair of no particular importance which had served to enliven an otherwise boring routine patrol, especially for a pilot who in the spring of that year, during the renewed night attacks on London, had been employed by the elite pathfinder *Gruppe* 1/KG 66 with the kind of success that had earned him the Knight's Cross only two months previously.

It had been something of a come-down to be transferred to KG 40 based at Trondheim, a unit specializing in shipping and weather reconnaissance, although the JU 88S they had given him to fly was certainly a superb plane – an all-weather machine capable of a top speed of around four hundred miles per hour.

His mission that morning had one purpose. To look for signs of a convoy expected to leave Liverpool for Russia that week, although the exact day of departure was unknown. He had crossed Scotland at thirty thousand feet to spend a totally abortive couple of hours west of the Outer Hebrides.

The sighting of the gunboat had been purest chance, following an impulse to go down to see just how low the cloud base was. The target, once seen, was too tempting to pass up.

As he climbed steeply after the second attack, Rudi Hubner, the navigator, laughed excitedly. 'I think we got her, Herr Hauptmann. Lots of smoke back there.'

'What do you think, Kranz?' Necker called to the rear gunner.

'Looks like they made it themselves to me, Herr Hauptmann,' Kranz replied. 'Somebody down there knows his business and they weren't *Tommis* either. I saw the Stars and Stripes as we crossed over the second time. Probably my brother Ernst,' he added gloomily. 'He's in the American navy. Did I ever tell you that?'

Schmidt, the wireless operator, laughed. 'The first time over London with the port engines on fire, and you've mentioned it on at least fifty-seven different occasions since. I suppose it shows that at least one person in your family has brains.'

Hubner ignored him. 'A probable then, Herr Hauptmann?' he suggested.

Necker was going to say no, then saw the hope in the boy's eyes and changed his mind. 'I don't see why not. Now let's get out of here.'

When Jago went up to the bridge there was no sign of Jansen. He leaned against the Browning and looked down. The smoke had almost cleared and Gould was kicking the burned-out flare under the rail into the sea. The deck was a mess by the port rail beside the anti-aircraft gun, but otherwise things didn't look too bad.

Jansen came up the ladder behind him. He was a tall, heavily-built man and in spite of the tangled black beard, the knitted cap and faded reefer coat with no rank badges, was a chief petty officer. A lecturer in Moral Philosophy at Harvard before the war and a fanatical weekend yachtsman, he had resolutely defeated every attempt to elevate him to commissioned rank.

'A lone wolf, Lieutenant.'

'You can say that again,' Jago told him. 'A JU 88 in the Hebrides.'

'And one of the Reichsmarschall's later models, to judge by his turn of speed.'

'But what in the hell was he doing here?'

'I know, Lieutenant,' Jansen said soothingly. 'It's getting so you can't depend on anyone these days. I've already checked below, by the way. Superficial damage. No casualties.'

'Thanks,' Jago said. 'And that smoke flare was quick thinking.'

He found that his right hand was trembling slightly and held it out. 'Would you look at that. Wasn't it yesterday I was complaining that the only thing we got to fight up here was the weather?'

'Well, you know what Heidegger had to say on that subject, Lieutenant.'

'No, I don't Jansen, but I'm sure you're going to tell me.'

'He argued that for authentic living what is necessary is the resolute confrontation of death.'

Jago said patiently, 'Which is exactly what I've been doing for two years now and you've usually been about a yard behind me. Under the circumstances, I'll tell you what you can do with Heidegger, Jansen. You can put him where grandma had the pain. And try to rustle up some coffee while I check over the course again.'

'As the Lieutenant pleases.'

Jago went into the wheelhouse and slumped into the chart-table chair. Petersen had the wheel – a seaman with ten years in the merchant service before the war, including two voyages to Antarctica in whalers.

'You okay?' Jago demanded.

'Fine, Lieutenant.'

Jago pulled out British Admiralty chart 1796. *Barra Head to Skye*. South Uist, Barra and a scattering of islands below it, with Fhada, their destination, at the southern end of the chain. The door was kicked open and Jansen came in with a mug of coffee which he put on the table.

'What a bloody place,' Jago said, tapping the chart. 'Magnetic anomalies reported throughout the entire area.'

'Well, that's helpful,' Jansen said. 'Just the thing when you're working out a course in dirty weather.'

'Those islands south of Uist are a graveyard,' Jago went on. 'Everywhere you look on the damned chart it says *Heavy Breakers or Dangerous Seas*. One hazard after another.'

Jansen unfolded a yellow oilskin tobacco pouch, produced a pipe and started to fill it, leaning against the door. 'I was talking to some fishermen in Mallaig before we left. They were telling me that sometimes the weather out there is so bad, Fhada's cut off for weeks at a time.'

'The worst weather in the world when those Atlantic storms start moving in,' Jago said. 'God knows what it must be like in winter.'

'Then what in the hell is Admiral Reeve doing in a place like that?'

'Search me. I didn't even know he was up here till I was told to pick up that dispatch for him in Mallaig and deliver it. Last I heard of him was D-day. He was deputy director of operations for Naval Intelligence and got himself a free trip on the Norwegian destroyer *Svenner* that was sunk by three Möwe-class torpedo boats. He lost his right eye and they tell me his left arm's only good for show.'

'A hell of a man,' Jansen said. 'He got out of Corregidor after MacArthur left. Sailed a lugger nearly six hundred miles to Cagayan and came out on one of the last planes. As I remember, he went down in a destroyer at Midway, was taken aboard the *Yorktown* and ended up in the water again.'

'Careful, Jansen. Your enthusiasm is showing and I didn't think that was possible where top brass was concerned.'

'But this isn't just another admiral we're talking about, Lieutenant. He's responsible for an excellent history of naval warfare and probably the best biography of John Paul Jones in print. Good God, sir, the man can actually read and write.' Jansen put a match to the bowl of his pipe and added out of the side of his mouth, 'Quite an accomplishment for any naval officer, as the Lieutenant will be the first to agree?'

'Jansen', Jago said. 'Get the hell out of here.'

Jansen withdrew and Jago swung round to find Petersen grinning hugely. 'Go on, you too! I'll take over.'

'Sure thing, Lieutenant.'

Petersen went out and Jago reached for another cigarette. His fingers had stopped trembling. Rain spattered against the window as the MGB lifted over another wave and it came to him, with a kind of wonder, that he was actually enjoying himself, in spite of the aching back, the constant fatigue that must be taking years off his life.

Harry Jago was twenty-five and looked ten years older, even on a good day, which was hardly surprising when one considered his war record.

He'd dropped out of Yale in March 1941 to join the navy and was assigned to PT boats, joining Squadron Two in time for the Solomons' campaign. The battle for Guadalcanal lasted six months. Jago went in at one end a crisp, clean nineteen-year-old ensign and emerged a lieutenant, junior grade, with a Navy Cross and two boats shot from under him.

Afterwards Squadron Two was recommissioned and sent to England at the urgent request of the Office of Strategic Services to land and pick up American agents on the French coast. Again Jago survived, this time the Channel, the constant head-on clashes with German E-boats out of Cherbourg. He even survived the hell of Omaha beach on D-day.

His luck finally ran out on 28 June, when E-boats attacked a convoy of American landing craft waiting in Lyme Bay to cross the Channel. Jago arrived with dispatches from Portsmouth to find himself facing six of the best that the Kriegsmarine could supply. In a memorable ten-minute engagement, he sank one, damaged another, lost five of his crew and ended up in the water with shrapnel in his left thigh, the right cheek laid open to the bone.

When he finally came out of hospital in August they gave him what was left of his old crew, nine of them, and a new job: the rest that he so badly needed, playing postman in the Hebrides to the various American and British weather stations and similar establishments in the islands in a pre-war MGB, courtesy of the Royal Navy, that started to shake herself to pieces if he attempted to take her above twenty knots. Some previous owner had painted the legend *Dead End* underneath the bridge rail, a sentiment capable of several interpretations.

Just for a month or two, the squadron commander had told Jago. *Look on it as a kind of holiday. I mean to say, nothing ever happens up there, Harry.*

Jago grinned in spite of himself and, as a rain squall hurled itself against the window, increased speed, the wheel kicking in his hands. The sea was his life now. Meat and drink to him, more important than any woman. It was the circumstance of war which had given him this, but the war wouldn't last forever.

He said softly, 'What in the hell am I going to do when it's all over?'

There were times when Rear Admiral Carey Reeve definitely wondered what life was all about. Times when the vacuum of his days seemed unbearable and the island that he loved with such a deep and unswerving passion, a prison.

On such occasions he usually made for the same spot, a hill called in the Gaelic *Dun Bhuide*, the Yellow Fort, above Telegraph Bay on the south-west tip of Fhada, and so named because of an abortive attempt to set up a Marconi station at the turn of the century. The bay lay at the bottom of four-hundred-foot cliffs, a strip of white sand slipping into grey water with Labrador almost three thousand miles away to the west and nothing in between.

The path below was no place for the fainthearted, zigzagging across the face of the granite cliffs, splashed with lime, seabirds crying, wheeling in great clouds, razorbills, shags, gulls, shearwaters and gannets – gannets everywhere. He considered it all morosely for a while through his one good eye, then turned to survey the rest of the island.

The ground sloped steeply to the south-west. On the other side of the point from Telegraph were South Inlet and the lifeboat station, the boathouse, its slipway and Murdoch Macleod's cottage, nothing more. On his left was the rest of the island. A scattering of crofts, mostly ruined, peat bog, sheep grazing the sparse turf, the whole crossed by the twin lines of the narrow-gauge railway track running north-west to Mary's Town.

Reeve took an old brass telescope from his pocket and focused it on the lifeboat station. No sign of life. Murdoch would probably be working on that damned boat of his, but the kettle would be gently steaming on the hob above the peat fire and a mug of hot tea generously laced with illegal whisky of Murdoch's own distilling would not come amiss on such a morning.

The admiral replaced the telescope in his pocket and started down the slope as rain drove across the island in a grey curtain.

There was no sign of Murdoch when he went into the boathouse by the small rear door. The forty-one-foot Watson-type motor lifeboat, *Morag Sinclair,* waited in her carriage at the head of the slipway. She was trim and beautiful in her blue and white paint, showing every sign of the care Murdoch lavished on her. Reeve ran a hand along her counter with a conscious pleasure.

Behind him the door swung open in a flurry of rain and a soft Highland voice said, 'I was in the outhouse, stacking peat.'

Reeve turned to find Murdoch standing in the doorway and in the same moment an enormous Irish wolfhound squeezed past him and bore down on the admiral.

His hand fastened on the beast's ginger ruff. 'Rory, you old devil. I might have known.' He glanced up at Murdoch. 'Mrs Sinclair's been looking for him this morning. Went missing last night.'

'I intended bringing him in myself later,' Murdoch said. 'Are you in health, Admiral?'

He was himself seventy years old, of immense stature, dressed in thigh boots and guernsey sweater, his eyes grey water over stone, his face seamed and shaped by a lifetime of the sea.

'Murdoch,' Admiral Reeve said. 'Has it ever occurred to you that life is a tale told by an idiot, full of sound and fury and signifying precisely nothing?'

'So it's that kind of a morning?' Murdoch wiped peat from his hands on to his thighs and produced his tobacco pouch. 'Will you take tea with me, Admiral?' he enquired with grave Highland courtesy.

'And a little something extra?' Reeve suggested hopefully.

'*Uisgebeatha?*' Murdoch said in Gaelic. 'The water of life. Why not indeed, for it is life you need this morning, I am thinking.' He smiled gravely. 'I'll be ten minutes. Time for you to take a turn along the shore with the hound to blow the cobwebs away.'

The mouth of the inlet was a maelstrom of white water, waves smashing in across the reef beyond with a thunderous roaring, hurling spray a hundred feet into the air.

Reeve trudged along in the wolfhound's wake at the water's edge, thinking about Murdoch Macleod. Thirty-two years coxswain of the Fhada lifeboat, legend in his own time – during which he had been awarded the BEM by old King George and five silver and two gold medals for gallantry in sea rescue by the Lifeboat Institution. He had retired in 1938, when his son Donald had taken over as coxswain in his place, and had returned a year later when Donald was called to active service with the Royal Naval Reserve. A remarkable man by any standards.

The wolfhound was barking furiously. Reeve looked up across the great bank of sand that was known as *Traig Mhoire* – Mary's Strand. A man in a yellow lifejacket lay face-down on the shore twenty yards away, water slopping over him as one wave crashed in after another.

The admiral ran forward, dropped to one knee and turned him over, with some difficulty for his left arm was virtually useless now. He was quite dead, a boy of eighteen or nineteen, in denim overalls, eyes closed as if in sleep, fair hair plastered to his skull, not a mark on him.

Reeve started to search the body. There was a leather wallet in the left breast pocket. As he opened it, Murdoch arrived on the run, dropping on his knees beside him.

'Came to see what was keeping you.' He touched the pale face with the back of his hand.

'How long?' Reeve asked.

'Ten or twelve hours, no more. Who was he?'

'Off a German U-boat from the look of those overalls.' Reeve opened the wallet and examined the contents. There was a photo of a young girl, a couple of letters and a leave pass so soaked in sea water that it started to fall to pieces as he opened it gingerly.

'A wee lad, that's all,' Murdoch said. 'Couldn't they do better than schoolboys?'

'Probably as short of men by now as the rest of us,' Reeve told him.

'His name was Hans Bleichrodt and he celebrated his eighteenth birthday while on leave in Brunswick three weeks ago. He was Funkgefreiter, telegraphist to you, on U743.' He replaced the papers in the wallet. 'If she bought it this morning, we might get more like this coming in for the rest of the week.'

'You could be right,' Murdoch crouched down and, with an easy strength that never ceased to amaze Reeve, hoisted the body over one shoulder. 'Better get him into Mary's Town then, Admiral.'

Reeve nodded. 'Yes, my house will do. Mrs Sinclair can see him this afternoon and sign the death certificate. We'll bury him tomorrow.'

'I am thinking that the kirk might be more fitting.'

'I'm not certain that's such a good idea,' Reeve said. 'There are eleven men from this island dead at sea owing to enemy action during this war. I would have thought their families might not be too happy to see a German lying in state in their own place of worship.'

The old man's eyes were fierce. 'And you would agree with them?'

'Oh no,' Reeve said hurriedly. 'Don't draw me into this. You put the boy where you like. I don't think it will bother him too much.'

'But it might well bother God,' Murdoch said gently. There was no reproof in his voice, in spite of the fact that, as a certificated lay preacher of the Church of Scotland, he was the nearest thing to a minister on the island.

There was no road from that end of Fhada, had never been any need for one, but during the two abortive years that the Marconi station had existed, the telegraph company had laid the narrow-gauge railway line. The lifeboat crew, mostly fishermen from Mary's Town, travelled on it by trolley when called out in an emergency, pumping it by hand or hoisting a sail when the wind was favourable.

Which it was that morning, and Murdoch and the admiral coasted along at a brisk five knots, the triangular strip of canvas billowing out to one side. The dead boy lay in the centre of the trolley and Rory squatted beside him.

Two miles, then three, and the track started to slope down and the wind tore a hole in the curtain of rain, revealing Mary's Town, a couple of miles further on in the north-west corner of the island, a scattering of granite houses, four or five streets sloping to the harbour. There were half-a-dozen fishing boats anchored in the lee of the breakwater.

Murdoch was standing, one hand on the mast, staring out to sea. 'Would you look at that now, Admiral? There's some sort of craft coming in towards the harbour out there and I could have sworn that was the Stars and Stripes she's flying. I must be getting old.'

Reeve had the telescope out of his pocket and focused in an instant.

'You're damned right it is,' he said as the *Dead End* jumped into view, Harry Jago on the bridge.

His hand was shaking with excitement as he pushed the telescope back into his pocket. 'You know something, Murdoch? This might just turn out to be my day after all.'

When the MGB eased into the landing-stage a woman was sitting on the upper jetty under an umbrella, painting at an easel. She was in her early forties, with calm blue eyes in a strong and pleasant face. She wore a headscarf, an old naval-officer's coat, which carried the bars of a full captain on the epaulettes, and slacks.

She stood up, moved to the edge of the jetty, holding the umbrella, and smiled down. 'Hello there, America. That makes a change.'

Jago went over the rail and up the steps to the jetty quickly. 'Harry Jago, ma'am.'

'Jean Sinclair.' She held out her hand. 'I'm bailie here, Lieutenant, so if there's anything I can do . . .'

'Bailie?' Jago said blankly.

'What you'd call a magistrate.'

Jago grinned. 'I see. You mean you're the law around here.'

'And coroner and harbourmaster. This is a small island. We have to do the best we can.'

'I'm here with dispatches for Rear Admiral Reeve, ma'am. Have you any idea where I might locate him?'

She smiled. 'We have a saying in these islands, Lieutenant. Speak of the devil and you'll find he's right behind you.'

Jago turned quickly and got a shock. When he'd received his Navy Cross from Nimitz at Pearl, Admiral Reeve had been one of those on the platform, resplendent in full uniform with three rows of medal ribbons. There was no echo of him at all in the small, dark man with the black eye patch who hurried towards him now wearing an old reefer coat and sea boots. It was only when he spoke that Jago knew beyond a doubt who he was.

'You looking for me, Lieutenant?'

'Admiral Reeve?' Jago got his heels together and saluted. 'I've got a dispatch for you, sir. Handed to me by the Royal Naval officer in command at Mallaig. If you'd care to come aboard.'

'Lead me to it, Lieutenant,' the admiral said eagerly, then paused and turned to Jean Sinclair. 'I found Rory. He was with Murdoch at the lifeboat station.'

Her eyes were lively now and there was a slight amused smile on her mouth. 'Why, Carey, I thought you were going to ignore me altogether.'

He said gravely, 'I found something else down there on Traig Mhoire. A body on the beach. A German boy off a U-boat.'

Her smile died. 'Where is he now?'

'I left him at the church with Murdoch.'

'I'd better get up there then. I'll pick up a couple of women on the way. See the lad's decently laid out.'

'I'll be along myself later.'

She walked away quickly, her umbrella tilted to take the force of the rain. 'Quite a lady,' Jago remarked.

The admiral nodded. 'And then some. As a matter of interest, she owns the whole damned island. Left it by her father. He was a kind of feudal laird round here.'

'What about that naval greatcoat, sir?' Jago asked, as they descended the ladder.

'Her husband's. Went down in the *Prince of Wales* back in forty-one. He was a Sinclair, too, like her. A second cousin, I believe.' He laughed. 'It's an old island custom to keep the name in the family.'

The crew were assembled on deck and as the admiral went over the rail, Jansen piped him on board. Reeve looked them over in amazement and said to Jago, 'Where did this lot spring from? A banana boat?'

'Chief Petty Officer Jansen, sir,' Jago said weakly.

Reeve examined Jansen, taking in the reefer, the tangled beard and knitted cap. He turned away with a shudder. 'I've seen enough. Just take me to my dispatch, will you?'

'If you follow me, Admiral.'

Jago led the way down the companionway to his cabin. He took a briefcase from under the mattress on his bunk, unlocked it and produced a buff envelope, seals still intact, which he passed across. As Reeve took it from him, there was a knock at the door and Jansen entered with a tray.

'Coffee, gentlemen?'

Reeve curbed the impulse to tear the envelope open and said to Jago as he accepted a cup, 'How's the war going, then?'

It was Jansen who answered. 'The undertakers are doing well, Admiral.'

Reeve turned to stare at him in a kind of fascination. 'You did say Chief Petty Officer?'

'The best, sir,' Jago said gamely.

'And where may I ask, did you find him?'

'Harvard, sir,' Jansen said politely, and withdrew.

Reeve said in wonderment, 'He's joking, isn't he?'

'I'm afraid not, Admiral.'

'No wonder the war wasn't over by Christmas.'

Reeve sat on the edge of the bunk, tore open the package and took out two envelopes. He opened the smaller first. There was a photo inside and a letter which he read quickly, a smile on his face. He passed the photo to Jago.

'My niece, Janet. She's a doctor at Guy's Hospital in London. Been there since nineteen-forty. Worked right through the blitz.'

She had grave, steady eyes, high cheekbones, a mouth that was too wide. There was something in her expression that got through to Jago.

He handed the photo back reluctantly. 'Very nice, sir.'

'You could say that and it would be the understatement of the year.'

Reeve opened the second envelope and started to read the letter it contained eagerly. Gradually the smile died on his face, his eyes grew dark, his mouth tightened. He folded the letter and slipped it into his pocket.

'Bad news, sir?'

'Now that, son, depends entirely on your point of view. The powers-that-be are of the opinion that the war can get on without me. That, to use a favourite phrase of our British allies, I've done my bit.'

Jago opened a cupboard behind him and took out a bottle of Scotch and a glass which he held out to the admiral. 'Most people I know wouldn't find much to quarrel with in that sentiment, sir.'

He poured a generous measure of whisky into the glass. Reeve said, 'Something else that's strictly against regulations, Lieutenant.' He frowned. 'What is your name, anyway?'

'Jago, sir. Harry Jago.'

Reeve swallowed some of the whisky. 'What kind of deal are you on here? This old tub looks as if it might be left over from the Crimea.'

'Not quite, sir. Courtesy of the Royal Navy. We're only playing postman, you see. I suppose they didn't think the job was worth much more.'

'What were you doing before?'

'PT boats, sir. Squadron Two, working the Channel.'

'Jago?' Reeve said and his face brightened. 'You lost an Elco in Lyme Bay.'

'I suppose you could put it that way, sir.'

Reeve smiled and held out his hand. 'Nice to meet you, son. And those boys up top? They're your original crew?'

'What's left of them.'

'Well, now I'm here, you might as well show me over this pig boat.'

Which Jago did from stem to stern. They ended up in the wheelhouse, where they found Jansen at the chart table.

'And what might you be about?' Reeve demanded.

'Our next stop is a weather station on the south-west corner of Harris, Admiral. I was just plotting our course.'

'Show me.' Jansen ran a finger out through the Sound into the Atlantic and Reeve said, 'Watch it out there, especially if visibility is reduced in the slightest. Here, three miles to the north-west.' He tapped the chart. 'Washington Reef. Doesn't it make you feel at home, the sound of that name?'

'And presumably it shouldn't?' Jago asked.

'A death trap. The greatest single hazard to shipping on the entire west coast of Scotland. Two galleons from the Spanish Armada went to hell together on those rocks four hundred years ago and they've been tearing ships apart ever since. One of the main reasons there's a lifeboat here on Fhada.'

'Maybe we'd be better taking the other route north through the Little Minch, sir.'

Reeve smiled. 'I know – it's a hell of a war, Lieutenant, but it's the only one we've got.'

Jansen said solemnly, 'As long as war is regarded as wicked it will always have its fascination. When looked upon as vulgar, it will cease to be popular. Oscar Wilde said that, sir,' he said helpfully.

'Dear God, restore me to sanity.' Reeve shook his head and turned to Jago. 'Let me get off this hooker before I go over the edge entirely.'

'Just one thing, sir. Do you know a Mr Murdoch Macleod?'

'He's coxswain of the lifeboat here and a good friend of mine. Why do you ask?'

Jago unbuttoned his shirt pocket and took out an orange envelope. 'The Royal Naval officer in command at Mallaig asked me to deliver this telegram to him, sir, there being no telephone or telegraph service to the island at the moment, I understand.'

'That's right,' Reeve said. 'The cable parted in a storm last month and they haven't got around to doing anything about it yet. In fact at the moment, the island's only link with the outside world is my personal radio.'

He held out his hand for the envelope which he saw was open. 'It's from the Admiralty, sir.'

'Bad news?'

'He has a son, sir. Lieutenant Donald Macleod.'

'That's right. Commanding an armed trawler doing escort duty on east-coast convoys in the North Sea. Newcastle to London.'

'Torpedoed off the Humber yesterday, with all hands.'

Reeve's voice dropped to a whisper. 'No one was saved at all? You're certain of that?'

'I'm afraid not, Admiral.'

Reeve seemed to age before his eyes. 'One thing they obviously didn't tell you, Lieutenant, was that, although Donald Macleod was master of that trawler, there were four other men from Fhada in the crew.' He passed the envelope back to Jago. 'I think the sooner we get this over with, the better.'

The church of St Mungo was a tiny, weatherbeaten building with a squat tower, constructed of blocks of heavy granite on a hillside above the town.

Reeve, Jago and Frank Jansen went in through the lychgate and followed a path through a churchyard scattered with gravestones to the porch at the west end. Reeve opened the massive oaken door and led the way in.

The dead boy lay on a trestle table in a tiny side chapel to one side of the altar. Two middle-aged women were arranging the body while Murdoch and Jean Sinclair stood close by, talking in subdued tones. They turned and looked down the aisle as the door opened. The three men moved towards them, caps in hand. They paused, then Reeve held the orange envelope out to Jean Sinclair.

'I think you'd better read this.'

She took it from him, extracted the telegram. Her face turned ashen, she was wordless. In a moment of insight, Reeve realized that she was re-living her own tragedy. She turned to Murdoch, but the admiral stepped in quickly, holding her back.

Murdoch said calmly, 'It is bad news you have for me there, I am thinking, Carey Reeve.'

'Donald's ship was torpedoed off the Humber yesterday,' Reeve said. 'Went down with all hands.'

A tremor seemed to pass through the old man's entire frame. He staggered momentarily, then took a deep breath and straightened. 'The Lord disposes.'

The two women working on the body stopped to stare at him, faces frozen in horror. Between them, as Reeve well knew, they had just lost a husband and brother. Murdoch moved past and stood looking down at the German boy, pale in death, the face somehow very peaceful now.

He reached down and took one of the cold hands in his. 'Poor lad,' he said. 'Poor wee lad!' His shoulders shook and he started to weep softly.

Barquentine *Deutschland*, 12 September 1944. Lat. 26°.11N., long. 30°.26W. Wind NW 2–3. Overcast. Poor visibility. A bad squall last night during the middle-watch and the flying-jib split.

Three

Some five hundred miles south of the Azores, Erich Berger sat at the desk in his cabin entering his personal journal.

. . . our general progress has, of course, been far better than I could ever have hoped and yet our passengers find the experience tedious in the extreme. For most of the time, bad weather keeps them below; the skylight leaks and the saloon is constantly damp.

The loss of the chickens and two goats kept for milk, all swept overboard in a bad squall three days out of Belém, has had an unfortunate effect on our diet, although here again, it has been most noticeable in the nuns. Frau Prager is still my main worry and her condition, as far as I may judge, continues to deteriorate.

As for the prospect of a meeting with an enemy ship, we are as ready in that respect as can reasonably be expected. The *Deutschland* is now the *Gudrid Andersen* to the last detail, including the library of Swedish books in my cabin. The plan of campaign, if boarded at any time, is simple. The additional men carried beyond normal crew requirements will secrete themselves in the bilges. A simple device admittedly, and one easily discovered by any kind of a thorough search, but we have little choice in the matter.

The *Deutschland* stands up well so far to all the Atlantic can offer, although there is not a day passes that shrouds do not part or sails split and, this morning, Mister Sturm reported twelve inches of water in the bilges. But, as yet, there is no cause for alarm. We all get old and the *Deutschland* is older than most . . .

The whole ship lurched drunkenly and Berger was thrown from his chair as the cabin tilted. He scrambled to his feet, got the door open and ran out on deck.

The *Deutschland* was plunging forward through heavy seas, the deck awash with spray. Leutnant Sturm and Leading Seaman Kluth had the wheel between them and it was taking all their strength to hold it.

High above the deck, the main gaff topsail fluttered free in the wind. The noise was tremendous and could be heard even above the roaring of the wind, and the topmast was whipping backwards and forwards. A matter of moments only before it snapped. But already Richter was at the rail, the sea washing over him as he pulled on the downhaul to collapse the sail.

Berger ran to join him, losing his footing and rolling into the scuppers as another great sea floated in across the deck, but somehow he was on his feet and lending his weight to the downhaul with Richter.

The sail came down, the *Deutschland* righted herself perceptibly, the continual drumming ceased. Richter shouted, 'I'd better get up there and see to a new outhaul.'

Berger cried above the wind, 'You wouldn't last five minutes out there on that gaff in this weather. It'll have to wait till the wind eases.'

'But that sail will tear herself to pieces, sir.'

'A gasket should hold her for the time being. I'll see to it.'

Berger sprang into the ratlines and started to climb, aware of the wind tearing at his body like some living thing. When he paused, fifty feet up and glanced down, Richter was right behind him.

There was a foot of water in the saloon, a sea having smashed the skylight and flooded in. Sister Angela went from cabin to cabin, doing her best to calm her alarmed companions.

When she went into the Pragers', she found the old man on his knees at his wife's bunk. Frau Prager was deathly pale, eyes closed, little sign of life there at all.

'What is it?' Otto Prager demanded in alarm.

She ignored him for the moment and took his wife's pulse. It was still there, however irregular.

Prager tugged at her sleeve. 'What happened?'

'I'll find out,' she said calmly. 'You stay with your wife.'

She went out on deck to find the *Deutschland* racing north, every fore and aft sail drawing well, yards braced as she plunged into the waves. Sturm and Kluth were still at the wheel. The young lieutenant called to her, but his words were snatched away by the wind.

She made it to the mizzen shrouds on the port side, the wind tearing at her black habit, and looked up at the ballooning sails. The sky was a uniform grey, the whole world alive with the sound of the ship, a thousand creaks and groans. And then, a hundred feet up, she saw Berger and Richter swaying backwards and forwards on the end of the gaff as they secured the sail.

It was perhaps the most incredible thing she had ever seen in her life and she was seized by a tremendous feeling of exhilaration. A sea slopped in over the rail in a green curtain that bowled her over, sending her skidding across the deck on her hands and knees.

She crouched against the bulwark and, as she tried to get up, Berger dropped out of the shrouds beside her and got a hand under her arm.

'Bloody fool!' he shouted. 'Why can't you stay below?'

He ran her across the deck and into his cabin before she had a chance to reply. Sister Angela collapsed into the chair behind the desk and Berger got the door shut and leaned against it. 'What in the hell am I going to do with you?'

'I'm sorry,' she said. 'There was panic down below. I simply wanted to know what had happened.'

He picked up a towel from his bunk and tossed it across to her. 'A line parted, a sail broke free. It could have snapped the topmast like a matchstick, only Richter was too quick for it.' He opened a cupboard and reached for the bottle. 'A drink, Sister? Purely medicinal, of course. Rum is all I can offer, I'm afraid.'

'I don't think so.' Berger poured himself a large one and she wiped her face and regarded him curiously. 'It was incredible what you were doing out there. You and Herr Richter, so high up and in such weather.'

'Not really,' he said indifferently. 'Not to anyone who's reefed main t'gallants on a fully-rigged clipper in a Cape Horn storm.'

She nodded slowly. 'Tell me, do you still think we're bad luck? A positive guarantee of contrary winds, wasn't that what you said at our first meeting? And yet we've made good progress, wouldn't you agree?'

'Oh, we're making time all right,' Berger admitted. 'Although she shakes herself to pieces around us just a little bit more each day.'

'You speak of her, the *Deutschland*, as if she is a living thing. As if she has an existence of her own.'

'I wouldn't quarrel with that. Although I suppose your Church would. A ship doesn't have one voice, she has many. You can hear them calling to each other out there, especially at night.'

'The wind in the rigging?' There was something close to mockery in her voice.

'There are other possibilities. Old timers will tell you that the ghost of anyone killed falling from the rigging remains with the ship.'

'And you believe that?'

'Obligatory in the Kriegsmarine.' There was an ironic smile on his face now. 'Imagine the shades who infest this old girl. Next time something brushes past you in the dark on the companionway, you'll know what it is. One Our Father and two Hail Marys should keep you safe.'

Her cheeks flushed but before she could reply, the door was flung open and Sister Else appeared, 'Please, Sister, come quickly. Frau Prager seems to be worse.'

Sister Angela jumped to her feet and moved out. Berger closed the door behind her, then picked up the towel she dropped and wiped his face. Strange how she seemed to bring out the worst in him. A constant source of irritation, but then perhaps it was simply that they'd all been together for too long in such a confined space. And yet . . .

For most of the afternoon, HMS *Guardian*, a T-class submarine of the British Home Fleet, en route to Trinidad for special orders, had proceeded submerged, but at 1600 hours she surfaced.

It was the throb of the diesels that brought her captain, Lieutenant-Commander George Harvey, awake. He lay there for a moment on the bunk, staring up at the steel bulkhead, aware of the taste in his mouth, the smell of submarine, and then the green curtain was pulled aside and Petty Officer Swallow came in with tea in a chipped enamel mug.

'Just surfaced, sir.'

The tea was foul, but at least there was real sugar in it, which was something.

'What's it like up there?'

'Overcast. Wind north-west. Two to three. Visibility poor, sir. Slight sea mist and drizzling.'

'Succinct as always, Coxswain,' Harvey told him.

'Beg pardon, sir?'

'Never mind. Just tell Mr Edge I'll join him on the bridge in five minutes.'

'Sir.'

Swallow withdrew and Harvey swung his legs to the floor and sat there, yawning. Then he moved to the small desk bolted to the bulkhead, opened the *Guardian*'s war diary and in cold, precise naval language, started to insert the daily entry.

There were three men on the bridge. Sub-Lieutenant Edge, officer of the watch, a signalman and an able seaman for lookout. The sea was surprisingly calm and there was none of the usual corkscrewing or pitching that a submarine frequently experiences when travelling on the surface in any kind of rough weather.

Edge was thoroughly enjoying himself. The rain in his face was quite refreshing and the salt air felt sweet and clean in his lungs after the hours spent below.

Swallow came up the ladder, a mug of tea in one hand. 'Thought you might like a wet, sir. Captain's compliments and he'll join you on the bridge in five minutes.'

'Good show,' Edge said cheerfully. 'Not that there's anything to report.'

Swallow started to reply and then his eyes widened and an expression of incredulity appeared on his face. 'Good God Almighty!' he said. 'I don't believe it.'

In the same instant, the lookout cried out, pointing, and Edge turned to see a three-masted barquentine, all sails set, emerge from a fog bank a quarter of a mile to port.

On board the *Deutschland* there was no panic, for the plan to be followed in such an eventuality had been gone over so many times that everyone knew exactly what to do.

Berger was on the quarterdeck, Sturm and Richter beside him at the rail. The bosun was holding a signalling lamp. The captain spoke without lowering his glasses. 'A British submarine. T-class.'

'Is this it, sir?' Sturm asked. 'Are we finished?'

'Perhaps.'

The *Guardian*'s gun crew poured out of her conning-tower and manned their positions. For a moment there was considerable activity, then a signal lamp flashed.

'Heave to or I fire,' Richter said.

'Plain enough. Reply: As a neutral ship I comply under protest.'

The shutter on the signal lamp in the bosun's hands clattered. A moment later, the reply came. 'I intend to board you. Stand by.'

Berger lowered his glasses. 'Very well, gentlemen. Action stations, if you please. Take in all sail, Mr Sturm. You, Richter, will see the rest of the crew into the bilges and I will attend to the passengers.'

There was a flurry of activity as Sturm turned to bark orders to the watch on deck. Richter went down the quarterdeck ladder quickly. Berger followed him, descending the companionway.

When he entered the saloon, four of the nuns were seated round the table listening to a bible-reading from Sister Lotte.

'Where is Sister Angela?' Berger demanded.

Sister Lotte paused. 'With Frau Prager.'

The door of the consul's cabin opened and Prager emerged. He seemed haggard and drawn and had lost weight since that first night in Belém so that his tropical linen suit seemed a size too large.

'How are things?' Berger asked.

'Bad,' Prager said. 'She gets weaker by the hour.'

'I'm sorry.' Berger addressed his next remark to all of them. 'There's a British submarine on the surface about a quarter of a mile off our port beam and moving in. They intend to board.'

Sister Käthe crossed herself quickly and Sister Angela came out of the Pragers' cabin clutching an enamel bucket, her white apron soiled.

When Berger next spoke, it was to no one but her. 'You heard?'

'Yes.'

'We had a bad night of it, Sister – a hell of a night. You understand me?'

'Perfectly, Captain.' Her face was pale, but the eyes sparkled. 'We won't let you down.'

Berger picked up a broom that leaned against the bulkhead, reached up and jabbed at the skylight again and again, glass showering across the table so that the nuns scattered with cries of alarm.

He tossed the broom into a corner. 'See that you don't,' he said and went back up the companionway.

There was total silence, the nuns staring at Sister Angela expectantly. With a violent gesture she raised the bucket in her hands and emptied the contents across the floor. There was the immediate all-pervading stench of vomit and Sister Brigitte turned away, stomach heaving.

'Excellent,' Sister Angela said. 'Now you, Lotte, go to the lavatory and fetch a bucket of slops. I want conditions down here to be so revolting those *Tommis* will be back up that companionway in two minutes flat.'

She had changed completely, the voice clipped, incisive, totally in command. 'As for the rest of you, complete disorder in the cabins. Soak your bedding in seawater.'

Prager tugged at her sleeve. 'What about me, Sister? What shall I do?'

'Kneel, Herr Prager,' she said. 'At your wife's bedside – and pray.'

As the *Guardian* moved in, Harvey observed the activity on the deck of the *Deutschland* closely through his glasses.

Edge came up the ladder behind him. 'I've checked Lloyd's Register, sir. It seems to be her all right. *Gudrid Andersen*, three-masted barquentine, registered Gothenburg.'

'But what in the hell is she doing here?'

Harvey frowned, trying to work out the best way of handling the situation. His first officer, Gregson, lay in his bunk with a fractured left ankle. In such circumstances to leave the *Guardian* himself, however temporarily, was unthinkable. Which left Edge, a nineteen-year-old boy on his first operational patrol – hardly an ideal choice.

On the other hand, there was Swallow. His eyes met the chief petty officer's briefly. Not a word spoken and yet he knew that the coxswain read his thoughts perfectly.

'Tell me, Coxswain, does anyone on board speak Swedish?'

'Not to my knowledge, sir.'

'We must hope they run to enough English over there to get us by, then. Lieutenant Edge will lead the boarding party. Pick him two good men – side arms only. And I think you might as well go along for the ride.'

'Sir.'

Swallow turned and at his shouted command, the forward hatch was opened and a rubber dinghy broken out. Edge went below and reappeared a few moments later buckling a webbing belt around his waist from which hung a holstered Webley revolver. He was excited and showed it.

'Think you can handle it?' Harvey asked.

'I believe so, sir.'

'Good. A thorough inspection of ship's papers and identity documents of everyone on board.'

'Am I looking for anything special, sir?'

'Hardly,' Harvey said drily. 'The Germans last used a sailing ship as a surface raider in nineteen-seventeen, if I remember my naval history correctly, and times have changed. No, we're entitled to check her credentials and I'm consumed with curiosity as to the nature of her business, so off you go.'

Sturm waited at the rail as the dinghy coasted in. Edge went up the Jacob's ladder first, followed by one of the ratings and Swallow, who carried a Thompson gun. The other rating stayed with the dinghy. Of Berger, there was no sign.

Sturm, who spoke excellent English, pointed to the ensign which fluttered at the masthead. 'I must protest, sir. As you can see, this is a Swedish vessel.'

'Ah, good, you speak English,' Edge said with a certain relief. 'Lieutenant Philip Edge of His Britannic Majesty's submarine *Guardian*. Are you the master of this vessel?'

'No, my name is Larsen. First mate. Captain Nielsen is in his cabin getting out the ship's papers for you. I'm afraid things are in a bit of a mess. We had a bad night of it. Almost turned turtle when a squall hit us during the middle watch. It caused considerable damage.'

Edge said to Swallow, 'You handle things here, Coxswain, while I have a word with the captain.'

'Shall we take a look below, sir?' Swallow suggested.

Edge turned, taking in the watchful gun crew on the *Guardian*, the Browning machine-gun which had been mounted on the rail beside Harvey.

'Yes, why not?' he said and followed Sturm towards the quarterdeck.

The young German opened the door to the captain's cabin and stood politely to one side. Edge paused on the threshold, taking in the shambles before him. A porthole was smashed, the carpet soaked, the whole place littered with books and personal belongings.

Berger stood behind the desk, face stern, the ship's log and other papers ready on the desk before him.

'I'm afraid Captain Nielsen doesn't speak English so I'll have to interpret for you.' Which was far from the truth for Berger's English, though modest, was adequate. 'The captain,' Sturm added, 'is not pleased at this forcible boarding of a neutral vessel about her lawful business.'

'I'm sorry,' Edge said, considerably intimidated by the stern expression on Berger's face, 'but I'm afraid I must insist on seeing your ship's papers and log, also your cargo manifest.'

Berger turned away as if angry. Sturm said, 'But we carry no cargo, Lieutenant, only passengers.' He picked up the ship's log, soaked in sea water, its pages sticking together. 'Perhaps you would care to examine the log? You will find all other relevant papers here also.'

Edge took it from him, sat down in Berger's chair and tried to separate the first two water-soaked pages which promptly tore away in his hand. And at that precise moment, Richter and the eleven other members of the crew secreted in the bilges with him, were lying in several inches of stinking water, aware of Swallow's heavy footsteps in the hold above their heads.

Edge left the cabin fifteen minutes later, having examined as thoroughly as he could an assortment of papers and clutching the Swedish passports offered for his inspection.

Swallow emerged from the companionway, looking ill. Edge said, 'Are the passengers down there, Coxswain?'

'Yes, sir.' Swallow was taking in deep breaths of salt air rapidly. 'Five nuns, sir, and an old gentleman and his wife – and she doesn't look too healthy.'

Edge advanced to the top of the companionway and Swallow said hastily, 'I wouldn't bother, sir. Not unless you feel you have to. They've obviously had a rotten time of it in last night's storm. Still cleaning up.'

Edge hesitated, turned to glance at Sturm, Berger glowering behind, then started down.

The stink was appalling, the stench of human excrement and vomit turning his stomach. The first thing he saw in the shambles of the saloon below were four nuns on their knees amongst the filth with buckets and brushes, scrubbing the floor. Edge got a handkerchief to his mouth as Sister Angela appeared in the doorway of the Pragers' cabin.

'Can I help you?' she asked in good English.

'Sorry to trouble you, ma'am. My duty – you understand?' He held out the passports. 'International law in time of war. I'm entitled to inspect the passenger list.'

He glanced past her at Prager who knelt beside his wife. Her face was deathly pale, shining with sweat, and she was breathing incredibly slowly.

'And this lady and gentleman?' He started to sort through the passports.

'Mr Ternström and his wife. As you can see, she is very ill.'

Prager turned to look at him, the agony on his face totally genuine, and Edge took an involuntary step back. Lotte chose that exact moment to be sick, crouching there on the floor like some animal. It was enough.

Edge turned hastily, brushed past Sturm and went back up the companionway. He leaned on the starboard rail, breathing deeply, and Swallow moved beside him.

'You all right, sir?'

'God, what a pest-hole. Those women – they've been through hell.' He pulled himself together. 'You've checked the holds thoroughly, Coxswain?'

'Clean as a whistle, sir. She's in ballast with sand.'

Edge turned to Sturm who stood waiting, Berger a pace or two behind. 'I don't understand.'

'For many months we work the coastal trade in Brazil,' Sturm told him. 'Then we decide to come home. As you may imagine, no one seemed anxious to risk a cargo with us.'

'And the passengers?'

'The good Sisters have been stranded in Brazil for more than a year now. We are the first Swedish ship to leave Brazil during that time. They were grateful for the opportunity for any kind of passage.'

'But the old lady,' Edge said. 'Mrs Ternström. She looks in a bad way.'

'And anxious to see her family again while there is still time.' Sturm smiled bitterly. 'War makes things difficult for us neutrals when we want to travel from one place to another.'

Edge made his decision and handed the passports back. 'You'll want these. My apologies to your captain. I'll have to confirm it with my commanding officer, but I see no reason why you shouldn't be allowed to proceed.' He moved to the head of the Jacob's ladder and paused. 'Those ladies down there . . .'

'Will be fine, Lieutenant. We'll soon have things shipshape again.'

'Anything else we can do for you?'

Sturm smiled. 'Bring us up to date on the war, if you would. How are things going?'

'All *our* way now, no doubt about that,' Edge said. 'Though they do seem to be slowing down rather in Europe. I don't think we're going to see Berlin by Christmas after all. The Germans are making one hell of a fight of it in the Low Countries.'

He went down the ladder quickly, followed by Swallow and the other rating, and they cast off. 'Well, Coxswain?' he asked as they pulled away.

'I know one thing, sir. I'll never complain about serving in submarines again.'

On the quarterdeck Berger smoked a cigar and waited, Sturm at his side.

'What do you think, Herr Kapitän?' Sturm asked. 'Has it worked?'

In the same moment, the signal lamp on the bridge of the *Guardian* started to flash.

'You may proceed.' Berger spelled out. 'Happy voyage and good luck.' He turned to Sturm, his face calm. 'My maternal grandmother was English, did I ever tell you that?'

'No, sir.'

Berger tossed his cigar over the side. 'She's all yours, Mr Sturm. Let's get under way again as soon as may be.'

'Aye, aye, sir.'

Sturm turned, raising his voice to call to the men below, and Berger descended to the deck. He stood in the entrance to the companionway, aware of the stench, of Sister Angela's pale face peering up at him.

'Did it work?' she called softly.

'Remind me, when I have the time, to tell you what a very remarkable woman you are, Sister.'

'At the appropriate moment, I shall, Captain. You may be certain of that,' she said serenely.

Berger turned away. The *Guardian* was already departing towards the south-west. He watched her go, and behind him Helmut Richter emerged from the forrard hatch and came aft. His body was streaked with filth, but he was smiling.

'Can the lads come on deck and wash off under the pump? They smell pretty high after those bilges.'

'So I observe.' Berger wrinkled his nose. 'Give it another twenty minutes until our British friends are really on their way, Helmut, then turn them loose.'

He went into his cabin and Richter stripped his shirt from his body, worked the deck pump with one hand and turned the hose on himself. As he did so, Sister Lotte came out on deck clutching a full pail of slops in both hands. She got as far as the starboard rail and was about to empty it when Richter reached her.

'Never into the wind,' he said. 'That way you get the contents back in your face.' He peered down in disgust. 'And that, you can definitely do without.'

He carried the pail to the port rail, emptied it over the side, then flushed it out under the pump. She stood watching him calmly.

She was small and very slightly built, a lawyer's daughter from Munich who looked younger than her twenty-three years. Unlike the other nuns, she was still a novice and had been transferred to Brazil, by way of Portugal, the previous year, only because she was a trained nurse and there was a shortage of people with her qualifications.

She picked up his shirt. 'I'll wash this for you.'

'No need.'

'And the seam is splitting on one shoulder, I'll mend it.' When she looked up, he saw that her eyes were a startling cornflower blue. 'It must have been horrible down there.'

'For you also.'

He handed her the pail, she took it and for a brief moment, they held it together. Sister Angela said quietly, 'Lotte, I need you.'

She was standing in the entrance to the companionway, her face calm as always, but there was a new wariness in her eyes when she looked at Richter. The girl smiled briefly and joined her and they went below. Richter started to pump water over his head vigorously.

Berger sat behind the desk, surveying the wreckage of his cabin – not that it mattered. It could soon be put straight again. He was filled with a tremendous sense of elation and opened his personal journal. He picked up his pen, thought for a moment, then wrote: *I am now more than ever convinced that we shall reach Kiel in safety* . . .

Barquentine *Deutschland*, 14 September 1944. Lat. 28°.16N., long. 30°.50W. Frau Prager died at three bells of the mid-watch. We delivered her body to the sea shortly after dawn, Sister Angela taking the service. Ship's company much affected by this calamitous event. A light breeze sprang up during the afternoon watch, increasing to fresh in squalls. I estimate that we are 1170 miles from Cobh in Ireland this day.

Four

Night was falling fast as Jago and Petty Officer Jansen went up the hill to St Mungo's. They found the burial party in the cemetery at the back of the church. There were twenty or so islanders there, men and women, Jean Sinclair and Reeve standing together, the admiral in full uniform. Murdoch Macleod in his best blue serge suit, stood at the head of the open grave, a prayer book in his hands.

The two Americans paused some little distance away and removed their caps. It was very quiet except for the incessant calling of the birds, and Jago looked down across Mary's Town to the horseshoe of the harbour where the MGB was tied up at the jetty.

The sun was setting in a sky the colour of brass, splashed with scarlet, thin mackerel clouds high above. Beyond Barra Head, the islands marched north to Barra, Mingulay, Pabbay, Sandray, rearing out of a perfectly calm sea, black against flame.

Reeve glanced over his shoulder, murmured something to Jean Sinclair, then moved towards them through the gravestones. 'Thanks for coming so promptly, Lieutenant.'

'No trouble, sir. We were on our way to Mallaig from Stornoway when they relayed your message.' Jago nodded towards the grave into which half-a-dozen fishermen were lowering the coffin. 'Another one from U-743?'

Reeve nodded. 'That makes eight in the past three days.' He hesitated. 'When you were last here you said you were going to London on leave this week.'

'That's right, Admiral. If I can get to Mallaig on time I intend to catch the night train for Glasgow. Is there something I can do for you, sir?'

'There certainly is.' Reeve took a couple of envelopes from his pocket. 'This first one is for my niece. Her apartment's in Westminster, not far from the Houses of Parliament.'

'And the other, sir?'

Reeve handed it over. 'If you would see that gets to SHAEF Headquarters personally. It would save time.'

Jago looked at the address on the envelope and swallowed hard. 'My God!'

Reeve smiled. 'See that it's handed to one of his aides personally. No one else.'

'Yes, sir.'

'You'd better move out, then. I'll expect to hear from you as soon as you get back. As I told you, I have a radio at the cottage, one of the few courtesies the Navy still extends me. They'll brief you at Mallaig on the times during the day I sit at the damned thing hoping someone will take notice.'

Jago saluted, nodded to Jansen and then moved away. As the admiral rejoined the funeral party, Murdoch Macleod started to read aloud in a firm, clear voice: 'Man that is born of woman hath but a short time to live, and is full of misery. He cometh up and is cut down like a flower . . .'

Suddenly it was very dark, with only the burned-out fire of day on the horizon as they went out through the lych-gate.

Jansen said, 'Who's the letter for, Lieutenant?'

'General Eisenhower,' Jago said simply.

In Brest, they were shooting again across the river as Paul Gericke turned the corner, the rattle of small-arms fire drifting across the water. Somewhere on the far horizon rockets arched through the night and in spite of the heavy rain, considerable portions of the city appeared to be on fire. Most of the warehouses which had once lined the street had been demolished by bombing, the pavement was littered with rubble and broken glass, but the small hotel on the corner, which served as naval headquarters, still seemed to be intact. Gericke ran up the steps quickly, showed his pass to the sentry on the door and went inside.

He was a small man, no more than five feet five or six, with fair hair and a pale face that seemed untouched by wind and weather. His eyes were very dark, with no light in them at all, contrasting strangely with the good-humoured, rather lazy smile that seemed permanently to touch his mouth.

His white-topped naval cap had seen much service and he was hardly a prepossessing figure in his old leather jerkin, leather trousers and sea boots. But the young lieutenant sitting at his desk in the foyer saw only the Knight's Cross with Oak Leaves at the throat and was on his feet in an instant.

'I was asked to report to the commodore of submarines as soon as I arrived,' Gericke told him. 'Korvettenkapitän Gericke. U-235.'

'He's expecting you, sir,' the lieutenant said. 'If you'd follow me.'

They went up the curving staircase. A petty officer, a pistol at his belt, stood guard outside one of the hotel bedrooms. The handwritten notice on the door said *Kapitän zur See Otto Friemel, Führer der Unterseeboote West.*

The lieutenant knocked and went in. 'Lieutenant-Commander Gericke, sir.'

The room was in half darkness, the only light the reading lamp on Friemel's desk. He was in shirt-sleeves, working his way through a pile of correspondence, steel-rimmed reading glasses perched on the end of his nose, and an ivory cigarette-holder jutting from the left corner of his mouth.

He came round the desk smiling, hand outstretched. 'My dear Paul. Good to see you. How was the West Indies?'

'A long haul,' Gericke said. 'Especially when it was time to come home.'

Friemel produced a bottle of Schnapps and two glasses. 'We're out of champagne. Not like the old days.'

'What, no flowers on the dock?' Gericke said. 'Don't tell me we're losing the war?'

'My dear Paul, in Brest we don't even have a dock any longer. If you'd arrived in daylight you'd have noticed the rather unhappy state of those impregnable U-boat pens of ours. Five metres of reinforced concrete pulverised by a little item the RAF call the Earthquake bomb.' He raised his glass. 'To you, Paul. A successful trip, I hear?'

'Not bad.'

'Come now. A Canadian corvette, a tanker and three merchant ships? Thirty-one thousand tons, and you call that not bad? I'd term it a rather large miracle. These days two out of three U-boats that go out never return.' He shook his head. 'It isn't nineteen-forty any longer. No more Happy Time. These days they send out half-trained boys. You're one of the few oldtimers left.'

Gericke helped himself to a cigarette from a box on the table. It was French and of the cheapest variety, for when he lit it and inhaled, the smoke bit at the back of his throat, sending him into a paroxysm of coughing.

'My God! Now I know things are bad.'

'You've no idea how bad,' Friemel told him. 'Brest has been besieged by the American Eighth Army Corps since the ninth of August. The only reason we're still here is because of the quite incredible defence put up by General Ramcke and the Second Airborne Division. Those paratroopers of his are without a doubt the finest fighting men I've ever seen in action, and that includes the Waffen SS.' He reached for the Schnapps bottle again. 'Of course they were pulled out of the Ukraine to come here. It could be they are still euphoric at such good fortune. An American prison camp, after all, is infinitely to be preferred to the Russian variety.'

'And what's the U-boat position?'

'There isn't one. The Ninth Flotilla is no more. U-256 was the last to leave. That was eleven days ago. Orders are to regroup in Bergen.'

'Then what about me?' Gericke asked. 'I could have made for Norway by way of the Irish Sea and the North Channel.'

'Your orders, Paul, are quite explicit. You will make for Bergen via the English Channel, as the rest of the flotilla has done, only in your case, someone at High Command has provided you with what one might term a slight detour.'

Gericke, who had long since passed being surprised at anything, smiled. 'Where to, exactly?'

'It's really quite simple.' Friemel turned to the table behind, rummaged amongst a pile of charts, found the one he was looking for and opened it across the desk.

Gericke leaned over. 'Falmouth?'

'That's right. The Royal Navy's Fifteenth MGB Flotilla operating out of Falmouth has been causing havoc on this entire coast recently. To be perfectly honest, it's made any kind of naval activity impossible.'

'And what am I supposed to do about it?'

'According to your orders, go into Falmouth and lay mines.'

'They're joking, of course.'

Friemel held up a typed order. 'Dönitz himself.'

Gericke laughed out loud. 'But this is really beautiful, Otto. Quite superb in its idiocy, even for those chairbound bastards in Kiel. What on earth am I supposed to do, win the war in a single bold stroke?' He shook his head. 'They must believe in fairy stories. Someone should tell them that when the tailor boasted he could kill seven at one blow he meant flies on a slice of bread and jam.'

'I don't know,' Friemel said. 'It could be worse. There's a protecting curtain of mines plus a blockship here between Pendennis Point and Black Rock and a temporary net boom from Black Rock to St Anthony's Head. That's supposed to be highly secret, by the way, but it seems the Abwehr still have an agent operational in the Falmouth area.'

'He must feel lonely.'

'Ships in and out all the time. Go in with a few when the net opens.

Drop your eggs, up here in Carrick Roads and across the inner harbour and out again.'

Gericke shook his head. 'I'm afraid not.'

'Why?'

'We may get in, but we certainly won't get out.'

Friemel sighed. 'A pity, as I'll be going with you. Not out of any sense of adventure, I assure you. I have orders to report to Kiel and as the land routes to Germany are cut, my only way would seem to be with you to Bergen.'

Gericke shrugged. 'So, in the end, all roads lead to hell.'

Friemel helped himself to one of the French cigarettes and inserted it in his holder. 'What shape are you in?'

'We were strafed by a Liberator in Biscay. Superficial damage only, but my engines need a complete overhaul. New bearings for a start.'

'Not possible. I can give you four or five days. We must leave on the nineteenth. Ramcke tells me he can hold out for another week at the most. No more.'

The door opened and the young lieutenant entered. 'Signal from Kiel, sir. Marked most urgent.'

Friemel took the flimsy from him and adjusted his spectacles. A slight, ironic smile touched his mouth. 'Would you believe it, Paul, but this confirms my promotion as Rear Admiral in command of all naval forces in the Brest area. One can only imagine it has been delayed in channels.'

The lieutenant passed across another flimsy. Friemel read it, his face grave, then handed it to Gericke. It said: CONGRATULATIONS ON YOUR PROMOTION IN THE FULL AND CERTAIN KNOWLEDGE THAT YOU AND YOUR MEN WILL DIE RATHER THAN YIELD ONE INCH OF SOIL TO THE ENEMY. ADOLF HITLER.

Gericke passed it back. 'Congratulations, Herr Konteradmiral,' he said formally.

Without a flicker of emotion, Friemel said to the lieutenant, 'Send this message to Berlin. Will fight to the last. Long live the Führer. That's all. Dismiss!'

The young lieutenant withdrew. Friemel said, 'You approve?'

'Wasn't that Lütjen's last message before the *Bismark* went down?'

'Exactly,' Rear Admiral Otto Friemel said. 'Another drink, my friend?' He reached for the bottle, then sighed. 'What a pity. We appear to have finished the last of the Schnapps.'

It was still raining heavily in London at eight-thirty on the following evening when JU 88 pathfinders of *Gruppe* 1/KG 66, operating out of

Chartres and Rennes in France, made their first strike. By nine-fifteen the casualty department of Guy's Hospital was working at full stretch.

Janet Munro, in the end cubicle, curtain drawn, carefully inserted twenty-seven stitches into the right thigh of a young auxiliary fireman. He seemed dazed and lay there, staring blankly at the ceiling, an unlit cigarette hanging from the corner of his mouth.

Janet was being assisted by a male nurse named Callaghan, a white-haired man in his late fifties who had served on the Western Front as a Medical Corps sergeant in the First World War. He strongly approved of the young American doctor in every possible way and made it his business to look out for her welfare, something she seemed quite incapable of doing for herself. Just now he was particularly concerned about the fact that she had been on duty for twelve hours, and it was beginning to show.

'You going off after this one, miss?'

'How can I, Joey?' she said. 'They'll be coming in all night.'

Bombs had been falling for some time on the other side of the Thames but now there was an explosion close at hand. The whole building shook and there was a crash of breaking glass. The lights dimmed for a moment and somewhere a child started to wail.

'My God, Jerry certainly picks his time,' Callaghan remarked.

'What do you mean?' she said, still concentrating on the task in hand.

He seemed surprised. 'Don't you know who's here tonight, miss? Eisenhower himself. Turned up an hour ago just before the bombing started.'

She paused and looked at him blankly. 'General Eisenhower? Here?'

'Visiting those Yank paratroopers in ward seventy-three. The lads they brought over from Paris last week. Decorating some of them, that's what I heard.'

She was unable to take it in, suddenly very tired. She turned back to her patient and inserted the last couple of stitches.

'I'll dress it for you,' Callaghan said. 'You get yourself a cup of tea.'

As she stripped the rubber gloves from her fingers, the young fireman turned his head and looked at her. 'You a Yank then, Doctor?'

'That's right.'

'Got any gum, chum?'

She smiled and took a cigarette-lighter from her pocket. 'No, but I can manage a light.'

She took the cigarette from his mouth, lit it and gave it back to him. 'You'll be fine now.'

He grinned. 'Can you cook as well, Doc?'

'When I get the time.'

Suddenly, the effort of keeping her smile in place was too much and she turned and went into the corridor quickly. Callaghan was right. She needed that cup of tea very badly indeed. And about fifteen hours' sleep to follow – but that, of course, was quite impossible.

As she started along the corridor, the curtain of a cubicle was snatched back and a young nurse emerged. She was obviously panic-stricken, blood on her hands. Turning wildly, she saw Janet and called out – soundlessly, because at that moment another heavy bomb fell close enough to shake the walls and bring plaster from the ceiling.

Janet caught her by the shoulders. 'What is it?'

The girl tried to speak, pointing wildly at the cubicle as another bomb fell, and Janet pushed her to one side and entered. The woman who lay on the padded operating table, covered with a sheet, was obviously very much in labour. The young man who leaned over her was a corporal in the Commandos, his uniform torn and streaked with dust.

'Who are you?' The tiredness had left her now, as if it had never been.

'Her husband, miss. She's having a baby.' He plucked at her sleeve. 'For God's sake do something.'

Janet pulled back the sheet. 'When did she start?'

'Half an hour, maybe longer. We was in the High Street when the siren went, so I took her into the underground. Borough Station. When she started feeling bad I thought I'd better get her to hospital, but it was hell out there. Bombs falling all over the place.'

Another landed very close to the hospital now, followed by a second. For a moment, the lights went out. The woman on the table cried out in fear and pain. Her eyes started from her head as the lights came on again and she tried to sit up.

Janet pushed her down and turned to the young nurse. 'You know what's wrong here?'

'I'm not sure,' the girl said. 'I'm only a probationer.' She looked at her hands. 'There was a lot of blood.'

The young Commando pulled at Janet's sleeve. 'What's going on? What's up?'

'A baby is usually delivered head first,' Janet said calmly. 'This is what's known as a breech. That means it's presenting its backside.'

'Can you handle it?'

'I should imagine so, but we haven't got much time. I want you to stand over your wife, hold her hand and talk to her. Anything you like, only don't stop.'

'Shall I get Sister Johnson?' the young nurse asked.

'No time,' Janet said. 'I need you here.'

Bombs were falling steadily now and from the sound of it, panic had broken out amongst the crowd that waited in general casualty for treatment. She took a deep breath, tried to ignore that nightmare world outside and concentrated on the task in hand.

The first problem was to deliver the legs. She probed gently inside until she managed to get a finger up against the back of one of the child's knees. The leg flexed instantly and so did the other when she repeated the performance.

The woman cried out and Janet said to the husband, 'Tell her to push. Push hard.'

A moment later, the legs delivered themselves. She held out her hands for the young nurse to wipe away the blood, then grasped the legs, fingers beneath the thighs and pulled down firmly until the shoulders were in sight.

Now the arms were extended. She twisted the child to the left until the shoulder flexed, hooked a finger under the elbow and delivered the left arm. Bombs were still falling but further away now as she repeated the performance with the right.

There was a tremendous hubbub outside, people running up and down the corridor and a smell of burning. She whispered to the young nurse, 'So far so good. Now for the head.'

She put her right arm beneath the child and got her forefinger into its mouth, then probed with her left hand for a grip on the shoulders and started to pull. Slowly, very slowly, it moved and yet the strength required was so considerable that sweat sprang to her forehead.

And then it was clear and safe in her hands. But it was obvious at once that it wasn't breathing and the whole body was deep purple.

'Cotton-wool, quickly!' The young nurse passed some across and Janet cleared the mouth and nostrils. 'Now you can get Sister Johnson, if she's available, or Callaghan. Anybody, only hurry.'

The girl went out on the run and Janet blew into the tiny mouth. Quite suddenly the child shuddered, gave an audible gasp and started to cry.

Janet looked up and found the young Commando staring at her wildly. 'A daughter,' she said. 'If you're interested.'

His wife gave a stifled moan and fainted. At the same moment the curtain was jerked back and Sister Johnson rushed in. Janet handed her the baby. 'This one's yours, Sister,' she said. 'I'll see to the mother,' and she elbowed the young Commando out of the way and leaned over his wife.

It was later, when the bombing had stopped and she had moved out on the porch to smoke a cigarette, that the tiredness hit her again.

'Oh God,' she said softly. 'Isn't it ever going to end, this war?'

There were fires on the other side of the Thames towards Westminster and the acrid smell of smoke filled the air. Behind her the blackout curtain opened briefly and Callaghan appeared, an American officer in raincoat and peaked cap with him.

'Oh, there you are, Doctor,' Callaghan said. 'Been looking all over for you. This gentleman would like a word with you.'

'Colonel Brisingham, ma'am.' He saluted punctiliously.

Callaghan withdrew, leaving them alone in the dimly-lit porch. 'What can I do for you, Colonel?' Janet asked.

'General Eisenhower would appreciate a word, ma'am, if you could spare him a few minutes of your time.'

He delivered the words gravely and courteously and yet, for Janet, the walls of the porch seemed to move in and out again, very slowly. She fell against the colonel, who caught hold of her arms.

'Are you all right?'

'It's been a long day.' She took a deep breath. 'Where is the General?'

'Just across the yard, ma'am, in his staff car. If you'd follow me. We haven't much time, I'm afraid. He has to be back in Paris by tomorrow morning.'

The car was parked in a corner by the main gate. She was aware of the jeeps surrounding it, the helmets of the military police, then Brisingham had the rear door open.

'Doctor Munro, General.'

Janet hesitated, then climbed inside and Brisingham closed the door. In the faint light from the dashboard she could only get the briefest impression. He was wearing a trenchcoat, a forage cap, she could see that, but not much of his face except for the brief gleam of teeth that went with the inimitable smile.

'Would it surprise you if I said I felt as if I already knew you?' Eisenhower said.

She frowned and then saw the solution. 'Uncle Carey?'

He chuckled. 'You were all he used to talk about over the coffee at SHAEF when we were putting Overlord together. But I knew him from long before then. Panama – nineteen twenty-two, twenty-three. I was a major and he, as I recall, was a lieutenant-commander with a reputation for being difficult to handle.'

'He hasn't changed.'

'Not in the slightest.' He hesitated. 'When he went down in that Norwegian destroyer on D-day, for example. He should never have been there. A direct contravention of his orders.'

'Which cost him an eye and most of one arm.'

'I know. Tell me. This place Fhada? This Scottish island he's staying on at the moment? What's he doing there?'

'His mother's family came from there originally. He was left a cottage by a cousin just before the war. He wanted somewhere to hide for a while and I suppose it seemed as good as any. It's a strange place.'

'You think he was looking for something?'

'Perhaps.'

The general nodded. 'Did you know he's been trying to get back into action?'

'No, but it doesn't surprise me.'

'Me neither. He couldn't change his nature this late in the day, but it just isn't possible, you must see that. One eye, an apology for an arm. He's given as much as any man could . . .'

'Except his life.'

'Dammit!' Eisenhower said. 'The Navy Department won't budge. They want him on the retired list now.'

'And you?'

He sighed heavily. 'He sent me a letter by hand, delivered by some young naval officer on leave. Lucky I happened to be in London today.'

'He asked for your help? Carey Reeve?' She smiled. 'Now that, General, is really something.'

'The same thought *had* occurred to me,' Eisenhower said.

'And can you help?'

'I've a job in Paris for him, starting the first of October. Supply and Personnel Co-ordination, Deputy Director.'

'A desk job?' Janet shook her head. 'It's action he's after.'

'Those days are over. If he wants a job, there's one for him. Otherwise it's the boneyard. He must understand that.'

'But will he?' she said softly and almost to herself.

Eisenhower said, 'Look, is there any chance you could get a few days off and go and see him?'

She hesitated. 'I suppose so. I haven't had more than a weekend in the past six months.'

'Wonderful,' he said. 'Naturally I'll have someone on my staff make all the necessary travel arrangements for you. I'll give you a letter, making clear the terms of my offer. But the real pressure must come from you.'

There was a tap on the window. Eisenhower lowered it and Brisingham leaned in. 'We'll have to get moving if we're to make that plane, General.'

Eisenhower nodded impatiently and wound up the window again.

'They won't leave me alone for a minute. A hell of a war, even for generals, believe me.'

Far out in the Atlantic, the horizon crackled with sheet lightning and rain started to fall heavily. The wind was Force 8 on the Beaufort scale, a mountainous sea running and the *Deutschland* fled under stay-sails only, Richter and Sturm at the wheel.

At four bells of the first watch a sudden vicious squall struck from the south-east with incredible force, driving hail before it like bullets. The *Deutschland* lurched to one side, swinging nearly five points off course, Sturm lost his balance and was swept into the scuppers by a cascade of water, leaving Richter to struggle desperately with the spinning wheel. The *Deutschland* staggered as the wind dealt her another savage blow and started to heel over.

Berger, unable to sleep, had been lying in his bunk for the best part of an hour, smoking a cigar and listening to the music of the gale. Every part of the ship creaked and groaned, and the wind whistled through the rigging with a hundred separate voices. He was wearing foul-weather gear, seaboots and oilskin coat, ready for any emergency.

The crisis, when it came, was so unexpected that he was thrown from his bunk before he knew what was happening and rolled across the cabin, fetching up against the desk.

The floor continued to incline as he tried to get up, 'Oh, dear God, she's going!' he said aloud. Then the tilting ceased. He scrambled across to the door, got it open and went outside.

The lightning that flickered constantly in the sky above illuminated an extraordinary scene. The *Deutschland* was lying over, almost on her beam ends, with her lee rail under and lower yardarm dipping into broken water.

Richter and Sturm were wrestling with the wheel and several members of the crew lurched and slithered across the sloping deck in complete panic.

'She's going! She's going!' one man screamed. Berger punched him in the jaw, sending him flat on his back.

He cried, 'Bring her round, for God's sake! Bring her round!'

Gradually and with considerable difficulty, the *Deutschland* started to turn into the wind, as Richter and Sturm got the helm up, but the deck remained at such a slope that no one could stand without hanging on to something.

Berger yelled at the two nearest men, 'Take the wheel and tell Richter and Mr Sturm to come to me.'

He managed to make it to the aft cargo hatch on his hands and knees and was wrestling with the ropes of the canvas cover when Sturm and Richter arrived. 'What do you think?' Sturm cried above the roaring of the sea.

'The ballast's moved, that's obvious,' Berger replied. 'But how much is the important thing. Let's have this hatch cover open and see the state of the game.'

Below, for the passengers, there was total confusion. When the squall struck, Sister Angela and Sister Else had been sitting together on the bottom bunk in their cabin, discussing a passage of the scriptures, the usual evening task before bed. They were both thrown to the floor and the oil lamp fell from its hook in the ceiling to smash beside them. The spreading pool of oil flared but was almost immediately extinguished as the cabin tilted, the door burst open and water poured in.

Sister Angela started to make a final act of contrition. 'Oh my God, who art infinitely good in thyself . . .' But she choked on the words, every instinct rebelling against such a calm acceptance of death. She crawled to the door, calling to Sister Else to follow her.

The saloon was in total darkness, water pouring in through the shattered skylight. It was a nightmare world. Voices called hysterically. Someone lurched into her, she reached out and touched a face as an arm fastened about her in panic. And then a cabin door opened and light flooded out as Otto Prager appeared with a lantern in one hand.

The floor of the saloon was tilted at an angle of forty-five degrees, the dining table and chairs, all bolted to the floor, still in place, but on the port side at the bottom of the slope, water had gathered to a depth of three feet. Each time the *Deutschland* rolled, more came in through the broken skylight, newly repaired only the previous day after the *Guardian* episode.

Sister Angela found herself held by Sister Lotte, the youngest of the nuns. The girl was out of her mind with fear, and Sister Angela had to struggle to tear herself free.

She shook the younger woman vigorously and slapped her face. 'Pull yourself together, Sister. Remember what you are.'

Sister Else managed to get to her feet beside her, waist deep in water, the skirt of her black robe floating around her and at that moment, the cabin door next to Prager's opened and Sisters Käthe and Brigitte peered through.

Prager, who seemed remarkably calm, said, 'Everything will be fine, Sisters, no need to panic. Make for the companionway.'

Sister Angela got there first, an arm around Sister Lotte. Prager handed her the lantern and assisted the others, one by one, until they were all on the tilting companionway.

As he moved up to join Sister Angela the door at the head of the companionway opened and Berger peered in, a storm lantern in one hand. 'Everyone all right?'

'I think so,' Sister Angela said.

He crouched down to speak to her. 'No point in putting you into one of the boats. It wouldn't last five minutes in this sea. You understand me, Sister?'

'What must we do then, Captain?'

'Stay here for the moment.'

'What's gone wrong, Erich?' Prager demanded.

'The ballast has shifted into the lee bow. Most of the crew are down there now trying to do something about it. We need you, too, Otto. If another squall hits while we're in this state she'll turn turtle.'

Prager moved out into the night without a word. Sister Angela said, 'Is there anything we can do, Captain?'

'Pray,' Eric Berger told her. 'Very hard,' and he slammed the door shut and disappeared.

When Otto Prager went down the ladder into the cargo hold it was like a descent into hell. The crew worked in the light of a couple of storm lanterns, furiously shovelling sand to windward. Each time the ship rolled men stumbled into each other and went down.

Prager stepped off the ladder and fell to one knee. Someone cried out in fear, but otherwise everyone shovelled away with a grim frenzy, the only sound the creaking of the ship's timbers and the gale outside.

A strong arm hoisted Prager to his feet and Helmut Richter grinned down at him. 'Just think, Herr Prager, you could have been safe in Rio at this very moment enjoying a drink before a late dinner, looking out from the terrace of the Copacabana at the lights in the bay . . .'

'Well, I'm not,' Prager told him, 'so just give me a bloody shovel and let's get to it.'

For some time now it had been obvious that the *Deutschland* was tilting to windward, but on the companionway in the half-darkness it seemed an eternity before the door opened again and Berger peered in. He managed a smile, but only just.

'Did you pray, Sister?'

'We did.'

'Well, for what it's worth, your prayers were answered. Somebody on this tub must live right. It isn't me, so it must be you.'

'I'm willing to admit that possibility, Captain.'

'Excellent. We'll have the pump working as soon as we can, but it may not be possible to light a fire in the galley again before morning. I'm afraid you're going to find it rather uncomfortable down there for the rest of the night.'

'We'll manage.'

In a sudden outburst, he added roughly, 'Dammit, Sister, it was you who insisted on coming. I warned you.'

'Yes, Captain, I believe you did,' she said. 'And for that I thank you, amongst other things.' She looked down at the faces of the others, upturned in the dim light of the lamp. 'Shall we pray, my beloved sisters?'

She began to recite aloud the prayers for thanksgiving after a storm. 'So they cried unto the Lord in their trouble; and he delivered them from their distress.'

Berger shut the companionway door and turned towards Prager who leaned wearily on the hatch beside him. 'What a woman,' he said. 'What a bloody infuriating . . .'

'Wonderful woman,' Prager finished.

Berger laughed, then turned to look up at the quarterdeck where Richter had the wheel on his own now, for the wind had dropped a little although there was still a heavy sea running.

Sturm came down the ladder to join him. 'I've got a party on the pump, sir. Any further orders?'

'Yes,' Berger said. 'Wood, Mr Sturm. Every plank you can find. Gut the ship if needs be. Every cabin and locker, but I want that sand decked-off within twenty-four hours so it can't damn well move again, whatever happens.'

'Aye, aye, sir.' Sturm hesitated. 'A close one, Captain.'

'Too close, Mister,' Erich Berger said. 'Let's try not to make a habit of it,' and he turned and walked towards his cabin.

Barquentine *Deutschland*, 17 September 1944. Lat. 38°.56N., long. 30°.50W. Wind hauled into the west during the middle watch and we braced the yards forward. Hove the log and found we were going 10 knots. Overcast cleared just before noon and allowed the sun to come through, the wind dropping to a flat calm.

Five

The *Deutschland* seemed to float in space, completely still, every sail set, yards braced, perfectly reflected in a sea of green glass.

It was hot and airless. Conditions below were unbearable and, on the captain's orders, a canvas awning had been rigged aft of the main mast so that the sisters might be protected to some degree from the fierceness of the sun.

Most of the crew and passengers were suffering from sea boils now, a product not only of the unsatisfactory diet, but of the constant action of salt water on the skin. One of the men, a brawny Hamburger named Schirmer, was virtually crippled by a whole crop of them on his left leg. He leaned back groaning in a canvas chair while Sister Angela went to work with a lancet.

Forward from the mainmast, under the supervision of Sturm, four of the crew worked the heavy metal bar of the ship's two suction pumps and water gushed across the deck in a brown stream.

Richter, who had just finished a thirty-minute stint himself, dipped a pannier into the water bucket, wrinkling his nose in disgust. 'Have you seen this, Herr Leutnant?' he asked Sturm, and poured the contents of the pannier back into the bucket. The water was dark red.

'Rust from the tanks, I expect.' Sturm grinned. 'On this ship we think of everything, Helmut. You don't just get a drink of water. We throw in an iron tonic as well. Good for the constitution.'

'My belly doesn't agree.' Richter ran a hand across his stomach. 'Sometimes the cramps are terrible. Most of the lads will tell you the same.'

Sister Lotte was standing by the mizzen shrouds on the port side. Like the other nuns, she had put on her white tropical habit again, because of the heat. And, as always, Richter wondered how on earth she managed to keep it so clean. She made a rather appealing figure as she stood there, one hand on a rope, gazing out to sea.

Walz, the cook, came out of the galley and emptied a pail of garbage over the rail beside her. She moved back hastily.

'Sorry, Sister,' he said, with total insincerity.

'That's all right, Herr Walz,' she answered in a low, sweet voice.

He looked her over boldly and grinned, showing bad teeth. The lust in his eyes was plain: her smile faded and she reached for the shrouds as if to support herself.

Walz turned back to the galley and found Richter leaning against the entrance. He was stripped to the waist, his muscular body burned brown by the sun, the long, blond hair and beard bleached white, a black Brazilian cigarillo between his teeth. A match flared in the bosun's cupped hands. As he leaned down to it, he said softly, 'Manners, you bastard. That isn't some San Pauli whore you're talking to.'

'So, you fancy her, too?' Walz grinned again. 'I don't blame you. It's a long trip home and women are women, as the captain said, whatever they choose to wear. It's what's between the legs that counts.'

He was hurled into the shadows of the galley, found himself back across the table, a hand of iron at his throat. There was a sharp click as the blade of the Finnish gutting knife in the bosun's right hand sprang into view.

'One wrong word, you lump of dung,' Richter said calmly, 'try even looking at her again as you did now and you go over the side – and I wouldn't like to guarantee it'll be in one piece.'

Walz almost fainted with terror, felt his bowels move. The bosun patted his face. 'That's it, Ernst. That's exactly the way I like you. Frightened to death.'

He snapped the blade of the gutting knife back into place and went outside.

Sister Lotte was still standing by the mizzen shrouds and, at that moment, an albatross swooped down to where the garbage floated, motionless as the ship itself.

She turned, as if by instinct, and became aware that Richter was watching her. She smiled and he crossed the deck to join her.

'Herr Richter.' There was no attempt to conceal the pleasure in her eyes. 'That bird – what was it?'

'An albatross, Sister. King of the scavengers. There'll be more around soon, when they get wind of our garbage.'

'So beautiful.' She shaded her eyes against the sun and watched it go.

And so are you, by God, Richter thought. 'They say an albatross is probably the ghost of a dead sailor.'

'And you believe that?'

Her eyes were very blue, her face a perfect oval framed by the white coif. Richter's throat was suddenly dry. He said, 'Of course not, Sister. Superstitious nonsense.' He took a deep breath. 'Now, if you'll excuse me, I must see the captain.'

He had a rope burn on his right wrist. She reached for his hand and frowned. 'That's nasty. It could get worse. You must let me see to it for you.'

Her fingers were cool. There was sweat on his brow and then, across her shoulder, he saw that Sister Angela, seated under the awning, her medical case open beside her as she treated one of the seamen, was watching him gravely.

Richter pulled his hand away. 'No need, Sister. It's nothing, believe me.'

Berger, seated at the desk in his cabin, was entering the log.

. . . 18 September 1944. A bad night. Rain and heavy seas. Lower t'gallant split during a sudden squall at six bells in the mid-watch. Weather changes again to flat calm in the forenoon. Mister Sturm reports sixteen inches of water in the bilges.

He put down his pen and sat back, aware of the dull monotonous thumping of the pump. Not good. Not good at all for her to be taking so much water. Although he had said nothing to Sturm and Richter about it, he knew that the seriousness of the situation must be as apparent to them as it was to him.

There was a knock on the door and Richter entered. 'Mr Sturm's compliments, sir. From the sound of things, she's just about dry again.'

Berger nodded. 'What do you think, Helmut?'

Richter shrugged. 'She's old, sir. Too old, and I shouldn't think the copper's been off her in years. God knows what state her timbers are in.' He hesitated. 'And when that squall struck the other night, when she nearly turned turtle . . .'

'You think she took some damage that we weren't aware of?'

Before Richter could reply, there was a confused shouting on the deck, mixed with cheering. And a strange drumming. Berger was on his feet in an instant, got the door open and rushed outside with Richter at his heels.

It was raining, a freak tropical downpour. Most of the crew were running about the deck like madmen, those who had been able to find buckets holding them up to catch the sweet water. The nuns, sheltering under the awning, were laughing like children as water poured from it in a torrent. Sturm stood underneath the impromptu shower, water cascading over his head. He turned and, seeing Berger, moved aside hurriedly.

'Sorry, Captain. Collective madness.'

He stood mopping his face with his neckerchief, like a schoolboy caught out. The rain ceased as suddenly as it had started, and steam began to rise from the decks.

Berger said, 'How's the pumping?'

'Sucked dry, sir.' Sturm hesitated. 'For the moment.'

Berger nodded, aware that most of the crew were hanging around, intent on picking up any information that was going. He made his judgement and acted on it. There was, after all, little point in pretending the situation didn't exist.

'Not good, Mr Sturm. Sixteen inches today. The same yesterday. Fourteen the day before. There has to be a reason.'

There was a heavy silence, broken only by the creaking of the rigging and the slapping of the empty sails.

Richter spoke first. 'Maybe I should go down and take a look, Captain.'

He was an excellent swimmer, and self-evidently strong as a bull. With the ship totally becalmed, there was little danger. Berger nodded. 'All right.' He took a key from his pocket and handed it to Sturm. 'Get a rifle from the gun locker, just in case.'

As Richter pulled off his canvas rope-soled shoes, Sister Angela moved to Berger's side. 'Why the rifle, Captain?'

Berger shrugged. 'Sharks. No sign now, but amazing how they appear with a man in the water, and all that garbage doesn't help.'

Sister Lotte turned pale. She moved to Richter's side where he stood at the rail, tightening his belt. 'It's – it's very deep, isn't it, Herr Richter?'

Richter laughed out loud, 'A thousand fathoms, at least. But don't worry, I'm not going all the way down.'

Berger, listening to this exchange, frowned, but the time was hardly appropriate to make any comment. Instead he said, 'You want a line, Helmut?'

Richter shook his head. 'Why bother? There isn't an inch of movement in her.' He put one foot on the rail, sprang up and dived cleanly into the water.

A shoal of small fish scattered before him, disintegrating in a silver cloud. He went down fast, through water that was like green glass, pale with sunlight. The planks of the hull of the *Deutschland* were coated with barnacles, and the seagrass sprouted everywhere in a gaudy carpet.

Years since her bottom's been scraped, he thought, and swam down to the keel, hanging on to it for a moment, then started to work his way along towards the prow.

On deck, they waited in silence. Richter surfaced once, for air, waved and went under again. Sister Lotte gripped the rail tightly, her knuckles white as she stared down into the water. Berger, watching her closely, glanced up and found Sister Angela looking at him. Her face was calm but there was something close to pain in her eyes. He took out his pipe and started to fill it from the worn oilskin pouch. More problems. As if he didn't have enough on his plate. And why did it have to be Richter, the finest seaman in the crew?

At that moment the bosun surfaced and floated at the port rail, coughing, his hair plastered to his skull. Someone tossed him a line and he was hauled over the rail.

He squatted on the deck for a moment, shivering. Berger said, 'How was it? You can speak out. Let everyone hear.'

'Nothing marked, Captain,' Richter said. 'No sign of any real damage. It's as we thought, she's a very old lady. In places there are gaps between her planks where you can stick two fingers. I'd say she needed recaulking ten years ago.'

Berger turned to address the men. 'You heard him. Nothing we can't handle. And with double the normal crew there won't be any difficulties in manning the pumps.'

The faces around him were still filled with uncertainty, but at that moment the mainsail flapped, as a tiny wind rippled the water from the south-east.

Berger looked up as the sails started to fill and laughed. 'There you are, a good omen. We're on the move again. Back to work, Mr Sturm, if you please.'

Sturm barked orders and the crew broke away. Sister Angela said, 'If you have a moment, Captain, I'd like a word with you.'

Berger glanced from her to Lotte who, with the other nuns, was clearing away her belongings from under the awning. 'All right, Sister.'

In his cabin, she faced him across the desk, perfectly composed, hands folded. 'Lotte is the most vulnerable of those amongst my charges, Captain. It is my sworn duty to see that nothing interferes with the path she has chosen.'

'What you're trying to say is that she isn't a proper nun yet,' Berger said. 'Not like the rest of you?' He shook his head. 'It doesn't make any kind of difference to me, I assure you. My orders to the crew are plain where you and your friends are concerned.'

'And Herr Richter?'

He leaned back and looked up at her. 'All right, so you've caught him looking at the girl a few times. What do you expect me to do about that?'

'She was afraid for him when he went over the side and she allowed it to show.'

'He's a good-looking boy.'

'Which is exactly what's worrying me.'

Berger said, 'Helmut Richter was Obersteuermann on a U-boat before he fetched up in Brazil like the rest of us. Chief Quartermaster, to you. Iron Cross, Second and First Class. The finest seaman I've ever known and a remarkable young man in every way. You've nothing to worry about, believe me.'

'I have your assurance in this matter, then?'

'Yes, dammit.' He was unable to contain his exasperation, went to the door, opened it and called to Sturm, 'Send Richter in here.'

As he went back to his desk, Sister Angela made a move towards the door. Berger said, 'No, don't go. You might as well hear this.'

She hesitated and at that moment there was a knock on the door and Richter entered. He had put on a heavy sweater and reefer, but still looked pale.

'You wanted me, Herr Kapitän?'

Berger produced a bottle and a glass from his desk cupboard. 'Scotch whisky, Haig and Haig. The very best. You've earned it.'

'It was colder than I thought down there.'

Richter drank some of the whisky and Berger sat down. 'How long have we known each other, Helmut?'

'A year, Captain. Fourteen months to be precise. Why do you ask?'

'The young nun,' Berger told him. 'Sister Lotte.' He hesitated, choosing his words. 'She was worried about you.'

Richter glanced at Sister Angela, his face paler than ever now, then placed his glass on the desk carefully. 'My affair, Herr Kapitän.'

'Don't play the fool with me, Helmut,' Berger snapped. 'The girl is still a novice. Do you know what that means to these people?'

'That she hasn't made up her mind yet,' Richter said evenly.

'And you'd like to make it up for her, is that it?'

Richter glanced at Sister Angela, then turned back to Berger. 'You don't understand, either of you, so let me make it plain.' He held up his left hand. 'Before I would see harm come to her from any man, I would cut this off. You understand me?'

'I believe you, boy. And what happens when we reach Kiel and dry land again will be none of my concern, but for the present, you'll stay away from her. I could make it an order, but I won't. I'll simply ask for your word instead.'

For a moment he thought that Richter was going to argue but the bosun's hesitation was only fractional. He braced himself, heels together. 'You have it, sir.'

'That's all right, then.'

Richter went out quickly and Berger said to Sister Angela, 'Was there anything else?'

'No, I don't think so. I appear to anger you at times, Captain. I wonder why?'

'God knows, Sister. I wish *I* did. I've experienced a few hard cases in my time: you get them in every crew. They can be handled well enough. With boot and fist if necessary, but you . . .'

She said gently, 'Poor Captain Berger. If only everything in life were capable of such a simple solution.'

She went out. Berger sat there, thinking about it, realizing suddenly that it was the first time he'd seen her smile.

Like many a distinguished sailor before him, sea-sickness was an old story to Rear Admiral Otto Friemel, and the foul weather which had allowed U-235 to make such an excellent surface run from Brest had had an unfortunate effect on his stomach. On arrival off the mouth of the Fal, he had accepted the offer of the bunk in Gericke's cabin on which to recover.

He slept surprisingly well and drifted up from darkness into a world of total silence. For a moment, he could not remember where he was and lay there frowning in the dim light. Then the curtain was pulled back and Gericke entered with a pot of coffee and two cups on a tray.

Friemel swung his legs to the floor. 'Things were a total blank. Does that ever happen to you?'

'Frequently.'

'A nasty feeling. Perhaps I'm getting too old. For this sort of thing certainly.'

Gericke said, 'It's the war, that's all. It's gone on too long.'

He took a chart from the shelf above the bunk and opened it out across the small table. Friemel said, 'It's damned quiet.'

'And so it should be. Most of the crew are lying down. Those who have to move are walking with rags round their boots.'

'How are they taking it?'

'The prospect of imminent death, you mean?' Gericke shrugged. 'They're good lads, and we've been together a long time. But they've been to Japan and back, remember, so there's a distinct feeling that we could be taking our pitcher to the well once too often.' He lit a cigarette and picked up a slide rule. 'Of course, it hasn't helped that I've taken the coding machine to pieces and distributed them around the crew in case the worst comes to the worst.'

'And you share their pessimism?'

'Not entirely.' Gericke traced a pencil across the mouth of the Fal from Black Rock Beacon to St Anthony's Head. 'According to the Abwehr's friendly local agent, the boom is positioned here. Getting in is no problem. There have been several ships in and out since we arrived, but so far they've always been singles. I'd rather follow a small convoy, if possible. It would give us better cover.'

Friemel inserted a cigarette in his holder. 'Another point in your favour, as I see it, is that at this stage in the war, the *Tommis* are hardly likely to expect a German U-boat to attempt to penetrate a major naval installation.'

'A comforting thought. But I'd rather not rely on it. Once in, we drop the mines through the stern tubes. Here in Carrick Roads; across the mouth of the Inner Harbour, what's left across the entrance to St Mawes . . .'

'And out again.'

'You forget the boom. We'll need a ship coming in or out for it to open again. We'll have to wait. And if anyone's unfortunate enough to touch off one of those mines in the meantime, the door, I assure you, will remain very tightly shut.'

'And what do we do then – scuttle?'

'There is another possibility. Not much of a one, but it's there.' Gericke ran his pencil across to Pendennis Point. 'Here, between the Point and Black Rock Beacon.'

'The minefield?' Friemel said. 'A death trap, surely.'

'Not the inshore run. South Passage, they call it. According to the Abwehr report, they haven't bothered to mine it. Simply stopped the hole by sinking an old merchant ship.'

Friemel looked at the map. 'In six metres. It would surprise me if a mackerel could find room to squeeze past.'

'Six metres now,' Gericke said. 'But at high tide, which tonight is at twenty-three hundred hours, nine metres at least in that slot.'

Friemel examined the map again. 'Sorry, Paul, but I just don't see it. Barely room to submerge, even at high water. And the navigation would be impossible.'

'But I wasn't thinking of submerging,' Gericke said. 'Not completely. I'd stay on the bridge and give steering directions. I've memorized the chart.'

'God in Heaven!' Friemel whispered.

The green curtain was pulled aside and Oberleutnant zur See Karl Engel, the first watch officer, appeared. 'Contact, sir. Ships moving in from the east, line astern. Three, possibly four.'

Gericke glanced at his watch. It was a few minutes past nine. 'Sounds exactly what we've been waiting for. You know what to do. Ready to

move out in five minutes from now. We follow them in blind. I'll take
the helm myself.'

'No periscope?' Friemel said.

'Not until we're well into Carrick Roads.'

Engel disappeared and the curtain dropped back into place.

Gericke opened a cupboard under the bunk and took out a bottle and
a couple of tin mugs.

'Schnapps?' Friemel asked.

'The best.' Gericke poured a generous tot into each mug. 'It's been to
Japan and back, this bottle. The one I keep only for the most special
occasions.'

'And to what shall we drink, my dear Paul?' asked Konteradmiral
Otto Friemel.

'Why, to the game,' Gericke said. 'That would seem appropriate. To
the bloody stupid and imbecile game we've all been playing for five
years, now which would once more appear, as they say, to be afoot.'

Janet Munro came awake reluctantly to the persistent buzzing of the
front doorbell. She had a splitting headache, her mouth was dry. She lay
staring up at the ceiling through the darkness, trying to pull herself
together, hoping that damn noise would cease. But it didn't. Suddenly
angry, she flung the bedclothes aside and reached for her bathrobe.

When she opened the front door, a tall, slightly-built young naval
officer in reefer coat and peaked cap was reaching for the bell push
again. He had stooped shoulders and seemed tired, particularly around
the eyes, and a bad scar ran down the right side of the face.

She glanced at her watch. It was just after ten. She'd had three hours'
sleep. Under the circumstances she found considerable difficulty in
keeping her temper.

'Yes, what is it?'

'Dr Munro? My name's Jago. Harry Jago.'

'I'm afraid you've chosen the wrong night. I don't know who sent
you, but I have to sleep. Maybe some other time.'

Jago's smile faded. He suddenly looked very young. 'You don't
understand.' He produced a letter from his pocket and held it out to
her. 'Your uncle asked me to deliver this.'

She frowned. 'Uncle Carey? I thought he was still in the Hebrides?'

'That's right. I spoke with him on Fhada the day before yesterday.'

She took the letter from him and nodded slowly as if still having
difficulty in taking it all in. 'And what are you doing up there,
Lieutenant?'

'Oh, I run a kind of postal service round the islands,' Jago said cheerfully.

'Hardly the dead centre of the only war we've got.'

'While good men and true are fighting and dying elsewhere? It's a point of view.' He was no longer smiling. 'Anyway, you've got your letter, Doctor, and if you're interested, the Admiral was in good health when I last saw him.'

She regretted the sarcasm instantly. She had become increasingly prone to such cruel remarks of late.

'Just a minute,' she said. Jago turned. She smiled. 'You'd better come in and have a drink while I read this.'

The living-room was small and untidy. She switched on the electric fire and sat down. 'Take off your coat and help yourself to a drink. You'll find some Scotch in the corner cupboard. No ice, I'm afraid. Something you learn to live without over here.'

'What about you?'

'A small one would be fine. Nice and straight.'

He took off his coat and cap and moved to the cupboard, and while he busied himself getting the drinks she read the letter. It told her nothing she had not already learned from General Eisenhower, and was mainly concerned with her uncle's desperate need to get back into the war again. Talking it out, she thought, just as if I was sitting in front of him, that's all he's doing.

She looked up as Jago came back with a couple of glasses and the first thing she noticed was the Navy Cross ribbon. She took the drink automatically, without even saying thank you.

'Sorry about the delay,' Jago said. 'The letter, I mean. I tried here yesterday evening but you were out, and when I called at the hospital today, they said you were too busy to see anyone.'

'You could have left it.'

'The admiral asked me to see that you got it personally.'

'You're a rotten liar, you know that?'

'I'm afraid so.'

'Why was it so important?'

'He showed me a photo of you.'

She laughed again. 'And what is that supposed to do – sweep me off my feet?'

'No, ma'am,' Jago said. 'You asked me, I told you, that's all.' He stood up and reached for his reefer. 'I'd better be moving.'

'Oh, be your age, for God's sake.' She was suddenly angry again. 'Let me tell you something, Lieutenant. Tonight, I feel not only totally exhausted but old enough to be your mother.'

'You're twenty-seven,' he said. 'Birthday, November ninth. That's Scorpio and I can certainly see why.'

'Did you get that out of Uncle Carey, too? All right, I surrender. What is it you do in the Navy in those circumstances?'

'Strike your flag.'

'I've had a rather heavy afternoon,' she said. 'Fourteen flying bombs hit London today. Maybe you heard the bangs but I saw the results. I fell into bed exactly three hours ago. Then you arrived.'

He was on his feet again in a moment. 'I'm sorry. I just didn't realize.'

'You brought a letter for Ike as well, didn't you?' He hesitated and she carried on. 'Don't worry, you aren't giving away state secrets. He spoke to me about it last night. My uncle's trying to get back into the glorious fight.'

Jago didn't know what to say. He was fascinated by this strange, abrasive girl, by her wide, almost ugly mouth and her harsh, distinctive voice.

She said, 'When are you going back? The weekend?'

'That's right.'

'Me too. I mean, I'm going to see my uncle, courtesy of the Supreme Commander, but they haven't given me a date yet.'

'Maybe we'll be on the same train.'

She took an English cigarette from a packet on the mantelpiece and he lit it for her. 'And the rest of your leave? What do you plan to do with that?'

'I don't really know.' Jago shrugged. 'There doesn't seem to be too much fun in this town these days.'

'Oh, I don't know,' she said. 'You Yanks seem to do all right, with your cigarettes and whisky. Why, you can even get a cab when you need one, which is more than the locals can, believe me.'

'Is that how you see yourself? A kind of American Cockney?'

'I came out of Paris in nineteen-forty. I've been here ever since.'

There was a hiatus and Jago couldn't think of anything to say. Janet said, 'Where are you going now? Out on the town?'

'I don't think so. I've got a bed in one of the officers' clubs.'

'And just think – you could be walking along the Embankment with me.'

He stared at her. 'The Embankment?'

'Sure, why not? I could do with the air. Give me three minutes to throw something on.' She crossed to the bedroom door and paused to look back at him. 'You don't mind, do you?'

* * *

In Falmouth, coasting along at periscope depth, U-235 discharged the last of her mines across the entrance to St Mawes harbour and started to turn away. Gericke was at the periscope, Admiral Friemel and Engel beside him, and the Obersteuermann, Willi Carlsen, at the helm. The tension had been incredible, the crew padding about like ghosts, no one speaking above a whisper.

There was sweat on Engel's face. He said eagerly, 'And now we go home?'

'Bergen is home?' Gericke said as he started his sweep, checking the situation in the harbour.

But at that moment a tug, emerging from Carrick Roads, struck one of the mines. There was an instant searing explosion, a tongue of flame that illuminated the entire harbour area. The concussion drummed on the hull of the submarine.

'Oh my God,' Engel moaned.

Friemel, face ashen, plucked at Gericke's shoulder. 'A mine?'

'I'm afraid so. Strike one.' And then he seemed to go rigid, his shoulders hunched. He turned to look at them. 'There are two River-class frigates moored almost side by side just north of the inner harbour.'

'Not even you could be crazy enough for such a thing,' Engel said desperately. 'We wouldn't stand a chance.'

'And what chance do we stand now?' Gericke demanded. 'Frigates, Karl. Two of them.'

He seemed to crackle with electricity, his face very white, his mad, dark eyes blazing. It was as if he had been sleeping and was now awake.

He turned on Friemel. 'Admiral?'

Friemel found himself shaking, not with fear, but with a kind of fierce joy. 'Why not, by God? A hell of a way to go, Paul.'

And Engel, touched now by the same madness, all fear leaving him, saluted, heels together. 'At your orders, Herr Kapitän.'

'Good man.' Gericke clapped him on the shoulder. 'Take her up. We'll have to do this the hard way. Prepare tubes one to four for surface firing.' He turned to Carlsen. 'You take the helm, Willi, and make it good.'

There was a sudden bustle of activity, the klaxon sounding battle stations. As Gericke moved towards the ladder, he added almost casually, over his shoulder, 'Perhaps you'd care to join me on the bridge, Herr Konteradmiral?'

At the top of the ladder he waited. There was a hiss of compressed air, a rushing of water and then Engel called, 'The hatch is above water.'

Gericke unclipped it and scrambled out on to the bridge of the conning-tower. Heavy rain smacked solidly into his face and the waters of the harbour heaved in turmoil. The tug was almost under now, but the oil around it was on fire and when he focused his night glasses, men jumped into view, hurling themselves into the icy water.

In the forward torpedo compartment the crew worked frantically to make ready. Engel was already aligning the attack periscope as Gericke swung his glasses to focus on the two frigates.

Beside him, Friemel said, 'A lot of activity on deck. I'd say you've got three minutes before they chop those anchors and get out of there.'

Alarm klaxons echoed stridently across the water. There was considerable movement now on the harbour wall. Suddenly, there was a hollow staccato booming and brilliant balls of fire seemed to cascade towards them in a great curve, falling into the water to port.

'That's it,' Friemel said grimly. 'They know we're here.'

U-235 surged forward. Gericke said calmly, 'Tubes one to four prepare for surface firing.'

Engel called into the voice pipe. There was the briefest of pauses before he looked up. 'One to four ready, sir.'

'Six metres,' Gericke said. 'Line of sight. One and two on the starboard frigate, three and four take care of the gentleman to port. Distance one thousand metres, speed thirty-five. Director angle blue four.'

Engel relayed the orders through the voice pipe to Leading Seaman Pich, who manned the TDC, the complicated electrical device linking gyro compass, attack periscope and torpedo circuits, which from now on would, in effect, be responsible for the success or failure of the operation.

He made the final connection. Engel guided the aiming cross of the attack periscope on to the starboard frigate which, relieved of its anchor, was starting to swerve to port.

'Blue four, ready to fire, sir!'

'Fire,' Gericke called.

'Tube one fire. Tube two fire!'

The U-boat staggered as the torpedoes broke free and raced towards the target at thirty-five knots. The port frigate was moving now, surging forward as her captain gave her everything she had, the bow wave rising.

'She'll make it, Paul. She'll make it!' Friemel cried, his binoculars glued to his eyes.

'Oh no she won't,' Gericke said calmly. 'This is my night. Hard a-starboard,' he called. 'It's all yours, Karl. Fire at will.'

Machine-gun bullets rattled against the conning-tower, several shells landed close enough on the port side to cause the U-boat to roll violently. But it was Karl Engel's night, too – calm, detached, cooler than he had ever been, as the captain of the frigate made his one mistake, turning to starboard to bring all guns to bear, momentarily exposing his entire port side, a perfect target.

As the torpedoes were released, the U-boat corkscrewed in the heavy seas. 'Hard a-port,' Gericke called. 'And tell Dietz to give them everything he's got.'

There was a muffled explosion, followed by another as the first two torpedoes struck home. A cheer drifted up from the control room. Across the water, orange fire erupted from the first frigate and black smoke billowed into the night. The second was turning frantically now, as if her captain already sensed that the axe was about to fall, her guns still firing.

A moment later, number three torpedo hit, closely followed by the fourth. The frigate staggered drunkenly, her prow seemed to lift high into the air, then plunged. There was a further great explosion and flames towered into the night.

'That's it,' Gericke said. 'The magazine. It has to be.' He called to Engel. 'I said speed, damn you! Speed! Let's get out of here.'

All hell had broken loose now, guns firing across the harbour from the shore installations. Friemel, ducking between the steel canopy as a bullet ricocheted close to his head, said, 'Gun crew, Paul?'

'No,' Gericke said. 'We'd only give them a better target. We'll be out of it soon, believe me. They won't be expecting us to try the South Passage run. It isn't supposed to exist, remember.'

The wind rolled thick, oily smoke in a black pall across the harbour, blanketing the entire scene, and U-235, hidden from view, made towards Pendennis Point at full speed.

The tide was running fast under the Point as they turned into the channel. In the control room, Engel had the helm, Friemel at his shoulder. Everyone seemed to have crowded in – Dietz, the Chief Engineering Officer, young Heini Roth, the Second Watch Officer.

The diesels had stopped and the propellers were being driven by the electric motors. It seemed very still and when Gericke's voice crackled over the Tannoy, Roth gave a startled gasp.

'We haven't got too much time to spare. The tide's beginning to ebb and there's a five or six knot current running, so let's get it right first time.'

His voice, clearly audible to every man on board, was properly calm. Engel, speaking into the microphone box above his head, barely managed to keep his voice steady as he replied, 'Aye, aye, sir. Ready when you are.'

Gericke, on the bridge, was colder than he'd ever been in his life before. Reaction, he told himself, to all that action and passion. He managed a smile. He wore a lifejacket, headphones and a throat microphone, and was up to his chest in water.

It was not totally dark for an eerie phosphorescence, and considerable broken water, gave him a far better view of the general situation than he had expected. The hubbub on the far side of the harbour seemed muffled and far away, without reality.

'Course one-eight-two,' he said.

Engel's voice crackled in his ears. 'Seven metres under the keel . . . six metres under the keel.'

They surged on, caught by the current, white water all around and somewhere high above in the night, the turret on Pendennis Point lifted into the darkness. Gericke could hear traffic, and wondered briefly whether there might be searchlights mounted.

There was sudden panic in Engel's voice, 'Two metres, sir. Only two metres under the keel . . . one metre.'

Gericke said calmly, 'Steady as she goes, Karl. Nice and easy. Half-ahead.'

'We would appear to have run out of water, my dear Paul,' Friemel's voice sounded equally calm.

U-235 seemed to shudder, there was a crunch, a long-drawn-out grating that set on edge the teeth of every man on board.

'Oh God, that's it,' Heini Roth said aloud in the control room.

And yet they were still moving, a long, continuous grating, that suddenly ceased as Gericke's voice called, 'Full ahead.'

There was a ragged cheer through the entire boat. 'He's done it!' Dietz said excitedly. 'As usual,' he added.

Gericke's voice sounded again, 'If you think we're out of the wood yet, forget it. We haven't passed the blockship. A hundred metres to go. I can see her plain. Half-engines and make ready to give me everything you've got when I give the word.'

On the bridge he faced the last obstacle. U-235 drifted forward in the grip of the current that coursed through South Passage as the tide started to ebb. The blockship was an old coaster, her single stack clear against the night sky, deck awash.

'Hard a-starboard,' Gericke said.

The slot between the rocks and the blockship seemed inconceivably narrow, but it was too late to turn back now. Again there was a grating under the keel.

Engel's voice was frantic. 'There should be six metres, sir. Six metres.'

The grating stopped as the U-boat slid on. 'Probably a chain,' Gericke said. 'Keep going, Karl. Not long now.'

Somewhere behind him, beyond the smoke on the other side of the harbour, there was a muffled explosion. He paid no heed, and gave all his concentration to the task in hand, gripping the rail with numbed fingers.

And then the boat seemed to be caught in a giant hand and pushed forward by a sudden fierce current. The blockship was alongside – the stack looming above him, rusting plates, bridge windows smashed, a ghost ship.

He leaned over the rail. This was the moment of maximum danger, the time for jagged metal or protruding girders to open them up like a sardine can.

There was a grating on the starboard side, the cliff seemed very close, too close, and then, as they swung to port in the current, the blockship seemed to drift away into the night, was suddenly abeam.

Gericke said hoarsely, 'We're into clear water. Heavy seas. Wind force six by my estimation. Full ahead, diesels too, if you please.'

The scene in the control room was incredible. Dietz burst into tears and Friemel, in an excess of emotion, grabbed Heini Roth and hugged him.

'Remarkable,' the admiral said. 'There I was, lying in my coffin ready to go. Now I've just been told it was all a mistake.'

On the bridge, Gericke hung on tight as U-235 rode into the full force of the wind, sweeping in from the Channel. It was very dark now, with no landmarks to guide him as one great wave after another slapped over him. Only the roaring of the sea was in his ears. Better to get out of it now. 'All right, Karl,' he said. 'Bring her up and let me get dry, then we'll submerge till we're in mid-channel.'

And suddenly the roaring was louder and it was no longer the sea. He became conscious of an enormous white bow wave to starboard. There was a tremendous crash, the tearing of metal as a dark, greyhound shape ploughed right across the U-boat's forecastle and plunged on into the night.

The U-boat rolled, the conning-tower swung to port and Gericke was tossed over the side.

'My night,' he thought, for some inane reason clutching at his cap. 'Wasn't that what I said?' and then he hit the water and the first wave rolled over him.

The dim shape Gericke had glimpsed momentarily as it ploughed across the U-boat's forecastle was a Vosper MTB of the Royal Navy's Fifteenth Flotilla, racing home from patrol at thirty-five knots on receipt of the news from Falmouth over the radio.

Now she drifted helplessly, making water, all engines stopped. On the bridge, her commander, an RNVR lieutenant named Drummond, was taking the damage report from the boat's chief petty officer.

'How long have we got, Chief?'

'In this sea, an hour at the most, sir. If they want to save her they'd better get a tug out here fast.'

'You're certain it was a submarine?'

'Definite, sir. Leading Seaman Cooper saw it, too.' He hesitated. 'But whether one of ours or theirs, I couldn't be sure.'

'My God,' Drummond said softly.

There was an excited cry aft of the bridge. 'Someone in the water, sir, off the port rail.'

'Searchlight,' Drummond said. 'Quickly now!'

The beam sliced across the broken water and picked out Gericke in his yellow lifejacket, his cap pulled down over his ears. He waved as he was swept in under the rail.

'Quickly!' Drummond called. 'He must be frozen half to death in there.'

Bell, the petty officer, ran down from the bridge to supervise. There was a flurry of activity at the rail and Gericke was hauled aboard. Drummond leaned over the bridge rail, watching anxiously, training the searchlight on them and then Bell looked up.

'Good God, sir, we've got ourselves a Jerry.'

In London, it was raining hard and fog crouched at the ends of the streets. Janet Munro's trenchcoat was soaked through, as was the scarf bound around her hair.

They had walked for several miles in the pouring rain – Birdcage Walk, the Palace, St James's Park and Downing Street, although Jago hadn't been able to see very much. Not that he cared.

'Sure you haven't had enough?' he asked as they moved down towards Westminster Bridge.

'Not yet. I promised you something special, remember?'

'Did you?' Jago looked puzzled.

They came to the bridge and she turned on to the Embankment. 'Well, this is it,' she said. 'The most romantic place in town. Every American in London should walk along the Embankment at least once, preferably after midnight.'

'It's almost that now,' Jago said.

'Good, we'll have another cigarette and wait for the witching hour.'

They leaned on the parapet and listened to the lapping of the water. 'Have you enjoyed it, your guided tour?' she asked.

'Oh yes, ma'am, you could say that,' Jago told her. 'I was a stranger in your city, but not any more.'

'I like that,' she said. 'You're a poet, too.'

'Not me,' Jago said. 'Thank the Gershwins.' He leaned over the parapet beside her. 'You really like this old town, don't you?'

'We have a special relationship. I've seen her through good times and bad, often burning like hell, and we're still here, both of us.'

'But you don't like people much?'

Her chin tilted. He could sense anger in her, barely contained. 'Should I, darling? I wish you could give me a good reason.'

'What is it, Doctor? Don't you think you're up to snuff? Do you have to let too many people die?'

'Damn you to hell, Jago.' Her hand went up as if she would strike him. Big Ben chimed the first stroke of midnight.

Jago put up his arms defensively. 'The witching hour – remember. And this is the Embankment, the most romantic place in London.'

She reached out to touch his face. 'Tell me, Jago, did they cut you up badly back there? Did they take a few years off your life?'

'Too many,' he said.

The last stroke of midnight boomed out. The rain increased into a drenching downpour and she seemed to be standing very close. Tentatively he put his hands on her shoulders. She ran a hand up behind his head and kissed him passionately on the mouth.

'Take me home, Jago,' she whispered.

Barquentine *Deutschland*, 19 September 1944. Lat. 43°.4N., long. 20°.55W. Last night in the middle watch, fore upper topsail split during a bad blow. Weather continues to deteriorate. Full gale in the morning watch with big sea running.

Six

In spite of the fact that it was only two bells of the afternoon watch, it was so dark in the saloon that Sister Angela had to light the lamp. She sat at the table which, like the chairs, was bolted to the floor. Her bible was open in front of her. Lotte sat opposite, busy with needle and thread as she mended a denim shirt.

Outside, the wind howled and the *Deutschland* rolled heavily to port taking her own time to come back again, an event which would once have caused them both considerable alarm, but not now. Water trickled down the companionway steps and slopped across the floor. It was cold and damp – everything was damp – even the blanket which she had draped around her shoulders.

Lotte, concentrating on her task in the poor light, smiled briefly, as if at some private thought. Sister Angela had seen that smile often of late; knew only too well what it meant. It was as if the girl was slipping away from her; from everything that had once seemed so important – and for what?

She was aware of anger rising inside as old wounds opened, but she resolutely held it in check. It was an unworthy emotion and solved nothing.

She said to Lotte, 'That shirt – isn't it Herr Richter's?'

Lotte looked up. 'Why, yes, Sister.'

Before the conversation could be taken any further, there was a clatter on the companionway and the bosun appeared, a billycan in one hand. His head was bare, the blond hair and beard beaded with rain, and his yellow oilskin ran with water.

He smiled as he placed the can on the table. 'Hot tea, ladies. All the galley can manage at the moment.'

'Is it bad up there, Herr Richter?' Sister Angela asked.

'Just another Atlantic gale, Sister,' he replied. 'Nothing special to an old hand like you.'

She smiled in spite of herself, for it was hard not to.

Lotte said, 'Your shirt, Herr Richter, will be ready for you this evening.'

'You'll spoil me, Fräulein.' The *Deutschland* lurched so that he had to brace himself against the table. 'I'd better get back up there. That wasn't too good.'

He mounted the companionway and Lotte paused in her sewing. 'He never stops. One would think at times that he was the only man in the crew.'

'The finest sailor, certainly,' Sister Angela said. She paused, then carried on, 'A fine young man altogether. Has he told you much about himself?' Lotte glanced up, her face colouring. 'I only ask because Sister Käthe mentioned that she had noticed you and Herr Richter enjoying a lengthy conversation on deck yesterday evening.'

Before the girl could reply, the ship staggered under another mighty blow, swinging off course. There was a cry of alarm on deck, the doors at the head of the companionway burst open and water cascaded in.

Berger had the wheel with two seamen to help him as the *Deutschland* ploughed on through a wilderness of white foam. In spite of their combined efforts, the ship was swinging a couple of points on each side of her course.

Sturm and Leading Seaman Knorr were attempting to reef the fore staysail and were having a hard time of it, for the sea constantly poured over the weather bulwark, covering the hatches, swirling waist-deep, so that again and yet again, they had to stop work and simply hang on to prevent themselves from being swept away.

Richter emerged from the companionway, closed the doors behind him and turned to move towards the quarterdeck ladder. An enormous wave raced in astern, towering into the rain as if intent on engulfing them. He cried a warning to Berger, pointing, but the wave broke full upon the poop, knocking the captain's two companions from their feet.

Richter grabbed for the weather-jigger rigging and held on. Water boiled around him as the wave passed, taking all before it, so that for a moment he believed she must certainly founder under all that weight.

Slowly, the *Deutschland* started to rise and, as the water receded, he saw that there was now only Sturm up there in the weather rigging by the fore staysail.

Knorr floundered in the lee scuppers, trying to get to his feet. Richter started towards him as the *Deutschland* continued to climb and then another great sea rolled in and knocked him off his feet again. He grabbed for the edge of the main-hatch cover and held on tight, but the same sea lifted Knorr over the rail. As Richter struggled to his feet, he caught a single flash of yellow out there that was quickly gone.

Sturm started to work his way along the deck using the weather lines. Berger and his two companions were winning in their battle to control the wheel. Richter saw that the doors at the head of the companionway swung open. He stepped inside, closed them behind him and went down.

There was a foot of water in the saloon and the other nuns had emerged from their cabins in some alarm to join Sister Angela and Lotte. 'It's all right, ladies,' Richter assured them. 'Everything is under control, but I would suggest you return to your cabins and strap yourselves into those bunks until the gale blows itself out.'

There was a certain hesitation, but Sister Angela said briskly, 'Herr Richter is right. We must all do as he says at once.'

The other nuns retreated to their cabins, ankle-deep in water, skirts raised but Lotte stayed, reaching up to touch the smear of blood on Richter's right cheek.

'You are hurt, Herr Richter.'

'Nothing,' he said. 'A scratch only. Please do as I say.' He turned to Sister Angela. 'We lost a man overboard just now. Knorr. You can tell the others in your own good time. I didn't want to alarm them unnecessarily.'

She crossed herself. 'Was there nothing to be done?'

'In these seas? He was swallowed whole.'

The ship staggered again and he turned, swearing, brushed past Lotte, and went up the companionway fast. She reached out as if she would hold him back.

'Helmut,' she whispered.

She stood there, her skirts dragging in the water that slopped around her feet, something close to despair on her face. 'He'll kill himself, I know it!'

Sister Angela said gently, 'You like him, don't you? Like him a great deal, I mean?'

'Yes, Sister,' Lotte replied in a low voice.

Sister Angela sat down at the table, her hands gripping the edge of the table. 'My child, you must remember that we are members of an order whose vows urge us to love all our fellow creatures equally. The danger for us in any kind of personal relationship is that it detracts from what one is able to give to others. Our vow is to be servant to humanity, Lotte.'

'I have taken no such vow, Sister.'

Sister Angela braced herself against the table as the floor tilted again. She was slightly breathless now and not from any physical exertion.

'Do you know what you are saying?'

'Yes,' Lotte replied, a new firmness in her voice. 'That I am no longer certain of my vocation.'

Sister Angela reached out, grasping the girl's hand tightly. 'Think well, Lotte,' she said urgently. 'To give up God's love for . . .'

'. . . a man?' Lotte asked. 'Is it not possible then to have both?'

Sister Angela tried to stay calm and yet that ancient bitterness floated up again like bile. 'Things are not always what they seem. Human beings are frail. Once, when I was even younger than you, I loved a man, gave him my heart and, God help me, gave him my body also – and in return . . .' She choked on the words. 'And in return . . .'

Lotte said gently, 'And because one man acted so, all men are tainted? Is this what you would have me believe, Sister?'

'No,' Sister Angela whispered. 'Of course not.' She squeezed Lotte's hand. 'We've talked enough for the moment. Go and lie down as Herr Richter ordered. He knows what is best for us.'

Lotte hesitated, but did as she was told. The door to her cabin clicked shut behind her. Sister Angela sat there at the table, her eyes vacant, staring into space.

'Why, Karl?' she whispered. 'Why?'

And then, as hot tears stung her eyes, the iron discipline of the years came to her aid as always. She took a deep breath to steady herself, folded her hands and started to pray for the repose of Leading Seaman Peter Knorr's soul; for all sinners everywhere whose actions only cut them off from the infinite blessing of God's love.

Towards evening the gale abated but it was still blowing very hard and high above the deck Helmut Richter, Sturm and Leading Seaman Kluth, balanced on the yardarm, struggled to refit the freshly-mended fore upper topsail. The rain, sweeping in from the south-east, was like bullets and bitterly cold as they punched the wet canvas, cursing as blood spurted from torn fingers.

Berger stood gazing up at the men aloft, Otto Prager at his side in black oilskin and sou'wester.

'It frightens me just to watch,' the consul said. 'I'd never get used to it, not if we sailed round the world and took a year over it.'

'It certainly separates the men from the boys,' Berger told him, as Sturm and the others started to come down.

The young lieutenant mounted to the quarterdeck. 'All square up there now, Captain.' His face was pale and drawn, the memory of Knorr still with him.

Berger said, 'Don't blame yourself, boy. There was nothing to be done.'

'I almost had him,' Sturm said. 'Then he slipped from my grasp.'

Berger put a hand on his shoulder. 'Get yourself some coffee.'

Sturm went down the ladder. Berger looked over the rail and saw Richter staunching blood with a handkerchief. 'Bad?' he called.

'Finger-end, that's all.'

'See Sister Angela. She'll fix you up.'

When the bosun went down the companionway, the saloon was deserted except for Lotte who sat at the table, a book open before her. She glanced up at the sound of his foot on the stair and smiled.

'Herr Richter.'

'Fräulein.' For some reason lately he found it impossible to call her Sister. 'You should be in your bunk.'

She reached for his damaged hand and started to unwrap the handkerchief. 'What have you done?'

'It's nothing,' he said. 'A split finger, that's all. Punching canvas. It happens all the time.'

The end of the middle finger was open to the bone. 'You must let me do something.'

'I'll see to it.' Sister Angela spoke from behind. 'Please return to your devotions and the task I set you. In your cabin,' she added.

Lotte coloured, picked up her book and went out quickly. It was very quiet in the saloon, the voice of the wind outside subdued, far away. Richter and Sister Angela confronted each other.

'I'll get my medical case.'

He sat at the table and lit a cigarette. 'You don't mind?' he asked when she turned.

'Your smoking? Oh no, Herr Richter. My father used to say that a man should have some vices. Of the right kind, that is.'

'A short leash, you mean?'

'Do I?' She examined the finger. 'This will need two stitches. You'd better look the other way.'

He drew on his cigarette, watching the door to Lotte's cabin, grunting a little as the needle entered his flesh.

'Where are you from, Herr Richter?'

'Vienna.'

She was surprised. 'A Viennese sailor? I didn't know there were such things. What did you do, run away to sea?'

'Strangely enough, that's exactly what I did,' Richter told her. 'My father, if you are interested, was a surgeon, and had a similar career mapped out for me.'

'And you had other ideas. Are you married?'

'No,' he said evenly.

The needle was inserted again. 'You should be. It's good for the soul, Herr Richter. There, I've finished.'

'How strange,' he said. 'I'd always understood it was good for the flesh.'

She kept her temper and contented herself with saying calmly, 'Leave her alone. She has better things to do with her life.'

'Why? Because that was the way it worked out for you?'

She stood abruptly, picked up the medical case and went into her cabin. Richter sat there for a moment longer. As he got up, Lotte's door clicked open. 'Are you all right now, Herr Richter?' she whispered.

'Fine,' he said. 'In fact, I've never felt better, Fräulein.'

She smiled again and withdrew. Richter went up the companionway steps two at a time.

For Paul Gericke things progressed with extraordinary rapidity. A preliminary interrogation at Falmouth during which his own clothes had been dried, then returned to him. He had then been moved by road to Portsmouth, where he had found himself in the hands of Naval Intelligence.

They had treated him with respect. He was, after all, something of a catch for them – the most important U-boat commander to be captured since Kretschmer.

For five straight hours they had interrogated him in shifts but with a total lack of success. Gericke had resolutely stuck to the personal information required under the Geneva Convention, and nothing more.

Just after noon he was informed that he was to be moved to London. He was transferred in a naval police van, handcuffed and escorted by a petty officer, two ratings and a sub-lieutenant, all armed.

And so it was that at four-thirty in the afternoon he was in the London District PoW Cage, a requisitioned house in Kensington Palace Gardens. This time, the treatment wasn't so good, particularly from the chief petty officer who took charge of him on arrival, a massively-built man of forty-six named Carver, with the broken nose of a boxer.

'If I had my way, son,' he informed Gericke, 'there's nothing I'd fancy more than getting you inside a ring for six straight rounds and I'd make sure you'd last right up to the final bell.'

'Oh, I don't know, Chief,' Gericke told him calmly. 'I should have thought you would have been at your best up a dark alley with a bottle in your hand.'

For a moment he thought Carver was going to strike him, but there were two ratings present in reception. The chief petty officer, shaking with rage, contented himself with stripping Gericke of his decorations.

The room to which he was finally taken was pleasant enough. More like a study than an office, books lining the wall, a fire in the grate and, although the tall window was heavily barred, there was a view of the garden outside. He was placed in a chair on one side of a wide desk, still handcuffed, and waited impassively for whatever was to come, an armed rating on either side of him.

After a while, the door opened. The man who walked round to the other side of the desk was a full captain in the Royal Navy. He had a DSO and ribbons for the First War – Gericke took that in automatically, along with the iron-grey hair and pale, ascetic face. He had a bad limp and leaned heavily on an ebony walking stick.

He placed a couple of manilla folders on the desk and said rather formally, 'Commander Gericke – my name is Vaughan.'

'I wish I could say I was happy to meet you.'

Vaughan nodded to one of the ratings. 'You can take the handcuffs off now, then wait outside.'

He waited for them to comply with his order and only sat down as the door clicked shut behind them. Gericke eased his cramped wrists. 'Thank you. They were beginning to be rather uncomfortable.'

'Cigarette?' Vaughan pushed a box across the table. 'Your English is really quite excellent, but then you did live over here for a couple of years, didn't you?' He opened one of the folders and put on a pair of half-moon reading glasses. 'Nineteen twenty-six to twenty-eight. Hull. You went to grammar school there.'

'You seem to know.'

'Yes, I do, Commander,' Vaughan told him, in the same calm, neutral voice. 'Everything about you. An excellent record by the way. I congratulate you.'

Gericke restrained an impulse to laugh. 'Of course.'

'Not only the Knight's Cross, but the Oak Leaves to go with it. A rare distinction.'

'It *was*.'

'Why do you say that?'

Gericke opened his leather jerkin to indicate the tunic underneath, bare of decorations. 'The spoils of war.'

For the first time, Vaughan showed emotion. A tiny muscle twitched in his right cheek. 'Your decorations were taken from you?'

'Yes.'

'In this establishment? You will be good enough to tell me when and by whom.'

'The chief petty officer in charge of reception,' Gericke said, and added maliciously, 'I had assumed it to be the normal run of things.'

'Not while I am in charge here, I can assure you, Commander.' Vaughan's face was white, pinched around the mouth as he picked up the telephone on the desk. 'Send Chief Petty Officer Carver up to twenty-two at once.'

He got to his feet and stumped across to the window, leaning on his cane. There was a knock at the door a moment later and Carver entered.

'You wanted me, sir?'

Vaughan spoke without turning round. 'Carver, I understand you have in your possession certain decorations belonging to this officer.'

'Sir?' Carver started to bluster.

Vaughan swung round to face him. 'Damn your eyes, man, get them out on the table. Now!'

Carver hurriedly produced Gericke's Knight's Cross, Iron Cross First Class and wound badge and laid them on the desk. 'Is that the lot?' Vaughan asked Gericke.

Gericke nodded.

Vaughan said to Carver harshly, 'I'll deal with you later. Get out.'

As the door closed behind Carver, Gericke picked up the medals and put them in his pocket.

Vaughan sat down, took a cigarette from the box on the desk and examined the file again. 'As I was saying, quite a record. Let's see now. You joined the Tenth Flotilla at Brest after your return from the Far East, didn't you?'

'I've told you who I am, that's all that's required of me. I'm sorry, Captain Vaughan, I have nothing else to say.'

'All right,' Vaughan said. 'You compel me to become unpleasant. You really leave me no other choice.'

'Bring on the rubber hoses by all means. But it won't change anything.'

Vaughan was annoyed. 'We're not the Gestapo. We don't operate that way.'

'Then I shall be even more fascinated to hear your proposal,' Gericke assured him.

Vaughan opened the second folder. 'On the fifth of April, nineteen-forty-two, you sank, in American waters near Rhode Island, an oil tanker named the *San Cristobal*.'

'Perfectly correct.'

'You are aware, of course, that this ship was a Spanish vessel registered in Bilbao and that to torpedo and sink her was contrary to the articles of war?'

'You don't say.'

'But I do and what is more to the point, our American friends intend to make you answer for it. As a courtesy, American Naval Intelligence was informed of your capture this morning. Within two hours they'd made a formal application to take you into custody. From what I hear, they intend to ship you to the States to stand trial.'

Gericke laughed. 'What nonsense! The *San Cristobal* was under charter to carry oil for the American War Department.'

'There's no mention of that fact here.'

'Strange – the rest of your information seems to have been so uniformly accurate.'

Vaughan shrugged. 'The Americans have asked for you, Gericke, that is fact, and the consequences if they do try you for this business could be most unpleasant.'

'But you could save me from all that?'

'If you were willing to co-operate.'

Gericke sighed. 'Sorry, but you really are wasting your time.'

Vaughan nodded calmly, put the manilla folder under his arm, got up and limped out without another word.

Left alone, Gericke, on impulse, pinned the Iron Cross and wound badge to his tunic and hung the Knight's Cross around his neck. Then he stood at the window and looked out through the bars. The garden was enclosed by a high wall and was badly overgrown. Rain drifted down through the branches of a large beech tree into a wilderness of rhododendrons. It was a melancholy sight.

The door opened behind him and Carver entered, followed by a rating carrying a covered tray. 'Put it down there, lad,' Carver ordered and added to Gericke. 'Something to eat, Commander?'

The rating withdrew and Gericke walked to the desk. Carver leaned across and grabbed him by the front of the tunic. The eyes were cold.

'I'm going to have you, you German bastard, you see if I don't,' he whispered. He hurled Gericke back into Vaughan's chair and hurriedly left the room.

Just after seven on the same evening Janet and Harry Jago arrived by taxi at the house in Kensington Palace Gardens. They went up the steps to the front door, which was guarded by two sentries, and into the entrance hall, where an Army Intelligence Corps sergeant sat at a trestle table.

Jago produced his pass. 'Lieutenant Jago. I'm supposed to report to a Captain Vaughan.'

'Oh yes, sir, he's expecting you. I'll get someone to take you up.'

The sergeant pressed a buzzer and Jago said, 'Okay if the lady waits for me here?'

'I don't see why not, sir.'

Jago turned to Janet, 'Sorry about this. Why the hell I'm supposed to report to a Royal Naval captain in the first place, God only knows. Let's hope it doesn't take long and we can get straight to the theatre.'

She patted his cheek. 'How could this mighty war machine of ours roll on without you?'

Before Jago could think of a suitable reply, a young ATS corporal appeared to escort him to Vaughan. Janet sat on a chair by the window, crossing one leg over the other in a manner which filled the intelligence sergeant at his desk with admiration.

'Not too bad today then, miss,' he ventured. 'Three in Hackney, two down Poplar way and one in Golders Green.'

'And that's good?' she said.

The flying bombs, the V1 variety, had been bad enough, the grating roar of their engines growing steadily louder as they approached, but at least you knew they were coming. With the V2 rockets, on the other hand, there was no warning: a supersonic bang, the roar of an explosion and total devastation.

A door on the far side of the hall opened and Gericke came through, flanked by two armed ratings. His hands were handcuffed in front of him, but he made a striking figure in the white naval cap with the Iron Cross on his tunic, the Knight's Cross around his neck.

He didn't appear to notice Janet, his head half-turned, laughing at something one of the guards had said, and they went up the stairs and disappeared from view.

The desk sergeant said, 'Jerry prisoner, miss. Naval officer. We get a lot of them through here.'

'Oh, I see.'

She stood up, crossed the hall and stood in the porch at the top of the steps. There was a staccato roaring high above in the darkness and she glanced up to see a V1 passing across the night sky, a short jet of flame sprouting from its tail.

'I wonder where that bastard will come down,' the sentry said beside her.

Death and destruction. She'd just seen one of the men responsible. *The enemy*. It was the closest she'd been to a German since before the war. For a moment, she saw Gericke again, laughing as he went up the stairs between the guards, and was conscious of a kind of anger.

Jago emerged behind her and took her arm. 'Okay, let's get out of here.'

They went down the steps and turned along the pavement. 'And what was all that about?'

'Well, I don't see why I shouldn't tell you. The British picked up a German U-boat commander last night, one of the really top boys. A guy named Paul Gericke. They've had him in here for interrogation. It seems they're giving him to us. He's being sent up to Glasgow on the night express tomorrow evening. He'll be handed over to our people and shipped out on a convoy leaving for the States three or four days from now.'

'And where do you come in to it?'

'Well, he'll have a British escort, but some bright boy at Naval

Headquarters remembered I was travelling on that train and decided it would be a good idea if I kept an eye out for our interests.'

'Did you meet him?'

'Just now.'

'Was he medium height – pale face, dark eyes, Iron Cross on his tunic?'

'That's our boy.'

'He was laughing as he went up the stairs,' she said. At that moment they were passing behind a row of half-demolished houses. 'He was laughing. He and his kind caused all this.'

'They tell me Berlin doesn't look too hot these days.'

She slipped an arm through his. 'You're too good to live, Harry Jago. By the way, I didn't get a chance to tell you, but Colonel Brisingham turned up at the hospital this afternoon with my travel warrant for tomorrow night's train.'

Jago was over the moon with delight. 'That means we can be together all the way to Mallaig.'

'I'm not so sure,' she said. 'Actually they've provided me with a sleeping compartment. A single berth all to myself.'

'They've what?' Jago said in astonishment. 'Have you any idea what it takes to get one of those things these days?'

'Yes,' she said. 'Eisenhower.'

Jago laughed. The rain increased and they ran across to the corner of the main road and she sheltered under a tree while he tried to whistle up a cab.

And as she waited, for some reason she kept seeing Gericke's face, laughing as he went upstairs.

The clock in the charthouse chimed seven bells of the first watch. Seated at his desk in the cabin, a cigar between his teeth, Erich Berger paused to listen and then returned to his journal, the scratching of his pen sounding unnaturally loud in the silence.

. . . the loneliest sound in the world, a ship's bell at sea by night, or is it that it simply accentuates for me the loneliness of command? I think to be a ship's master no simple task, especially in the conditions under which I find myself at the moment . . .

There was a knock on the door and Sturm entered in a flurry of rain. He wore black oilskins and sou'wester and water glistened on him in the light of the oil lamp.

'Well, Mr Sturm?' Berger said.

Sturm saluted. 'I've just made the rounds, sir. Everything nice and tight. Kluth and Weber have the wheel at present. Heading north-west by west at ten knots by estimation.'

'Full sail?'

'Every stitch she can carry.'

'And what about the weather?'

'Wind force five with heavy rain, but it's surprisingly warm.'

'Excellent,' Berger went to the cupboard and found the rum bottle and two glasses. 'How long were you operating the radio for yesterday?'

Sturm accepted the glass gratefully. 'An hour and a half exactly.'

'What about the batteries?'

'Not too good, sir, but then they never were. It's not much of a set. The best Herr Prager could manage at short notice, I know. Still . . .' He hesitated. 'Do you want me to stop listening in, sir?'

'No, I don't think so. Those British and American weather reports are too useful, and the war news. But it's when we're close to home and wanting to transmit that we're going to need the power. I want to be sure we have enough in reserve.'

'Shall I leave it for tonight?'

'Half an hour,' Berger said. 'When you go off watch. I think that should suffice.'

'Very well, sir.' Sturm drained the last of his rum with reluctance. 'If you'll excuse me, I'd better get back on the quarterdeck.'

He turned and put his hand to the door – and from somewhere outside came the agonized cry of a woman.

It was hot below and very close. To Lotte, this voyage seemed interminable. From nowhere to nowhere. There was a gentle and continuous snoring from beneath her. Sister Angela had moved Sister Else into the cabin without any explanation.

Lotte lay on the top bunk, the roof no more than two feet above her face, hot and uncomfortable in spite of the fact that she was wearing only a linen nightdress. She was thinking of Helmut Richter, concentrating with an intensity that was almost frightening, trying to conjure him up from the darkness – the slow smile, the wild blond hair and beard.

Lotte was a quiet, self-contained girl. Most of her life had been totally enclosed – first by the demands of a rigidly orthodox Catholic family, and then by the self-discipline of nursing training. And afterwards, the Order of the Sisters of Mercy. Nothing more demanding than God.

She had learned to live within herself. But Richter – Richter was something different – a totally new experience. When she thought of him, she smiled spontaneously.

Her body was damp with sweat. It was impossible for her to stay in that cabin another minute. She needed air – clean salt air. She dropped to the floor softly, reached for her cloak and slipped outside.

Lightning flickered on the far horizon, moving nearer. There was an eerie phosphorescence to everything, so that the ship was a place of darkness and light, warm rain drifting across the deck in a silvery haze.

Kluth leaned on the wheel, his foot against the binnacle, thoroughly enjoying himself as the *Deutschland* stormed on through the night, every sail full. Weber leaned on the rail beside him, smoking a pipe. Neither saw Lotte emerge from the companionway.

But Walz, making himself coffee in the galley, saw her. The girl kept to the shadows by the port rail and paused at the mizzen shrouds, head lifted to feel the rain.

She moved away from the rail and as she passed the galley entrance, Walz reached out and caught her round the waist.

Lotte was not certain what was happening. From surprise as much as fear she cried out – a sharp cry of terror that sounded clearly above the wind and rain.

Helmut Richter, asleep in one of the hammocks which had been rigged in the fo'c'sle to take care of the extra crew, was awake in an instant, was up the ladder and out on deck before even Berger and Sturm had emerged from the captain's cabin.

Lotte staggered across the deck, losing her balance as the ship heeled and falling at Richter's feet. As he picked her up, the cloak fell back from her shoulders.

Sister Angela emerged from the companionway. 'Lotte!' she called.

Richter put the girl to one side and took a pace forward to stand waiting as Walz came hesitantly from the galley.

'Walz!' Richter said softly.

He stood there, bare feet apart, dressed only in seaman's denims. Lightning flickered overhead as the storm moved in. St Elmo's Fire flared at each masthead, so that the entire ship seemed to glow as it plunged forward.

'Richter!' Berger cried.

The bosun ignored him and moved forward. Walz, terrified, sprang into the ratlines and started to climb the foremast. Richter went after him picking his way with care as if he had all the time in the world.

Walz moved with remarkable speed. When he reached the lower topsail yard, he paused to look down, then drew the knife at his belt and slashed at the ratlines. Lotte cried out. There was a sudden groan from the assembled crew, followed by total silence as they held their breath.

The ratlines parted and Richter reached for the downhaul nearest to hand, swinging from it to a shroud line with the skill of a trapeze artist.

He hung there for a moment before starting upwards again. Walz, holding on to the yard, waited for him, reaching down to slash at the bosun's hand with the knife. Richter twisted out of the way, but Walz kicked him in the side of the face.

Richter slipped several feet down the line, then came to a halt spinning round. Lotte stared up, her knuckles tight against her teeth. Sturm took a step forward.

Berger grabbed his arm. 'Leave it!' he said in a low voice.

'In God's name, Captain Berger,' Sister Angela said. 'Do something.'

'What would you suggest, Sister?' Berger asked, without taking his gaze away from the scene above for a moment.

It was an extraordinary sight, with sheet lightning exploding from one horizon to the other, the strange ball of light of the St Elmo's Fire pulsating at each masthead, the eerie phosphorescence of the electrical discharge flowing along every rope and stay, picking Richter and Walz out of the darkness with total clarity.

With an incredible effort, the bosun went up the line hand over hand, grabbed for the lower topsail yard and a moment later was secure in the foot-ropes.

Walz backed away and started upwards again, climbing towards the upper topsail yard. Each flash of lightning had a dazzling white intensity to it that seemed to imprint the scene on the brain for those on deck, but in between was a brief interval of total darkness so that they might have been looking through the eyeholes of an old-fashioned moving picture machine, the action moving jerkily forward, scene by scene.

As Walz reached the yard, the bosun swung to one side on a lift, pulled himself up to a position on the extreme end of the yardarm and began inching along the foot-ropes. Walz backed away, out towards the other end of the yardarm.

Richter was very close now. He hung there no more than three feet away from Walz who struck out blindly. The point of the knife caught the bosun's right cheek. He came forward implacably and Walz gave a cry of despair.

He grabbed for the main upper topsail brace and slashed at it in a frenzy with the knife. The line parted and the yardarm, freed from restraint, swung viciously from one side to the other, the sail flapping as air spilled from it.

Richter should have been hurled into space, but managed to scramble to the temporary safety of the lower topgallant yard.

Walz swung crazily backwards and forwards. A particularly wild roll of the *Deutschland* sent him half over the yard and he only managed to save himself by hooking an arm in the footrope.

Richter worked his way across the back of the lower topgallant from one lift to another. He paused, suspended in space, watching carefully, judging his moment, as Walz, on the end of the yardarm, swung far out over the sea.

The ship heeled, Walz swung in very fast, hanging on with one arm, striking with the knife. Richter, a rope in each hand, gave him both feet in the face. Walz cried out and went back over the yard into space.

He hit the water some distance from the starboard rail. His arm swung up in mute appeal, but in spite of the wildly flailing sail, the *Deutschland* was still making ten knots, and he receded, became one with the night, taken by the sea.

'We're heaving to, Mr Sturm. Douse jibs, if you please. Clew up forecourse, topsails and t'gallants, then get to work and repair that damage. I want to be under way again in an hour,' Berger ordered.

'Is that all you have to say?' Sister Angela's voice was low, intense. 'A man is dead.'

'It shall be so noted in the log,' Berger said impassively.

Richter dropped to the deck and Lotte ran forward, arms outstretched. When she was a yard or two away from him she swayed, half-fainting. Richter caught her quickly. He stood there for a moment looking down at her, blood oozing from his slashed cheek, then went towards the companionway.

The others nuns gathered together at the bottom, got out of the way quickly. Sister Käthe said, 'Is she all right, Herr Richter?'

Richter didn't reply. He walked across the saloon to Lotte's cabin, went in and laid her on the lower bunk. He reached for a blanket to cover her and the girl's eyes fluttered.

For a second only she stared blankly into space, then recognized him. 'Herr Richter?'

'It's all right,' Richter said.

He made a movement as if to turn away and there was instant panic. 'Don't leave me.'

He took her hand and crouched beside the bunk stroking her forehead as one might gentle a child. 'Never,' he said softly. 'Never again. Sleep now.'

She closed her eyes, the face growing calm. After a while, the breathing became slow and regular, the hand slackened in his.

He got to his feet and turned to find the nuns peering in at the doorway, a uniform look of astonishment on their faces in the dim light. Sister Angela stood at the foot of the bed, pale and composed, hands folded. He waited for her comment, drained of emotion, quite indifferent and as always, she surprised him.

'And now, I think you'd better come with me, Herr Richter,' she said calmly. 'From the looks of things, I'd say you need another stitch or two.'

In the grey light of dawn far to the north-east, U-235 surfaced at the rendezvous buoy a mile off Bergen. She presented an extraordinary sight, for in place of her prow there was only a jagged stump of twisted, rusting metal. In mid-Channel it had been discovered that eight metres of the forecastle was bent to one side. Friemel had managed to detach the damaged portion by alternating as rapidly as possible between full speed ahead and full speed back.

But the rest of the trip had been an unqualified nightmare. He had not closed his eyes in thirty-six hours and when he followed Engel up the ladder to the bridge, it was very slowly indeed.

An escort of two armed trawlers raced out to meet them, signal lamps flashing. Engel examined them through his binoculars, then turned. His face was grey, the eyes dark, no life there at all. The bandage round his forehead didn't help the general appearance.

'We made it, Herr Admiral?'

'So it would appear.'

A seaman came up the ladder behind them quickly and passed a flimsy across. 'Signal, sir.'

He offered it to Friemel, who shook his head. 'You read,' he said to Engel.

'Well done, Otto. Dönitz, Commander-in-Chief of the Kriegsmarine and BdU,' Engel said in a low voice. 'That's all it says, sir.'

'Well done.' Friemel laughed harshly. 'Well done indeed.'

There was a further flurry of activity as the minesweepers circled to take up position, men cheering from the rails as U-235 ploughed forward slowly.

From somewhere below there was a cry, a muffled cheer, feet scrambling on the iron ladder and Heini Roth erupted on to the bridge, another flimsy in his hand. His face was white with excitement. 'What is it, for God's sake?' Friemel said.

'Further signal from BdU, Herr Admiral. It simply says: Information from Abwehr that Gericke arrived London Cage on the nineteenth.'

He turned, leaned heavily on the rail, totally overcome. Friemel took a crumpled cigarette pack from his breast pocket. There was one left which he carefully inserted into his holder. Heini gave him a light, hand shaking.

Friemel inhaled deeply, then sighed. 'The last of those lousy French weeds and yet I don't think a cigarette ever tasted better in my life.'

Barquentine *Deutschland*, 20 September 1944. Lat. 46°.55N., long. 17°.58W. Another bad night. Wind Force 7. Rain and heavy seas. At four bells of the morning watch outer jib parted at the clew and jib boom ripped away when a huge sea came up to windward. Leading Seamen Kluth and Schmidt who had jumped to the mizzen pipe-rail were hurled into the lee scuppers. I expected to see them swept away, but by some miracle, they survived, Schmidt sustaining a fracture of the left forearm. As it was imperative to go about with such a sea running, I decided to wear ship to give Mr Sturm a chance to repair damage. At two bells of the forenoon watch, Bosun Richter reported eighteen inches of water in the bilges. I immediately ordered him to call the starboard watch from below and to commence pumping. It was two bells of the first dog-watch before Mr Sturm was able to report all damage secure. Bosun Richter's watch having pumped her dry again and the storm having abated a little, I was able to bring her round and resume our original course, having lost some forty miles as we drifted to leeward. I estimate we are now some seven hundred miles due west of the Bay of Biscay.

Seven

It was considered useful propaganda to let the public see German prisoners-of-war being led through Euston station. Sub-Lieutenant Fisher was in charge of the escort which consisted of Carver and two leading seamen, Wright and Hardisty. They all wore gaiters and webbing belts carrying Webley .38 revolvers like any normal shore patrol, but they took Gericke through the crowd as unobtrusively as possible, just another naval prisoner, a blue raincoat draped over his shoulders.

Fisher identified himself to the guard, who led them into a luggage van. The rear section was walled off by a metal grille behind which lay a jumble of red GPO bags.

The guard produced a key. 'He can go in there if you like.'

'Fine,' Fisher said. 'Can I keep the key?'

'Don't see why not,' the guard said. 'I've got a spare. I don't suppose you're likely to steal the mail.'

He went out. Fisher unlocked the iron gate and Carver nodded to Gericke, scrupulously polite, 'If you don't mind, sir.'

Gericke moved inside, the sub-lieutenant locked the gate and handed the key to Carver. 'Right, Chief. You look after things here while I see if I can find Lieutenant Jago.'

'You take your time, sir. We'll be fine in here,' Carver told him. 'A damn sight better off than they are further up the train.'

Fisher went out and Carver passed a pound note across to Leading Seaman Hardisty. 'You and your mate cut along to the station buffet and grab what you can in the way of sandwiches and fags.'

'But we've brought a load of stuff with us from the canteen, Chief,' Hardisty told him.

'I know, son, I know,' Carver said. 'Which is fine, till we roll into Leeds or somewhere like it at two in the bloody morning and find the cupboard's bare. Now do as I say.'

Gericke leaned against the metal grille and examined a notice on the wall. It said:

If an air raid occurs while you are on the train:
1 *Do not attempt to leave unless required by the guard to do so. You are safer where you are.*
2 *Pull the blinds down, both by day and night, as a protection against flying glass.*
3 *If room is available lie down on the floor.*

Carver said, 'Thanks to you buggers, that little lot's there.'

'Tell me something, Chief Petty Officer,' Gericke asked. 'How long have you been in the Service?'

'Thirty years. I joined up in nineteen-fourteen when I was sixteen.'

'Ah, a regular,' Gericke nodded. 'You surprise me. War, after all, is the name of the game for the professional. Yet you seem to object to the fact that there's one on. Perhaps the only reason you stayed on after the first lot was to wear a pretty uniform and have a girl in every port.'

Carver was furiously angry. 'You wait, you bastard.'

They heard Fisher's voice approaching. The sub-lieutenant entered followed by Captain Vaughan and Harry Jago to find Carver passing a cigarette through the mesh to Gericke.

'Care for a smoke, Commander?' he was asking with perfect civility.

'That's very kind of you, Chief.' Gericke accepted the cigarette and a light.

Vaughan said, 'A little primitive, but it could be worse. Any complaints, Commander?'

Gericke raised his handcuffed wrists. 'Could I possibly have these removed? After all, I *am* caged in.'

'Sorry.' Vaughan shook his head. 'But if it makes you feel any better, we had an intelligence report in from our Norwegian friends in Bergen a couple of hours ago. It seems U-235 under the command of Konteradmiral Otto Friemel arrived safely, minus seven or eight metres of her bows.'

For a moment, Gericke couldn't take it in, but in any case, there was no time to say anything for outside the guard's whistle blew, there was the sound of running feet.

Vaughan said stiffly in that careful, precise voice, 'Well, Commander, I can only wish you a safe voyage, in spite of the exigencies of the North Atlantic.'

Gericke smiled. 'Ironic to find myself in the periscope sights of an old comrade.'

Vaughan saluted, beckoned to Fisher and limped out on the platform. Jago said to Gericke, 'I'll look in from time to time. It can take twelve hours or more to make Glasgow.'

'I'm in no particular hurry.'

Jago went out and Carver moved across to the grille. 'And neither am I, son,' he said softly. 'But just for starters, let's have those medals back.'

On Fhada, rain blew in across the harbour and drummed against the windows of the old cottage. Reeve was seated at his desk, his diary open before him. His daily entry was an old habit, engaged in from his earliest days at sea. Not so much a record of events as an attempt to formulate his thoughts. He put a match to his pipe, picked up his pen and started to write.

> . . . this life of mine, if life I can call it, has become a strange affair, a kind of metamorphosis in which everything has changed. Oliver Wendell Holmes once said that it was required of a man that he should share the action and passion of his times at peril of being judged not to have lived, and for most of my life I have followed his precept with uncommon faithfulness. But now, I find myself caught in a web of days, time passing in a kind of slow motion and to what purpose? What end?

He put down his pen and stirred the wolfhound, sprawled on the rug before the hearth, with his foot. 'Out of the way, you red devil.'

Rory moved reluctantly and Reeve added a few turves to the peat fire, then glanced at his watch. 'Almost time, Rory. Shall we see if they've anything for us today, eh? Maybe someone out there will actually remember that we still exist.'

The radio was on a table by the window. He sat down, adjusted the headphones and started to transmit. 'This is Sugar One on Fhada calling Mallaig. Are you receiving me?'

Rory crouched beside him and Reeve fondled the dog's ears and tried again. There was an almost instanteous response. 'Hello, Sugar One, this is Mallaig receiving you loud and clear. Stand by, please. I have a message for you.'

Reeve was aware of a sudden excitement.

'Admiral Reeve? Murray here, sir.'

'What can I do for you?' Reeve demanded.

'Had a signal from London for you, sir. Just to let you know that your niece is on her way to stay with you for a few days.'

Reeve said automatically, 'That's wonderful. When does she arrive?'

'Sometime tomorrow. I can't be more exact than that, I'm afraid. You know what the trains are like these days. What about transport to Fhada, sir? I don't think I'll have anything official available.'

'That's all right,' Reeve said. 'I'll see to that end of things.' He braced himself. 'Anything else for me, Murray?'

'I'm afraid not, sir,' Murray said, and added, 'I'm sorry, Admiral.'

'Don't be,' Reeve said bitterly. 'I don't think anyone else is, so why should you be different? Over and out.'

He switched off the set and sat staring into space, one hand idly playing with Rory's ears. It would be nice to see Janet again, to hear her news, but it wasn't enough. Not nearly enough.

The dog whined as his hand gripped too tightly and he stood up quickly. 'Sorry, boy. I'm not at my best today. Let's get a little fresh air.'

He took down his reefer from behind the door and went out, Rory at his heels. The wind was in the wrong direction to use a sail so he hand-pumped his way on one of the trolleys for the entire length of the line to South Inlet. When he went down to the lifeboat station the rear door of the boathouse was open. Murdoch was sitting on an old chair, sheltered from the rain, mending a net across his knee.

He looked up, the weatherbeaten face showing no emotion, his hands still working. 'A good day or a bad day is it, Carey Reeve?'

'Since when have I had a choice?'

'Like that, is it? Would you care for a dram?'

'Maybe later. My niece is arriving at Mallaig tomorrow on the London train.'

'That will be nice for you.' Murdoch spread his net. 'Young Lachlan MacBrayne is coming home on leave off that same train. His mother told me yesterday.'

'A paratrooper, isn't he?'

'That is so. If you've no objection I've promised to run across in your *Katrina* and pick him up. You would like me to bring your niece back also?'

'That would be fine,' Reeve said.

On the train, Gericke sprawled back on the mail sacks, eyes closed, apparently asleep. Carver and the two leading seamen were playing cards. Fisher was reading a book.

There was a knock on the door and when Fisher unlocked it, Harry Jago stepped in. 'Everything okay?'

'I think so,' Fisher said. They walked across to the wire mesh screen. 'He's been asleep for the past hour.'

'Fine. If you've got time I'd like you to come up to the sleeping car and meet Dr Munro. There's a bottle of Scotch in my bag we could do a little damage to.'

'Sounds good to me,' Fisher said as they went out.

Carver lit a cigarette and scratched himself. 'They've got it made, these bloody Yanks.'

'How's that, Chief?' Hardisty asked.

'This Dr Munro. A nice bit of skirt, I can tell you, going all the way to Mallaig. Her uncle's an American admiral living on some island in the Outer Hebrides. She's got a private berth up there in the sleeping car. Jago's shacked up with her.' He threw in his cards. 'Another lousy bloody hand. Deal 'em again, Wright, only make sure you give me some good ones this time.'

He got up and stared through the mesh at Gericke. 'You awake, Commander?'

Gericke made no sign, breathing softly, eyes closed and Hardisty said, 'Leave him, Chief, for Christ's sake. He isn't going anywhere.'

Carver turned away reluctantly, sat down and picked up his cards. Behind him, Gericke's eyes opened for a brief moment.

It was raining in Trondheim, heavy, drenching rain as Horst Necker went up the steps of the main entrance to the Operations building with Rudi Hubner. They were still in flying gear, having just returned from an eight-hour operational flight that had taken them far out into the Barents Sea and back again.

Necker was tired and bad-tempered. 'They'll have to do something about that port engine. It sounds more like a bloody tractor every time we go out.'

'I know, Herr Hauptmann,' Rudi said soothingly. 'I spoke to Vogel myself. He said he was waiting for our next standdown.'

'Christ Almighty, we could be dead by then.'

He pushed open the door of the intelligence room, expecting to find Altrogge, the intelligence officer, and pulled up short, for Colonel Maier, the Gruppenkommandeur, was sitting on the edge of the desk, smoking a cigarette and leafing through some papers.

He glanced up. 'You don't look too pleased with life, Horst. Did you have trouble?'

'You could say that.' Necker dropped his parachute on a convenient chair and accepted a cigarette. 'Eight hours of nothing but bloody sea and a port engine with asthma. Otherwise the flight was sheer delight.'

Maier grinned. 'Never mind. I've brought your two-day standdown forward. That should please you.'

'Why should it?' Necker demanded sourly. 'You'll have a damn good reason, I'm sure.'

'A change of routine. Our masters would like you to concentrate on the West Coast of Scotland and the Hebrides again for the next couple of weeks.' He smiled. 'You wanted action, Horst. You've got it. Two new Spitfire squadrons moved up to the east coast this week. That should make it interesting for you.'

'Thanks very much,' Necker said suddenly feeling surprisingly cheerful considering the circumstances. 'What's it all about?'

'Convoys from Canada have been using the northern run lately according to Intelligence. Coming up a lot closer to Iceland. From now on your patrol must take you much further out into the Atlantic. At least five hundred miles west of the Outer Hebrides.'

'We won't be able to stay there long.'

Maier pulled a chart across the desk and nodded. 'We'll give you improved drop tanks. That should add another five hundred miles. And there's a modification to your GMI system that should make it possible for you to cross Scotland without dropping below thirty-five thousand. They claim forty, but I wouldn't count on it. In any case, it should keep you out of the way of those Spitfires.'

The GMI system employed nitrous oxide which was injected into the superchargers where, during high altitude flights, it supplied additional oxygen for combustion, increasing the engine power by twenty per cent.

Necker examined the chart and nodded. 'That's a long way to go.'

Maier smiled and slapped him on the arm. 'It will seem shorter when you've had a couple of days' rest.'

★ ★ ★

The wind dropped considerably towards evening and the *Deutschland*, under full sail, moved on into the gathering darkness, pushed by a light breeze from the south-west.

Richter had the first watch, alone on the quarterdeck except for a Petty Officer Torpedo Mechanic named Endrass who was at the wheel. The bosun stood at the rail smoking one of his cigarillos, enjoying the night, the horned moon, the stars scattered to the far horizon, their glow diffused by a damp clinging sea mist.

At nine o'clock he went forrard to speak with the lookout in the bows. On his way back, he paused by the mizzen shrouds on the port side to check a lashing which had worked loose on the mainsail boom. There was a movement behind him and Lotte stepped out of the shadows between the lifeboats.

'Helmut!'

Her hands reached out through the darkness, her face a pale blur. Richter took them instinctively. 'Lotte – what are you doing here?'

'I've been watching you for the past half-hour, pacing from one side to the other of that wretched quarterdeck. I was beginning to think you were never coming down.'

'You must return below,' he said. 'At once.'

'Why?'

'Because Sister Angela is concerned for your welfare, I've given my word to the captain that I'll stay away from you for the rest of the voyage.'

'And you?' she said. 'Are you concerned for my welfare?'

'God help me.' He tried to release his hands. 'Let be, Lotte. I've given my word – don't you see?'

'I understand only one thing,' she said. 'That all my life I have been afraid. But when I am with you . . .' Her hand tightened on his. 'Is that what love is always like, Helmut? Have you known love like this before?'

His arms went round her as his last defences crumbled. 'No, never like this, Lotte.'

She tilted her chin to peer up at him. 'As a novice, I can leave the order at will and with a minimum of fuss when we reach Kiel. And then . . .'

He kissed her gently. 'What happens in Kiel is one thing. As for now, there can be no more such meetings.'

'How much longer?' she asked.

'Two weeks if we're lucky, though we'll need to make better time than this.'

'Shall I whistle up a wind for us?' she demanded. 'A real wind?'

'No need.' He looked up at the night sky. 'I think this is only a temporary lull. Storm before morning.'

There was a slight movement behind. They turned quickly and found Sister Angela standing by the mainmast.

'Herr Richter – Lotte,' she said calmly. 'A fine night.'

It was Lotte who spoke first, reacting instinctively in Richter's defence. 'This was my fault, Sister, believe me. None of Herr Richter's doing.'

'I'm well aware of that, child. I've been here for the past five minutes. But now, I really do think you should go below.'

Lotte hesitated, then started towards the companionway reluctantly. When she was half-way there, Sister Angela added, 'I'm sure Herr Richter will be happy to talk to you again tomorrow, if his duties permit.'

The girl caught her breath, paused, then turned and fled down the companionway.

Richter said, 'Do I understand from this, Sister, that I actually have your permission to . . .'

'. . . pay your addresses, Herr Richter?' She smiled faintly. 'How old that makes me feel. So old.'

She turned from him and walked to Berger's door. Richter watched helplessly as she knocked and entered.

Berger was at his desk, writing. Otto Prager lay on the bunk reading a book. The consul sat up, swinging his legs to the floor and Berger laid down his pen.

'Sister?' he said politely.

Prager stood up. 'You would like me to leave, perhaps?'

He took a step towards the door, but she shook her head. 'A moment of your time only, Captain. In the matter of Herr Richter and Lotte.'

'Well?' Berger asked bleakly, ready for trouble.

'I would be obliged if you would release him from his promise not to speak to her again until we reach Kiel.'

'A rather surprising change of attitude on your part, wouldn't you say?'

'A new viewpoint, perhaps. All I have ever wanted was what was right for Lotte. Her decision as to her future when we reach Kiel must be made of her own free choice with no voice to aid her but God's, I see that now. In the meantime, it would seem pointless to keep her and Herr Richter apart artificially. As I have discovered for myself, he seems a singularly honourable young man.'

Berger couldn't think of a thing to say. She gave him a moment, then added, 'And now, if you gentlemen will excuse me. I'm really very tired.'

The door closed behind her. The consul turned, total astonishment on his face. Berger, without a word, opened the cupboard and took out the rum bottle and two glasses.

It was very dark as the train ploughed on into the night, rain lashing against the windows. When Harry Jago knocked on the door of the sleeping compartment and went in, Janet was in the single bunk, a blanket pulled up to her chin.

'I'm freezing.'

'Well, I could suggest a remedy for that condition,' he told her cheerfully.

'Not tonight, darling. I've had it. I could sleep for a week. You'll have to make do with the floor and a blanket.'

He shrugged his shoulders. 'Okay,' he said. 'There are guys sleeping in the luggage racks back there.' He took off his shoes, wrapped himself in one of the blankets, lay on the floor, head pillowed on a canvas holdall and was almost instantly asleep.

They reached Glasgow at six-thirty on a grey, sullen morning. Janet had slept badly and awakened to find that Jago had gone. It took her a moment or so to pull herself together – to realize that they were standing still.

As she threw the blanket aside and sat up, there was a tap at the door and he looked in. 'Alive and well,' he commented. 'That's nice.'

He passed a Thermos. 'Coffee. We're in Glasgow, by the way. They seem to be disconnecting about half the coaches.'

'Then what happens?'

'We pull out in about ten minutes. Bridge of Orchy, Rannoch, Fort William and Mallaig. Another five hours if all goes well. I'm just saying goodbye to Fisher and our mutual friend, Gericke. I'll be straight back and we can have breakfast. It's all arranged.'

He went out before she could reply. For a moment only, she sat there, then got up, raised the blind and pushed down the window. The platform was almost deserted. Jago was hurrying along to a small group consisting of Lieutenant Fisher and the escort, Gericke standing in the centre, the blue raincoat over his shoulders again.

As she watched, Fisher and Jago moved to one side. She caught a brief glimpse of Gericke's sardonic face and then Carver turned him round and gave him a push. They went through the door of the station waiting-room leaving Fisher and Jago talking on the platform. Quite suddenly, Janet had had enough. She pushed up the window and pulled down the blind. When she turned back to the bunk, she was trembling.

'I'm tired,' she said softly. 'Too little sleep for too damned long. That's what it is.' And she got back into the bunk and pulled the blankets up.

'I was expecting your people to meet us,' Fisher said. 'I wonder what's keeping them?'

'God knows.' Jago looked at his watch. 'Say, I'd better get back on board. This thing pulls out again at any moment.'

'I can't hand him over quickly enough, believe me,' Fisher said. 'There's something about him. The way he looks at you.'

'I know exactly what you mean.' Jago shook hands. 'A good trip back, anyway.'

He got into the train and Fisher turned and walked towards the waiting-room where a coal fire burned in a small grate. Hardisty and Wright warmed themselves in front of it, smoking cigarettes.

'Where's the prisoner?' Fisher demanded.

'He wanted to go to the lavatory, sir.' Hardisty nodded towards a green door with the sign *Gentlemen* painted on it. 'The Chief said he'd see to it.'

Fisher turned and at that moment the door opened violently and Carver staggered through, half-doubled over. He seemed to find difficulty in speaking, his mouth opening and closing as he gasped for air.

Fisher grabbed him by the lapel. 'What is it, man?' he demanded.

'He – he's got away, sir,' Carver groaned, clutching at his groin. 'The bastard's got away.'

Gericke had asked to go to the lavatory for the most genuine of reasons. The idea of escape at this stage hardly seemed to be on the cards, especially when one considered those damned handcuffs. What had happened had been a spur of the moment decision, the briefest of opportunities instantly seized.

'I'll see to this, lads,' Carver pushed him towards the door and kicked it open. 'You two have a quick smoke while the going's good.'

Inside, there was a row of stalls, a urinal, a broken washbasin, the rain drifting in through the open window above the basin. It was the sight of that window that stirred Gericke.

The chief petty officer leaned against the door. 'All right, get on with it.'

Gericke moved towards one of the stalls, turned and held out his handcuffed wrists. 'A little awkward with these things.'

'Oh, a sit-down job, is it?' Carver laughed, eager to extract every last ounce of humiliation from the situation. 'I think we might stretch a point there, Commander.' He produced the key and unlocked one handcuff. 'There, that will do you. And you'll have to leave the door open, of course. I'm sure you won't mind me watching, under the circumstances.'

'Thank you, Chief,' Gericke said calmly, and lifted his right knee into Carver's crutch.

Barquentine *Deutschland*, 21 September 1944. Lat. 49°.52N., long. 14°.59W. Wind Force 5–6. Intermittent squalls. Heavy rain. It is now necessary to pump four hours out of each twenty-four, which seems to suffice and thanks to the size of the crew is less of a burden than it otherwise would have been. Our position now approximately 220 miles south-west of Ireland.

Eight

Fisher moved out of the parcels' office with Carver hobbling at his heels, and paused outside the waiting-room. 'God damn you, Carver, I'll have you for this.'

Hardisty and Wright came round the corner on the run. 'He hasn't gone through the barrier, that's definite, sir.' Hardisty said. 'Two redcaps on duty there. They're putting the word out now.'

'Go through that damned luggage-room again,' Fisher ordered. 'He's got to be here somewhere. Nowhere he could go, not in the time.'

The two leading seamen went off. Carver said bitterly, 'When I get my hands on that German bastard I'll . . .'

'Oh, shut up, for God's sake and let me think,' Fisher said.

There was the shrill blast of a whistle, the guard's flag fluttered. A sudden hiss of steam and the train started to ease forward. One or two sailors leaned out of carriage windows to see what the fuss was about, but most of the passengers on board were still hardly stirring.

'I mean, where in the hell could he have gone?' Fisher demanded and then, as realization dawned, he almost choked. 'The train, Chief!' he shouted. 'He must have got back on the train. It's the only possible explanation.'

It was already moving fast, but there was still time and he jumped for the open door of the guard's van as it passed, turning to pull Carver up behind him. Hardisty and Wright, running along the platform to join them, were too late.

'Here, what's going on?' the guard demanded.

Fisher ignored him, drew his revolver and turned to Carver. 'All right, Chief, let's rout him out,' he said.

Janet Munro's travel voucher being marked top priority, the sleeping car steward served her first that morning, a good English breakfast of bacon, scrambled egg, marmalade and toast and tea.

Jago could hardly believe his eyes. 'Did I say there was a war on?'

'Not for people with my influence, darling.'

'I certainly joined the right ship this time.'

He sat down on the other side of the small table which the steward had pulled up from under the window. Janet poured the tea.

'You know, I've actually managed to acquire a taste for this stuff,' Jago said.

There was a knock at the door. Janet, who was nearest, reached to open it, Fisher moved in, revolver in his right hand, Carver behind him.

'What in the hell is going on?' Jago demanded.

'He gave Carver the slip back there in the station, sir,' Fisher told him. 'Asked to go to the lavatory . . .'

'Save it for your court-martial, Lieutenant,' Jago said brutally. 'Just tell me one thing.' He turned to Carver. 'Did you unlock his handcuffs?'

Carver licked his lips nervously. 'Just one, sir. I mean, he wanted . . .'

'I can't believe it,' Jago exploded. 'One chance – any chance – that's all a guy like that needs.' He turned away, white with anger. 'So, he's on the train, is that what you're saying?'

'I think so, sir.' Fisher hesitated and then added awkwardly, 'I mean, there wasn't anywhere else for him to go. There wasn't time.'

'You *think* so?' Jago said. 'All right then, Lieutenant, where is he? German Korvettenkapitäns must be kind of thin on the ground, wouldn't you say, especially on the West Highland Line?'

Fisher glanced nervously at Carver, then back at the American. 'I – I just don't know, sir. We started with the guard's van and worked our way forward.'

'And there was no sign of him. Well, that figures. He'd hardly advertise. Is he armed?'

Carver hesitated, debating whether to lie or not, but one look from

Jago was enough. 'I'm afraid so, sir. I was carrying a spare, sir. A Mauser. Just in case.'

'In case of what?' Jago demanded and then waved a hand. 'Don't bother, Chief, we've got more important things to consider.' He opened his holdall and took out a service issue Colt automatic and slipped it into one pocket. 'Put those pistols away for the moment. No need to set the entire train on its ear. If he is on board, which I doubt, any confusion can only assist him.'

Fisher, delighted to hand over the reins, said eagerly, 'What are we going to do, sir?'

'Carver stays up here at one end, you and I go back to the guard's van and work our way forward. Every compartment, every lavatory. We'll find him – if he's here at all. In my personal opinion, he's on a street car right now, heading for Glasgow docks and a Portuguese or Spanish boat if he can find one.'

'In German uniform?' Janet said. 'He wouldn't last five minutes.'

'Last year a London journalist walked down Oxford Street to Piccadilly dressed as an SS colonel,' Jago said grimly. 'And no one took any kind of notice. There are so many uniforms around these days people are punch drunk.' He nodded to Fisher and Carver who moved outside. 'You stay close to home. I'll be back soon.'

It was a good hour later and the train was approaching the northern end of Loch Lomond when they reappeared, Fisher paler than ever, a picture of total dejection. Carver lurked in the corridor outside.

'No Gericke?' Janet said.

'What do you think?'

The guard, an old man long past his prime who had only stayed on because of the war, appeared behind Carver. 'Any luck, sir?'

Jago shook his head. 'Wherever he is, it isn't on board this train. We've checked every inch.'

The guard said, 'Not quite, sir. They coupled a flat-top on at Glasgow behind my van with three jeeps on it for delivery to the Royal Navy at Mallaig. Mind you, there's no way he could have got out there as far as I can see.'

'Is that so?' Jago said and he reached up and pulled the communication cord.

Gericke had enjoyed a surprisingly comfortable trip in the back of one of the jeeps on the flat-top. He was out of the rain and the views were spectacular – just the kind of country he liked.

He had no set plan, allowing things to happen as the cards fell. The opportunity to put Carver down had been too good to miss – the decision to get back on the train so obvious that he hadn't really thought about it. He'd simply jumped for cover, head down.

And one thing was in his favour. The fact that, in regard to uniform, most naval officers looked the same the world over. All he had to do was remove the swastika and eagle from the Kriegsmarine badge on his uniform cap: and he was doing just that, the handcuffs swinging from his left wrist, when the train started to grind to a halt with such violence that he was thrown from the seat.

The game was up, so much seemed obvious, for the train was passing through a long narrow cut with sides that were almost perpendicular. Yet Gericke was reluctant to throw in the towel. He had nothing to lose. While the train was still sliding to a halt, he moved along the flat-top to the rusting iron ladder at the rear of the guard's van.

There was a catwalk on the roof and he ran along it, jumping to the first coach, almost losing his balance as it swayed violently from side to side. He made it to the next roof and threw himself flat on his face as the train came to a halt.

There was silence, only the heavy rain, the hiss of steam and then windows going down, doors opening – excited voices. Someone was running along the side of the track. He heard Fisher say, 'Nowhere for him to go this time.'

'Exactly,' Jago called. 'So play it cool. No need for gunplay. Much better to get him back in one piece.'

They moved on. Gericke, daring all, went over the edge and slipped down the ladder to the bridge between the coaches. He opened the door before him and moved inside.

The corridor was lined with people, mostly sailors on their way to the naval depot at Mallaig, leaning out of the windows, looking back along the track. There was a great deal of speculation going on as to what it was all about. Gericke moved along the corridor, thrusting his left hand and the dangling handcuffs into his pocket.

No one took the slightest notice of him until he reached the end and then a young sailor, moving back from a window, pushed into him. He turned, took in the raincoat and uniform cap and said quickly, 'Sorry, sir.'

'That's all right.'

'What's going on back there, sir?'

'God knows,' Gericke said. 'I saw a couple of officers with guns in their hands. Maybe some prisoner or other has given them the slip.' He stood at a window for a while, just one of the crowd watching, and saw Jago and the others climb back on board. The guard's whistle sounded, there was a hiss of steam, the wheels spun and the train moved forward again.

People started to go back into their compartments and he carried on. He crossed to the sleeping car and immediately found himself in a calmer, more ordered world. The corridor was deserted and as he started along it, a door at the far end opened and the steward came out of his tiny kitchen.

He paused, 'Can I help you, sir?'

Gericke, improvising fast, remembered the conversation he had overheard earlier about Jago and the girl he was sharing a sleeping compartment with. What was her name again? Dr Munro; an American admiral's niece. It had a certain black humour to it.

'I'm Lieutenant van Lott, Royal Netherlands Navy,' he said smoothly. 'I was looking for Dr Munro.'

'Compartment fourteen. This way, sir.'

He turned, moved a little way along the corridor and knocked at a door. Gericke followed.

The door opened and Janet peered out. 'Gentleman here was looking for you, Doctor. Lieutenant van Lott of the Dutch Navy.'

Janet looked Gericke over calmly. 'Thank you,' she said and added to Gericke, 'Won't you come in?'

The steward departed and Gericke moved past her into the compartment. When he turned, she was standing against the door, arms folded, watching him gravely. 'You don't look too good to me, Lieutenant. What's the trouble?'

'I'm not sure. I wasn't feeling marvellous in Glasgow. Nearly got off the train there, but it's essential I get to Mallaig today. Someone told me there was a doctor on the train so I asked the steward.'

'You'd better sit down.'

He perched on the edge of the bunk. She put a hand on his forehead. 'You could be running a fever.'

'You think so?'

'But definitely.'

She was close enough for him to smell her perfume, she sat down beside him and took his pulse, crossing one knee over the other.

'You've got excellent legs, Doctor.'

'It's been said before,' she said calmly and stood up. 'A large Scotch, I think, is my prescription for you.'

'You think so?'

'I'd say you're going to need it.'

She found the bottle in Jago's holdall, took a glass from the small washbasin in the corner and poured him a large one.

'Good health,' Gericke said.

'Prosit,' she replied and smiled. 'How stupid of me. That's German, isn't it?'

Gericke sighed and took the whisky down in a single swallow, 'That was really most kind of you,' he said and reached out and shot the bolt on the door.

Jago made his way along the swaying train, Fisher and Carver behind him. 'But what in the hell am I going to do, sir?' Fisher asked plaintively.

'Run for the hills. Blow your brains out. Why ask me?' Jago demanded. 'It's your problem, Fisher. I wasn't even there. I was back on the train.'

He had no intention of being dragged down by this young fool's incompetence. As he opened the door and entered the sleeping car, the steward was just emerging from the end compartment with a tray.

'We'll have some tea or coffee,' Jago told him. 'Anything you can rustle up.'

'In Dr Munro's compartment?' The steward hesitated. 'Actually she has someone with her at the moment, sir. A Lieutenant van Lott. Dutch naval officer.'

Jago looked at him. 'A small guy with a pale face,' he said carefully. 'White cap, navy blue raincoat?'

'That's right, sir. I'm short of coffee, but I think I can manage tea for you gentlemen. I'll see to it directly.'

He moved along to his kitchen. Jago took the Colt automatic from his pocket and turned to Fisher. 'Well?' he said.

'I can't believe it.' Fisher looked stunned. 'It doesn't make sense.'

'Just give me a minute, sir,' Carver said eagerly, 'and I'll have the sod out of there.'

'Like hell you will. We've got Dr Munro to consider, so we play this very carefully indeed till we know what's going on. Understand?'

He moved quietly along the corridor to Janet's compartment. He tried the door handle gently without success, took a deep breath and knocked. 'Janet, you in there?' His voice was muffled.

She took a step towards the door but Gericke pulled her back, the handcuffs dangling from his wrist, plain to see now. 'I don't think so. Not at the moment.'

Jago rapped on the door again, a little more insistently. 'Heh, come on, Janet. Open up.'

Gericke sat on the edge of the bed. 'How did you know?'

'When I first saw you at the London Cage there was an eagle and swastika above the badge of that rather sweet, white cap you're wearing.'

He smiled good-humouredly. 'How could I have missed you?'

'One of your bad days, I expect. Charm, like most things, has its limitations. Now would you mind very much if we bring this little farce to an end?'

She put a hand to the bolt and Gericke produced the Mauser from his pocket and cocked it. 'I don't suppose you'd like to take my pulse again?'

'Not today, I'm fully booked.'

'Ah well, I shall always have the memory.' He clicked his heels, gave a little bow and handed the Mauser across butt first. 'Isn't that how Conrad Veidt does it in all those Hollywood movies?'

She stopped smiling. 'You fool,' she whispered. 'And in the end, where has it got you?'

He shrugged. 'The rules of the game, Doctor. You have to keep moving.'

She pushed back the bolt, opened the door and stood to one side. Jago and the others crowded in, Carver grabbing Gericke roughly and turning him round, jerking his arms behind his back.

'You all right?' Jago demanded.

She handed him the Mauser. 'He behaved like a perfect gentleman.'

'I'm sorry about that,' Gericke said cheerfully over his shoulder.

She laughed harshly. 'Get him out of here, for God's sake.'

Carver shoved Gericke, whose wrists were by now handcuffed behind him, into the corridor. Jago handed him the Mauser. 'Try not to lose it again. Or him.'

'I won't, sir. You can count on that,' Carver said grimly and he put a knee behind Gericke and sent him staggering.

The train stood in Fort William for twenty minutes while Fisher used the phone in the stationmaster's office. Finally he came out, climbed into the guard's van and knocked on the door of the luggage compartment. As Carver opened it, the train started to move again.

'What's the form, sir?'

'We're taking him on to Mallaig. Back to Glasgow on the afternoon train. How is he?'

'Trussed up like a Christmas turkey.'

Fisher walked over to the cage and looked inside. Gericke sprawled across the mailbags, wrists handcuffed behind him, ankles tied together with twine. The lieutenant sat down, suddenly very tired indeed, and lit a cigarette. Thank God the nightmare was over at last. No court-martial, no enquiry. Well, an enquiry perhaps, but then he might not come too badly out of that. After all, it had been Carver's fault in the first place, the whole wretched affair.

On the *Deutschland*, there were rumblings of discontent amounting almost to mutiny when Richter descended to the forecastle for his midday meal.

'Something's crawled in there and died if you ask me,' he heard Leading Seaman Roth observe.

The watch below were grouped around the narrow central table on which stood the cause of their dissension – two large pans which had just been brought down from the galley. The smell, when someone raised a lid, was really quite special, Richter had to admit that. Enough to take the edge off the strongest appetite.

'What's all this?' he demanded, pushing his way through.

'The food again,' Endrass told him. 'Not fit for pigs. Weber's gone too far this time.'

'He's no cook,' Richter admitted, peering into one of the pans with distaste.

'Which Walz was, whatever else he might have been.'

There was an uncomfortable silence for it was an undeniable fact of life that the cook's death had left a gap which had proved almost impossible to fill. Richter, by implication, did bear a certain responsibility for the present situation.

Riedel said, 'I served my time in sail, Herr Richter, you know that. I was with the old Kommodore Johnsen out of Hamburg in the last grain race just before the war. One hundred and seven days, Australia to Queenstown. I know my rights and according to regulations, each man is entitled to one and a quarter pounds of salt beef and three-quarters of a pound of pork per day.' He dipped the ladle into the pan. 'And what do we get? A mouthful each if we're lucky.'

'Supplies are running low,' Richter said. 'That pork is half-rotten when it comes out of the barrel. You can't blame Weber for that.'

'Which is still no excuse to serve what little there is like something off the pavement,' Endrass said. 'I think we should see the captain.'

'All right.' Richter nodded. 'You and Riedel here, and you'd better bring one of those pans so he can see what we're talking about.'

Not that there was any need, for when the bosun knocked at Berger's door and entered, he found the captain and Prager seated opposite each other, plates of stew before them.

'What's this?' Berger demanded.

'Deputation from the crew, Captain. Petty Officer Endrass and Leading Seaman Riedel ask leave to speak for the men.'

Berger looked at Endrass coldly. 'Well?'

'The food, Herr Kapitän,' Endrass said. 'It's getting so the men can't stomach it any more and the stink . . .'

He lifted the lid of the pan which Riedel was holding. Berger grimaced at the first whiff. 'You've made your point. Get it out of here.' Riedel retreated. 'All right, so it's not too good, but we're all in the same boat.' He indicated his own plate and said to Richter, 'Who's in the galley now? Weber, isn't it?'

'That's right, sir, and he had to be pressed into service. Nobody wanted the job so the men drew lots.'

Berger nodded. 'I don't really see that there's anything much I can do about this. It's an old problem on sailing ships, as you know. Once the food starts going off, especially the meat, it needs an experienced cook to handle it and that's something we just don't have. I'm sure Weber is doing his best.'

'I beg leave to doubt that.' Sister Angela stood in the doorway, a pan in one hand, the other nuns behind her. She lifted the lid. 'What would you say this is exactly?' she asked Berger.

He eyed the greasy scum on the surface with distaste. 'Pea soup, I think, Sister.'

'So dirty that it's almost black,' she said. 'A rare phenomenon which is explained by the simple fact that the cook has omitted to wash the peas.'

'All right.' Berger held up a hand. 'No need to go on. So what do you want me to do about it?'

She handed the pan to Sister Käthe. 'We could start with an inspection of the galley. With your permission, of course.'

Berger, for once allowing himself to go with the tide, reached for his cap. 'For you, Sister, anything. If you'd follow me, please?'

So it was that the unfortunate Weber, sitting disconsolate in the tiny galley surrounded by greasy pans and dirty plates, observed through the open doorway, a sizeable group bearing down on him headed by the captain.

He got to his feet, wiping his hands hastily on his soiled apron and Berger said, 'Outside, Weber. On the double.'

Weber did as he was told. Sister Angela paused in the doorway. She surveyed the scene inside, briefly leaning down to sniff at the rotting pork in its barrel, then turned.

'Take off your apron,' she said to Weber.

He glanced nervously at Berger, then did as he was told. She took it from him, holding it at arm's length for a moment, then tossed it over the side.

'I suggest you return this man to his normal duties. This is obviously not the place for him.'

'And the cooking?' Berger asked.

'There, you will have to show a little faith, Captain. But first, I want every inch of this disgusting hovel scrubbed clean.' She turned to the nuns. 'Every pan sparkling. Then and only then will we be in a position to do something about the food. You agree, Captain?'

'We are, as you so frequently remind me, in the good Lord's hands,' Berger told her.

But later, towards evening, when he went up on the quarterdeck with Prager, the aroma which drifted up from the galley on the damp air was so appetizing that for the first time in days, he felt genuine hunger.

'What's that?' he demanded of Richter who had the watch.

'I think it's what's called the woman's touch, Herr Kapitän.'

'And thank God for it,' Prager added piously.

Janet stood at the window of her sleeping compartment, looking out morosely, but even the spectacular beauties of Ben Nevis didn't improve the way she felt. She sat down at the table and picked up a book.

An hour passed, an hour and a half, and Jago continued to sleep as they moved on, passing through some of the most spectacular mountain scenery in Scotland. Glenfinnan, Lochailort and then the sea and the Sound of Arisaig, shrouded in mist and rain.

She had long since discarded the book. She sat smoking a cigarette, watching raindrops roll down the window, thinking of Gericke, mainly because the thought of him simply wouldn't go away. And that would never do. She picked up the book again and forced herself to read.

Lying face-down on the mailbags Gericke couldn't see Carver, but he was conscious of his approach. The chief petty officer squatted beside him, a knife in his hand, and jerked Gericke's head round.

'Very foolish,' Gericke said. 'You'd never be able to explain it away.'

Carver took the Knight's Cross from his pocket. 'Did you do something special for this one then? Big hero, is that it?' The anger welled up in him like hot lava. He sliced through the cords that bound Gericke's ankles and grabbed his arm. 'Come on – on your feet.'

Gericke stood there swaying, almost crying out with pain as blood moved in his cramped legs. Carver pushed him out through the gate, then tripped him so that he fell to his knees, head resting on the floor. Carver booted him in the ribs.

'You feel better now, sir?'

Gericke pushed himself up on his knees. 'Was this how you won those fights of yours, Chief? Using men with their hands tied behind their backs as punchbags?'

Carver produced the keys to the handcuffs and swung him round. 'I'll show you if I can use myself or not.'

Gericke, his wrists free, shrugged off his raincoat, a smile on his face. Carver rushed in and swung a wild punch which the German side-stepped with ease, dropping into a fighting crouch, his right arm extended in front of him, fist clenched, his left guarding the body. And there was something terribly professional-looking about the way he moved.

The chief stamped in again, swinging a punch which Gericke once more evaded with ease, this time pivoting and delivering a left to Carver's kidneys. Carver cried out in agony and turned to face him.

'Yes, I'm afraid I haven't been really honest with you, Chief,' Gericke said, sinking another left under Carver's ribs followed by a right which landed high on the cheek, splitting flesh. 'As a young man, I served my apprenticeship in a clipper ship on the nitrate run to Chile. A hard school. Plenty of discipline enforced by belaying pin, knuckle-duster and boot. I grew up fast.'

He seemed to be moving in a kind of slow motion, one punch after another finding its target and Carver's blows repeatedly landed on thin air.

The chief petty officer was in a bad way, face covered in blood, unable to speak, gasping for breath as the German drove him back across the van relentlessly.

'My friend, you are a disgrace to the uniform you wear and the country which nurtured you. Someone should have cut you down to size long ago,' Gericke said, striking Carver three terrible blows on the face that sent him back against the wall of the cage.

He slid to the floor, head lolling to one side. Gericke stood there looking down at him, then dropped to one knee and went through his pockets, retrieving his decorations.

He found the Mauser which he slipped into his own pocket, picked up his cap and put on the raincoat. He pulled back the sliding door and rain flooded in.

Janet, standing at an open window in the corridor of the sleeping car, caught a brief glimpse of him landing in heather and rolling over and over down the slope. And then there was only the mist and the rain.

Barquentine *Deutschland*, 22 September 1944. Lat. 50°.59N., 15°.35W. At six bells of the mid-watch, the iron collar of the mainsail boom fractured. In the ensuing tangle, the mainsail itself was split from top to bottom and we had to heave to for repairs, drifting under sea anchor until Mr Sturm reported all clear and ready to proceed at noon. The weather deteriorated into heavy rain and mist soon after. Wind NW 5–6.

Nine

The *Mary Masters*, a nine-thousand-ton Liberty ship out of Halifax, Nova Scotia, with a cargo of pig iron destined for the steelworks of South Wales, had just gone through a very bad twenty-four hours. Most of the crew, including the captain, were snatching a couple of hours' sleep below.

Visibility was poor owing to driving rain and mist and the third officer, alone on the bridge, was tired. When he raised his binoculars for perhaps the twentieth time in half an hour and the *Deutschland* sprang into view, he received a considerable shock.

He went to the voice pipe to call up the captain. 'Braithwaite, sir. Sorry to bother you, but I've sighted a sailing ship.'

'What did you say?'

'A sailing ship, sir. A quarter of a mile away on the port quarter.'

'I'll be right up.'

Braithwaite turned to examine the *Deutschland* again and a few moments later, Captain Henderson hurried on to the bridge. He was a small, white-haired man who should have retired in nineteen-forty and had stayed on for the duration.

He reached for the binoculars and focused them. 'You old beauty,' he said softly. 'Alter course, Mr Braithwaite. I think we'll take a closer look.'

There were no more than half-a-dozen men visible on the decks of the *Deutschland* as Berger and Sturm stood together on the poop, watching the other vessel move in towards them.

Sturm lowered his glasses. 'A *Tommi*, Herr Kapitän. The *Mary Masters*, registered Liverpool.'

Richter came up the ladder holding the signalling lamp. 'What happens now, sir?'

'That's a merchant ship out there, not the Royal Navy.' Berger glanced up at the Swedish ensign. 'We're still the *Gudrid Andersen* until someone proves different.'

A signalling pennant was hoisted on the *Mary Masters* and Sturm examined it quickly through his glasses. 'May I be of assistance?'

Berger frowned, one hand gripping the rail. She was very near, moving on a course that would take her astern, close enough for him to see the men on the bridge clearly.

'I think we'll try a real bluff this time. You speak the best English, Mr Sturm, so you take the signalling lamp. Get ready to transmit on my orders. Plain language, if you please.'

'Aye, aye, sir.'

Sturm made a preliminary signal. There was a pause and then an answering flash.

'Here we go then,' Berger said softly. '*Gudrid Andersen* twenty-eight days out of Belém for Gothenburg. Thank you for your offer, but in no need of assistance.'

The lamp flashed in reply from the bridge of the *Mary Masters*, even closer now. Sturm waited until it had finished, then translated.

'Out of Halifax, Nova Scotia, for Swansea. Compelled to drop out of convoy yesterday owing to temporary engine fault.' The lamp flashed again. 'Do you wish me to report your position?'

'Accept his offer. After all, we don't really have a choice. You agree, Helmut?'

Richter nodded, his face grim. 'I'm afraid not, Herr Kapitän.'

'With luck, it will take them a couple of days, perhaps three, to discover that the real *Gudrid Andersen* is still in Gothenburg harbour and we'll change course as soon as they're over the horizon.'

The signal lamp clattered in Sturm's hands, the *Mary Masters* acknowledged. Most of her crew seemed to be lining the port rail, waving, calling cheerfully through the rain.

'Ask him if they are still winning the war,' Sturm turned, mouth open in astonishment. 'Get on with it, man!' Berger told him impatiently.

The reply was noticeably brief. 'Definitely. That's all he says, sir.'

'Somehow I thought they might be,' Berger said. 'Thank you and goodbye, Mr Sturm.'

The lamp clattered for the last time and as the *Mary Masters* passed astern, they heard three long blasts on her steam whistle.

'Mr Richter, return the salute.'

The bosun hurried down the ladder and ran along the deck to dip the ensign. The hooter sounded again, a lonely echo drifting across the water.

'Right, Mr Sturm, let's get to hell out of here,' Berger said.

On the bridge of the *Mary Masters*, Henderson watched the *Deutschland* slip away and she was already partly obscured by rain and mist when he lowered his binoculars.

'Everything I ever learned at sea, everything worth knowing, I learned by the age of eighteen on an old hooker just like her.'

'Is that so, sir?' Braithwaite said.

The old captain nodded. 'Watch her go, mister. Drink your fill. I don't think you'll get a second chance – not in your lifetime.'

There was mist on the hills, but in Mallaig it was relatively clear. Janet waited in the outer office of the naval commander's headquarters, staring out across the harbour. It was busier than when she was here before, fishing boats, several naval patrol craft, a submarine even, and a lighter unloading at the pier.

Her eyes were gritty from lack of sleep and she was impatient to be on her way. She had answered their questions, made an official statement and signed it, and still there were delays.

A young Wren was typing at a desk in the corner, but in spite of that the murmur of voices was clearly audible from the inner office. She turned from the window as the door opened. Fisher hurried out, his face flushed, and brushed past her without a word.

Jago appeared with Captain Murray, the base commander, a pleasant, grey-haired man of fifty or so. He smiled. 'Sorry about the delay, Miss Munro, but we're all through now.'

'I can go?'

'I don't see why not. You've told us all you know. As regards your passage to Fhada, Murdoch Macleod hasn't arrived yet. The arrangement was that he would report here when he did. If I were you, I'd book in at the hotel for the moment. I've told them to expect you.'

'And Gericke? What about him?'

Murray smiled. 'My dear Miss Munro, I'm filled with admiration for the gentleman.'

She was suddenly angry again. 'Good God, he *is* on the other side. Or had you forgotten that?'

'Not at all, I assure you. Professional regard for a superb seaman, that's all. However . . .' Here he turned to a one-inch ordnance survey map of the Western Highlands which was pinned to the wall. 'If he came straight over the mountain from where he left the train he would find his way blocked by Loch Morar. If he cut down to the coast road, it would only bring him to Mallaig – and he won't come here.'

'So where will he go?'

'Not very far, I'm afraid, because there isn't anywhere for him to go.

One road and the railway line coming in, as you can see. Only a question of time. He won't stay up on those hills for long, not in this weather.'

Jago picked up her bag. 'I'll walk you to the hotel.'

Murray shook hands. 'I'll send word the moment Murdoch arrives. Have a nice trip.' And he turned and went back into his office.

They walked back towards the station, heads down against the rain. Janet said, 'What about Lieutenant Fisher?'

'They'll probably post him to Cape Wrath.'

'And Carver?'

'Patching him up now at the base hospital. That must have been something to see. I mean, Gericke really sorted him out. He's finished, of course. I'm not saying he'll end up in the brig, but he'll lose all rank.'

As they came abreast of the station, a voice called, 'Dr Munro?'

A young paratrooper in red beret and camouflage jump jacket hurried across the road.

'Why, Lachlan,' Janet said. 'Were you on the train?' She turned to Jago. 'This is Lachlan MacBrayne, Harry. He's from Fhada, too.'

'Is that so?' Jago held out his hand.

Lachlan was eighteen and his untidy red hair, freckles and snub nose made him look even younger. 'Fourteen days' leave. I've just finished jump training. Murdoch is supposed to pick me up but when I checked down at the harbour he hadn't arrived.'

'He's taking me, too,' she said. 'I'm going to wait at the hotel. They'll send word when he arrives. Why not join us?'

He glanced at Jago awkwardly. 'Would it be all right, do you think?'

'Sure it would,' Jago said. 'You get your gear and follow us on.'

The boy ran back across the road.

Janet and Jago paused outside the hotel as the rain increased in a sudden rush and Janet looked up to the peaks on the other side of Loch Morar, shrouded in mist.

'I shouldn't think it would be too comfortable up there on a day like this,' Jago said.

'An understatement.'

They went up the steps into the hotel.

Gericke was slightly north-west of Sitheon Mor. His intended destination was Mallaig. There was nowhere else to go; he remembered enough of the charts for the west coast of Scotland to realize that. All he had to do was keep going, straight over the top and down to Loch Morar, impossible to miss even in the worst of weather, then along the shore to the coast road. That he could last longer than a day seemed highly improbable, but at least there were boats at Mallaig. Some kind of a chance, however remote. And it was good to be free. Anything was worth that.

After jumping from the train, he had started up the hillside, coming across a mountain stream after ten minutes or so. He followed its course, moving fast with mist pressing in on either hand that gave him a safe, enclosed feeling, somehow remote from the world outside. There were birch trees at first which grew sparser as he climbed higher, working his way through bracken that in places was waist-high.

Occasionally, grouse or plover lifted out of the heather, disturbed by his passing. He kept on the move, stopping after an hour to catch his breath, sheltering under an overhang from the rain. Not that it mattered by now, for his raincoat was soaked through.

He set off again, climbing strongly. Three miles to the loch, perhaps four, and the mountains to pass over, but he was conscious of no feeling of fatigue, the first elation of freedom still carrying him on.

Half an hour later the burn petered out in a small loch and he moved on to the flank of South Morar, climbing across a boulder-strewn hillside. The mist totally enveloped him and he was by now soaked to the skin, for the first time aware of the cold.

He climbed on doggedly and two hours after leaving the train, scrambled over the edge of a great up-tilted slab of granite and found himself on a plateau. There was a special kind of cold here, a wind on his face that told him he was on top. Then a sudden current of air snatched away the grey curtain.

The view was incredible. Loch Morar below him, Mallaig on the far point four or five miles beyond and, out to sea, the islands crouching in the rain, Eigg, Rhum and Skye across the Sound of Sleat. There was a cairn of stones ten or fifteen yards away, a track snaking down towards the loch. The curtain of mist dropped back into place but he had seen enough. With renewed energy, he started down the mountainside.

The *Deutschland* was making good time, plunging into the waves, carrying every stitch of canvas she possessed. From the quarterdeck, Berger addressed the crew and passengers.

'The final run,' he said. 'Our meeting with the *Mary Masters* was unfortunate but we've had a lot of luck on our side. I altered course as soon as I could, just in case anyone should come looking but I don't think it likely. However, one thing is essential. Now, more than ever, we must watch those lights at night. There have been occasions when carelessness in this regard has been much in evidence.'

There was a moment of silence, every face turned up to him, expecting more and there was so little to give. He clutched the rail tightly and tried to put confidence into his voice. 'Look, it's going to be all right. Another seven or eight days, that's all, and those of you with families to think of will be greeting them again, I promise you. We've come too far to fail now.' He nodded to Sturm. 'Dismiss the crew, please, Mr Sturm.'

There was a general movement as the starboard watch returned to their duties and the others went below. Berger checked the course, then descended the ladder and went into his cabin. He was pouring himself a glass of rum when there was a knock on the door and Prager entered.

'Join me?' Berger held up his glass.

'No, thanks,' Prager said, 'but I'll have one of your cheroots if you have any left.'

'Help yourself.'

Berger sat down at his desk and pulled a chart of the Western Approaches forward. Prager said, 'You sounded good out there, Erich.'

'Did I?' Berger said wearily. 'That's something anyway.'

'Where are we? Is it permitted to ask?'

'Here,' Berger tapped on the chart with his forefinger. 'Now all we have to do is work our way up west of Ireland, the Outer Hebrides, Shetland, across to Norway. We should be safe enough then. Follow the coastline down through the Kattegat and Kiel.'

'It seemed like a dream when we started,' Prager said. 'An impossible dream.'

'Yes, it did, didn't it?'

And something touched him, a wave of greyness running through his entire body, like a cold wind brushing the face on deck at night, first warning of a storm to come.

In the galley, Sister Angela and Lotte, sleeves rolled up to the elbows, worked together preparing the evening meal. The door was pushed open and Richter entered, an enamel washbasin in his hands.

He dropped it on the table. 'Salt beef. The last of the crop and it doesn't smell too good.'

Sister Angela prodded it with a knife.

'Half of it rotten, the rest teeming with life.'

'Not to worry, Sister. I'm sure you'll manage to do something with it.'

He exchanged glances with Lotte, who smiled as she kneaded dough, flour to her elbows. She wasn't wearing her coif and the slender neck and cropped hair made her look strangely defenceless. Richter would have liked nothing better than an opportunity to take her in his arms.

He pulled himself together hurriedly. 'Anything else I can do?'

'Yes,' Sister Angela told him. 'There are still a few potatoes left. You can peel them. Outside.'

He took the bowl she indicated, went out and squatted by the port rail. He took out his gutting knife, sprang the blade and started on the potatoes. They were mainly rotten, sprouting roots, but he did the best he could, whistling between his teeth as he worked.

After a while, Lotte appeared, a bucket of garbage in one hand. He got up quickly, took the bucket from her and emptied it over the side. When he returned it, their hands touched briefly and she smiled. As a token, he had given her his signet ring. Impossible to wear it, of course, and for the moment she kept it hidden in her bunk under a corner of the mattress.

'It will be all right, Helmut?' she said. 'We will get through?'

'Of course we will. Why do you ask?'

'Captain Berger. It was something in his voice. Something I can't explain.'

'Nonsense, he's tired, that's all. We all are. It's been a hell of a trip.' He reached up and held her hand. 'You've nothing to worry about.'

She smiled. 'And when we get to Kiel?'

'You'll never be alone again, I promise you. From now on nothing parts us. Not ever. I swear it.'

She smiled warmly. 'Then that's all that matters,' she said and returned to the galley.

Janet peered out across the harbour from the bridge of the *Dead End*. 'I always forget when I'm away just how much it rains up here.'

'Five days out of seven,' Jago said.

Jansen entered, a cup of coffee in each hand. 'Just had our orders, sir. Stornoway, by dawn's early light.'

Noting Janet's expression, Jago explained. 'He always speaks that way. In quotations.'

'A well-known disease,' Jansen told her. 'It's called education.'

A sea-going launch rounded the pier and moved into harbour. Janet leaned forward. 'I believe that's the *Katrina* now. Yes, I'm sure of it.'

Jansen said, 'I'll go and tell him you're here.'

He went out. She turned to Jago. 'Well, Harry – the end of something.'

'Or the beginning.'

'That's what I like about you, darling. The last of the great romantics and that's a quality hard to come by these days.'

★   ★   ★

There was a surprising amount of light on the pier in spite of the blackout. A crane was working, powered by a diesel engine that thumped hollowly through the night as a party of sailors unloaded oil drums from a lighter into two large trucks.

At least it gave Gericke, standing in the shadows, a view of the general state of things. There was an old gunboat which looked pre-war, with a couple of ratings on the deck. Americans, to judge from their headgear.

Beyond the gunboat was a coaster, a single stacker of eight or nine hundred tons and then a gaggle of fishing boats. And perhaps twenty yards further on as the light faded, the dim shape of a sea-going launch.

He glanced at his watch. It was just coming up to nine. Those sailors couldn't work all night, at least he hoped not, for to attempt to reach that boat as conditions were presently on the pier, was obviously impossible.

He needed somewhere to lie up for three or four hours, preferably with a roof over his head for the rain showed no sign of abating. There were half a dozen naval trucks parked at one side in a rather confined space, crammed together nose to tail.

He made a cautious reconnaissance, but there seemed to be no guard, probably because they were empty. He climbed over the tailgate of one, made himself as comfortable as possible on the floor and waited.

Janet and Harry Jago were sitting in a corner of the bar of the Station Hotel when Murdoch came in. He wore seaboots and his reefer coat, a yellow oilskin over one arm, a splendidly archaic figure that made heads turn as he moved past.

'Can I get you a Scotch, Mister Macleod?' Jago asked, standing up.

'Murdoch, lad, Murdoch to my friends,' the old man said. 'And yes, a wee dram would go down just fine, you being the one with the influence to get it.'

Jago moved over to the bar and Murdoch took out his pipe. 'Do you mind, girl?'

'Not at all,' she said. 'Now tell me about the island. How's my uncle?'

Murdoch filled the pipe methodically from his oilskin pouch. Instead of answering her question, he said, 'Where would young Lachlan be?'

'In my room. I thought the bed might as well get some use and he looked as if he needed the sleep.'

Jago returned with Murdoch's Scotch. The old man raised the glass and examined the contents in the light with a connoisseur's appreciation. 'How in the devil do you manage it, Lieutenant?'

'Oh, I let them have a couple of bottles now and then so they always keep one under the bar for me.'

'How is Uncle Carey? You still haven't told me?' Janet demanded.

He said carefully, 'Have they work for him yet? Have you news?'

'Yes, I think you could say that.'

He nodded. 'His only problem.'

'Mind you, it's not what he's hoping for. No more boarding parties, sword in hand, if you know what I mean.'

'I was afraid of that.' Murdoch sighed. 'He has – how can I explain it to you – a hunger for action. It is, I think, meat and drink to him. A great pity he cannot bide still for a while and a good woman to hold his hand.'

'Jean?'

'That is the impression I get.'

'And the best thing for him.' Janet was pleased. 'I'll have to see what I can do.'

'Look to your own affairs, girl,' he told her gently. 'Some things grow better on their own.'

Jago was vastly amused to see her slapped down. She kicked him under the table. 'When do you plan to leave?'

'Oh, about two o'clock in the morning if that will suit. The tide will be flowing well by then. I'll leave you now, if you don't mind. I'm promised to supper with my sister.' He produced an old tin watch from some inner pocket and consulted it gravely. 'I should have been there ten minutes ago. She'll have the skin off me. Terrible sharp since her husband died last year.'

'Is it far?' Jago stood up. 'I could get the jeep.'

'The top end of the main street. A step only. I'll see you here at one-thirty.'

He moved away through the crowded bar and Jago sat down. 'There goes one hell of an old man. Pity you had to be so open-handed with young Lachlan. There's a perfectly good bed going to waste up there.'

'Good deeds is my second name.'

He leaned across, offering her a cigarette. 'As it happens, being a young man of some resource, I have a special arrangement with the landlord.'

'Somehow I thought you might.'

'You know how it is. Home is the sailor and all that. Somewhere to lay his weary head. There *is* only one difficulty. It's a single bed.'

'And two into one won't go?'

'I was always lousy at mathematics.'

'Me too.'

They got up and moved out of the bar into the hall. Rain rattled against the door in a sudden flurry of wind and she paused, one hand on the bannister. 'A hell of a night to be out.'

'Not fit for man, beast or an old stray tomcat,' he told her cheerfully. 'As my old grannie used to say.'

'I was thinking of Gericke,' she said and started upstairs.

Gericke actually dropped off to sleep, waking in something of a panic to find that a good two hours had passed. Not that it mattered for it was one o'clock before the sailors on the pier finished unloading. The lights were extinguished, the trucks driven away.

It was very quiet now. A dog barked hollowly somewhere in the distance. He waited for another quarter of an hour just to make sure that no one was coming back, then moved out from the shelter of the trucks and went cautiously down to the pier.

He kept to the shadows, pausing to remove his seaboots and stuffing his white cap inside his raincoat. There was a murmur of voices as the two men on watch in the gunboat chatted, the glow of a cigarette inside the wheelhouse. He moved on, soundlessly in stockinged feet, past the coaster and the fishing boats.

The launch was tied up at the bottom of a flight of stone steps. He stepped over the rail, put his seaboots down gently and descended the companionway, the Mauser in one hand.

There was a decent-sized saloon, a cabin aft with two bunks, both unoccupied, and a small toilet. The galley was forrard. Nothing could have been more satisfactory. He found a towel, dried his feet, then went back up the companionway and pulled on his seaboots.

Next, he made a cautious exploration of the wheelhouse. This was no fisherman's boat, so much was certain. A rich man's craft. Penta petrol engine, twin screws, a depth sounder, automatic steering. Such boats commonly had a range of seven or eight hundred miles, perhaps more. It all depended on what was in the tanks.

He found the correct dial which seemed to indicate that they were full or nearly so. What he needed now was an oar so that he might sweep her out of harbour before switching on the engine. He moved out on deck cautiously and pulled back into the wheel-house at the sound of voices, footsteps approaching along the pier.

He stayed in the shadows, waiting for them to stop, perhaps at one of the fishing boats, already aware with a strange kind of fatalism that they would keep right on coming.

Someone laughed clear on the damp air, harsh, distinctive and familiar. Gericke smiled incredulously as Janet Munro said, 'Don't you ever take anything seriously, Harry?'

'Not if I can help it,' Jago told her. 'You know, I've had a great idea, Murdoch. Why don't you choose the deepest spot you can find between here and Fhada and put her over the side with about eighty pounds of old chain round her ankles? I'd say the world would be a whole lot more comfortable for all of us.'

'Bastard,' she replied.

'Mind your manners, girl,' Murdoch said in reproof. 'For if you do not act in a more seemly fashion, I might take the lieutenant, here, up on his suggestion.'

Gericke, smiling again, was already out of sight and half way down the companionway.

Barquentine *Deutschland*, 23 September 1944. Lat. 53°.59N., long. 16°.39W. Wind NW 6–7. Rain and intermittent squalls. During the mid-watch, Mr Sturm requested permission to shorten sail as we were taking so much water inboard that life was becoming very uncomfortable for the passengers. I refused his request, anxious to make as much time as possible now.

Ten

Jago switched on the light in the saloon. The blackout curtains were neatly drawn and he turned as Janet followed him down. 'This is nice. Where do you want these, by the way?'

'The aft cabin,' she said.

He kicked open the door and dropped the suitcases and medical bag on one of the bunks. As he went back into the saloon, Lachlan came down the companionway, his rifle slung over one shoulder, a kitbag under his arm.

The boy made a face. 'So help me, Doctor, but I feel sick already.'

He dropped his kitbag on the floor and Janet took the rifle from him and pushed it out of sight under one of the divan seats. 'I hate those things. Never mind, Lachlan, I've got some pills in my bag. I'll give you a couple and you can get your head down and sleep all the way across.'

The boy went into the galley and she turned to Jago. 'He's always been like that, ever since he was a kid. Believe it or not, but his father was captain of a local fishing boat out of Fhada.'

'Was?'

'Apparently he was killed in action recently serving as a petty officer under Murdoch's son.'

'I know,' Jago said. 'About what happened, I mean. Not about Lachlan's father, though. They were torpedoed in the North Sea. I had the unpleasant task of bringing the good news. As I told you before, I'm just a bloody postman.'

She was suddenly angry, irritated at the recurrence of the same old theme. 'For God's sake, grow up, Harry. Stop feeling sorry for yourself.' She grabbed hold of his sweater. 'You try turning up at Fhada in that mood and I'll throw you straight back into the sea.'

'Yes, ma'am.'

He tried to kiss her, but she slipped from his arms and made for the companionway. 'I want to get out of here.'

They found Murdoch in the wheelhouse with Jansen. 'I've been trying to suggest to Mr Macleod,' the chief petty officer said, 'that maybe it would be a good idea to wait for a little more light.'

'And what was his reaction?'

'As I have been sailing these waters man and boy for at least seventy years now, I told him to mind his own business and go to hell,' Murdoch said. 'A terrible sentiment for a man of my persuasion, but there it is.'

'Admirably put,' Jago observed.

Murdoch took out his pipe. 'A couple of plates of good Scots porridge in you and you'll be ready for that dawn start to Stornoway.'

'Porridge?' Jansen said. 'A grain which in England is given to the horses, but in Scotland supports the people. It was Dr Samuel Johnson who said that first, by the way. Not me. As a matter of interest, he actually travelled in these parts.'

'Lieutenant Jago,' Murdoch said grimly, 'will you get him off now or do I pitch him headfirst over the side?'

'No offence, sir.' Jansen backed out hurriedly and stepped over the rail.

'I'm sorry,' Jago said. 'He isn't really responsible. Something they gave him when he was very young.'

'On your way, Harry.' Janet gave him a push.

Jago joined Jansen at the bottom of the steps and they cast off the lines. Janet hauled them in, then stood watching them, hands on hips. Jago blew her a kiss. She waved and went into the wheelhouse.

She stood at Murdoch's elbow peering out into the darkness. 'What's the forecast?'

'Three to four winds with rain squalls. A light fog generally in the Sea of the Hebrides just before dawn.'

'How disappointing.'

'Oh, so it's excitement you're seeking? You must wait a day or two.'

'Why do you say that?'

'Heavy weather coming.'

'Something really bad, you mean?' Janet frowned, for she knew that it was not uncommon for Fhada to be cut off from the mainland for weeks at a time. But that was usually in the winter. 'How do you know?'

'It is to be found in the wind's breath, the touch of the rain. The smell of things.' He smiled. 'Or in the sum total of a lifetime at sea, perhaps.'

She stuffed her arm through his. 'I know – you're just an old highland mystic. Can I take the wheel?'

'Later. Go you and see to the boy. You know how this trip distresses him.'

She left him and went downstairs. Lachlan was seated at the table and already looked ghastly. She went into the aft cabin, opened it and found the pills she'd promised.

'Take these with a glass of water, then get on one of the bunks. I'll bring you a cup of tea.'

She went out to the galley. Lachlan stood there by the bunk for a moment then, stomach heaving, reached for the handle of the toilet door. When he pushed it open, Gericke was sitting there, the Mauser in his right hand.

Janet leaned against the bulkhead in the galley and smoked a cigarette, arms folded as she waited for the kettle to boil. She was aware of the creak as the door swung open, turned casually and saw Lachlan standing there, hands clasped behind his neck.

Gericke peered over the boy's shoulder, smiling. 'Ah, there you are, Doctor.'

Her heart pounded and so great was the shock that she had difficulty in speaking at all.

'You,' she whispered.

'I'm afraid so.' He stepped back, motioning with the Mauser. 'Now you will please be so good as to come out here and tie this young gentleman's hands behind him.'

He threw her a coil of thin rope which he had found behind the cabin door. Janet folded her arms quite deliberately and it landed at her feet.

'You won't shoot me. You couldn't on the train – you won't now.'

He smiled calmly. 'You're quite right. But the boy here – now he is something different. A paratrooper as well, so it may be argued that I am helping the war effort. The left kneecap first, I think.'

She picked up the coil of rope hurriedly. Lachlan looked sicker than ever. 'Sorry, Doctor, but he was in the lavatory when I opened the door, sitting there bold as brass. Would he be the U-boat captain they were on about in Mallaig?'

'At your service,' Gericke said. 'Now lie down like a good boy and all will be well.'

Lachlan lay on one of the divans and Janet lashed his wrists, Gericke observing her closely.

'Satisfied?' she demanded.

'Not bad. Now the ankles.'

She did as she was told and when she was finished he said, 'And now we will go to see your friend upstairs, Mr Murdoch Macleod. Have I got the name right?'

She had recovered enough from her initial astonishment to be able to assess the situation more coolly and became aware, with a kind of clinical detachment, that she was not afraid of Gericke in the slightest. Which was interesting. On the other hand he was very obviously a man who would kill, if he had to, without a second's hesitation.

He smiled at her. 'Of what are you thinking?'

The feeling of intimacy was really quite disturbing, but she forced herself to stay calm. 'Murdoch's an old man. One of the finest men I know. I don't want him hurt.'

It was delivered almost as a command. Gericke inclined his head. 'Very well, Doctor, let's see if we can deal with this in a civilised manner, then.'

She led the way up the companionway and opened the wheelhouse door. Murdoch stood there, his head disembodied in the light of the binnacle.

Gericke leaned in the doorway and thumbed the hammer on the Mauser very deliberately. 'You will please do exactly as you are told, Mr Macleod.'

Murdoch looked him over calmly. 'And who might you be, laddie?'

'He's Gericke, the U-boat commander who escaped from the train,' Janet informed him.

'I see,' Murdoch said. 'It's the boat you're after, is that it? And where exactly do you intend to take her?'

'Norway, by way of the Orkneys.'

'A possibility. But only just. You'd need to know what you were doing. A lot different from those sardine cans you're used to.'

'I have a master's certificate in sail,' Gericke told him. 'Is that good enough?'

Murdoch nodded gravely. 'Like that gun of yours – difficult to argue with. And what about us?'

'I'll drop you off on the way. Somewhere nice and remote on the coast of one of the larger islands. Lewis, perhaps. And now, as I am perfectly capable of reading a chart, you will oblige me by putting her on automatic pilot and coming below.'

'You feel you are familiar enough with these waters?'

'I do.'

'Then who am I to argue.'

He locked the automatic steering device in position and moved out, Janet leading the way. They descended to the saloon where he lay on the opposite divan from Lachlan and allowed her to lash his wrists and feet.

When she was finished, she said, 'Now it's my turn I suppose.'

'Good heavens no. I shouldn't dream of such a thing,' Gericke said. 'You, my dear Doctor, are far too useful. First, you will make a flask of hot tea and some sandwiches, then we will continue in the wheelhouse.'

'Continue what?' she demanded suspiciously.

'Why, where we left off in the train if you like.' He smiled. 'The galley, by the way, is right behind you.'

It was very peaceful in the wheelhouse. Janet swung from side to side in the chart-table chair and watched Gericke at the wheel.

'You like that, don't you?' she said.

'A deck under the feet, a wheel kicking in the hands?' He smiled. 'The finest feeling in the world. Well, almost.'

'Aren't you ever serious?'

'Not possible. I realized rather early in life what a bloody unpleasant business it all was. No man of intelligence could possibly take it seriously. We had a hard time when I was a boy, you see. My father was killed on the Western Front.'

'Was he a soldier?'

'No, a fighter pilot. One of the first. He lasted three years. A long time, but not long enough.'

'And your mother?'

'Died in the influenza epidemic of 1918. I went to live with her brother, my uncle Lothar in Hamburg. Poor as a church mouse, but one of the kindest men I've ever known. He was a teacher of mathematics. Had a house at Blankanese on the Elbe from which you could see every ship that entered or left Hamburg. I used to sit in my room at night for hours with the window open, watching the lights on cargo boats slipping out to sea. Going somewhere romantic – always that. And I wanted to sail with them.'

'The beginning of a love-affair?'

He carried on, 'And if it was too foggy to see them there were always the foghorns growling out there somewhere at the edge of things.'

He took one of her cigarettes from the packet on the chart table. Janet said, 'When I was a girl I used to spend summers at my uncle's place on Cape Cod. Lots of fog there. Sometimes at night you could hear the fishing boats calling to each other far out to sea.'

Gericke nodded. 'A lonely sound for a lonely place.'

She swung round on the swivel seat to face him. 'You know it?'

'I sank eleven ships off that coast between mid-March and late April of forty-two.' There was a slight ironic smile on his mouth. 'The Happy Time all over again. For five consecutive minutes the thought actually crossed my mind that we might win the war.'

'American ships?'

'All except one. A Spanish tanker which got in the way of the action, so to speak.'

'I see,' she said. 'So even a neutral wasn't safe from your attentions?'

He smiled sardonically. 'Sea Wolves. Isn't that what they call us?'

'And you're proud of that?' She reached for the Thermos, mainly to give her hands something to do, and poured tea into the plastic cup. 'Now let me tell you something. Lieutenant Jago let me read the report on you back there on the train.'

'Strictly against regulations that, I should imagine.'

'That Spanish boat was an oil tanker, the *San Cristobal* out of Bilbao. There was a big fuss in the newspapers at the time because she was a neutral, then it turned out that she'd been chartered by the American War Department. You knew that when you sank her.'

'Naturally.' He peered down at the compass and altered course a point to starboard.

'Then why try to make me think something different?'

He smiled good-humouredly. 'But I thought that was what you wanted to believe. The brutal Hun about his evil work. Machine-gunning the lifeboats, after making sure there weren't any women available amongst the survivors, of course.'

'Damn you, Gericke!'

'Taken care of long since.'

She lit another cigarette and sat leaning her elbows on the chart table, frowning and staring into the dark glass. 'You love ships, yet you destroy them.'

'I'm perverse by nature. You should try me sometime.'

'No thanks – and still not good enough.'

'What would you prefer – some neat psychological explanation on the lines that each man kills the thing he loves? Come now, Doctor. Even the great Freud once said that sometimes a cigar is only a cigar.'

'They certainly didn't teach us *that* in medical school.'

'Just put it down to the bloody war, then.'

There was a savage tone in his voice that had not been present before. For a moment she stood on the edge of something, peered into a dark and private place and drew back.

He checked the course again and stared grimly in the dark, his face set, that slight, perpetual smile missing for the first time.

'Your English,' she said lamely, 'is really very good.'

'We lived in Hull for a while. That's a port on the east coast of England.'

'I know.'

'My uncle taught English there for two years.' He smiled. 'People tell me I have a Yorkshire accent. When we returned home, I tried a year at university. Philosophy and mathematics because Uncle Lothar wanted it. It didn't work out so he allowed me to enrol in the school for naval petty officers at Finkenwärder in Hamburg. After that I went to sea as an apprentice on a squarerigger.'

'A hard school.'

'As friend Carver discovered earlier today. I sailed in clippers for a while. The Chilean nitrate trade, grain from Australia by way of the Horn. Then I served as third officer on a cargo boat to complete my navigational training. I was all of twenty-two when I took my masters' tickets in both sail and steam.'

'And then?'

'Nobody wanted me. I tramped the streets of Hamburg. Visited every ship owner there was, but nothing doing. Times were hard, the Depression was at its height. We all used to meet at a bar in the Davidstrasse called the Star of David. The man who ran it had served as a bosun under sail and gave credit. I finally shipped as first mate on a clipper doing the big circle. Chile, the States, then across to Australia and home again. When I got back, everything was changed.'

'What was that?'

'It was nineteen thirty-three and the Kriegsmarine was offering equivalent rank to officers of the merchant service. I couldn't get to Stralsund fast enough to sign on.'

'To learn how to sink ships?'

'It's a living.'

There was silence between them for a while. The wind had shifted and the sea was rising, the *Katrina* rocking in the turbulence. Janet said carefully, 'And women? A family? No mention of them. Haven't they ever had a place in your scheme of things?'

'Not really. Women, yes, in the most basic way. But shore leave, as I have always found, seldom lasts long enough for more permanent arrangements to grow.'

'Strictly ships that pass in the night?'

'An apt analogy.' He shrugged. 'And then the important things in life have one hell of a way of happening at exactly the wrong time. At least as regards being able to do anything about it. Don't you find that?'

He turned to face her. She was aware of a cold excitement, a need to breathe deeply – then a sudden violent squall struck *Katrina*, swinging the boat to port. Janet fell from her seat.

Gericke wrestled with the wheel and brought her head round. 'Are you all right?'

She scrambled to her feet, white and shaken. 'Yes, but I'd better get below and check on the others.' She hesitated, peering out into the dark. 'You think it will get worse?'

'I should imagine so. I'll put on the automatic steering device and come down myself.'

'Is it safe to have only that thing in control in this kind of weather?'

'A whole lot safer than allowing you to go below on your own.'

She slipped through the door and was gone. He cursed, locking the steering and went after her, already too late, for when he entered the saloon, she had Lachlan's Lee-Enfield in her hands. She thumbed off the safety-catch, worked the bolt, ramming a cartridge into the breech, and backed off.

'Loaded, I presume?' he enquired.

'You can take my word for it,' Lachlan said, struggling to sit up.

Gericke produced his Mauser and cocked it. 'Stalemate, I think.'

'Don't make me shoot you, darling,' she said harshly. 'I will if I have to and I could hardly miss at this range.'

There was determination on her face, but a kind of panic also, as if she knew that whatever happened, he would not pull the trigger. Suddenly, there was a desperate appeal in her eyes.

Gericke smiled very gently and placed the Mauser on the table. 'Ah well,' he said. 'It was fun while it lasted,' and he clasped both hands behind his neck.

Richter, flat on his face because of the confined space, was examining the bilges with the aid of a storm lantern. The pumps had been working constantly for two hours but it was still a foot deep in there. Every so often, as the *Deutschland* plunged over a particularly large wave, filthy, rancid water washed over his head.

He finished his inspection and came up through the hatch in the aft hold, passing his lantern to Sturm. 'God, but you stink,' the young lieutenant observed.

'I know,' Richter said in disgust. 'It's like crawling along a very old sewer down there.'

'How does it look?'

'It could be worse.'

'Good.' Sturm was relieved. 'Better let the old man know straight away.'

When they went out on deck there was a terrific beam sea running and Berger, in oilskin coat and sou'wester, leaned on the quarterdeck rail.

'Just in time, Mr Sturm,' he called. 'Clew up the topsails and fore lower t'gallant and make them fast, quick as you like.'

'Aye, aye, sir.'

'And get the foresail off her.'

Berger went down to his cabin and the crew tumbled into action as Sturm relayed the orders, Richter springing into the ratlines and leading the way aloft, no place for the faint-hearted in such weather. But on deck, conditions were just as hazardous. The men at the clew lines were up to their necks in water, hanging on for dear life every time another sea washed over them.

Richter, on his way down to the deck again, saw Lotte emerge from the galley. She carried a bucket in each hand and was wearing an old oilskin coat and sou'wester. At the same moment, he noticed a huge sea coming aboard.

He cried a warning, jumped for the nearest line and slid down to the deck very fast. There was a tremendous crash as the sea poured aft. Richter caught a brief glimpse of Lotte washing along with it, dropped into the welter of foam and went after her.

The *Deutschland* pointed into the slate grey sky, riding high over the next wave. Richter hauled the girl to her feet and discovered that she was still clutching the two buckets, both quite empty now. And she was laughing.

'Little fool,' he cried. 'How often do I have to tell you?'

'I don't think I'll ever be dry again,' she answered.

He put a hand under her elbow and helped her along the deck to the galley. When he opened the door, there was a couple of feet of water inside, pots and pans swilling around, Sister Angela on her hands and knees.

From the look on her face, that inexhaustible patience had finally run out. Richter retreated, leaving Lotte to handle the situation.

Berger towelled his head dry, then sat down at his desk, selected a cheroot and lit it. The last box and only a dozen left. He inhaled the fragrance of Brazil with conscious pleasure, reached for his pen and started the daily entry in his private journal.

. . . we are, by my estimation, perhaps a hundred miles due west of Galway Bay in Ireland and make excellent time, mainly because I have maintained a policy of carrying as much canvas as possible in rough weather. An unfortunate consequence of this is the fact that we take water inboard in large quantities and this makes things difficult for both crew and passengers. The fanlight has smashed again, water cascades into the saloon without pause, making life wet and uncomfortable for the nuns who pray constantly during such weather, although whether their plea is for the Good Lord to take them up to heaven or save them from it, I have never been able to determine . . .

There was a knock at the door and Richter entered. Berger put down his pen. 'How was it down there, Helmut?'

'Smelly, but sound, Herr Kapitän. We worked the pumps for two hours before I went in and there was still twelve inches, but when you consider this weather and how much water we've been shipping that seems to me not too bad.'

'Good,' Berger said. 'Very good. I've a feeling we may hit rough weather all the way now and it's a comfort to know things are still no worse than they were below the waterline.'

He reached for his pen and had already started to write in his journal again as Richter went out.

It was just after eighty-thirty as the *Katrina* moved in towards Fhada. Gericke, seated in the swivel chair at the chart table, hands tied behind his back, looked out with interest at the grey-green hump crouching there in the rain, cliffs splashed with lime, seabirds wheeling in great clouds, cormorants, razorbills, gulls of every description.

'So this is Fhada?'

Murdoch, at the wheel, nodded. 'They say the name is derived from an old Gaelic word *Fuideidh* meaning an island that lies apart from other islands.'

'Interesting.' Gericke filled his lungs. 'I like islands. They have a special quality. In April, nineteen forty-one, I did a patrol in the Aegean and came down with some kind of fever. I convalesced on the island of Corfu. A marvellous place. It was April. The most beautiful wild flowers I've ever seen in my life and the butterflies . . .'

'Whatever else it is, Fhada isn't like that, darling.' Janet came in through the door carrying a mug of tea. 'I thought you might like to have yours below,' she said to Murdoch. 'Put her on automatic pilot and I'll keep my eye on things while I feed the pride of the Kriegsmarine.'

Murdoch hesitated, then locked the steering device in position. 'Ten minutes, that's all you get,' he said and went out.

'It would seem he assumed you wanted to be alone with me,' Gericke observed. 'How romantic.'

'Nothing could be further from the truth,' she said. 'I just wanted him to sit down for ten minutes and have a hot drink. He's an old man, or hadn't you noticed?'

'The doctor in you coming out. Does this happen often?'

'Not on Fhada, believe me. They're a healthy lot here.'

She unlocked the automatic pilot and took the wheel herself.

'You love the place, I think,' he said.

'It has a strange attraction for me. It's as if the outside world has ceased to exist, which it very frequently does. On Fhada, they boast winds four to seven for two-thirds of the time as early as April. From September on, anything goes. They tell a story of a constable sent from the mainland to escort a local man to serve a six weeks' sentence at Stirling prison.'

'What happened?'

'The weather was so bad that by the time it was fit for the boat to leave, the sentence was finished.'

'So – I may be in for a long stay?'

'They also boast the worst hazard to shipping on the entire west coast. The Washington Reef. That's why they stationed the first lifeboat here back in eighteen eighty-two. Murdoch's the present coxswain.'

'Isn't he a little old for such work?'

'He handed over to his son in thirty-eight. Came back into harness when Donald was called up by the Navy. Uncle Carey says he's a genius. One of the greatest coxswains in the history of the Lifeboat Institution.'

'I see. And how do people live here?'

'A little crofting. Sheep. A few cattle. Fishing. The population's very small now. A place of women, children and old men. All the others are away, mostly serving in merchant ships.'

As they drew nearer to the island they met the only four fishing boats still working from Fhada moving out to sea.

Janet waved. Gericke said, 'Old men.'

'And boys,' she said. 'All that will be left soon if this damned war lasts much longer.'

They moved into harbour and Gericke noticed a small dark man with a black eye patch in old seaboots and reefer coat standing at the edge of the upper jetty.

Janet placed her hands lightly on his shoulders. 'And that,' she said, 'believe it or not, is my uncle, Rear Admiral Carey Reeve, United States Navy, not quite retired.'

Barquentine *Deutschland*, 23 September 1944. Further entry. Sister Angela and Herr Prager visited me formally to raise the question of low morale amongst the crew and passengers because of the lack of hot food and drink owing to the impossibility of keeping a fire going in the galley under the present weather conditions. Sister Angela made the point, which I had to accept, that my own cabin was the driest in the ship owing to its position and prevailed upon me to allow her to use it for cooking purposes with the aid of a portable oil stove. A run of 225 miles this day.

Eleven

It was very quiet in the small study where Gericke sat, hands still tied behind his back. Murdoch leaned in the window seat, filling his pipe.

'This house,' Gericke said. 'Quite impressive. Who does it belong to?'

'Mrs Sinclair. She owns the island. What we call the laird in these parts. Also bailie – that's magistrate. And coroner and harbourmaster.'

'A remarkable woman.'

'You'll see soon enough. She is responsible for you in a sense. The only law we have here. Her husband was in the same trade as yourself. He went down with the *Prince of Wales* in the Pacific. That would be in nineteen forty-one.'

'I see,' Gericke said. 'I shouldn't imagine I'll be too popular in that quarter.'

'We are not savages, Commander. Put that from your head. During the past fortnight we have buried eight of your comrades, washed up from a U-boat that was sunk in this area on the ninth of the month. I took the services myself and almost every soul on this island attended.'

There was a moment's silence. Gericke, for once at something of a loss, said, 'I thank you. On their behalf, I thank you, sir.'

The door opened and Reeve came in. He was still wearing his reefer coat and there was rain on his face. 'I've been in touch with Captain Murray at Mallaig. He insists that under no circumstances should any attempt be made to take you back to the mainland in anything other than an official vessel. Lieutenant Jago is apparently en route for Stornoway now. He'll receive instructions by radio to call in here for you, sometime tomorrow.'

'Another day's grace before the door closes finally.'

Reeve said, 'And now Mrs Sinclair would like to see you.'

He nodded to Murdoch who moved out and Gericke followed, the admiral bringing up the rear. They went along a corridor, passed through a large stone-flagged hall and paused at a green baize door. Reeve opened it and motioned Gericke through.

It was a pleasant room, two of the walls lined with books from floor to ceiling, french windows giving a view of the garden outside. Janet and Jean stood in front of the log fire.

They turned at once. Gericke came to a halt and inclined his head formally. 'Ladies.'

'Korvettenkapitän Paul Gericke,' Reeve said. 'Mrs Sinclair.'

A handsome woman, she was wearing a Shetland sweater, brogues and a kilt, which he presumed to be in her clan's tartan, and her hair was tied back with a blue velvet bow.

She looked him over calmly and her voice was formal. 'I don't know if Admiral Reeve has explained, Commander, but I am bailie here and responsible for you at law.'

'That has been made clear to me.'

'There is no policeman stationed on the island, but the police station is still here from the old days and I do have to make use of its cells on occasion.'

'I understand.'

'You will be locked up there until Lieutenant Jago arrives to take you into custody tomorrow. And you will be guarded, naturally.'

There was really nothing to say. Janet had moved to the window and was looking outside. Reeve touched Gericke's arm. 'Let's go. Murdoch and I will take you down.'

Gericke hesitated, glancing towards Janet. She did not turn round. He inclined his head again, turned without saying anything and went out followed by Reeve and Murdoch.

The door closed. 'Damn you, Paul Gericke,' Janet whispered, still staring out into the rain. 'I wish I'd never set eyes on you.'

★ ★ ★

The three men went down the cobbled main street, Gericke in the centre. The heavy rain kept most people indoors, but here and there a woman stood on a step watching curiously and two small boys trailed behind until Murdoch chased them away.

The old police station was at the bottom of the street and faced out over the harbour, solidly built of granite like every other dwelling in Mary's Town, with only the bars at the windows to distinguish it.

Reeve tried to open the oaken door that was bound with iron, but it refused to budge. Murdoch hammered with the toe of his boot. 'Lachlan, are you asleep in there?'

There was the sound of heavy bolts being withdrawn and Lachlan MacBrayne peered out. He wasn't wearing his jump jacket, but was otherwise in uniform, the battledress blouse open at the neck.

'Time to lock up when we've got him inside,' Murdoch said.

There was an old desk in one corner, a chair and not much else, and a peat fire smouldered in a tiny grate.

Lachlan picked up his rifle, slung it from his shoulder, then took a large bunch of keys down from a nail on the wall. 'Will we be putting him straight in, Admiral?'

'The sooner the better,' Reeve said.

They went down a flight of steps to a narrow corridor. There were three cells on either side, each closed by a gate of iron bars. Reeve untied Gericke's wrists and pushed him inside. There was an iron bed, three or four army blankets and a bucket. Lachlan closed the gate and locked it.

'That's it then.' Reeve slipped a packet of cigarettes, a box of matches and a newspaper through the bars. 'Something to read. Three days old, but you'll see you're still losing the war.'

Murdoch took a small bottle from his pocket. 'It will be cold in there after a while, I'm thinking.'

'A surfeit of riches indeed.' Gericke clicked his heels. 'Gentlemen – my thanks.'

Reeve smiled in spite of himself and they went back to the office and left Gericke alone. He crossed to the barred window, peered out across the harbour, then sat on the edge of the bed, unscrewed the neck of the bottle Murdoch had given him and sampled the contents. It burned all the way down, exploding in the pit of his stomach.

He gasped for breath. 'God Almighty!' he said and stiffened as he heard steps in the corridor.

Lachlan was on the other side of the gate, the rifle still hanging from his left shoulder. He unslung it awkwardly and stood staring at Gericke, gripping the rifle lightly in his two hands. Gericke got up slowly, muscles tightening. As casually as possible, he took out the cigarettes Reeve had given him and put one in his mouth.

'Do you smoke?' He moved to the bars, holding out the packet.

The boy shook his head and when he spoke his voice was hoarse. 'You had a round up the spout of that Mauser. I unloaded it myself. I saw it.'

'That's right.'

'You could have shot her. Why didn't you?'

'Could I?' Gericke said gently. 'You think that?'

The boy sighed, relaxing suddenly, and rested the butt of the rifle on the floor. 'No, I don't suppose you could.' He moved away, then paused. 'I'll be making a cup of tea in a little while. Do you want one?'

'I don't think I'd like anything better.'

Lachlan said very slowly, 'I thought I could shoot you. I had it all worked out, because of my father, but when it came to it, I couldn't do it.'

'I know,' Gericke said.

The footsteps died away along the corridor. He sat down on the edge of the bed again very carefully and when he struck a match to light his cigarette, his hand was shaking.

The *Dead End* was five miles south-west of Idriggil Point on the Isle of Skye and making heavy weather of it. Petersen had the helm and Jago sat at the chart table checking their course. When the door swung open behind him he turned, expecting coffee and found instead Jansen, a signal flimsy in one hand and a peculiar glint in his eye.

'I think the lieutenant might find this one particularly interesting.'

'A signal?' Jago said. 'From Mallaig. Christ, we only left the damned place an hour ago. Read it to me.'

'As the lieutenant pleases.' Jansen was enjoying himself. 'Korvetten-kapitän Gericke apprehended as stowaway on *Katrina*. Now on Fhada. Request you call there on your way back from Stornoway tomorrow and take into custody.'

Jago looked at him incredulously, then snatched the flimsy and read it for himself. 'It's not possible.'

'I'm afraid it has to be, sir. The good word came direct from Captain Murray himself.'

'All right – if you can find a brief moment in that crowded schedule of yours, signal Mallaig message received and understood. Will leave Stornoway at dawn tomorrow, weather permitting, and should arrive Fhada around noon. Now kindly get to hell out of here.'

Jansen withdrew, grinning hugely, and Jago picked up a pencil from the chart table and snapped it between his fingers.

* * *

Janet put another log on the fire, pushing it into place with a long brass poker, then sat back and waited. Her uncle stood at the window reading the letter she had brought him.

'He says here that he's spoken to you personally.'

'That's right,' she said. 'In the back of his staff car at Guy's.' There was no immediate response and she was seized with a sudden impatience. 'He's offered you a job, Uncle Carey. The Supreme Commander himself. A chance to get back in the thick of things. Isn't that what you wanted?'

'Deputy Director, Supply and Personnel Co-ordination,' he said bitterly, and crumpled the letter in his hand.

'For God's sake, what do you want – blood?'

The door opened and Jean came in with tea things on a silver tray. 'Family argument?' she asked cheerfully. 'Or can anyone join in?'

'Show her,' Janet ordered. 'Go on – show her. She's as much right to know as anyone.'

Jean put the tray down on a small brass table by the fire. She crossed to Reeve, prised the letter from his grasp, smoothed it out and read it.

'But that's wonderful, Carey.' She kissed him on the cheek. 'I'm so pleased for you.'

'Good God, woman, you're as bad as she is. A desk job, don't you understand? A glorified clerk, signing papers all day.'

Jean pulled him towards the fire and Janet shook her head. 'You and Harry Jago. You just can't wait to get back into the glorious fight. Death before dishonour.'

Jean said, 'You two should be celebrating, not fighting. I've got a marvellous dinner laid on for tonight. Game pie, jugged hare and there are still four bottles of that special champagne Colin laid down in the cellar.'

'I'm sorry, Jean,' Janet told her, 'and thank you. That sounds wonderful. I'd love to come.'

Reeve stood in front of the fire, filling his pipe. 'You know Gericke interests me. It's not often one gets a chance to meet a legend face-to-face.'

'Is he really that special?' Jean asked.

'In naval circles certainly. Probably the most successful submarine commander on either side in the war. That information's not exactly on release for public consumption, mind you. But he's a remarkable man, no doubt about it.'

'Whose side are you on, for God's sake?' Janet demanded.

'Oh, don't misunderstand me. Respect of one professional for another, that's all. Mind you that attack on Falmouth was quite something. I'd love to know just how he pulled it off.'

'Then ask him to dinner, why don't you? Make up the four – isn't that the civilized thing to do? You can talk war to your heart's content.'

The sarcasm was heavy in her voice together with a certain anger.

Reeve frowned, a slight fixed smile on his mouth. 'That's not a bad idea.'

'You've got to be joking.'

'But why not?' He turned to Jean. 'Would you mind?'

She hesitated. 'I'm not sure, Carey. If you'd asked me that yesterday I'd have thought you were mad, but now . . .' She frowned. 'The enemy – everything I should hate – and yet I liked him. He's a human being.'

'Does he come or doesn't he?' Reeve demanded impatiently. 'Your decision. You are the civil power here, after all.'

'Are you suggesting he gives his parole for the evening?'

'Nothing so old-fashioned. Young Lachlan in attendance with that rifle of his, of course.'

'Why?' Janet asked. 'Why are you doing this?'

'Why not? At least I'll hear how the war's going at first hand for a change.' There was a glint in his eye, a hint of that wild and unpredictable Carey Reeve she knew and mistrusted. 'And anyway – I would have thought it might make for a rather entertaining evening.'

Gericke, lying on the bed, was surprised to hear that distinctive laugh from the office. He got to his feet as her step sounded in the corridor.

She stood on the other side of the gate. 'I've seen them do this scene so often in the movies that I have the dialogue off by heart. Are they treating you all right?'

'No complaints. To what do I owe the pleasure of this visit?'

'An invitation to dinner from Jean Sinclair.'

Lachlan appeared behind her looking slightly bewildered.

'A joke perhaps?' Gericke suggested.

'Half-seven for eight. As you don't have a black tie, uniform will do. Lachlan will bring you up to the house – and please don't try to do anything silly like starting to run in the wrong direction. He'll shoot you if he has to.'

He bowed slightly. 'How could I refuse such a charming invitation.'

'I know,' she said. 'The honour of the Kriegsmarine is at stake.'

She walked away briskly and the boy stared at Gericke, mouth open. Gericke smiled. 'Don't fight it, Lachlan, just go with the tide like me.'

He lay down on the bed and pillowed his head on his hands.

Berger's cabin was a scene of confusion. The oil stove stood on the cabinet in a corner and his desk had been cleared to take a selection of pans. Sisters Käthe, Else and Brigitte were serving food to some of the crew and not without considerable difficulty. Outside, the wind howled in full gale and the floor tilted beneath their feet as the *Deutschland* rolled through heavy seas.

The captain stood in a corner out of the way, a glass of rum in one hand, the bottle in the other. He was just in from the quarterdeck, chilled to the bone, his oilskin streaming.

Sister Käthe looked across at him. 'Something to eat, Herr Kapitän?'

Berger shook his head. 'No time, Sister. I've things to do. Any problems?'

'The men come in when they can. Three or four at a time. At least we're managing to keep a stove going in here.'

'Meaning hot food?' Berger said. 'All the difference in weather like this. I'm very grateful to you ladies. We all are, believe me.' He drained his glass. 'I'd better get back to it.'

He opened the door and went out, struggling to close it again in the high wind. The *Deutschland* fought her way through heavy seas under full sail, water pouring over the bulwarks as she rolled. There were two men on the wheel and her hatches were buried under a maelstrom which on occasions was waist-deep as he made his way to the companionway. He entered with a flood of water, got the doors closed again and went down.

Water, a foot deep, swirled about the floor of the saloon. The fanlight had been boarded over and two storm lanterns swung from hooks in the ceiling.

Four of the crew waited their turn for attention at Sister Angela's afternoon clinic. A young electrician's mate named Sporer lay on the table, his left sleeve rolled up exposing a ring of very bad sea boils on his wrist.

Sister Angela stood on one side of him, the hem of her skirt tucked into her belt. Lotte faced her holding a tray containing instruments and a small basin. Richter stood at the head of the table.

'What's all this?' Berger demanded.

'The infection is now so bad that his arm is almost paralysed.' Sister Angela reached for a scalpel. 'Hang on, Karl, like a brave boy. I'll be as quick as I can.'

Sporer, only eighteen, was frightened to death, his face damp with sweat. She nodded to Richter who placed his hands on the boy's shoulders. The *Deutschland* staggered in a sudden squall, a minor wave flowing from one side of the cabin to the other.

One of the crew lost his balance and ended on his hands and knees in the water, but Sister Angela, bracing herself against the table, leaned down and went to work.

The scalpel lanced into the boils one after another, there was an immediate stench of corruption as pus spurted. The boy cried out, bucking, in spite of Richter's weight on him – and then he fainted.

She worked on at an incredible speed, no need to be gentle now, Lotte handing her one instrument after another without a word. As she started to bandage the suppurating sores, Berger said, 'Are many of the crew suffering with those things now?'

'About half,' she said.

Berger turned and found Richter watching him. 'A long voyage, Herr Kapitän.'

Berger nodded wearily. 'So it would appear.'

It was just before seven-thirty and dusk when Gericke and Lachlan turned in through the wide gate of Fhada House and moved along the gravel drive. They went up the steps and the German tugged at the chain of the old-fashioned bell-pull.

Steps approached and the door was opened by a pleasant-looking woman of sixty or so, grey hair pinned back in a bun. She was wearing a black bombazine dress and a starched white apron.

She smiled, showing no surprise at all. 'Won't you come in, sir?'

'Thank you.' Gericke stepped into the hall, Lachlan behind, the Lee-Enfield ready in both hands.

'Let me take your coat, sir.' She vanished into a small cloakroom and was back in a moment. 'The others are in the drawingroom. If you'll come this way.' She paused, a hand on the door. 'Who is it again, sir?'

Gericke, convinced more than ever that he was engaged in some privileged nightmare, said, 'Korvettenkapitän Paul Gericke. I'm expected,' he added gravely.

'Oh yes, sir.' She opened the door and led the way in. 'Korvettenkapitän Gericke, madam.'

'Thank you, Mary.'

Jean Sinclair, Reeve and Janet were by the fire drinking sherry, Rory sprawled across the carpet. She held out her hand. 'I'm so glad you could come, Commander.' She turned to Reeve, 'Do get Commander Gericke a drink, Carey.'

Lachlan took up a position beside the door. She said, 'Good evening, Lachlan. How is your mother?'

'She is well, Mrs Sinclair.'

'You will tell her I was asking after her.'

Gericke found himself a moment later in front of the fire, slightly bewildered, a glass of excellent sherry in one hand, a cigarette in the other.

'I hope they've made you as comfortable as possible down there,' Jean said.

But it was a remark not to be taken seriously for there was a glint in her eye, laughter hardly contained.

'I should describe the facilities at your police station as adequate rather than comfortable,' he replied smoothly.

Reeve burst out laughing. 'I like that.' He took Gericke by the arm. 'Let's leave these two to cackle on and come over here and tell me about Falmouth.'

He and Gericke moved over to the window and stood heads together. Jean said, 'He's a handsome man, isn't he?'

'Which one?' Janet said.

The older woman smiled. 'Point taken, but you know what I mean.'

Janet nodded. 'He's like no other man I've ever known. There is a quality to him I can't define. I've always been too busy for men, Jean. For any deep relationships, I mean. Medical school, then the war. Work and sleep mostly, with the occasional affair when I felt the need.'

'And Gericke?'

'I'm just a little bit afraid of him.'

'I know what you mean.'

'It's there in the eyes mostly,' Janet said.

'Or not there, haven't you noticed that? Nothing shows for he gives nothing away. He seems a man remote from life, that constant wry smile of his a sign perhaps that he thinks it all a rather black little joke. A brilliant officer, a seaman of genius; his record, those decorations prove that. And like all such men, totally unpredictable. No rule that was ever made was made for him.'

A gong sounded outside and Mary appeared in the doorway. 'Dinner is served, madam.'

Jean stood up. 'Shall we go in, gentlemen?'

She moved out with Reeve, Janet and Gericke following, Lachlan bringing up the rear.

The meal, served in a dining-room of baronial proportions, was everything Jean had promised. There was a minstrels' gallery at one end, the most enormous fireplace Gericke had ever seen, three great logs burning brightly on the open hearth. Above it hung two tattered battle flags.

There were mounted animal heads on the stone walls. Everything from leopard to Thompson's Gazelle, taking in most things in between.

A magnificent suit of medieval armour, halberds, targes, and crossed claymores, muskets of every description.

'Extraordinary,' he said. 'You have a very remarkable place here, Mrs Sinclair.'

'We know,' Janet said. 'Stage six at MGM. All we need is Errol Flynn in a kilt, swinging down from that gallery, claymore in hand.'

Jean Sinclair laughed. 'Actually she's not too far from the truth, Commander. This place is really the most awful fraud. Victorian Gothic. An ancestor of mine, one Fergus Sinclair, was responsible.'

'The trophies, are they from his time also?' Gericke asked.

'No, those were my grandfather's. Hunted all over the world. He was one of those men who would rather shoot anything than nothing. He used to insist on taking me deer-stalking in season when I was quite young. Something of an experience.'

'I just bet it was,' Janet commented.

'Oh yes, I learned many things. That you must never hurry. That you must never stalk and stay downwind, even at a thousand yards and always to shoot low if the target is downhill.'

'Interesting,' Gericke said. 'I must remember.'

'To weave from side-to-side when making a run for it?' Reeve said.

He was already opening a third bottle of champagne, fumbling with the cork, supporting his bad arm on the edge of the table. There was a touch of aggression in his voice that had not been there earlier. Janet stopped smiling.

Jean went round the table and reached for the bottle. 'Let me, Carey. They can be difficult, those corks.'

'I can manage.' He tried to jerk the bottle away from her, one-handed, lost his grip and it smashed on the floor. 'Would you look at that,' he said bitterly.

'It's all right, Carey.' She picked up a napkin and wiped down his uniform where it had been splashed.

'That was a good year,' Reeve said slowly. He passed a hand over his eyes for a moment, then turned to Janet and Gericke. 'I must apologize. I haven't been quite myself lately.'

Jean patted him on the shoulder. 'Coffee in the drawing-room, I think.'

She nodded to Janet who glanced at Gericke, then pushed back her chair. They returned to the drawing-room and Lachlan followed without a word.

'He's not well?' Gericke asked.

She took a cigarette from a box and he gave her a light. 'You noticed his arm, and there's the eye. He got that little lot on D-day going into action when he shouldn't. The story of his life. He's been trying to get back into the fight ever since.'

'I know the type well. His last words in this life will probably be: Follow me, men.'

She shook her head. 'The only job he's been offered, and that took all the influence in the world, is behind a desk. That's what I've come up to see him about.'

'And he didn't like it?'

'He has nothing,' she said. 'In *his* eyes, he has nothing.'

'A beautiful woman is nothing?'

'To some men.'

'But not all, I think.'

She put a hand to her throat, at a loss for words, then turned quickly, sat down at the grand piano and lifted the lid.

'But then, how seriously can one take that kind of thing? The war can do strange things to people, make them act in a way they otherwise would not.'

'Or with complete honesty for once. A Bechstein, I see? Only the best. I didn't know you could play.'

'One of the more useful by-products of an expensive education, but if it's Beethoven you're after, I'm afraid I'm not your man.'

She started to play 'A Nightingale Sang in Berkeley Square' and Gericke leaned on the piano, watching her. 'You're good.'

The wolfhound came over from his place in front of the fire and flopped down beside her. 'I'm afraid so. Isn't it a bore? Even Rory agrees.'

He burst out laughing and Reeve and Jean Sinclair came in. The admiral looked considerably more cheerful and crossed to the piano. 'That really takes me back. What about "Moonlight in Vermont"?'

She moved smoothly into the new melody and Reeve went and sat by the fire with Jean, who was pouring coffee. They had their heads together and were talking softly.

'Doesn't that make you feel the world's a better place?' Janet asked.

'Envious,' Gericke whispered. 'It makes me feel envious.'

She started to play 'Lilli Marlene'. 'Is that any better?'

'Not really. Reminds me too much of the way the war is going, the British having taken that over too. Do you know "A Foggy Day in London Town"? It was extremely popular with the Luftwaffe for a while.'

She hesitated, remembering that night on the Embankment with Harry Jago. 'No, I'm afraid I never did get round to that one.'

Reeve had taken Jean Sinclair's hand. They were totally engrossed in each other. Janet closed the lid and stood up. 'I think I'd like a little air. Could I have my wrap, please?'

It was hanging over the back of a chair. Gericke got it at once and draped it around her shoulders. 'We're going on the terrace for a while to look at the evening,' she called and smiled up at Gericke. 'An old Scottish custom. Coming, Lachlan?'

Reeve glanced across. 'Oh, sure – fine.' He turned back to Jean and took her other hand.

'You see?' Gericke said. 'How a good woman can work wonders?'

'In this case, a miracle,' Janet said. 'Believe me.'

She opened the french window and moved out on the terrace. The sky was very dark, streaked with orange flame on the horizon so that to the north, the islands stood up starkly and the sea was perfectly calm.

They stood on the edge of the terrace, shoulders touching, and Lachlan paused beside the french windows. 'It's as if everything is waiting for something,' she said.

Gericke nodded. 'Once in the West Indies we surfaced off Martinique at night to charge the batteries. It was just like this. Incredibly quiet.'

'That's what I like about it here,' she said. 'The stillness. At least in the brief interludes when the wind isn't blowing.'

'The following day it blew the worst hurricane they'd known in those islands in living memory. We had to go down and stay down. Nature took care of the convoy we were after. Eleven ships out of twenty-six were sunk.'

'Did you claim a medal for that, too?'

'Now why didn't I think of that?' he said lightly.

In the pale evening light her face was barely visible. 'I'm sorry.'

Reeve appeared behind Lachlan. 'Heh, you two, the coffee's getting cold.'

'We're coming,' Janet replied.

Her wrap slipped from her shoulders, falling to the ground. Gericke picked it up and handed it to her. The last flicker of orange on the horizon seemed to flare suddenly – was extinguished as total darkness fell.

At Trondheim, Necker walked across to the Operations building. He was in a thoroughly bad temper. His eyes were sore as if from lack of sleep, though he'd been sitting around for three days now with absolutely nothing to do.

When he went into the intelligence room Colonel Maier was sitting behind Altrogge's desk. The major leaned over beside him and they were examining a chart of the Western Approaches together.

Maier glanced up. 'There you are, Horst. A little action for you at last.'

'It would be nice to think so,' Necker said with a certain amount of sarcasm in his voice, 'but as the Herr Oberst is well aware, I've been called out on three separate occasions during the past thirty-six hours, only to have the operation cancelled at the last moment.'

'Not this time,' Maier said. 'It's too important. To put it briefly, you take off at 0200. Your flight plan will take you over Scotland, then south of the Outer Hebrides and west of Ireland to this map reference.' He indicated the spot with a pencil. 'According to the Abwehr, there should be a large convoy homeward bound from Halifax, Nova Scotia, in that area about now. It's essential they have the information regarding its position in Kiel before noon tomorrow.'

'Or we'll lose the war, I suppose.'

'Very funny,' Maier said coldly and got to his feet. 'You're a good pilot, Horst, but there are times when you behave with the intelligence of a fourteen-year-old. One of these days, you will make that kind of remark just once too often.'

'I'm sorry, Herr Oberst.'

'No you're not.' Maier smiled and clapped him on the shoulder. 'Altrogge will fill you in on the wearisome details and I'll expect a personal report the moment you get back.'

He went out and Necker examined the chart. 'I'd say it's a nine hundred mile flight to that map reference.'

'And nine hundred back, which leaves you with six to play with when you get there. Say two hours' flying time in the target area, just to give you a margin for error.'

'I don't make them,' Necker said. 'That's why I'm still here. What about those Spitfire squadrons?'

'Up here near Inverness, but they'll give you no trouble if you stay at thirty-five to thirty-eight thousand, which you can do in comfort with the improvements we've been installing. The outward journey will be in darkness anyway. A milk run.'

'If you say so,' Necker said acidly and sat down. 'All right, let's get into it in detail.'

Reeve opened the police station door and he and Gericke walked in, followed by Lachlan. The boy got his keys and led the way down the steps to the passageway. Gericke moved into his cell and Lachlan double-locked it.

'Herr Konteradmiral.' Gericke saluted. 'My thanks for your part in a delightful evening.'

Reeve hesitated. For a moment it seemed that he might speak. Instead, he returned the salute punctiliously and moved away along the passageway to the office, Lachlan following.

The door closed. Gericke stood there for a moment, listening, hands on the bars, then moved to the window. The stonework of the sill was cracked, the cement where the bars fitted into it, old and crumbling. He lifted his mattress, removed one of the coil springs from the iron bed and went to work on that cement with the hooked end.

There were steps in the corridor. He sat down quickly and Lachlan appeared on the other side of the gate, rifle over his shoulder, a sleeping-bag under one arm.

'What's all this?' Gericke demanded.

The boy placed a Thermos flask on the floor, unrolled the sleeping-bag, stepped into it and zipped it up around his body. Then he sat down, back against the opposite wall, rifle across his knees.

'Just keeping an eye out for you, Commander. Admiral Reeve thought you might sleep better knowing I was close by.'

Gericke smiled. 'You know something, Lachlan? I think he may very well have a point there.'

He lay down on the bed, pulled the blankets up to his chin and was asleep almost instantly.

Barquentine *Deutschland*, 24 September 1944. Lat 56°N., long 9°.51W. 110 miles south-west of the Outer Hebrides. Starts calm and strangely still as I cannot remember it in these waters within my experience. Just after midnight a ship crossed our bow for we heard her engines and saw a light plainly, presumably carelessness on the part of her crew. In the mid-watch it began to rain again and the wind freshened considerably. At four bells in the morning watch, it being Sunday, Sister Angela held her usual early-morning service on deck in spite of the inclement weather.

Twelve

The *Deutschland*, with every stitch of canvas set, was making twelve knots. The sea was beginning to lift into white caps under a sky of uniform slate grey.

Rain was driving in from the south-west, yet Sister Angela stood at the rail in front of him and addressed the other nuns on the deck below with the dozen or so crew members who had felt religious enough to turn out.

Although a few of the men were Roman Catholic, the rest, when they were anything at all, were Lutherans and she had opted for a service of such a nature that it would offend no one.

She was just coming to the end of general confession, her voice clear on the damp air.

. . . and grant, O most merciful Father, for His sake, that we may hereafter live a godly, righteous, and sober life, to the glory of thy holy name.

There was a moment of silence as she prayed, eyes closed, hands clasped. She crossed herself and said, 'We will now sing a hymn, specially for those at sea and well known to you all. "Eternal Father, strong to save, whose arm doth bind the restless wave".'

Lotte and the other nuns took up the words bravely and Richter, standing behind her, joined in, taking the other crew members along with him in a ragged chorus. Sister Angela turned once to glance at Berger and Sturm and the captain found himself joining in helplessly.

'Oh hear us when we cry to Thee for those in peril on the sea.'

And then, as the chorus started to peter out, there was a roaring in the heavens and Berger swung round in alarm to see a black plane coming in over the sea from the south-east at no more than a hundred and fifty feet.

God in heaven, this is it! At last this is it! he thought and in the same moment grabbed Sister Angela and pulled her down. There was total confusion on the deck below as the crew scattered and Sister Käthe screamed piercingly.

Sturm, crouching on one knee beside Berger, cried excitedly, 'Herr Kapitän – look! It's one of ours!'

Berger caught a glimpse of the Junkers as it passed over, saw the crosses on the wings clearly, the swastika tailplane, and then it banked to port and started to climb.

On the deck below men were running to the rail, two or three actually climbing the rigging, everyone cheering, and Richter and Lotte stood together, the bosun's arm around the girl's waist as they stared up into the sky.

'Now what, Herr Kapitän?' Sturm demanded.

Berger, recovering his scattered wits, got to his feet. He leaned over the rail and bawled, 'Richter, run that Swedish flag down. You'll find a Kriegsmarine ensign in the main locker in my cabin.' He turned to Sturm. 'Get on the radio, quick. Let's see if we can make contact.'

*   *   *

'Swedish?' Necker demanded. 'Are you certain?'

'Definitely, Herr Hauptmann,' Rudi assured him. 'I saw the flag plainly.'

Kranz, the rear gunner, cut in on them. 'I can confirm that, Herr Hauptmann.'

'A sailing ship,' Necker said. 'If I hadn't seen it for myself I'd never have believed it. Let's take another look.'

He throttled right back, making his pass at no more than a hundred and fifty this time, aware himself as they approached, that the Swedish flag was fluttering down.

'What on earth are they striking their colours for, Herr Hauptmann?' Rudi Hubner asked in bewilderment.

'Search me,' Necker said and then grunted in astonishment as another flag was run up.

As they flashed past, the flag stretched in the wind and Kranz called excitedly, 'A Kriegsmarine ensign, Herr Hauptmann! I swear it!'

'Don't worry,' Necker called. 'I saw it too. But it doesn't make any sense. I'm going round again.'

Schmidt, the wireless operator, touched his shoulder. 'I'm getting something now, Herr Hauptmann. It must be them. I'll switch over.'

A moment later, to his total astonishment, and with a clarity only to be expected at such short range, he heard Johann Sturm's voice clearly in his headphones saying. 'This is the *Deutschland* calling Big Black Eagle. Are you receiving me?'

'Big Black Eagle?' Schmidt said in bewilderment. 'What's he talking about?'

'He doesn't want to identify us, you fool, in case anyone else is picking the message up,' Necker said. 'Here, let me speak to him.'

Jean Sinclair was having a last cup of tea before leaving for church when Reeve and Janet arrived.

'This is a pleasant surprise,' she said. 'I don't usually have much success when I try to persuade him to turn out on a Sunday morning.'

'Business, I'm afraid,' Janet said. 'But I persuaded him to put his uniform on anyway, so grab him if you can.'

Jean looked puzzled. Reeve said, 'I've had word from Mallaig that Lieutenant Jago's got engine trouble. His deadline for fixing it is the middle of the afternoon, otherwise they'll send someone else to pick up Gericke. Whoever it is, they obviously can't make it before late evening. Possibly even tomorrow morning.'

'I see.' She glanced at her watch. 'The service, I might remind you, starts in fifteen minutes and unless you want one of Murdoch's public rebukes as we creep in at the back of the congregation, we'd better hurry.'

'All right,' he said heavily. 'I'll come, only I'll have to catch you up. I want a word with Mary about butter and eggs. I'm fresh out.'

The door closed behind him and Jean turned to Janet. 'What about you?'

'I don't think so – not this morning.'

'What are you going to do?'

'I'll think of something.'

Jean smiled. 'I'm sure you will.'

Gericke had breakfasted well on porridge and fried bacon and tomatoes supplied, surprisingly enough, by Lachlan's mother. After she had gone, Lachlan resumed his place against the wall.

Gericke said, 'Sleep, Lachlan. When do you expect to get some sleep?'

'Och, I need terrible little of that. An awful problem I was to my mother as a wee boy.' Lachlan glanced at his watch. 'No sweat, Commander. Murdoch takes over from me at eleven o'clock after morning service.'

'Ah yes,' Gericke said. 'He is some kind of pastor is he not?'

'That's right – and coxswain of the *Morag Sinclair*.'

'The *Morag Sinclair*?'

'The great love of Murdoch's life. She's a forty-one foot Watson-type motor lifeboat. The station's at South Inlet at the other end of the island and Murdoch lives there.'

Gericke said, 'I don't understand. Why not here?'

'Because in really rough weather the sea builds up so bad across the harbour bar it's impossible to get out. Much easier from South Inlet.'

'And this is always so?'

'No – once or twice a year it's impossible to launch from the inlet.'

'And what happens then if there is a call?'

'There's another lifeboat stationed at Barra.'

'And you, Lachlan, were you a member of the lifeboat crew before joining the army?'

'Not with my belly,' Lachlan said. 'But my father was.'

He stopped smiling and Gericke, at a loss for words, stood there gripping the bars. The outer door banged and Janet called, 'Anyone home?'

She was wearing a sheepskin coat, tweed skirt, knee-length boots and Tam o' Shanter. 'Has he been behaving himself, Lachlan?'

'No choice,' Gericke said. 'Young Lochinvar having sat against the wall looking in on me all night with that rifle across his knees.'

She passed a packet of cigarettes and a couple of magazines between the bars. 'To help you pass the time.'

'Not long now,' he said. 'Lieutenant Jago will be here at noon to take me away. Is it not so?'

'Engine trouble at Stornoway. Tonight at the earliest – maybe even tomorrow.'

He stood there looking at her through the bars as if waiting for something. Suddenly, she felt awkward, half-angry with herself for being there at all.

'I'll have to go now. I've got things to do.'

'My thanks,' Gericke said gravely and held up the magazines. 'For these – amongst other things.'

She turned and walked out quickly.

In the intelligence room at Trondheim, Necker paced up and down moodily, smoking a cigarette. He still wore flying clothes, his face streaked with dirt and sweat, the marks of his goggles plain.

Altrogge, at his desk, glanced up from the report he was writing. 'That won't help, Horst. Why don't you sit down. Have some coffee.'

He reached for the pot on the tray at his right hand and Necker shook his head. 'No, thanks.' And then he exploded. 'Why all the delay? I mean, what in the hell goes on?'

'The Gruppenkommandeur is handling it personally, you know that, but with a thing like this, there are bound to be delays in channels. You'll have to be patient.' He leaned back and added carefully, 'I suspect, my friend, that you may also have to prepare yourself for a rather large rocket.'

Necker stopped his pacing. 'What are you talking about?'

'You didn't do as you were told, Horst. You didn't follow orders.'

Necker gaped at him in astonishment. 'Didn't follow orders? For God's sake, Hans, what did you expect me to do?'

The door opened and Maier entered. He carried several signal flimsies and his face was grave. 'I've been on to the Kriegsmarine in Kiel and the news has gone right up to Dönitz himself. I've had a signal acknowledging and thanking us for the information.'

'Is that all?'

'No, they also sent another signal expressing their extreme displeasure at the lack of information concerning the whereabouts of the Halifax convoy.'

'Never mind that,' Necker said. 'What about the *Deutschland*?'

Maier sat on the edge of the desk and selected a cigarette carefully. 'They know all about her from intelligence sources in the Argentine.

Left Brazil some weeks ago with a crew of assorted Kriegsmarine types under a Fregattenkapitän Berger. They also have some civilian passengers on board – nuns, I believe.'

'How fantastic,' Necker said. 'To sail a thing like that from one end of the Atlantic to the other right under the noses of the British and American navies. It'll set the country on fire.'

'No it won't, my friend, for the good and sufficient reason that the news will not be released. For such an intelligent man, Horst, you can on occasion be exasperatingly stupid. You kept your radio contact with *Deutschland* to a minimum, didn't you? Improvised a crude code, for example. Why did you do that?'

'In case anyone picked up the transmission and was able to get a fix.'

'Exactly. The British Navy, Horst, can have had no more than a passing interest in the activities of a broken-down old sailing ship attempting to reach Kiel from Brazil, mainly because no one would have given a snap of the finger for her chances of getting even half way.'

'So?'

'But now the situation changes. Our friends on the other side of the North Sea are as alive to the value of propaganda of the right sort as we are. Let them even suspect that the *Deutschland* is in that area and so close to home and they'll do anything, deploy every ship they have in those waters, to stop her getting through.'

There was silence for a moment and it was Altrogge who said, with considerable sympathy in his voice, 'So you see, Horst, no one must know. Any public announcement at this stage would be fatal.'

Necker nodded slowly, suddenly very tired, and slumped into a chair. 'The *Deutschland*, Horst, must be left to her own devices,' Maier said. 'You understand this? We can pray for her, but no more than that.'

'Yes, Herr Oberst.'

'And you were wrong, Horst. You had no right to break off from your search pattern. You could have stayed in the area another hour and a half at least. You may very well have sighted the Halifax convoy.'

Necker nodded wearily and Maier put a hand on his shoulder. 'We all make mistakes, but of this kind you are permitted only one. You understand?'

'Yes, Herr Oberst.'

'Good, now go and get something to eat, then sleep, Horst. Lots of sleep. Sometime during the next twenty-four hours you'll be going out again.'

Necker stood up. 'The same area?'

'The same.' Maier nodded. 'But the Halifax convoy this time, Horst.'

Necker went out slowly, boots drubbing. The door swung behind him. There was silence for a moment, then Maier sighed heavily. 'A funny thing, Hans,' he said to Altrogge. 'And I'll always deny having said it, of course.'

'What's that, Herr Oberst?'

'Oh, just that in his place, I've a nasty suspicion I'd have done exactly what he did.'

In Stornoway, the mist had been swept away by the rising wind and rain drove in from the sea as Jago went down the ladder from the bridge and moved aft. He dropped to one knee by the open hatch and peered into the cramped engine-room.

'How's it going in there?'

Jansen squatted beside Astor and Chaney. 'Another hour, sir.'

'And are you certain it will work?'

It was Astor who looked up, slightly aggrieved. 'Me and Chaney and that limey warrant officer up at the RAF workshop, we made the new parts ourselves. Solid brass. She'll be as good as new, Lieutenant.'

Jansen came up the ladder. 'He's right, sir, they've done an excellent job.'

'Good,' Jago said, hauling himself up on the bridge. 'Signal Mallaig we expect to be able to leave in one hour.' He glanced at his watch. 'Which means we'll only have overstepped Murray's deadline by ten or fifteen minutes. I'll confirm actual departure, naturally.'

He pushed open the door, went in and sat at the chart table. Jansen hesitated and said, 'The glass has fallen quite substantially within the past hour, Lieutenant.'

'So?'

'And the general forecast, not to put too fine a point on it, sir, stinks.'

Jago laughed. 'Aren't you the guy who once crossed the Atlantic single-handed?'

'The sea, Lieutenant, has fulfilled a need in me for most of my life,' Jansen said gravely. 'We enjoy a very special relationship. She has shaken me up a time or two, but I have always come back for more. A game we play.'

Jago felt unaccountably chilled. 'What in the hell are you talking about?'

'God knows.' Jansen seemed embarrassed. 'Perhaps I'm getting old.' He peered out through the doorway. 'These islands are different from anything I've ever known. The sea's different.'

'Oh, I get it,' Jago said mockingly. 'You mean it's been waiting for you up here all your life?'

'Or I've been waiting for it,' Jansen said. 'Which is something else again. Anyway, I'd better get that signal off, sir.'

He went out. Rain dashed against the bridge windows and outside the wind moaned through the steel rigging. Jago, still caught by what Jansen had said, sat there, head slightly turned as if listening for something.

There was a weather report on the desk and he picked it up. Sea areas Rockall, Bailey, Malin, the Hebrides; the picture was uniformly black. A deep depression moving in fast from the Atlantic. Heavy rain, winds four to five increasing to full gale by evening.

He crumpled the flimsy and tossed it into a corner. 'Ah well,' he said softly. 'I guess it just isn't my day.'

On the *Deutschland*, Berger sat at the charts in his cabin, plotting the course for the next few days. He was aware of the pump clanking monotonously outside, the rising wind. Otto Prager lay on the bunk reading a book. He sat up and removed his spectacles.

'That damn thing seems to be going on for ever.'

'You think so?'

There was a knock at the door and Sturm entered, 'You wanted me, Herr Kapitän?'

'How goes it?'

'Two hours yesterday – two and a half today.'

'And still not dry?'

'Almost.' Sturm hesitated. 'We ship water constantly, Captain, which doesn't help. It seems to me, sir, that if we took in sail . . .'

'Not a stitch, Mr Sturm.' Berger slammed a hand on the table. 'Not one rag do you touch without my permission. You understand?'

'As you say, sir.'

'Now return to your duties and send Richter in here.'

Sturm withdrew and Prager got up and crossed to the desk. 'He's changed, that boy. A month ago he would have jumped to attention and clicked his heels if you'd spoken to him like that, but now . . .'

'. . . he is a man,' Berger cut in. 'He has the *Deutschland* to thank for that. Nothing will ever be the same again.'

'He is right then?'

'Only in part. That we are shipping a great deal of water is true, which doesn't help an already indifferent situation below the waterline. That the main reason for this is my insistence on hanging out all my canvas in rough weather is also true. But bad weather is the best friend we have, for it makes us difficult to find. We can use it, Otto, to make time, which at this stage in the game is what we need to do at all costs.' He smoothed the chart with both hands. 'I mustn't fail. Not now. Not having come so far.'

Prager put a hand on his shoulder. 'We owe you a great deal, Erich. All of us.'

There was a knock at the door and Richter came in. He wore an oilskin jacket and his hands were covered in Stockholm tar. 'Herr Kapitän?'

'Ah, Richter. You've been aloft, I see.'

The bosun glanced at his hands. 'A block came loose on the top foremast.'

'Have you attended to the saloon skylight?'

'We've boarded it up permanently, Herr Kapitän. Dark for the ladies down there now, but better than water flooding through at all hours.'

'Good,' Berger said. 'Now, I'd like your opinion on our general situation.'

Richter appeared to hesitate. 'You are the master, sir, not I.'

'I know, man,' Berger said impatiently. 'But except for myself, you've had more time at sea under sail than anyone else. You, at least, know what I'm talking about.'

Richter shrugged. 'As the Herr Kapitän pleases.'

Berger half-turned the western-approaches chart and tapped it with his fingers. 'Most blockade runners in the past have attempted the Denmark Strait between Greenland and Iceland, then across to Norway. You agree?'

'One doesn't exactly expect to find traffic up there, Herr Kapitän.'

'But not for us, eh? Why?'

'A possibility of spare ice floating around in the Greenland section and we'd have to spend too much time north of the Arctic Circle.'

'I agree. And once past the Hebrides, where should our present route take us? The Orkneys passage?'

'No, sir,' Richter said. 'In my opinion we'd do better to make our turn somewhere north of the Shetlands, then cut straight across for Bergen.'

'Good, Helmut. Very good. It's nice to have one's judgement confirmed.' Berger rolled up the chart. 'There is just one other thing. Mr Sturm thinks we're carrying too much canvas. Do you agree with him?'

'Not if the Herr Kapitän wishes to make time,' Richter said. 'However, I would point out that the glass is falling. In my opinion, we're in for a bad night.'

Berger, who had started to smile, frowned in irritation. 'All right, I wasn't born yesterday. You think I don't know the glass is falling?'

The bosun went out. Berger unrolled the chart and looked down at it, scowling.

Gericke moved his bed towards the gate to avoid the rain which was driving in through the broken window every so often when the wind gusted. When he had things arranged to his satisfaction, he went back and peered through the bars.

It was just after seven, night falling fast and as wild a scene as he had ever seen, ragged waves stretching to the horizon, driving rain, sky of lead verging to black, yet here and there slashed with orange and gold.

Suddenly, far out to sea beyond the end of the pier, he saw the *Dead End* rise high over a wave, then plunge down again, her prow biting deep.

There was a step in the passageway and he turned to see Janet on the other side. She wore a sou'wester and an oilskin coat that glistened with rain and she carried a covered basket. She dropped to one knee and pushed the basket through the small flap at the bottom of the gate.

'That should keep you going. What the Scots call a good ham tea.'

Gericke picked the basket up and put it on his bunk. 'Your friend, Lieutenant Jago. He's making his run into harbour now and from the looks of that sea, I'd say he must be damn glad to get in.'

'Harry?' she said, her face lighting up. 'Here?'

She turned and ran out and Gericke reached for a cigarette as Lachlan came along from the office, a mug of tea in his hand which he passed through.

'Have you a match, Lachlan?'

'I have, Commander.' Lachlan gave him a box between the bars. 'You can keep them.'

Gericke lit his cigarette and moved to the window. The gunboat was bouncing against the pier now, her crew hanging on to her lines.

He saw Jago come out on the bridge, then Janet, her yellow oilskin clear against the evening light, running along the pier. Jago waved, came down the ladder and stepped over the rail. A moment later she was in his arms.

'So that's the way of it,' Gericke whispered. And as the wind gusted, driving rain in through the bars, he turned away.

At Fhada House the wind howled down the chimney, sending the logs roaring. Jago reached out his hands to the blaze. 'That's marvellous, Mrs Sinclair. I was beginning to think I'd never get warm again. One hell of a trip.'

'Another coffee?'

'No, thanks. I've really done very well.'

He glanced across at Janet who played the piano softly. Jean said, 'I'm sorry the Admiral couldn't come.'

'Well, as he said, he prefers to stick close to the radio on a night like this.'

'I know,' she said. 'There could be a call for the lifeboat. I wish they'd get that submarine cable connected. It makes things very difficult for everyone. Carey, you know, is our only link with civilization.'

The clock chimed eleven and Jago smiled. 'I really think I should be getting back now. Early start in the morning.' He turned. 'I'm ready when you are, Janet.'

'I'm staying the night, darling,' Janet said, still continuing to play.

'Oh, I see. Well, I'd better get going then.'

She showed no inclination to move. Jean Sinclair took him out into the hall. As she helped him into his reefer, she said, 'You did say an early start in the morning, didn't you, Lieutenant?'

'That's right, ma'am.'

She shook her head. 'I don't think so. Not tomorrow, probably not for two or three days now.' She smiled. 'I know what I'm talking about. When the wind starts blowing over Fhada like this, anything can happen.'

Jago grinned, suddenly much more cheerful. 'Can you positively guarantee that?'

'I think so.'

As she opened the door, struggling to hold it still against the wind, he kissed her on the right cheek. 'Anyone ever tell you you're an angel?' he said and plunged out into the gale.

When Jean returned to the drawing-room, Janet was standing by the fire pulling on her sheepskin. 'Has he gone?'

'Obviously.'

'Good.' Janet moved past her into the hall and Jean followed.

'What are you playing at?'

'To be perfectly honest, I don't know,' Janet said and added, 'I've just had a great idea. To hell with men.'

'It's a thought.' Jean opened the door. 'I'd sleep on it if I were you.'

'Exactly,' Janet said and she moved out into the driving rain.

'Personally I think the search for the Halifax convoy to be a waste of time,' Hans Altrogge said. 'But they still insist you have a look.'

It was just before midnight and the intelligence room was a place of shadows. Necker leaned over the chart and nodded. 'I agree. A waste of fuel, the whole exercise.'

'Not entirely, Horst.' Altrogge opened a briefing file. 'There's something building up out there in the Atlantic, something pretty unusual according to our weather station at Kap Bismarck in Greenland.'

'How unusual?'

'Deep depression coming in very fast and exceptionally severe storms forecast. Nothing to worry you, of course, not at thirty-five thousand.'

'And what if I have to go down?'

'We must hope you won't have to. One thing is certain, the trip should be worthwhile for the weather statistics you can bring back, if nothing else.'

'All right,' Necker said. 'When do we leave?'

'O-five-hundred,' Altrogge glanced at his watch. 'Time to get some sleep in. You could manage three or four hours.'

'I'll think about it,' Necker said and went out.

Barquentine *Deutschland*, 25 September 1944. Lat. 56°.20N., long. 9°.39W. A bad night. Winds force 6–8 increasing. Heavy rain and a pounding sea. At two bells in the mid-watch I gave orders to furl the fore upper top-gallant and fore upper topsail. This was accomplished with considerable difficulty. Richter, Winzer and Kluth have the wheel at this moment which I snatch to enter the log. The barometer continues to fall. I greatly fear things will get worse before they get better.

Thirteen

On Fhada it was Reeve who first became aware for certain, that something completely out of the ordinary in the way of weather was building up. High winds always had made him nervous and restless. Unable to sleep, he got out of bed around two a.m., made a pot of coffee and sat at the radio for a while to see what he could pick up.

The air seemed alive with voices, crackling through the static. Some were faint and far away, others close at hand, but all had one thing in common; fear. Those who could were already running for shelter.

At one point a Royal Naval supply ship, south of Iceland, came in urgently to report a wind speed of seventy-five knots increasing, with heavy seas and rain. She was trying to make Reykjavik.

It was almost three o'clock when he tuned in to the first really vital transmission from RAF Coastal Command at Stornoway.

Suspect polar air depression imminent in sea areas Malin and Hebrides. Be prepared for winds of hurricane force within the next few hours. Expected direction north-east.

Reeve sat thinking about it for a moment, then padded into the kitchen, closing the door quietly behind him. He had often joked that the telephone in the wall was so old that Alexander Graham Bell himself must have installed it, but just now it was a lifeline. He turned the handle vigorously for some considerable time, knowing there would be no one on duty at the post office on the quay. It would be necessary to raise Mrs MacBrayne from her bed.

There was no response at first. He tried again and as he did so, the kitchen door opened and Janet entered, her dressing-gown over her shoulders. 'What's going on?'

He waved her to silence as Mrs MacBrayne's sleepy voice said, 'Hello?'

'Katrina? Reeve here. Can you put me through to Murdoch at South Landing. Sorry to bother you, but it's urgent.'

She was instantly alert. 'Is the boat called out, Admiral?'

'Not yet, but it could be before too long, the way things are building up.'

'Hold on now. I'll put you through directly.'

He turned to Janet. 'Put the kettle on, sweetheart, we'll have some coffee. We could be in for a long night.'

She was still slightly bemused, but went obediently to the stove, opened it and fed wood into the still glowing ashes.

Reeve waited impatiently. After a while, Katrina MacBrayne came back on. 'I can't get through, Admiral.'

'You mean there's no reply?'

'Och, no. The line's dead. Down in this wind, I'm thinking. Is there anything I can do?'

'No, I'll see to it. But I think the crew should be alerted.'

'But there is no crew, Admiral. The fishing boats were working the grounds South Uist way this afternoon. They'll run for shelter to Lochboisdale to wait for it to blow over. If they call the boat out tonight, there'll be no one fit to handle her except old men and boys.'

'Right, Katrina,' Reeve said briskly. 'Leave it to me. I'll be in touch.'

He replaced the receiver and turned to Janet. 'I've got a job for you.' He took her by the hand, led her into the living-room and sat her down at the radio. He adjusted the dial quickly and locked it in. 'That's the band that most of the local stuff comes through on. You can get dressed if you want, make your coffee, only keep listening. Any messages for me or for Fhada direct, write them down.'

'But what about you?' she demanded. 'Where are you going?'

'To see Murdoch,' he said simply, went into his bedroom and started to dress quickly.

Reeve carried a storm lantern, but it only seemed to accentuate the darkness. Rain fell relentlessly and the wind gusted with such force that it was out of the question to raise the sail on the trolley.

He pumped his way across the spine of the island one-handed, rain cascading from his oilskins. The wind snatched away the storm lantern when he was half way there and he completed the journey in darkness.

He negotiated the track down to the lifeboat station with the aid of the electric torch he'd slipped into his pocket in case of emergencies before leaving. He could hear Rory barking and then the cottage door was opened, light flooding out, and Murdoch appeared. The wolfhound bounded through the rain to greet Reeve. His hand fastened in its ruff and they went down to the cottage together.

Murdoch drew him inside. 'A bad night to be out, Admiral.'

'Worse at sea.' Reeve took off his sou'wester and oilskin and crouched at the fire. 'I've been trying to get you on the telephone. The line must be down.'

'Is the boat called out then?'

'No. Not that you could do much if it was. You haven't got a crew, Murdoch. The fishing boats didn't get back in this evening.'

'I wouldn't say that,' Murdoch told him calmly. 'There is Hamish Macdonald, Francis Patterson, James and Dougal Sinclair.'

Reeve stared at him. 'Hamish Macdonald is seventy if he's a day. The Sinclair brothers must be the oldest twins in the business. I don't know about Patterson . . .'

'We were born in the same year, Admiral.'

'Come off it, Murdoch,' Reeve said angrily. 'There's a world of difference between you and those old guys and you know it.'

'The *Morag* is a fine boat. If she capsizes, she rights herself again. Even if her engine compartments flood, her engines will still keep turning. You know the *Morag*, Admiral. It is not like the old days when young muscle was needed for the oars. Hamish and the others have fished these waters all their lives. They know their business. It is enough.'

'Well, I hope to God they don't have to be put to the test.'

Murdoch produced a bottle from a cupboard by the fire and found a couple of glasses. 'Here, now, this will put marrow in your bones again.'

Reeve gulped, tears springing to his eyes as the *Uisgebeatha* exploded in the pit of his stomach. 'Damn you, Murdoch, that not only hits the spot – it takes it right out. Anyway, you need eight to man the boat so you're still three short. What would you do about that?'

'There is always Lachlan.'

'Who spews his guts at the first ripple on the water. You must be joking.' A sudden gust of wind slammed solidly against the roof of the house and the building shook. He shivered. 'I don't like the sound of that. I caught a storm warning from Coastal Command on the radio before leaving. Winds of hurricane force within the next few hours from the south-west.'

Murdoch frowned. 'Let us hope they are wrong. If that is the way of it, it's the devil's own job we'd have in launching.'

'You think so?'

'I know it, Admiral.'

Reeve reached for his oilskin. 'I'd better be getting back. At first light we'll see if we can find where your line's down.'

'And if I'm needed before then?' Murdoch took his own yellow oilskin down from behind the door. 'Better I come with you now and see what is happening out there in the wide world.'

It was a quarter to five when they reached Reeve's cottage and when they went into the living-room, Jean was sitting with Janet at the radio.

'Hello, Carey,' she said. 'I couldn't sleep in this wind so I thought I'd come along and see how you were making out. I'll get some tea.'

She went into the kitchen. Janet said, 'Things have been warming up. The Stornoway boat was called out an hour ago to assist a fleet tanker in difficulties off Cape Wrath. Barra, twenty minutes later.'

'Where to?'

'Somewhere up in the North Minch.'

'Our turn soon, I'm thinking,' Murdoch said as Jean returned with cups of tea on a tray. 'No, not now, Mrs Sinclair. I have one or two people to see. I'll be back later.'

He went out and Janet said, 'Where's he off to?'

'Oh, rousting out Hamish Macdonald, the Sinclair twins and a few other members of the pensioners' club, just in case they're needed,' Reeve told her.

'You must be joking. They're old men.'

'You try telling Murdoch that.' There were various other notes on the table and he picked one up. 'What's this, another weather report?'

'That's right. From the Meteorological Office.'

It was substantially the same as before. *Sea areas Hebrides, Bailey, Malin, an intense depression giving rise to hurricane force winds with heavy rain and sleet.*

A moment later, a voice crackled over the radio, 'Mallaig calling Sugar One on Fhada. Mallaig calling Sugar One on Fhada.'

The reception was poor, crackling with static, other voices crowding in. Reeve took the mike. 'Reeve here. Receiving you strength five, Mallaig.'

'I have Captain Murray for you, Admiral.'

There was only the static for a moment and then Murray's voice broke in. 'Hullo, sir, how are things with you?'

'Terrible. What about your side of the pond?'

'Total chaos. Two lighters sunk right here in the damned harbour and a nine-hundred-ton coaster loaded with fuel drums broken loose from her moorings. We've been trying to contact Jago during the past hour; routine check on all naval vessels. No success, I'm afraid. Any suggestions?'

'Last I saw of him he was safely tied up at the pier. I'll take a look and call back.'

'Be obliged if you would, Admiral. By the way, you're in for at least another really bad day. We've reports of winds gusting up to a hundred knots. The weather boys tell me we can expect an almost vertical fall in barometric pressure.'

'For those few kind words, I thank you,' Reeve told him. 'Over and out.'

It was bitterly cold in the cell. Gericke had slept little during the night and at five-thirty, he got up and went to the window, pulling a blanket around his shoulders.

It was still dark outside, but occasionally the horizon exploded with electricity, giving a split-second instant picture of the scene in the harbour. There were several small boats adrift down there as far as he could see, two of them upturned.

The noise of the wind was higher now, a grating moan that was a constant irritation. He looked out again and in another flash of sheet lightning saw a figure in an oilskin, lantern in hand, ploughing along the pier towards the gunboat. There was a step in the passageway and Lachlan peered through the bars, an oil lamp in one hand.

'You must be cold in there, Commander.'

'Yes, I think you could say that.'

'I've a good fire up there in the office. If you'd give me your hand on it, I'd let you sit by it for a while.' The boy grinned. 'Not that there's anywhere for you to go – not in this lot.'

'Why, thank you, Lachlan,' Gericke said without hesitation. 'My hand and my word. You are very kind.'

The boy unlocked the gate and Gericke followed him up to the office. The peat fire glowed white-hot in the draught. Lachlan handed him a mug of tea as a great gust of wind struck the roof, loosening tiles.

'God help me, but it frightens me, that wind, Commander. Frightens me to death. The same since I was a wee boy. Isn't that a terrible thing to have to confess?'

'That one is afraid?' Gericke smiled and offered him a cigarette. 'Have one of these, Lachlan, and join the club.'

Mary's Town had never been a good anchorage and though sheltered from the wind when it was from the south-west, a considerable sea was apt to build up inside the harbour.

The *Dead End* had had a bad night. Twice she had dragged her lines, on the first occasion being hurled back against the pier by a severe gust with considerable force, and she was under regular attack from loose boats in the harbour.

Jago and his crew had been at action stations for much of the night, engaged in a constant battle to save the old gunboat from dashing her brains out against the pier. By five thirty, he was exhausted.

He was aware of the storm lantern on the pier, but didn't realize it was Reeve coming aboard until the admiral mounted the ladder to the bridge.

'How goes it?'

'We're hanging on, sir, that's about all. I think I'd rather be taking my chances in the open.'

'Don't kid yourself. You think this is bad? Wait till it gets worse. Murray's been in touch. He can't raise you.'

'I know, our radio's taken a pounding. I'll be surprised if they can ever put it together again.'

'Okay, I'll notify Murray you're still in one piece. If you can spare an hour when it gets lighter, come on up to my cottage. I've an idea I might need you.'

'Will do, sir.'

Reeve judged his moment to step over the rail and hurried back along the pier.

Berger kicked open the door of his cabin and lurched inside followed by a tremendous gust of wind and rain. The oil lamp above his desk was swinging in its gimbals, light and dark chasing each other back and forth in the corners.

Otto Prager, who had been lying on the bunk, sat up in alarm. 'What is it, Erich?'

Berger was soaked to the skin in spite of his oilskins. His face was wild. 'I lost another man.'

He leaned heavily on the desk for a moment, then made his way round to the other side with all the care of a drunken man as the floor heaved. He sagged into his chair.

'I'm sorry,' Prager said.

'Aren't we all?'

Berger opened the top drawer, took out the ship's log and picked up his pen.

. . . Five bells in the morning watch and conditions as bad as I have ever known. We have reduced sail to main lower topsail and storm staysail with great difficulty. Conditions aloft were atrocious. At four bells two enormous waves swept down upon the ship. She rose the first, but while in the trough on the other side, the second wave struck, reaching halfway up the foremast. There were eight men in the rigging at that time by my orders, amongst them Leading Electrician's Mate Hans Bergman who was swept away.

'So far,' Berger said bitterly. 'Poor lad. All this bloody way – and for what?'

'You need sleep, Erich.'

'You're right,' Berger said. 'Wake me in half an hour.'

He laid his head on his hands and closed his eyes. Prager sat watching him, the light from the wildly swinging oil lamp flickering backwards and forwards across the room and outside the thousand several voices of the wind seemed to rise to a crescendo.

'It's the sea, Otto,' Berger said softly without opening his eyes, 'I think maybe it's decided to come for us.'

In the saloon, the nuns grouped around the table, heads bowed, hands clasped. Water dripped in through the skylight, but the boards, for the present, seemed to be holding. And here, as in the rest of the ship, there was not a dry inch to be found, water pouring down the companionway, swilling in and out of the cabins.

Sister Angela prayed aloud in a firm, steady voice: 'Thou, O Lord, that stillest the raging of the sea, hear, hear us and save us, that we perish not . . .'

The doors at the top of the companionway opened and Richter

clattered down the steps, carrying a large billy-can which he set on the table. His cap was soaked, his tangled beard and oilskin streaming with water. He stood there waiting, chest heaving. Sister Angela faltered, then continued her prayer to the end and crossed herself.

'Captain's compliments, Sister. Hot coffee. Just made on the oil stove in his cabin.'

'My thanks to Captain Berger. How are things?'

'Bad,' Richter said. 'We lost another man. Young Bergman. Swept from the rigging.'

'We will pray for him.'

'Yes, you might well do that, Sister.'

He turned and went back up the companionway. 'Let us pray, Sisters, for the soul of Hans Bergman, that he may find peace.'

But Lotte, at the other end of the table, turned suddenly, mounted the companionway before a word could be said and went out on deck.

It was a sight to take her breath away. Although it was well past dawn there was no day: the sky was black, mountainous swirling clouds touched with violet and red as if somewhere beyond in the gloom great fires burned. Lightning flickered constantly and the wind howled like a mad dog, slashing at her face.

Everyone on deck had his hands full and no one noticed her. Sturm had the wheel, with Winzer and Kluth, and four men manned the pump, each one tethered to the mainmast by a line.

The sea swept in over the ship in a solid mass, taking all before it. Lotte hung on to the ladder. The *Deutschland* seemed to lie right over, then righted herself.

Without their lifelines the men on the pump would have been washed away. They floundered on the deck like stranded fish and Richter, who had jumped into the ratlines, dropped down to go to their aid.

There was a sudden violent report, almost like an explosion, high above. He looked up. The lifts had parted on the fore top-gallant. As he watched, the yard swung violently and the sail broke free.

It fluttered wildly in the gale, the entire mast vibrating. Richter knew that it could only be a question of time before it snapped the fore topmast itself like a rotten stick. He ran to the galley, snatched one of the fire-axes from its mounting, and sprang into the ratlines.

He paused to jam the axe into his belt, turned and saw Berger on the quarterdeck waving wildly. Impossible to hear what he was calling, but it was plain enough from his gestures that he wanted Richter down out of there.

But if that sail was left and brought the mast down . . . Richter kept on climbing, gritting his teeth. His oilskin was worse than useless, more a hindrance than a help for it offered little protection against such heavy and continuous rain. The rigging was swollen, every rope stiff, and each time he raised an arm to pull himself up, a cold stream of water slopped in between clothes and skin. The wind was pulling and tearing at his clothes like a living thing.

He paused on the foretop for a moment to catch his breath. The sea boiled white foam as far as the eye could see, rain and hail driving in, lightning glimmered balefully in the blackness of the sky.

He paused beneath the sail. It thundered free with a terrible roar. Facing death now, judging his moment, he moved close to the mast, got inside the flailing sail, hung on tight with one hand and swung the fire-axe, attacking the ring that held the yard to the mast.

The sail enveloped him, almost tearing him away. Then the line from one corner tightened, pulling it straight for a moment. He glanced down and found Berger standing on the foretop just below him, hanging on to the line.

He nodded, Richter swung the axe again, aware of the entire topmast vibrating. Once, twice, the axe cut clean through metal, the yard swung, the line parted. Berger released the line – only just in time, as the yard, the lower topgallant sail still fluttering wildly from it, whirled away on the wind.

Berger clapped Richter on the shoulder. Slowly, painfully, they descended, taking their time. Richter dropped to the deck and as he moved forward, saw Lotte by the quarterdeck ladder. She was gazing at him, a kind of awe on her face. As if by instinct, he held out his arms and she ran into their shelter.

Jago and his men moved the gunboat into the inner harbour at first light where the groundswell was less of a problem. As soon as the *Dead End* was secure he left Jansen in charge and went up to the cottage. Jean Sinclair let him in the front door and when he went into the living-room, Reeve and Murdoch were at the radio.

'How goes it?'

'Terrible,' the admiral said. 'A bloody shambles.'

In Mallaig, another coaster had been driven ashore and two more lighters sunk. Three trawlers had foundered off Stornoway so quickly that nothing could be done, overwhelmed in that terrible sea. South of Iceland, the Royal Canadian Navy corvette *Macmichael* had disappeared, never to be seen again, along with the eighty-five officers and men who comprised her crew. And the Halifax convoy, striking for the North Channel into the Irish Sea, was hopelessly scattered.

But still, there had not been a specific call for the Fhada lifeboat.

Murdoch sat patiently smoking his pipe, listening to the jumbled messages over the radio. Jago went into the kitchen where he found Janet with Jean making sandwiches.

'Heh,' he said. 'You're a woman after all.'

'Watch it, darling.' She pointed the knife under his chin.

He helped himself to tea. 'I see the boat hasn't been called out.'

'It will be. That's what Murdoch's waiting for. The crew are all ready down at the lifeboat station.' She shook her head. 'Honest to God, Harry, you've never seen anything like it. There isn't one of them who isn't a grandfather. It's pathetic.'

'Pathetic? A bunch of guys are willing to put themselves on the line in the worst sea I've ever seen in my life and that's all you can find to say?'

'They wouldn't last five minutes out there. What would be the point?'

He went back into the living-room and took a chair next to Reeve. It was just after seven-thirty. At ten to eight there was another weather forecast from Stornoway.

US Destroyer Carbisdale a hundred-ten miles north-west of Butt of Lewis reports winds of hurricane force, gusting to one-hundred-twenty knots.

'A hundred and twenty,' Jago said in awe.

'A bad blow indeed,' Murdoch said gravely. 'As bad as I have known.'

Janet brought in tea and sandwiches on a tray, put them down and went back to Jean in the kitchen without a word. Jago helped himself to a sandwich and leaned forward to pat Rory on the head. The clock on the mantelpiece struck eight times.

As the last stroke died away, a voice sounded over the radio in broken English. 'Three-masted barquentine *Deutschland* adrift and helpless. I estimate my present position some twenty miles south-west of Fhada in Outer Hebrides. For God's sake help us. I have women on board.'

The message faded, drowned in a sea of static. Reeve turned to stare at Jago. 'Did he say *Deutschland*?'

'That's what it sounded like to me, Admiral.'

'A three-masted barquentine,' Murdoch said. 'I did not think I would live to see the day.'

Janet and Jean had come from the kitchen and stood listening. Reeve said, 'It just can't be, for Christ's sake.'

Berger's voice swelled through the static. 'This is barquentine *Deutschland* in urgent need of assistance, twenty miles south-west of Fhada. I have women on board.'

'There he is again, Admiral,' Jago said. 'That guy *has* to be for real.'

Reeve reached for the microphone, and then, as Berger started to repeat his message again, another voice broke in on channel. '*Deutschland*, hier ist Grosser Schwarzer Adler.'

What followed was wholly in German. Reeve sat back helplessly. 'What in the hell goes on here? One minute we have some guy screaming for assistance – the next, a lot of Kraut I don't understand a word of.'

There was a moment's silence before Janet said carefully, 'Gericke would, Uncle Carey.'

On the *Deutschland* things had gone from bad to worse. By seven-fifteen it became obvious that she could no longer support the main lower topsail and Berger gave Sturm the necessary orders.

To clew up that sail proved to be incredibly difficult. Although the men had to work at no great height above the deck, they still had the appalling wind to contend with. Every rope was foul, swollen to twice its normal size, the blocks jammed at a touch, and all the time the wind tore at them, keen as a surgeon's lancet, splitting flesh with its driven spray.

Finally it was done and the men descended wearily to the deck. The wind now dominated everything, striking the ship one blow after another as it gusted. Ragged clouds passed by overhead, seeming low enough to touch the mastheads, sheet lightning flickered and the rain fell relentlessly.

Another four men worked frantically at the pump. Berger, as he watched them at the quarterdeck rail, felt strangely impotent. Such puny insignificance in the midst of all this vastness. What could it hope to achieve?

He turned to check on Sturm and the two men who had the wheel with him, and his mouth opened in a soundless cry as a tremendous following sea rolled in across the stern.

The *Deutschland* shuddered, Berger found himself on his back, clutching at the rail for life itself, as hundreds of tons of water swept on towards the prow. There was no sign of Winzer or Kluth, but Sturm was still there, hanging on to the wheel.

Berger staggered across the quarterdeck to join him. The *Deutschland* put her lee rail under the water. They fought like demons, Berger cursing in a frenzy, and slowly, so slowly, she started to answer the helm. But the blow had been mortal. The mizzen topmast and much of the rigging had gone. The life-boats had been swept away. The galley shack had totally disappeared.

Richter came up the ladder. Berger shouted in his ear, 'Two more men on this wheel, Richter, then a damage report, quick as you can.'

The bosun disappeared. A few moments later Holzer and Endrass came up to take over the wheel. 'You're in charge here, Mr Sturm. I'll see what the situation is below.'

As Berger reached his cabin door, Richter came up the companionway. 'Are the Sisters safe?'

Richter nodded. 'Shaken up and badly scared. But we've other problems now, Herr Kapitän. Twenty inches of water in the bilges and rising.'

Berger turned to look at the *Deutschland*. Rigging lines danced on the wind, the fore lower topsail had torn free and half of it still fluttered from the yardarm like a ragged grey flag. Here and there planking protruded from the deck and the pipe rails were smashed. The entire ship shuddered as she wearily climbed another great wave and a squall hit her.

Richter knew what he was thinking; could smell defeat. 'It's no good, is it, Helmut?' the captain said. 'We're finished.'

'I'm afraid so, Herr Kapitän.'

Berger nodded. 'Take over from Mr Sturm and tell him to bring the radio to my cabin right away.'

Necker had left Trondheim at five and the flight over Scotland at thirty-five thousand feet, far above the weather, had been completely without incident. He had arrived in the target area, however, to find a very different situation.

Clouds boiled below him, dark and menacing, tinged with orange and fire, twisting and curling like black smoke. Schmidt said, 'They're having a hell of a time down there today. My English is only fair, but I know SOS when I hear it. I'll cut you in, sir.'

There was another message coming through now. *Sea areas Malin and Hebrides. Wind gusting to one-hundred-thirty. Barometer reading nine-seven-o and still falling.*

It was Schmidt who said, 'I know one thing, Herr Hauptmann. The Halifax convoy won't be a convoy any longer. She'll have been smashed to pieces.'

But Necker, gazing down into that black smoke below, was thinking of the *Deutschland*. He said to Rudi, 'You've got the position where we saw the *Deutschland* yesterday. Average let's say ten knots on a north-east by north course. See what your dead reckoning can do with that for her present whereabouts.'

'But Herr Hauptmann,' Rudi protested. 'Our orders . . .'

Necker said coldly, 'Do as you're told, and shut up.'

It only took the boy a couple of minutes to produce the desired information and he passed it across. Necker altered course immediately, switching on his intercom at the same time.

'Listen to me, you lot. They told us this was the finest all-weather plane in the world. Claimed it would even operate under hurricane conditions. Let's see if they're right. I'm going down into that shit to find out what's happening to the *Deutschland*. My decision.'

He pushed the column forward, taking the Junkers into a shallow dive, and started to descend. Within a few minutes they were enveloped in cloud and heavy rain, lightning flickering at the wing tips.

They continued to descend at speed, buffeted from side to side in the heavy wind. Necker had to hang on to the column with all his strength. At one point, they slewed to port, the wind striking a series of blows on the fuselage that stripped pieces from the wings, but he regained control and maintained his dive.

They were at ten thousand and still descending, still enveloped in dark, swirling clouds. Rudi had unclipped his oxygen mask and stared out through the windscreen, his face very white.

And it was all a waste of time, Necker told himself. In such weather it was highly unlikely that the *Deutschland* would have been able to maintain her original course, and her speed, after all, was only an estimation.

At three thousand, the Junkers burst out of the clouds into a great bowl of luminous light and torrential rain, a sea of foam stretching to the horizon. And there she was – quite incredibly, about half a mile away to the south-west.

'Rudi,' Necker said, 'I owe you a bottle of champagne,' and he banked steeply to port.

Rudi had the binoculars out. 'She looks in bad shape, Herr Hauptmann.'

Schmidt broke in, 'Something's wrong, sir. They're transmitting a distress call. In English. Berger is asking for help.'

'Hook me in,' said Necker grimly. 'And I'll talk to him myself.'

Barquentine *Deutschland*, 25 September 1944. Winds of hurricane strength and the *Deutschland*, being in my opinion in imminent danger of foundering, I started to transmit distress calls at the end of the morning watch. Our signal, I fear, is very weak owing to the effect of salt water on the batteries. However, shortly afterwards our friend from the Luftwaffe reappeared. To our mutual astonishment, a third party joined in from the neighbouring island of Fhada.

Fourteen

'*Deutschland* calling. Are you still with us, Necker? We lost you in low cloud.'

'I still have you in sight,' Necker replied. 'Don't worry. I'll stay close.'

The exchange crackled through static, remote and somehow far away. Gericke, at the radio, said slowly, '*Deutschland*?'

'Well, speak to him,' Reeve said. 'Find out what's going on.'

'Very well.' Gericke reached for the microphone and started to transmit in German. '*Deutschland*, this is Fhada calling. Come in, please.'

There was silence and then Berger's voice crackled faintly. 'Necker, who was that, for God's sake?'

'I don't know.'

'*Deutschland*. Fhada calling. Will you please come in with fullest details on your present position. We may be able to assist.'

There was a further silence and then Necker's voice: '. . . haven't any idea . . . suggest you answer . . . see what happens.'

Once more there was silence, other fainter messages crowding in as if from far away. Jago said, 'What's going on out there, Commander?'

'We're only picking up one side of the conversation now. Necker, whoever he is. As for the *Deutschland*, she's either foundered or lost radio contact.'

'There's only one sure way to find out,' Reeve said. 'Speak to Necker this time.'

'All right.' Gericke tried again. 'Fhada calling Necker. Come in, please. Fhada calling Necker. Come in, please. I cannot raise the *Deutschland*. Urgent I speak with you.'

Only the silence. Jean Sinclair said softly. 'He doesn't trust you, Commander.'

Gericke tried again. 'Necker, this is Korvettenkapitän Paul Gericke of the Kriegsmarine calling from Fhada. I beg you to reply to me.'

There was more static, then Necker's voice strongly. 'Paul Gericke – the U-boat ace?'

'That's right.'

'But how can this be?'

'I am a prisoner of war. Those in charge here have asked me to monitor your calls because they cannot understand German. Who are you?'

'Hauptmann Horst Necker serving with KG 40 out of Trondheim. Shipping and weather reconnaissance. I'm circling the *Deutschland* at the moment in a Ju 88.'

'I can't get any kind of reply from them.' Gericke said. 'What's wrong?'

'Their signal has weakened. Sea water in the batteries.'

'Can you still monitor them?'

'Yes, if I stay close.'

The admiral said impatiently, 'Come on, Gericke, what's going on out there?'

Gericke told him. Reeve turned to Murdoch. 'Think you can reach them?'

'We can try,' Murdoch said. 'It would help if that aircraft stayed overhead to give us a mark. Visibility at sea level will be very bad.'

'That's asking one hell of a lot,' Jago said. 'Of Necker, I mean. Can you imagine what it's like trying to keep that plane in the air in this weather?'

Gericke reached for the microphone again. 'Gericke calling Necker. We have a lifeboat here ready to leave at once. It would greatly assist if you could stay in the area as marker.'

Necker replied: 'In the worst conditions I've ever known. But she's handling all right so far. We'll do what we can. Present position is as follows.' He gave the essential facts slowly and clearly. 'How long before this lifeboat reaches us?'

Gericke passed the details to Murdoch. The old man nodded. 'About an hour. I'm leaving now.'

'I'm coming with you.' Reeve reached for his oilskin. But Murdoch shook his head. 'You are welcome to watch, Admiral – nothing more. I have my crew.'

'Now look here,' Reeve started to say hotly.

'I am coxswain of the Fhada lifeboat, Carey Reeve,' the old man said. 'Life or death this day, by my decision only. You can see us off with pleasure, but no more.'

Reeve turned to Gericke. 'Stay on that radio. I'll be back as soon as I've seen the boat launched.'

'Very well,' Gericke said.

Murdoch plunged out into the gale with Reeve and Jago at his heels.

* * *

High up on the spine of the island the wind was ferocious, a living thing that seemed to be doing its utmost to force the trolley back. It took the combined efforts of Murdoch and Jago pumping together to make any kind of progress.

When they came to end of the track above the lifeboat station, the sea was enough to take the breath away. A ragged broken carpet of white water, one enormous wave after another flowing in a kind of slow motion. Now and then in the trough, the jagged black teeth of the reef gaped beyond the mouth of the inlet.

'Think you can make it?' Reeve bawled into Murdoch's ear.

'Perhaps,' the old man replied.

There were people clustered around the lifeboat house. Mainly women and a few children. As the three men hurried down the track there was the sound of running behind and Lachlan overtook them.

'I came as soon as I heard,' he said, slightly breathless. 'And half Mary's Town behind me. Will you be needing me, Murdoch?'

'There are six of us, Lachlan. We can manage fine.'

Murdoch moved on through the small crowd and entered the boat-house. His crew already waited in the boat wearing yellow oilskins and lifejackets.

The doors at the end of the slipway were open. He pulled on an oilskin and moved a yard or two down the slope from where he could see into the mouth of the inlet. He looked up at his crew.

'There is a chance it can be done. One in ten only, but worth a try. There is a ship out there in a bad way and women on board. And if we don't go now, we don't go at all, not the way the sea builds up out here. If any one of you thinks better of it, speak up and get out of the boat.'

This last remark was delivered in the same calm, matter-of-fact tone as the rest. White-bearded Francis Patterson replied with a touch of impatience, 'Can we be off now, Murdoch, or are we going to hang about and jaw all day?'

'So be it,' Murdoch said and went up the ladder.

The women in the small crowd moved down to the Strand, talking anxiously amongst themselves in low voices.

The *Morag Sinclair* emerged from the mouth of the boathouse a moment later, sliding down the slipway at considerable speed, and entered the water, her prow biting deep, spray fanning high into the air.

She moved on through the heavy swell, lifting as a great wave smashed in through the narrow mouth of the inlet. For a moment, the reef gaped again through broken water. There was silence from the crowd, only the wind howling.

'It's no good,' Reeve said. 'They'll never make it. It's madness. Those waves must be thirty feet high. If they hit at the wrong moment, they'll be chewed to pieces out there.'

But the *Morag* kept going, out through the entrance in a burst of speed. 'He's trying to catch the next big swell for clearance over the reef,' Jago cried.

Perhaps it might have worked, Murdoch's one chance in ten. But at that moment, the wind gusted with such violence that a woman screamed somewhere in the crowd. The *Morag Sinclair* staggered, then veered sharply to port and seemed to poise high on the swell above the black rocks suddenly revealed.

'She's going to strike!' Reeve cried.

An enormous wave bored in, rising thirty or forty feet into the mouth of the inlet, carrying the lifeboat broadside on, helpless before it. She struck close inshore, water boiling over her in fury, washing two of the crew straight over the side.

Harry Jago was running now, down into the surf, reaching out for a yellow oilskin. He was aware of Francis Patterson's face surfacing beside him, eyes closed, teeth bared.

And then there were others beside him, waist-deep in the freezing water. Admiral Reeve, with his one good arm, floundering, the black patch lifting to reveal the ugly puckered scar, the eyeless socket. Jago turned the yellow oilskin over to find James Sinclair and heaved him backwards through the surf to where willing hands stretched out to help.

The next few minutes were a total confusion of shouts and screams, the *Morag Sinclair* grinding in through the surf on each succeeding wave. A line was thrown, another, and people running from the boathouse brought more.

Jago found himself heaving, bending his back in the surf, Lachlan and Reeve beside him. Once, falling flat on his face, he took a moment to collect himself and was astonished to see a dozen women on the next rope, skirts swirling up about their hips.

The wind blew sand straight into his face. He closed his eyes and kept on hauling, the rope burning his shoulder. Then he was on his hands and knees. This time, when he opened his eyes painfully and looked about him, everyone seemed to be roughly in the same position. And the *Morag Sinclair*, tilted to one side, was safe on the beach.

Jago and Reeve got to their feet and went forward. Murdoch appeared at the rail above them. His face was very pale and twisted with pain.

'Are you all right?' Reeve called.

'I took a knock when we broached. It's nothing.'

Jago circled the boat. 'Only superficial damage and the screws are intact.'

'That's something,' Reeve said. 'At least there's been no loss of life. A miracle.'

Murdoch hooked a ladder over and came down it awkwardly as the crowd surged forward. His left arm swung loosely at his side in a way which Jago thought was distinctly unhealthy.

The old man swayed and Jago tried to steady him. 'Are you all right?' Murdoch pushed him away. 'Never mind me.' He turned to Reeve. 'There is a boat out there helpless, and women on board, and nothing to be done about it.'

Jago heard someone say, 'There's always the *Dead End*.' Only afterwards did he realize it was he himself who had spoken.

Jago sat at the chart table, Jansen at his side and the crew crowded in around the door. 'That's it,' he said. 'Now you know the score. It's going to be rough out there. Volunteers only this trip. Any man who wants to can collect his duffel and step over that rail to the pier and I won't think any the worse of him. Not to put too fine a point on it, I'd say that should particularly commend itself to those of you who are married.'

It was Petersen who spoke for all of them. 'We've been together a long time, Lieutenant. We've been in the water together more than once and this is the first time I ever heard you talk crap. Begging your pardon, sir.'

'I think what he's trying to ask in his own delectable way, Lieutenant, is when do we leave?' Jansen said.

Jago glanced at his watch. 'The Admiral's due at any moment with the *Deutschland*'s present position. I'd say we'll be moving out of here within the next ten to fifteen minutes.' He looked up. 'So what are you all hanging about for?'

Janet left Murdoch lying on the bed, closed the door softly and went into the living-room. Gericke was at the radio, Reeve and Jean beside him.

The admiral turned. 'How is he?'

'The arm's broken. I've put it in a splint for the time being and given him a pain-killing injection. He should sleep for a while. How are things going?'

'Not so good. We've not been able to raise Necker again. Probably an electrical storm.'

Gericke was still trying in the background, speaking urgently into the mike in German. 'Come in, Necker. Come in, please.'

Necker's voice sounded faint, but clear enough for them all to sense the urgency. 'Necker here, Gericke. I've been calling for the past half-hour. What's happening?'

'We've not been connecting, that's all.' Gericke told him. 'Too much disturbance. There's been a delay. The lifeboat couldn't get away, but there's a gunboat leaving now from Mary's Town. Please confirm present position.' Necker did so and Gericke went on, 'What about the *Deutschland*? Are you still in touch?'

'Only with difficulty. The signal is very weak. Another hour to wait, then?'

'I'm afraid so.'

Gericke had written the details of the *Deutschland*'s position on a scrap of paper which he pushed across at Reeve. The admiral slipped it into his pocket. 'I'll get this down to Jago.'

As he turned to the door, Jean caught his sleeve, 'Carey, you wouldn't do anything silly, like try to go along for the ride, would you?'

'At my age?' He grinned and kissed her lightly. 'Sweetheart. You've got to be joking.'

He went out quickly. Jean turned, her face troubled. 'He's going to go, Janet. I know it.'

Janet said bitterly, 'What did you expect?'

She went into the kitchen and slammed the door. Gericke reached for Jean's hand and held it tight for a moment. Necker's voice cut in on them.

'Have they left yet?'

'On their way.'

'I have a problem. An hour and fifteen minutes, then we must head for home. A question of fuel.'

'I understand,' Gericke said. 'You must leave when you think fit. Your decision.'

He switched off and turned to Jean with a smile. 'And now, if you dare venture in there, I think we could all do with one of your nice hot cups of tea.'

The *Dead End* was ready and waiting, her engines turning, when Reeve went on to the bridge. Jago was bending over the chart and the admiral passed Gericke's message across.

Jago quickly worked out the target position and nodded. 'That's it, sir. We can get moving now.'

'I'd like to come with you.'

Petersen, at the wheel, glanced sideways, Jansen looked stolidly ahead. Jago said, 'Well, now, Admiral, I'm not so sure that's a good idea.'

'I could order you to take me.'

'And I could point out, with the utmost respect, that as commander of this old bucket, I'm the only one whose words count round here.'

Reeve came right down. 'All right, Lieutenant, I'm asking, not ordering. I'll even say please if that helps.'

'My command, sir. You understand that?'

'Perfectly.'

Jago nodded and turned to Jansen. 'Okay, Chief, let's move it.'

Necker's voice exploded from the radio, full of excitement. 'Come in, Gericke! Come in!'

'Receiving you loud and clear,' Gericke replied. 'What is it?'

'I can see it. I can see the gunboat, half a mile to starboard, in heavy seas, but making progress.'

'He can see the *Dead End*,' Gericke said.

'My God,' Janet breathed and her hand fastened tightly on his shoulder.

'I'll stay on the air,' Gericke said. 'Please keep close contact from now on.'

The bedroom door clicked open and Murdoch appeared, his left arm in a sling. His face was drawn and full of pain, a slightly dazed expression in the eyes. 'What is it?' he demanded.

Janet went to his side and drew him towards a chair. 'You shouldn't be up. You should have stayed in bed.'

The old man sat down heavily and it was to Gericke he spoke now. 'What is happening, Commander?'

'Lieutenant Jago has gone out there in the gunboat.'

'And the Admiral?'

'We think he has gone with them.'

'They should have taken me. I know how this game is played. They do not.' There was only resignation in Murdoch's voice now. 'God help all of them.'

The *Deutschland* wallowed in gigantic seas, plunging drunkenly down the slope of each successive wave, climbing with extreme difficulty to the crest of the next. There was two or three feet of water in the saloon and it was rising. The nuns, in Prager's charge, were secure for the moment in Berger's cabin.

On the quarterdeck, Richter and two of the men had the wheel. Berger stood at the rail, hanging on tightly as one sea after another washed in. Below, four of the crew, tethered to the mainmast, pumped frantically, a losing battle.

He looked up to the Junkers, circling overhead, his brain numbed by the incessant cold, faintly surprised to find that she was still there. Sturm stumbled out of the cabin below and hauled himself up the ladder.

The wind tore away his voice even when he put his mouth close to Berger's ear. The captain shook his head. Sturm grabbed his arm and pointed to starboard. As Berger turned, the *Dead End* came over the crest of a wave two hundred yards away, poised dramatically, then plunged down out of sight.

Every window on the bridge of the gunboat was smashed, the door ripped from its hinges and Petersen and Chaney struggled to hold the wheel between them. Reeve had jammed himself into a corner and Jago and Jansen crouched at the chart table, observing the *Deutschland*.

Jago had long since passed the point of feeling the intense cold, indeed of feeling anything. His body had ceased to exist, only the brain turned still, sharp and keen. The trip had been a nightmare. He knew that to have got this far was some kind of miracle. But that didn't matter. They were here.

'Now what?' Jansen cried into his ear.

The *Deutschland* leaned over, her lee rail under water, then swung to port again.

'I don't know,' Jago said. 'Perhaps if we go in there under the lee. If they're quick.'

This was unknown territory, a situation so extreme that it was not covered by any manual of seamanship. He was hesitating. And that was fatal. Two men at the quarterdeck rail were waving frantically. One of them, he presumed, was Berger, beckoning him to come in.

Reeve broke the spell, crying hoarsely, 'Let's go, for God's sake! Let's go!'

Jago turned to Petersen. 'Okay, straight in to her lee rail. This is crunch time.'

He went out on the bridge, followed by Reeve. Jansen went down to the deck, calling the other five crew members to him and they moved to the rail to get ready.

The *Dead End* went in fast and Chaney turned the wheel frantically at the last moment as a wave caught them. Her prow smashed into the barquentine's rail. As the wave receded, the *Deutschland* rolled to port and the *Dead End* dropped sickeningly fifteen feet below her. In the same moment a great sea rolled in across the *Deutschland*'s port rail, rising forty feet up her masts, sweeping everything before it.

Jago, on his knees in a world of green water, hanging on to the rail, felt the gunboat sag beneath him. Another wave washed in as he grabbed for Reeve, throwing both of them bodily forward. When it receded, he found himself face-down beside the admiral on the deck of the *Deutschland*.

Berger reached them a moment before the next wave struck and hauled Jago to his feet. The lieutenant grabbed at the mainmast ratlines to steady himself, turned and saw to his horror, the *Dead End* in the process of going down close to the rail, the *Deutschland*'s mizzen mast, torn from its mountings by the first enormous sea, lying across her in a tangle of wreckage.

The surviving members of his crew were already on the move, jumping for their lives to the deck of the *Deutschland*. Petersen, blood on his face, but not Chaney. Crawford, Lloyd – but no sign of Jansen.

Another wave swept in and Jago held tight, aware that the *Deutschland* was foundering beneath his feet, already up to his waist in water, as the combined weight of the mizzen mast and the gunboat pulled her over.

Richter came down the quarterdeck ladder, an axe in one hand, and started to attack the tangled web of lines that still held them tied to the mast. In a daze Jago turned to watch him. And then Reeve was tugging at his arm and pointing.

Jansen was out there, head and shoulders above the tangle where the mast had struck. He was bareheaded, one arm free. Jago stumbled towards Richter and pulled him away.

The German had him by the oilskin with one hand holding him off and Reeve was screaming into his ear. 'It's got to be done, Jago. Otherwise we all go.'

Jago turned to look out at Jansen as if in a dream, could have sworn he smiled and then quite distinctly heard the chief call, 'Get it done, Lieutenant.'

Suddenly, unable to breathe, he tore the axe from Richter's grasp. 'Damn you,' he cried. 'Damn you all to hell!'

There were tears in his eyes. The axe rose, descended, cutting deep, rose again and again in a frenzy.

The *Deutschland* lifted as the mast tore away from the gunboat and Jago was hurled on his back. He got to his feet in time to see the mast and what was left of the *Dead End* drifting rapidly away. He caught a final glimpse of Jansen, his arm moving in slow motion, as if in a kind of benediction. Then another wave rolled in and there was nothing.

Jago hurled the axe into the sea, turned and stumbled away.

At almost the same moment Necker's voice sounded on the radio again. 'She's foundering. The gunboat has foundered.'

Gericke turned and said gravely, 'I'm afraid the *Dead End* has gone down.'

Jean Sinclair slumped into a chair, stunned. Janet said frantically, 'It can't be.'

'Come in, Necker. Come in. Please confirm your last message.'

There was silence, the crackle of static. Janet said in a dull voice, 'All gone. All of them. Uncle Carey, Harry . . .'

Necker's voice cut in on her. 'Have been in communication with the *Deutschland*. The gunboat foundered under her lee rail when the mizzen mast fell on her. There were six survivors from her crew, all of whom are now safe on board *Deutschland*.'

'Six survivors,' Gericke translated rapidly.

Jean grabbed his arm. 'Who? I must know who?'

'Admiral Reeve, Lieutenant Jago and four others,' Necker continued.

Gericke turned to Jean. 'He's safe, Mrs Sinclair, for the moment at any rate, on board the *Deutschland*.' He glanced at Janet. 'And so is your lieutenant.'

Necker's voice broke in again. 'What happens now? What shall I say to the *Deutschland*?'

Gericke sat there for a long moment. Then he told him.

When he had finished, Necker said, 'Are you sure? You will see to it personally?'

'My word on it.'

'I'll tell them what you say. The trouble is, I'm already ten minutes past the critical point as regards my fuel for the return trip.'

'There is nothing more you can do here, my friend. Speak to the *Deutschland* and go home.'

There was a brief pause. Janet said, 'What's going on? What have you been saying?'

Gericke motioned her to silence. Necker's voice sounded again. 'I've spoken to Berger. Told him what you intend.'

'Has he told the Admiral?'

'Yes, he's sent a rather peculiar message for you.'

'What is it?'

'He says isn't it about time you realized you'd lost the war. Does that make any sense?'

'Of a sort. And now, my friend, you must be leaving.'

Necker said, 'Goodbye, sir. It's been an honour to know you.'

'And you, Herr Hauptmann.'

And then there was only that damned static again. Gericke switched off the set and reached for a cigarette. 'So,' he said.

'What's going on?' Janet began, but Murdoch waved her down.

'Be still, girl.' He leaned close to Gericke. 'Well, Commander?'

'Necker's had to leave. He's already dangerously short of fuel, but before he went, I asked him to send a last message to the *Deutschland*.'

'And what would that be?'

'I told them to hang on because we'd be coming for them in the lifeboat.'

'But that's impossible,' Jean said. 'She's on the beach at South Inlet.'

'And even if we could launch her again,' Murdoch said, 'she will never make it over that reef and out to sea, not as the wind is. I told you that.'

'I'm not suggesting that you launch her from South Inlet, but from here in the harbour.'

Murdoch shook his head. 'Madness. It can't be done and if it could – if you dragged that boat from one end of the island to the other, who could take her out there?' He looked down at his broken arm. 'One hand is not enough – not in weather like this.'

'I told them I would come myself,' Gericke said simply. 'I told them exactly what I intended.' He turned to the two women. 'The Admiral knows and so does Jago. They must also know that it is their only chance of life now.'

The door burst open and Lachlan ran in to collapse against the table, chest heaving as if he had run for some considerable distance.

'What is it, lad?' Murdoch demanded sternly. 'Pull yourself together now.'

'I've been up on Feith na Falla,' Lachlan said, struggling for breath. 'Along with half the town. The *Deutschland* has just come into view.'

As Janet and Gericke went over the crest and stood on top of the hill the wind almost knocked them back again. She held on to his arm tightly and Murdoch and Lachlan, Jean Sinclair between, followed after them.

There were dozens of women there many of them wearing the oilskins of absent husbands, most with shawls bound tightly around their heads against the wind.

The sea raged in fury, a boiling cauldron. Visibility, because of blown spindrift and sleet, was poor and yet they were able to see her a couple of miles out, lifting on the crest of a wave, two masts only now and the rag of a staysail still intact.

Murdoch raised his binoculars. 'Aye, she is in a bad way sure enough,' he said and then swung the binoculars slightly to the north-west.

Lachlan said, 'She is going straight on to the Washington.'

'I fear so.'

Someone in the crowd cried out and then another voice was raised – another. Women were moving forward, arms outstretched – calling out, as if by the simple power of their voices, they could haul her back. Prevent what was happening.

Gericke said nothing, but simply reached for Murdoch's binoculars and focused them on that place where the sea boiled in fury, spray lifting a hundred feet into the air over jagged rocks. The *Deutschland* was no more than three hundred yards away from the reef, drifting in fast to a rising chorus from the women on the hill.

'She'll strike,' Murdoch said, taking back the binoculars. 'Can't avoid it now.'

He stood there, legs apart, watching intently through the binoculars and when he finally turned, his face was surprisingly calm. 'The old Washington will hold her tight for a while. Time enough if we move fast.' He waved his arm at the crowd. 'Follow me – all of you!'

He went straight down the hill. Gericke and Janet, Jean Sinclair and Lachlan followed. As the word spread, others went after them until, in a few moments, the top of the hill was deserted.

The track emerged at the side of the church. When they reached that point, the old man went through the lych-gate, hurried up the path and entered the porch. A moment later, the bell started to toll.

Horst Necker burst out of cloud at eight thousand feet over the Moray Firth, in serious trouble and still descending. Things hadn't been right since leaving the *Deutschland*, but it was only within the past five minutes that the source of the trouble had become apparent – a fracture in one of the fuel pipes connecting the GMI system.

'I'll have to go down to floor level,' he said over the intercom. 'No choice. Anyone who wants to pray, start now.'

There was a chance that in this weather the *Tommis* would be too preoccupied to bother about one stray intruder on their radar screen. In fact, although Necker wasn't aware of it, Spitfires had already scrambled at Huntly airfield near Inverness and were seeking him out.

'I have a Kurier! I have a Kurier!' Kranz the rear gunner's voice sounded in his ears.

Necker went into a corkscrew instantly, the reflex of several years of combat flying coming to his aid. He was aware of the chatter of the machine-guns, glanced up to see a Spitfire zoom overhead and turn away to port, and then the entire aircraft seemed to stagger. Miraculously he was still in control.

'Everyone still in one piece?' he said over the intercom.

There was no reply. Rudi, blood on his face where a splinter had sliced his cheek, scrambled to the rear. Necker kept on going down, jinking from side to side, aware of the shock waves as cannon shell punched holes in the fuselage.

Rudi got back into his seat. 'Kranz is dead. Schmidt is unconscious. Some sort of head wound. I've put a field dressing on him.'

'Good boy. Now hang on while I show these bastards how to fly.'

He took the Junkers right down to sea level – a hazardous undertaking; with forty foot swells, it was possible to find on occasion that the seas ahead were above the plane.

And the Spitfires didn't like it, although two of them still hung on grimly for a while, even at that suicidal level.

Once, Necker looked down and observed strange waterspouts all around and wondered for a moment what they were – until the Junkers shuddered again under the impact of cannon shell.

Twenty minutes at three hundred miles an hour. Not so good with that fractured pipe. The engines would be overheating, but not long now, unless he had hopelessly miscalculated.

The aircraft staggered under a well-aimed burst of machine-gun fire. The windscreen shattered, Necker felt as if he had been kicked in the left shoulder, turned and found the port engine smoking. He feathered it at once and switched to the extinguishers. The Junkers slowed, the needle falling right down to one hundred and fifty.

He hung on grimly, still no more than fifty feet above the sea. Rudi plucked at his arm excitedly. 'They've gone, Herr Hauptmann. Cleared off. I don't understand.'

'That's what I was hoping for. We're just over a hundred miles from the coast. That's usually the limit of their radius on a sea chase.'

Rudi was staring at the blood on his glove and touched Necker's arm again gingerly. 'You're wounded.'

'So I believe,' Necker said. 'You know at flying school, they told us it was impossible to keep one of these birds in the air on one engine. Let's see if we can prove them wrong.'

'What shall I do, Herr Hauptmann?'

'Take off your belt, fasten it round the left rudder pedal.'

Rudi did as he was told and with his help, it was now possible to hold the crippled Junkers on course again.

'Pull tight, Rudi, all the way home.' Necker grinned, beginning to feel the pain in his shoulder now and not caring. 'See how simple it is when you know how? Stick with me and you'll live forever.'

When Murdoch mounted into the pulpit at St Mungo's there were something like seventy people in the congregation, mainly women, a handful of old men and children. It was strangely silent, the wind muted by the thickness of massive stone walls.

He stood for a moment, head bowed in prayer, then looked up. 'There is a boat out there on the Washington. You all know this. And the *Morag Sinclair* is beached at South Inlet. The only question is what can be done.' No one said a word. 'Commander Gericke has a solution. That we haul the *Morag* from South Inlet to Mary's Town and launch her in the harbour.'

There was a gasp from the congregation. Someone said clearly, 'Impossible.'

'Not so,' Murdoch said. 'Such a thing has been done before. In Northumbria, early in the war, at Newbiggin. Should we be capable of less? Or must those poor souls on the Washington perish?'

Katrina MacBrayne answered him in a clear savage voice. 'Bloody Germans all. Why should we lift a finger?'

'I could say that Admiral Reeve is out there, too, and five survivors from that Yankee gunboat. I could say that there are women out there, for there are. But what would be the point? I am not here to argue. I am here to tell you. Is this all your God means? Is this what our worship together has meant? You have lost a husband to the war, Katrina MacBrayne. I have given a son – a week back some of you women wept at the graveside of German boys laid to rest in our own churchyard. Pain is the same both sides. Everyone loses. But what does that prove? That there is no God in this life? No, by heaven, for he gives us choice in our actions. We choose the way, not he.'

The silence was intense; total. 'People die out there if we do nothing and who they are doesn't matter. You see the state I'm in. Not fit to handle a wheel. But when the *Morag* leaves harbour, Commander Gericke stands in my place and I, by God, will be at his right hand.' He slammed his fist down hard on the lectern. 'There has been enough of talking. I am going to South Inlet to get that boat. Those who will can follow. As for the rest – to hell with you.'

He came down out of the pulpit and marched up the aisle like a strong wind.

Barquentine *Deutschland*, 25 September 1944. At four bells in the forenoon watch in winds of hurricane strength we struck on the Washington Reef three miles north-west of Fhada in the Outer Hebrides. We are in the hands of the Almighty now and although help is promised, I fear there is little hope for us.

Fifteen

The *Deutschland* lay hard on the reef, her back broken, the fore topmast swinging down in a tangle of rigging, the sea breaking over her, one wave after another. Her stern jutted high into the air. Those who had been able to make their way aft in time, clustered on the quarterdeck. There were still several men forrard, some tied to the mainmast, others high in the rigging.

Berger, Reeve and Jago huddled together at the quarterdeck rail. Sturm hauled himself up the ladder and crouched beside them and spoke to Berger, shouting to make himself heard.

Berger's English, though far from perfect, was good enough to get by. He turned to Reeve, his mouth close to the admiral's ear. 'The women seem safe enough for the moment, in my cabin. Sturm says the bulkhead's breached but it's mainly holding together.'

'Not for long,' Reeve said as the *Deutschland* lifted, then crunched down on to the reef again.

'Gericke will come. He said he would.'

For a moment Reeve saw again the *Morag Sinclair* on the beach at South Inlet and wanted to tell the German the truth. But what would be the point? At least the end, when it came, would be quick.

Berger leaned over the rail, in spite of the breaking waves, and tried to count the men in the rigging and on the deck by the mainmast. 'Not good. It looks like we lost five when we struck.'

The telegraphist was forty feet up in the ratlines where he had climbed to avoid the worst of the waves. Jago saw him plainly. The man waved and actually managed a smile. A mountain of water curled in. When it subsided, he was gone.

'We've got to get those men out of there,' Jago shouted.

Reeve plucked at his sleeve. 'Don't be crazy. You won't last two minutes on that open deck.'

Jago shook him off, crawled to the quarterdeck ladder and descended cautiously. He hung on at the bottom as another wave washed in, holding his breath, refusing to let go. As it subsided, Richter dropped down beside him.

He carried a coil of rope over one shoulder and tied one end quickly about Jago's waist, then looped the rest around the ladder. Jago started forward and Richter paid the rope out gradually.

Jago struggled desperately alone in a world of cold green water. He lost his footing at one point, fetching up in the scuppers, but braced himself hard against the rope, and carried on, sometimes on hands and knees, until he was almost within touching distance of Petersen, tethered to the mainmast. Another wave bounced Petersen towards him on the end of his line and Jago grabbed him by the leg, then the belt, hauling himself over Petersen's prostrate body until he reached the mainmast and was able to stand.

He unfastened the rope from around his waist and tied it to the mast, then waved to Richter. The German lashed the other end securely to the ladder so that there was now a lifeline stretching to the mast three feet above deck level.

Jago gestured to the men in the rigging and they started to descend. Petersen and the others, who had been tethered to the mast, had already untied themselves and were making their way across one by one, the rest followed. Jago waited until last, made a final check to make absolutely certain the deck and rigging were clear and went after them.

In Berger's cabin, Prager and the nuns were still reasonably protected from the full fury of the storm, in spite of breaches in the bulkhead. Prager crouched against the bunk, the rum bottle in both hands. He had almost emptied it, had ceased to feel the cold.

'Not long now, Gertrude,' he whispered. 'Not long.'

Sister Angela prayed aloud at one end of the desk, hands clasped. 'Save, Lord, or else we perish. The living, the living shall praise thee. O send thy word of command to rebuke the raging winds and the roaring sea; that we, being delivered from this distress, may live to serve thee, and to glorify thy name all the days of our life.'

The door opened and Richter entered, slamming it behind him. He looked around the cabin, frowning. Sister Angela said, 'Herr Richter?'

'Where's Lotte?'

She was very cold and when she unclasped her hands, she found, to her surprise, that they were shaking. 'Lotte?' She looked around, a dazed expression on her face. 'Has anyone seen Lotte?'

Sister Brigitte was sobbing. No one seemed to have anything to say. Richter crossed to Prager and hauled him to his feet. 'You were supposed to bring them up from the saloon just before we struck. Didn't Lotte come with you?'

'Definitely,' Prager said. 'I was right behind her.'

Sister Käthe said, 'She went back.'

Richter started violently. 'That's not possible.'

'I heard her say she'd forgotten something,' Sister Käthe said vacantly. 'Then she went out.'

Richter wrenched open the door and plunged outside. He started down the companionway, but the deck and entire superstructure was buckled and twisted, the way into the saloon blocked by a tangle of wreckage.

'Lotte?' he cried. 'Lotte?' But there was no reply.

It was Jago who saw him first, crossing the deck below, using the lifeline they had rigged. He tugged at Berger's sleeve. 'What's he up to?'

'God knows,' Berger replied.

As they watched, Richter took out his gutting knife, sprung the blade, slashed at the ropes securing the cargo hatch, surprisingly still intact, and disappeared into the forrard hold.

The *Morag Sinclair* was almost at the top of the track leading up from the lifeboat station. She sat on a trolley with enormous broad iron wheels, not used since the time of the pulling lifeboat, when muscle and oars provided the power. Gericke had thought it impossible to lift her into position. But the solution was simple. They had pushed her out into the surf, as in the old days, floated her on to the trolley and hauled them in together.

Now, close to the crest of the hill, the lines were hauled by eleven farmhorses, forty-one women, eighteen children and eleven men.

Gericke and Lachlan moved behind, blocking the wheels every few yards with baulks of timber. Sleet mingled with the rain, cutting cruelly into the flesh.

Someone in a long oilskin coat fell down a yard or two ahead of Janet. She left her place on the line and ran to help, discovering, to her horror, that it was a frail, white-haired woman of seventy at least. There was blood on her hands. She looked down at it, a dazed expression on her face, then raised her long skirt and tore strips from her petticoat.

She started to wind them around her hands and Janet tried to pull her over to the side of the track. 'You must sit down.'

The old woman pushed her away. 'Leave me be, girl.' She staggered up the track and resumed her place.

'Oh God, this is madness,' Janet said to herself.

Murdoch was beside her, pulling her to her feet. 'Are you all right, girl?'

'Yes – yes, I'm fine.'

'Then why have you left your place?'

He glared at her like some Old Testament prophet about to invoke the wrath of God and smite the wrongdoer. She turned from his anger and, slipping and stumbling, ran forward along the column to resume her place beside Jean.

Time was meaningless now, a long agony as she strained, and voices swelled around her, women urging each other on, reaching beyond the agony to another place. Then, quite suddenly and to a ragged cheer, they went over the crest and started to move faster, following the path beside the railway track.

There was five to ten feet of water in the forrard hold; depending on where he stood, for it was inclined sharply to starboard. The storm lantern hung from a hook in the bulkhead, its light playing across the dark water, which erupted suddenly as Richter surfaced.

But there was no route through there. The communicating hatchway was hopelessly jammed. And even if it hadn't been, it was debatable whether he would be able to hold his breath for long enough to get through all that wreckage under water.

So there was only one way, it seemed. He rapped at the bulkhead with his knuckles. Still reasonably sound. It would take time. But then he didn't really have anywhere else to go. He picked up the two-handed fire-axe he'd brought down with him and swung it over his head.

The *Morag Sinclair* was half way along the track beside the railway line, high up on the spine of the island, progress slowing a little as they moved, totally exposed, into the full fury of the wind.

The scene behind was like a battlefield, people huddled beside the track at intervals where they had dropped, totally exhausted. It was a nightmare that couldn't be allowed to continue, Janet knew that, and yet still she bowed her back beside Jean, the rope biting cruelly into her shoulder and her hands dripping blood.

When she looked out over the sea, it seemed more troubled than ever, a vast wash of foam, a sky of writhing black smoke that boiled down as if it would envelop the earth.

Ahead of her, old Dougal Sinclair stumbled out of the line, crossed the railway track and fell down in the heather. Janet relinquished her grip and went after him wearily. He looked very peaceful lying there on his back, the blue eyes staring up into the dark sky. It was a moment or two before she realized how fixed that stare was and quickly unbuttoned his oilskin and jacket, reaching inside to feel for the heart.

Gericke dropped to one knee beside her. 'What is it?' he demanded. 'Are you all right?'

'He's dead,' she said bitterly. 'Are you satisfied now?'

Reeve crouched against the quarterdeck rail of the *Deutschland*, his pocket telescope raised, and looked towards Fhada. 'No good,' he cried to Jago. 'They can probably see us from up there on Feith na Falla, but I can't even see the island.'

'They're not coming, Admiral. Nobody's coming. We've had it.'

At least in the Solomons it had been warm. He closed his eyes and a wave washed in, lifting the *Deutschland* bodily and crashing her down again.

'Christ Jesus, but I thought we were going straight over the edge of the reef that time,' Reeve said.

Berger shouted in his ear. 'She's breaking up now. Next time that happens, or the time after, she comes apart at the seams.'

Reeve's face was bleached from the constant salt water, wrinkled like a fish's belly, and he looked a hundred years old. Jago leaned close. 'You wanted action, Admiral. You got it in spades. What a way to go.'

Richter had just smashed his way through from the forrard hold when the *Deutschland* lifted and started to roll. *Oh God, he thought, this is it.*

She settled on the rocks again, with a nasty grating sound as more planks tore loose. He waited for the swirling water to subside. Strangely enough he wasn't afraid, consumed totally by a passionate need to know what had happened to Lotte.

He squeezed past the mainmast mounting and the pump, found a nail on which to hang the storm lantern and started to attack the bulkhead which would give him access to the aft hold.

The *Morag Sinclair* was beginning to move fast now as the track sloped down to cross the railway line above Mary's Town, and suddenly the situation was totally changed. The forty or so people who were left on the lines, their roles reversed, were hanging on grimly to stop the boat running away from them on its trolley.

Murdoch hurried alongside, shouting instructions to Gericke and Lachlan as they attempted to slow her by blocking the wheels with the same baulks of timber they had used at South Inlet.

The *Morag* was really moving – rocking alarmingly on her trolley, swinging from side to side, leaving a trail of smashed windows as she coasted down the High Street. She emerged on to the front by the pier at some considerable speed, Gericke and Lachlan running alongside, frantically jamming the wheels with their timber pieces and slowly and very, very gradually, she started to slide to a halt.

There was the silence of total exhaustion. Murdoch heaved himself up the ladder and over the side and nodded to Gericke. 'You, too, Commander.'

Gericke followed him, aware with something of a surprise, that his arms were having difficulty in holding the weight of his body.

Murdoch looked out over the crowd. 'What is wrong with you, then? She's only fifteen tons. One more heave now.'

No one made a sound and then, somehow, women who had collapsed were on their feet again, reaching wearily for their lines. They dragged the lifeboat forward to the top of the stone slipway at the head of the pier and ran her down into the harbour.

Watching her there, grinding against the pier, Janet couldn't quite take it all in. She was aware of Jean crying helplessly beside her, tears pouring down her cheeks, heard Gericke say, 'Get those petrol drums along here quickly now,' for they had emptied the tanks at South Inlet to lighten her.

Murdoch, in the aft cockpit, was calling up to the pier. 'Lachlan, are you there, boy? No time for your sick belly now. I need you – and you, Hamish, and Francis Patterson. Are you still game?'

They went forward, those old men, even James Sinclair, whose brother lay dead back beside the track. Janet turned, started to run back up the High Street, finding a new strength in her purpose, never stopping until she reached the cottage. She went inside, snatched her medical bag and ran back down the hill to the harbour.

She pushed her way on to the pier through the crowd and saw them on deck below, fastening their lifejackets, each man in yellow oilskins, even Gericke. She went down the stone steps to the lower landing and scrambled over the rail.

Murdoch turned to confront her. 'And what is this, girl?'

'There are six of you, Murdoch. Five and a half if you consider that arm of yours. You should crew eight.'

Gericke got between them, his hands on her shoulders. 'This is no job for a woman, Janet. You must see that.'

'Who got your bloody boat here for you?' She held up her medical bag. 'I'm not here as a woman. I'm here as a doctor. And you might be damned glad to have me along before this is through.'

Gericke opened his mouth to reply, but Murdoch pulled him out of the way. 'No time to argue. You go to hell your own way, girl. Get down in the cockpit.' He gave her a push. 'You'll find an oilskin and lifejacket. Put them on and stay out of the way.'

Gericke's face was pale. He hesitated, then moved to the wheel. A second later, Lachlan, who was acting as bowman, had cast off and they were moving away from the pier out into the harbour.

At the quarterdeck rail, Jago, Reeve and Berger still huddled together. The *Deutschland* had eased herself over a little further to starboard and seemed to lift now with each wave.

It was Reeve who, turning to look in the direction of Fhada for the hundredth time, caught the first glimpse of the *Morag Sinclair* a mile to starboard.

'She's coming!' he cried, tugging frantically at Jago's arm. 'I see her.'

Jago pulled himself to his feet, holding on to the rail and peered into the rain through swollen eyelids. 'No,' he said hoarsely. 'You're imagining things.'

But Reeve cried out again excitedly, clutching at Berger. This time the lifeboat was plain and a sudden cheering broke out amongst the men assembled on the quarterdeck.

Berger waved Sturm across. 'Go down to my cabin and bring up the Sisters.'

Sturm crawled away wearily. At that moment another wave thundered against the *Deutschland* sliding her bodily across the reef. Part of the prow broke off and the storm staysail, intact all this time, fluttered away like a great bird.

'They'd better hurry,' Jago said. 'From the feel of that last one, I'd say we don't have too much time.'

Richter had hacked his way through three bulkheads and scrambled into the aft hold as the men on deck started to cheer. He hesitated, put down the axe, turned and crawled back through the hole he had just made. He clung on to the base of the mainmast as the ship moved again on the reef, but emerged from the forrard hatch a few moments later in time to catch a glimpse of the *Morag Sinclair* on the crest of a wave some distance away.

How much time did he have? Impossible to know. He dropped down into the hold, forced his way back through the water, negotiating the holes he had made in the bulkheads, until he stood again in the aft hold.

At some time in the *Deutschland*'s earlier history, the hold had been halved to make room for the additional cabin accommodation. The intervening bulkhead having been added at a later date, it had nothing like the strength of construction of the ones he had already negotiated. He picked up his axe, waded towards it and started to attack it furiously.

★　★　★

The *Morag Sinclair* took water constantly, green sheets passing over her from stem to stern, exploding into the aft cockpit with stunning force. Janet was terrified. The waves seemed so enormous that each time they attempted to scale one, the task seemed an impossibility, the *Morag* climbing in slow motion. When she swooped down the other side into the trough, it was as if she never intended to come up again.

But Gericke seemed unperturbed as he wrestled with the wheel, Murdoch at his shoulder.

Lifeboatmen, as a rule, don't wear lifelines, believing them to be too constricting in an emergency. So it was that at one moment, as Lachlan turned from beside her, reaching up to the rail and slipped, a sea washed in, taking him out with it over the starboard rail. Janet screamed and as Gericke glanced over his shoulder in alarm, the starboard rail dipped under and the boy miraculously floated inboard.

Murdoch reached down and shook him like a rat. 'Lifeline!' he shouted. 'Get a lifeline on!' He turned to Hamish MacDonald. 'Lifelines for everyone. My orders – like it or not.' He crouched down over Janet. 'You too, girl.'

She reached for the line that was passed to her and had barely hooked herself on when disaster struck. The *Morag* hovered on the crest of a mountainous wave, broached as she went down. At the same moment, the wind gusted in fury, striking her starboard bow. She capsized.

To Janet, the world was stinking green water, washing over, filling heart and mind and brain, kicking and struggling in a desperate desire to live. The *Morag* was partially under, still pushing forward, screws turning.

Slowly, she righted herself. Janet was aware of Gericke clinging to the wheel with one hand, reaching out to her with the other, Murdoch pulling himself up beside them. Lachlan was safe, Hamish MacDonald, Sinclair. But Francis Patterson had gone.

From then on, so vicious was the weather, so impenetrable the curtain of rain and sleet and flying spindrift that they caught no further sight of the wreck until they lurched over the top of an enormous wave and saw her a hundred and fifty yards away, the survivors clustered on the quarterdeck, waving.

'Now what?' Gericke demanded.

'Take your time, boy,' Murdoch said. 'And let me work this out.'

Richter broke through the final bulkhead. He crawled into the saloon. It was dark in there, only the gurgle of the water, the howling of the gale outside. As with the rest of the ship, it was steeply inclined, the starboard cabins under water.

'Lotte?' he called.

There was no reply. Could be none. He had been a fool to think otherwise. He floundered through the water, crawled up the slope to where the door of her cabin swung crazily, braced himself in the entrance and raised the lamp.

She lay trapped across the bunk, a tangle of wreckage across her stomach and legs. Her face was very pale, her eyes closed, but now she opened them slowly.

'Helmut,' she whispered. 'I knew you would come.'

'What happened? Why did you come back?'

'Your ring, Helmut. I'd hidden it here under the mattress in the corner of my bunk. I forgot it when we were ordered on deck. Wasn't that silly of me?'

He was already heaving on the beam, straining with all his strength, but it refused to budge. 'How strange,' she said. 'I've been so cold for days, so very cold, yet now, I can't feel a thing.'

The *Deutschland* shook herself and started to move as if ready now to ease off the reef. He wrenched frantically at the beam again, then said, 'I must get help, Lotte. I'll be back in a little while. I'll have to take the lantern, but don't be afraid.'

'You won't leave me?'

'Never again. Remember my promise?'

He left her there and ploughed back through the water, working his way from hold to hold. The *Deutschland* was in constant motion, nosing forward, slithering further over the edge of the Washington, her prow dipping.

Richter hauled himself up the ladder in time to see the *Morag* moving in. The nuns were already making their way across from the shelter of Berger's cabin, the men on the quarterdeck crowding down the ladder.

There were cries of fear and one of the women screamed high and shrill as the *Deutschland* moved again with a terrible rending and tearing sound.

Richter had to hang on tight to the ladder for a moment. He dropped down, waist-deep in water, waded towards the hole in the bulkhead and climbed through. The *Deutschland* was in constant motion now, water swirling all around him, but when he reached the saloon, there was that strange eerie quiet. And she was still there waiting for him when he went into the cabin. He hung up the lantern and sat down beside her.

'You came back.'

'Of course.'

'What's happening, Helmut?'

'They're coming for us, Lotte. They finally got here.' He took her hand and held it tightly.

To Murdoch, debating on the best way to go in, that sudden tremble as the *Deutschland* slid towards the edge was enough.

'She's going, lad, she's going!' He slapped Gericke on the shoulder. 'Give her everything you've got, full power and straight in over the rail. Two minutes is all we get.'

Gericke boosted power, the *Morag* surged forward, catching even those on the quarterdeck by surprise, slicing in across the rail until her bows rested on the deck.

There was no need to say a word for already the nuns were scurrying from Berger's cabin, shepherded by Sturm, and Prager and Reeve, Jago and the rest of them, were getting off the quarterdeck fast.

The *Deutschland* shook herself again and men cried out in fear, Sister Käthe screaming, falling across the rail. Janet reached over, dragged her bodily, pushed her down into the cockpit and the cabin.

'She'll take us with her, boy!' Murdoch shouted. 'Reverse those engines. Get ready!' He waved his arm and called furiously, 'Come on, damn you! She's going!'

There was a final mad scramble, men vaulting over the rails in panic, Berger last of all, the ship's log and his personal journal in an oilskin wrapper under his arm. Gericke reversed the engines full power as the *Deutschland* sagged again, and the *Morag* shot away.

Sister Angela crouched in a corner of the small cabin. She tried to get up, peering at the faces crowded around her. 'Lotte?' she said. 'Where's Lotte?'

There was no reply – could be none. She turned, grabbed Janet's arm fiercely and said in English. 'Lotte isn't here – neither is Herr Richter. They must still be on board.'

Janet scrambled out of the cabin into the cockpit. Jago was there, Reeve above him crouched beside Gericke and Murdoch. She shook Jago's arm. 'There's still someone on board.'

He seemed to find difficulty in speaking. 'Not possible.'

She reached up and pulled at Gericke's oilskin. 'Paul – there's still someone on board.'

He glanced down at her, startled. In the same moment, the *Deutschland* started to slide off the reef.

Berger, at the starboard rail, had tears in his eyes. As water boiled around her, his hand went up in a brief salute. For a moment, the main topmast was visible, then that too dropped beneath the surface and there was nothing – only the sea's leavings. A few planks, a tangle of rope, a barrel spinning.

Gericke, his face grave, turned the wheel, taking the *Morag* away from the Washington, round in a great curve, ready to start the slow and painful fight back through those mountainous seas to Fhada.

Barquentine *Deutschland*, 25 September 1944. At three bells of the afternoon watch with the *Deutschland* sinking beneath us, the sixteen survivors of her original complement were snatched from the Washington Reef by the lifeboat *Morag Sinclair*, Coxswain Murdoch Macleod and Korvettenkapitän Paul Gericke of the Kriegsmarine combining in a remarkable feat of seamanship. Afterwards they conveyed us to the neighbouring island of Fhada through heavy and mountainous seas. I was distressed to learn that in one way or another seven people gave their lives to save ours. Words, for the first time, fail me. So ends this log.
Erich Berger, Master

Sixteen

Reeve poured himself a large Scotch and drank it slowly. He was tired right through, more conscious of his age than he had ever been. The wind hammered against the roof of the cottage, and he winced.

'No more, please,' he whispered. 'Enough is enough.'

He hobbled painfully across to his desk. What he needed now was sleep, but first there was work to be done. He reached for his pen and opened his journal. There was a knock at the door and Harry Jago entered, struggling to close it again against the wind. His face was swollen, the flesh split in a dozen places. Like Reeve, he seemed to find difficulty in walking.

'You don't look too good, Harry.' The admiral pushed the bottle of Scotch across the desk, 'Help yourself.'

Jago went into the kitchen and came back with a glass. When he spoke, it was very slowly. 'I feel like a dead man walking.'

'I know what you mean. How's Janet?'

'Indestructible. It's like a field hospital at Fhada House, and she hasn't stopped since we got in.'

'She's had plenty of practice. It's been a long war,' the admiral said. 'Still foul out there?'

'Nothing like as bad. Winds seven to eight, I'd say, and falling a little. She'll have blown herself out by morning.'

He emptied his glass and Reeve filled it again. 'I've been in touch with Murray on the radio. Chaotic over there apparently, but he's going to send a boat in the morning. Says he'll try and make it himself.'

'What about the survivors? What will happen to them?'

'I don't know. Internment for the nuns, prison camp for Berger and his men.' There was a long pause and Jago stared down into his glass. 'You don't like that, do you?'

'It just doesn't have any meaning for me any more. Not any of it.'

'I know how you feel. All that bloody way and they nearly made it.'

The Scotch by now was dulling the pain. 'And Gericke?' Jago asked.

'What about him? There's still a war on, Harry.'

'I know,' Jago said. 'There always is some place. Does he go back in his cell?'

'That isn't my decision. Jean's the civil power here, you know that.'

Jago emptied his glass at a swallow. 'Well, I think I'll get back up to the house and see how my boys are doing.'

'Then bed, Harry. Go to bed.' Reeve managed a smile. 'That's an order.'

'Admiral.' Jago drew himself up and managed a salute.

He had almost reached the door, had his hand out, when Reeve said softly, 'Harry?'

Jago turned. 'Yes, sir.'

'All of a sudden I feel old, Harry. Too damned old. I just wanted to tell somebody that.'

There was still quite a swell in the harbour as Gericke went along the pier, head down against the rain. The *Morag Sinclair* danced at her moorings, a brave sight in her blue and white paint. Only a closer inspection revealed the ferocious battering she had taken from the sea.

He stood there, hands thrust deep into the pockets of the reefer someone had given him, and suddenly he heard himself hailed. He turned and saw Murdoch on the lower landing further along the pier, standing beside the *Katrina*.

As Gericke went down the stone steps, Lachlan came out of the wheelhouse. There was an oil drum on deck and he levered it over on to the landing with an ease which indicated that it was empty.

'What's this?' Gericke asked.

'Lachlan and I have been filling the *Katrina*'s tanks,' the old man said. 'That she may be ready for sea if wanted.'

The boy nodded to Gericke. 'Commander.'

'I didn't have a chance to tell you before, but you were fine out there, Lachlan.' Gericke held out his hand. 'I was proud to know you.'

Lachlan flushed crimson, stared at the hand for a moment, grabbed it briefly, then turned and hurried away.

'There is good stuff there, I am thinking,' Murdoch said. 'Too good to be off to bloody war again in a few days.' He started to fill his pipe, awkwardly because of his broken arm. 'Have you spoken with Janet since returning?'

'She's had her hands more than full.'

'Things must have eased considerably for her by now.' The old man turned and looked out to sea through the driving rain. 'Still rough, but not too rough.'

'I suppose not.'

Murdoch nodded. 'Go see her now, boy.'

'Yes, I believe I will.'

He started to walk away and Murdoch called, 'Commander.'

'Yes?'

'Good luck to you.'

For a long, long moment they looked at each other, then Gericke turned and hurried away along the pier.

As he went into the kitchen of Fhada House, Jean Sinclair turned from the stove with a bowl of hot water. 'Hello,' she said. 'Are you looking for Janet?'

'Yes. Is she available?'

'Pretty busy last time I saw her. She has one of the sailors from the *Deutschland* on the table in the dining-room. A broken arm.'

'And the rest?'

'Mostly sleeping now. I think every bed in the house must be in use.' She held up the bowl. 'Sorry, I'll have to move on. Janet's waiting for this.'

He opened the door. 'And Captain Berger. Where is he?'

'First bedroom on the right, top of the stairs.'

She went away quickly and Gericke climbed the stairs. He paused at the door she had indicated, knocked and entered. Johann Sturm and Leading Seaman Petersen lay on top of the bed, side by side, sleeping heavily. Berger was seated in a chair at a small table by the window, his head resting on his arms.

The log of the *Deutschland* was open before him. Gericke stood at his shoulder for a moment and read its last entry, then turned and tiptoed out.

As the door clicked behind him, Berger stirred and looked up, peering around the room through swollen eyelids. 'Who's there?' he called hoarsely.

But there was no one. No one at all. His head sank down on his arms. He slept again.

Reeve was writing in his journal with care and considerable precision, mainly because he was more than a little drunk, when the door opened violently and Janet came in, Jago at her heels.

'Is Paul here?'

He laid down his pen and regarded her with drunken gravity. 'Ah, Gericke, you mean. I didn't realize you two were on firstname terms.'

He was mocking her and she flared angrily. 'Has he been here?'

'Half an hour ago. Maybe a little longer. As a matter of fact we had a drink together, then he asked if he could leave something for you.'

'What?' she demanded.

'He said it was a private matter. I think you'll find it in the bedroom, whatever it is.'

She went out quickly into the hall and opened her bedroom door. The Knight's Cross with Oak Leaves for a second award lay, neatly arranged, on her pillow. She stared down at it, stupefied for a moment, then picked it up and ran back into the livingroom.

'Uncle Carey!' She held it out to him, her voice breaking.

Reeve nodded. 'Now I understand. On his way out he said tell her she's earned it.'

There was a knock at the door and Murdoch moved in. 'Ah, there you are, Admiral.'

'And what can I do for you?'

'A matter of official business only. The *Katrina* appears to be missing from her moorings.'

'Is that a fact!' Reeve said. 'It's a damned good thing I'm insured.'

Janet ran out of the door. Jago turned to Reeve, leaning on the desk. 'Are you going to notify Mallaig? They'll get to him soon enough up there in the Minch.'

'Very unfortunate, Harry, but the radio appears to have packed in since I last talked to Murray. Valve gone, I think, and I don't have any spares. Just have to wait till they get here tomorrow. Nothing else to be done.'

Jago took a long, long breath, then turned and went out. Murdoch said gravely, 'Is that good Scotch you have there in that bottle, Carey Reeve?'

'And another in the cupboard when we've finished that. I've been holding out on you.'

'Later, then, I will come back if I may. But now, I must see to my people.'

He walked out. Reeve poured himself another whisky and resumed his writing.

. . . and so I see, when all is said and done, that this has been an old story. Murdoch, Harry Jago and Gericke – men against the sea, who have won this time. But in the end, what is the nature of their achievement . . .?

God, but he was tired – more tired than he had ever been. The wind rattled the window as if trying to get in, but it could not touch him now. He pillowed his head on one arm for a moment and was instantly asleep, the pen still firm in his good hand and resting on that final entry.

NIGHT OF
THE FOX

1

The Romans used to think that the souls of the departed stayed near their tombs. It was easy to believe that on a cold March morning, with a sky so black that it was as if night was about to fall.

I stood in the granite archway and looked in at the graveyard. The notice board said *Parish Church of St. Brelade* and the place was crammed with headstones and tombs, and here and there a granite cross reared up. There was a winged angel on the far side, I noticed that, and then thunder rumbled on the horizon and rain swept in across the bay.

The porter at the hotel had given me an umbrella and I put it up and ventured in. On Sunday in Boston I'd never heard of the British Channel Islands off the coast of France or the Island of Jersey. Now it was Thursday and here I was having traveled halfway round the world to seek the final answer to something that had taken three years out of my life.

The church was very old and built of granite. I moved toward it through the tombstones, pausing to look out over the bay. The tide was out and there was a fine sweep of golden sands extending to a concrete seawall and I could see my hotel.

I heard voices and, turning, saw two men in cloth caps, sacks over their shoulders, crouching under a cypress tree by the far wall of the graveyard. They stood up and moved away, laughing together as if at some joke, and I noticed they were carrying spades. They disappeared around the back of the church and I crossed to the wall.

There was a freshly dug grave, covered with a tarpaulin although the tree gave it some protection from the rain. I don't think I've ever felt so excited. It was as if it had been waiting for me and I turned and moved through the headstones to the entrance of the church, opened the door and went inside.

I'd expected a place of darkness and gloom, but the lights were on and it was really very beautiful, the vaulted ceiling unusual in that it was constructed of granite, no evidence of wooden beams there at all. I walked toward the altar and stood for a moment, looking around me, aware of the quiet. There was the click of a door opening and closing. A man approached.

He had white hair and eyes of the palest blue. He wore a black cassock and carried a raincoat over one arm. His voice was dry and very old and there was a hint of Irish to it when he spoke. 'Can I help you?'

'Are you the rector?'

'Oh, no.' He smiled good-humoredly. 'They put me out to grass a long time ago. My name is Cullen. Canon Donald Cullen. You're an American?'

'That's right.' I shook hands. He had a surprisingly firm grip. 'Alan Stacey.'

'Your first visit to Jersey?'

'Yes,' I said. 'Until a few days ago I never knew the place existed. Like most Americans, I'd only heard of *New* Jersey.'

He smiled. We moved toward the door and he carried on, 'You've chosen a bad time of the year for your first visit. Jersey can be one of the most desirable places on earth, but not usually during March.'

'I didn't have much choice,' I said. 'You're burying someone here today. Harry Martineau.'

He had started to pull on his raincoat and paused in surprise. 'That's right. I'm performing the ceremony myself, as a matter of fact. Two o'clock this afternoon. Are you a relative?'

'Not exactly, although I sometimes feel as if I am. I'm an assistant professor of philosophy at Harvard. I've been working on a biography of Martineau for the past three years.'

'I see.' He opened the door and we went out into the porch.

'Do you know much about him?' I asked.

'Very little, besides the extraordinary way he met his end.'

'And the even more extraordinary circumstance of his last rites,' I said. 'After all, Canon, it isn't often you get to bury a man forty years after his death.'

The bungalow was at the other end of St. Brelade's Bay, close to L'Horizon Hotel where I was staying. It was small and unpretentious, but the living room was surprisingly large, comfortable and cluttered, two walls lined with books. Sliding windows opened to a terrace and a small garden, the bay beyond. The tide was rushing in, the wind lifting the sea into whitecaps, and rain rattled against the window.

My host came in from the kitchen and put a tray on a small table by the fire. 'I hope you don't mind tea.'

'Tea will be fine.'

'My wife was the coffee drinker in the family, but she died three years ago. I could never abide the stuff myself.'

He filled my cup and pushed it toward me as I sat down on the other side of the table from him. The silence hung between us. He raised his cup and drank very precisely, waiting.

'You're very comfortable here,' I said.

'Yes,' he said. 'I do very well. Lonely, of course. The great weakness of all human beings, Professor Stacey, is that we all need somebody.' He refilled his cup. 'I spent three years in Jersey as a boy and grew to love the place very much.'

'That would be easy enough.' I looked out at the bay. 'It's very beautiful.'

'I returned on holiday on many occasions. When I retired, I was a canon of Winchester Cathedral. Our only son moved to Australia many years ago, so . . .' He shrugged. 'Jersey seemed an obvious choice as my wife had owned this bungalow for many years. A legacy from an uncle.'

'That must have been convenient.'

'Yes, especially with the housing laws the way they are here.' He put down his cup, took out a pipe and started to fill it from a worn leather pouch. 'So,' he said briskly. 'Now you know all about me. What about you and friend Martineau?'

'Do you know much about him?'

'I'd never heard of the man until a few days ago when my good friend, Dr. Drayton, came to see me, explained the circumstances in which the body had been recovered and told me it was being shipped from London for burial here.'

'You're aware of the manner of his death?'

'In a plane crash in 1945.'

'January 1945, to be precise. The RAF had a unit called the Enemy Aircraft Flight during the Second World War. They operated captured German planes to evaluate performance and so on.'

'I see.'

'Harry Martineau worked for the Ministry of Economic Warfare. In January 1945, he went missing when traveling as an observer in an Arado 96, a German two-seater training plane being operated by the Enemy Aircraft Flight. It was always believed to have gone down in the sea.'

'And?'

'Two weeks ago it was found during excavations in an Essex marsh. Work on the building site was halted while an RAF unit recovered what was left.'

'And Martineau and the pilot were still inside?'

'What was left of them. For some reason the authorities kept a low profile on the affair. News didn't filter through to me until last weekend. I caught the first plane out. Arrived in London on Monday morning.'

He nodded. 'You say you've been working on a biography of him. What makes him so special? As I told you, I'd never even heard his name before.'

'Nor had the general public,' I said. 'But in the thirties, in academic circles . . .' I shrugged. 'Bertrand Russell considered him one of the most brilliant and innovative minds in his field.'

'Which was?'

'Moral philosophy.'

'An interesting study,' the canon said.

'For a fascinating man. He was born in Boston. His father was in shipping. Wealthy, but not outrageously so. His mother, although born in New York, was of German parentage. Her father taught for some years at Columbia then returned to Germany in 1925 as professor of surgery at Dresden University.' I got up and walked to the window, thinking about it as I peered out. 'Martineau went to Harvard, did a doctorate at Heidelberg, was a Rhodes scholar at Oxford, a Fellow of Trinity College and Croxley Professor of Moral Philosophy by the age of thirty-eight.'

'A remarkable achievement,' Cullen said.

I turned. 'But you don't understand. Here was a man who was questioning everything. Turning his whole field upside down. And then the Second World War broke out and the rest is silence. Until now, that is.'

'Silence?'

'Oh, he left Oxford, we know that. Worked for the Ministry of Defence and then the Ministry of Economic Warfare, as I told you. Many academics did that. But the tragedy was that he seems to have stopped working altogether in his chosen field. No more papers and the book he'd been writing for years was left unfinished. We've got the manuscript at Harvard. Not a line written after September nineteen thirty-nine.'

'How very strange.'

I went back and sat down. 'We have all his papers in the Harvard Library. What really intrigued me on going through them was a personal thing.'

'And what was that?'

'When I finished high school at eighteen, instead of going straight to Harvard I joined the Marines. Did a year in Vietnam until a bullet in the left kneecap sent me home for good. Martineau did the same sort of thing. Joined the American Expeditionary Force in the last few months of the First World War, underage, I might say, and served as an infantry private in the trenches in Flanders. I was fascinated by the fact that in turning from what we'd gone through, we'd both sought another answer in the same way.'

'From the hell of war to the cool recesses of the mind.' Canon Cullen knocked out his pipe in the hearth. 'I can't remember who said that. Some war poet or other.'

'God save me from those,' I said. 'Nam cost me a permanently stiff left leg, three years in the hands of psychiatrists and a failed marriage.'

The clock on the mantelpiece struck twelve. Cullen got up, moved to the sideboard and poured whisky from a cut glass decanter into two glasses. He brought them back and handed me one. 'I was in Burma during the war myself, which was bad enough.' He sipped a little whisky and put down his glass on the hearth. 'And so, Professor, what about the rest?'

'The rest?'

'Priests are supposed to be ingenuous souls who know nothing of the reality of life,' he said in that dry, precise voice. 'Rubbish, of course. Our business is confession, human pain, misery. I know people, Professor, after fifty-two years as an ordained priest, and one learns to know when they are not telling you everything.' He put a match to his pipe and puffed away. 'Which applies to you, my friend, unless I'm very much mistaken.'

I took a deep breath. 'He was in uniform when they found him.'

He frowned. 'But you said he was working for the Ministry of Economic Warfare.'

'German Luftwaffe uniform,' I said. 'Both he and the pilot.'

'Are you certain?'

'I have a friend from the Vietnam days in the Marines called Tony Bianco. He's with the CIA at our embassy in London. They get to know things, these people. I had problems with the Ministry of Defence the other day. They were giving very little away about Martineau and that plane.'

'Your friend checked up for you?'

'And found out something else. The newspaper report about that Arado being from the Enemy Aircraft Flight. That's suspect, too.'

'Why?'

'Because they always carried RAF rondels. And according to Bianco's informant, this one still had Luftwaffe markings.'

'And you say you couldn't get any more information from official sources?'

'None at all. Ridiculous though it may seem, Martineau and that flight are still covered by some wartime security classification.'

The old man frowned. 'After forty years?'

'There's more,' I said. 'I had this kind of problem last year when I was researching. Ran into roadblocks, if you know what I mean. I discovered that Martineau was awarded the Distinguished Service Order in January 1944. One of those awards that appears in the list without explanation. No information about what he'd done to earn it.'

'But that's a military award and a very high one at that. Martineau was a civilian.'

'Apparently civilians have qualified on rare occasions, but it all begins to fit with a story I heard when researching at Oxford three years ago. Max Kubel, the nuclear physicist, was a professor at Oxford for many years and a friend of Martineau's.'

'Now I *have* heard about him,' Cullen said. 'He was a German Jew, was he not, who managed to get out before the Nazis could send him to a concentration camp?'

'He died in nineteen seventy-three,' I said. 'But I managed to interview the old man who'd been his manservant at his Oxford college for more than thirty years. He told me that during the big German offensive in nineteen forty that led to Dunkirk, Kubel was held by the Gestapo under house arrest at Freiburg, just across the German border from France. An SS officer arrived with an escort to take him to Berlin.'

'So?'

'The old boy, Howard his name was, said that Kubel told him years ago that the SS officer was Martineau.'

'Did you believe him?'

'Not at the time. He was ninety-one and senile, but one has to remember Martineau's background. Quite obviously he could have passed for a German any time he wanted. He not only had the language but had the family background.'

Cullen nodded. 'So, in view of more recent developments you're prepared to give more credence to that story?'

'I don't know what to think anymore.' I shrugged. 'Nothing makes any sense. Martineau and Jersey, for example. To the best of my knowledge he never visited the place and he died five months before it was freed from Nazi occupation.' I swallowed the rest of my whisky. 'Martineau has no living relatives, I know that because he never married, so who the hell is this Dr. Drayton of yours? I know one thing. He must have one hell of a pull with the Ministry of Defence to get them to release the body to him.'

'You're absolutely right.' Canon Cullen poured me another Scotch whisky. 'In all respects, but one.'

'And what would that be?'

'Dr. Drayton,' he said, 'is not a he, but a she. Dr. Sarah Drayton, to be precise.' He raised his glass to toast me.

I am the resurrection and the life, saith the Lord: he that believeth in me, though he were dead, yet shall he live.

Cullen sounded even more Irish as he lifted his voice bravely against the heavy rain. He wore a dark cloak over his vestments and one of the funeral men stood beside him holding an umbrella. There was only one mourner, Sarah Drayton, standing on the other side of the open grave, an undertaker behind her with another umbrella.

She looked perhaps forty-eight or fifty although, as I discovered later, she was sixty, small and with a figure still trim in the black two-piece suit and hat. Her hair was short, expertly cut and iron gray. She was not in any way conventionally beautiful, with a mouth that was rather too large and hazel eyes above wide cheekbones. It was a face of considerable character with an impression of someone who had seen the best and worst that life had to offer, and there was an extraordinary stillness to her. If I had seen her only in passing, I'd have turned for a second look. She was that sort of woman.

She ignored me completely and I stayed back under what shelter the trees provided, getting thoroughly damp in spite of my umbrella. Cullen concluded the service, then moved toward her and spoke briefly. She kissed him on the cheek and he turned and moved away toward the church, followed by the funeral men.

She stayed there for a while at the graveside and the two gravediggers waited respectfully a few yards away. She still ignored me as I moved forward, picked up a little damp soil and threw it down on the coffin.

'Dr. Drayton?' I said. 'I'm sorry to intrude. My name is Alan Stacey. I wonder if I might have a few words? I'm not a reporter, by the way.'

Her voice was deeper than I had expected, calm and beautifully modulated. She said, without looking at me, 'I know very well who you are, Professor Stacey. I've been expecting you at any time these past three years.' She turned and smiled and suddenly looked absolutely enchanting and about twenty years of age. 'We really should get out of this rain before it does us both a mischief. That's sound medical advice and for free. My car is in the road outside. I think you'd better come back for a drink.'

The house was no more than five minutes away, reached by a narrow country lane along which she drove expertly at considerable speed. It stood in about an acre of well-tended garden surrounded by beech trees through which one could see the bay far below. It was Victorian from the look of it, with long narrow windows and green shutters at the front and a portico at the entrance. The door was opened instantly as we went up the steps by a tall, somber-looking man in a black alpaca jacket. He had silver hair and wore steel-rimmed glasses.

'Ah, Vito,' she said as he took her coat. 'This is Professor Stacey.'

'Professore.' He bowed slightly.

'We'll have coffee in the library later,' she said. 'I'll see to the drinks.'

'Of course, Contessa.'

He turned away and paused and spoke to her in Italian. She shook her head and answered fluently in the same language. He went through a door at the rear of the hall.

'Contessa?' I asked.

'Oh, don't listen to Vito.' She dismissed my query politely, but firmly. 'He's a terrible snob. This way.'

The hall was cool and pleasant. Black and white tiled floor, a curving staircase and two or three oil paintings on the wall. Eighteenth-century seascapes. She opened a double mahogany door and led the way into a large library. The walls were lined with books, and French windows looked out to the garden. There was an Adam fireplace with a fire burning brightly in the basket grate and a grand piano, the top crammed with photos, mostly in silver frames.

'Scotch all right for you?' she asked.

'Fine.'

She crossed to a sideboard and busied herself at the drinks tray. 'How did you know who I was?' I asked. 'Canon Cullen?'

'I've known about you since you started work on Harry.' She handed me a glass.

'Who told you?'

'Oh, friends,' she said. 'From the old days. The kind who get to know things.'

It made me think of Tony Bianco, my CIA contact at the embassy, and I was immediately excited. 'Nobody seems to want to answer any of my questions at the Ministry of Defence.'

'I don't suppose they would.'

'And yet they release the body to you. You must have influence?'

'You could say that.' She took a cigarette from a silver box, lit it and sat in a wing chair by the fire, crossing slim legs. 'Have you ever heard of SOE, Professor?'

'Of course,' I said. 'Special Operations Executive. Set up by British Intelligence in 1940 on Churchill's instructions to coordinate resistance and the underground movement in Europe.'

'"Set Europe ablaze," that's what the old man ordered.' Sarah Drayton flicked ash in the fire. 'I worked for them.'

I was astonished. 'But you can't have been more than a child.'

'Nineteen,' she said. 'In 1944.'

'And Martineau?'

'Look on the piano,' she said. 'The end photo in the silver frame.'

I crossed to the piano and picked the photo up and her face jumped out at me, strangely unchanged except in one respect. Her hair was startlingly blonde and marcelled – that's the term I think they used to use. She wore a little black hat and one of those coats from the wartime period with big shoulders and tight at the waist. She also wore silk stockings and high-heeled shoes and clutched a black patent-leather bag.

The man standing next to her was of medium height and wore a leather military trenchcoat over a tweed suit, hands thrust deep into the pockets. His face was shadowed by a dark slouch hat and a cigarette dangled from the corner of his mouth. The eyes were dark, no expression to them at all, and his smile had a kind of ruthless charm. He looked a thoroughly dangerous man.

Sarah Drayton got up and joined me. 'Not much like the Croxley Professor of Moral Philosophy at Oxford there, is he?'

'Where was it taken?' I asked.

'In Jersey. Not too far from here. May nineteen forty-four. The tenth, I think.'

'But I've been in Jersey long enough to know that it was occupied by the Germans at that time,' I said.

'Very much so.'

'And Martineau was here? With you?'

She crossed to a Georgian desk, opened a drawer and took out a small folder. When she opened it I saw at once that it contained several old photographs. She passed one to me. 'This one I don't keep on top of the piano for obvious reasons.'

She was dressed pretty much as she had been in the other photo and Martineau wore the same leather trenchcoat. The only difference was the SS uniform underneath, the silver death's-head badge in his cap. 'Standartenfürer Max Vogel,' she said. 'Colonel, to you. He looks rather dashing, doesn't he?' She smiled as she took it from me. 'He had a weakness for uniforms, Harry.'

'Dear God,' I said. 'What is all this?'

She didn't answer, but simply passed me another photo. It was faded slightly, but still perfectly clear. A group of German officers. In front of them stood two men on their own. One was Martineau in the SS uniform, but it was the other who took my breath away. One of the best-known faces of the Second World War. Field Marshal Erwin Rommel. The Desert Fox himself.

I said, 'Was that taken here too?'

'Oh yes.' She put the photos back in the desk and picked up my glass. 'I think you could do with another drink.'

'Yes, I believe I could.'

She got me one, handed the glass to me, and we moved to the fire. She took a cigarette from the box. 'I should stop, I suppose. Too late now. Another bad habit Harry taught me.'

'Do I get an explanation?'

'Why not?' she said, and turned as rain drummed against the French windows. 'I can't think of anything better to do on an afternoon like this, can you?'

London 1944

2

It started, if one can ever be certain where anything starts, with a telephone call received by Brigadier Dougal Munro at his flat in Haston Place, ten minutes' walk from the London headquarters of SOE in Baker Street. As head of Section D at SOE he had two phones by his bed, one routed straight through to his office. It was this that brought him awake at four o'clock on the morning of April 28, 1944.

He listened, face grave, then swore softly. 'I'll be right over. One thing, check if Eisenhower is in town.'

Within five minutes he was letting himself out of the front door, shivering in the damp cold, lighting the first cigarette of the day as he hurried along the deserted street. He was at that time sixty-five, a squat, powerful-looking man with white hair, his round, ugly face set off by steel-rimmed spectacles. He wore an old Burberry raincoat and carried an umbrella.

There was very little of the military in either his bearing or his appearance, which was hardly surprising. His rank of brigadier was simply to give him the necessary authority in certain quarters. Until 1939, Dougal Munro had been an archaeologist by profession. An Egyptologist, to be more precise, and fellow of All Souls at Oxford. For three years now, head of Section D at SOE. What was commonly referred to in the trade as the dirty tricks department.

He turned in at the entrance of Baker Street, nodded to the night guard and went straight upstairs. When he went into his office, Captain Jack Carter, his night duty officer, was seated behind his desk. Carter had a false leg, a legacy of Dunkirk. He reached for his stick and started to get up.

'No, stay where you are, Jack,' Munro told him. 'Is there any tea?'

'Thermos flask on the map table, sir.'

Munro unscrewed the flask, poured a cup and drank. 'God, that's foul, but at least it's hot. Right, get on with it.'

Carter now got up and limped across. There was a map of the southwest of England on the table, concentrating mainly on Devon, Cornwall and the general area of the English Channel.

'Exercise Tiger, sir,' he said. 'You remember the details?'

'Simulated landings for Overlord.'

'That's right. Here in Lyme Bay in Devon there's a place called Slapton Sands. It bears enough similarities to the beach we've designated Utah in the Normandy landings to make it invaluable for training purposes. Most of the young Americans going in have no combat experience.'

'I know that, Jack,' Munro said. 'Go on.'

'Last night's convoy consisted of eight landing craft. Five from Plymouth and three from Brixham. Under naval escort, of course. They were to do a practice beach landing at Slapton.'

There was a pause. Munro said, 'Tell me the worst.'

'They were attacked at sea by German E-boats, we think the Fifth and Ninth Schnellboote Flotillas from Cherbourg.'

'And the damage?'

'Two landing craft sunk for certain. Others torpedoed and damaged.'

'And the butcher's bill?'

'Difficult to be accurate at the moment. Around two hundred sailors and four hundred and fifty soldiers.'

Munro said. 'Are you trying to tell me we lost six hundred and fifty American servicemen last night? Six hundred and fifty and we haven't even started the invasion of Europe?'

'I'm afraid so.'

Munro walked restlessly across the room and stood at the window. 'Has Eisenhower been told?'

'He's in town, sir, at Hayes Lodge. He wants to see you at breakfast. Eight o'clock.'

'And he'll want the facts.' Munro turned and went to his desk. 'Were there any Bigots among those officers lost?'

'Three, sir.'

'Dear God, I warned them. I warned them about this,' Munro said. 'No Bigot to in any way undertake hazardous duty.'

Some months previously it had become regrettably clear that there were serious breaches of security, in some cases by high-ranking American officers, in connection with the projected invasion of Europe. The Bigot procedure had been brought in as an answer to the situation. It was an intelligence classification above Most Secret. Bigots knew what others did not – the details of the Allied invasion of Europe.

'The three are missing so far,' Carter said. 'I've got their files.'

He laid them on the desk and Munro examined them quickly. 'Stupid,' he said. 'Unbelievably stupid. Take this man, Colonel Hugh Kelso.'

'The engineering officer?' Carter said. 'He's already visited two of the Normandy beaches by night, courtesy of Four Commando, to check on the suitability of the terrain for vehicles.'

'Sword Beach and Utah Beach.' Munro groaned. 'For God's sake, Jack, what if he was picked up by one of those E-boats? He could be in enemy hands right now. And they'll make him talk if they want to, you know that.'

'I don't think it's likely that any of those missing were picked up by the Germans, sir. The captain of the destroyer *Saladin*, which was one of the escorts, said the E-boats attacked at a range of fifteen hundred meters, then got the hell out of it fast. Typical hit and run. A lot of darkness and confusion on both sides. And the weather isn't too good. Wind force five to six and freshening, but I'm informed that the way the currents are in Lyme Bay, most of the bodies will come ashore. Already started.'

'Most, Jack, most.' Munro tapped the map on the table. 'The Germans know we're coming. They're expecting the invasion. They're ready for it. Hitler's put Rommel himself in charge of all coastal fortifications. But they don't know where and they don't know when.' He shook his head, staring down at the map. 'Wouldn't it be ironic if the greatest invasion in history had to be called off because one man with all the right information fell into the wrong hands.'

'Not likely, sir, believe me,' Carter said gently. 'This Colonel Kelso will come in on the tide with the rest of them.'

'God help me, but I pray that he does, Jack. I pray that he does,' Dougal Munro said fervently.

But at that precise moment, Colonel Hugh Kelso was very much alive, more afraid than he had ever been in his life, cold and wet and in terrible pain. He lay huddled in the bottom of a life raft in several inches of water about a mile offshore from the Devon coast, a contrary current carrying him fast toward Start Point on the southernmost tip of Lyme Bay, and beyond Start Point were the open waters of the English Channel.

Kelso was forty-two, married with two daughters. A civil engineer, he had been managing director of the family firm of construction engineers in New York for several years and had a high reputation in the field. Which was why he'd been drafted into the Engineering Corps in 1942 with the immediate rank of major. His experience with the engineering problems involved in beach landings on various islands in the South Pacific had earned him a promotion and a transfer to SHAEF Headquarters in England to work on the preparation for the invasion of Europe.

He'd taken part in Exercise Tiger on the request of the commanding officer for one reason only. The American 1st Engineer Special Brigade was one of the units assigned to take the beach designated as Utah during the coming Normandy landings, and Hugh Kelso had actually visited Utah Beach six weeks previously, under cover of darkness, guarded by British commandos. Slapton Sands was as close to the terrain as they could get. It had seemed sensible to seek his opinion, which was why he'd sailed on LST 31 from Plymouth.

Like everyone on board, Kelso had been taken totally by surprise by the attack. A considerable number of flares had been noticed in the distance which had been assumed to be from British MTBs. And then the first torpedo had struck and the night had become a living hell of burning oil and screaming men. Although Kelso didn't know it then, 413 men were killed from LST 31 alone. In his own case, he was blown off his feet by the force of the explosion and slammed against a rail, toppling into the water. His life jacket kept him afloat, of course, but he lost consciousness, coming to his senses to find himself being towed through the icy water.

The flames were a hundred yards away and in the reflected light he was aware only of an oil-soaked face.

'You're okay, sir. Just hang on. There's a life raft here.'

The life raft loomed out of the darkness. It was the new model of inflatable developed from Pacific experience. A round, fat orange sphere riding high in the water and intended to carry as many as ten men. There was a canopy on top to protect the occupants from wind and weather, the entrance flap standing open.

'I'll get you in, sir, then I'll go back for some more. Come on, up you go.'

Kelso felt weak, but his unknown friend was strong and muscular. He pushed hard, shoving Kelso in headfirst through the flap. And then Kelso was aware of the pain in his right leg, like a living thing and worse than anything he had ever known. He screamed and fainted.

When he came to, he was numb with cold and it took him a few moments to work out where he was. There was no sign of his unknown friend. He felt around in the darkness, then peered out through the open flap. Spray dashed in his face. There was no light anywhere, only the dark and the wind and the sound of the sea running. He checked the luminous dial of his waterproof watch. It was almost five o'clock and then he remembered that these life rafts carried an emergency kit. As he turned to feel for it, the pain started in his leg again. He gritted his teeth as his hands found the emergency kit box and got the lid open.

There was a waterproof flashlight in a clip on the inside of the lid and he switched it on. He was alone, as he had thought, in the orange cave, about a foot of water slopping around him. His uniform trousers were badly torn below the right knee, and when he put his hand inside gingerly he could feel the raised edges of bone in several places.

There was a Verey pistol in the box and he fingered it for a moment. It seemed the obvious thing to send up one of its parachute distress flares, but then he paused, trying to make his tired brain think straight. What if the German naval units that had attacked them were still in the area? What if it was the enemy that picked him up? He couldn't take that chance. He was, after all, a Bigot. In a matter of weeks an armada of six thousand ships would sail across the narrow waters of the English Channel and Kelso knew time and place. No, better to wait until dawn.

The leg was really hurting now and he rummaged in the box and found the medical kit with its morphine ampules. He jabbed one in his leg and, after a moment's hesitation, used another. Then he found the bailer and wearily started to throw water out through the open flap. God, but he was tired. Too much morphine perhaps, but at least the pain had dulled and he dropped the bailer and pulled the plastic zip at the entrance and leaned back and was suddenly asleep.

On his right, a few hundred yards away, was Start Point. For a while he seemed to be drifting toward the rocks and then a contrary current pulled him away. Ten minutes later, the life raft passed that final point of land and a freshening wind drove it out into the cold waters of the English Channel.

Eisenhower was seated in the Regency bow window of the library at Hayes Lodge having breakfast of poached eggs, toast and coffee when the young aide showed Dougal Munro in.

'Leave us, Captain,' the general said and the aide withdrew. 'Difficult to smile this morning, Brigadier.'

'I'm afraid so.'

'Have you eaten?'

'I haven't eaten breakfast for years, General.'

For a moment, Eisenhower's face was illuminated by that famous and inimitable smile. 'Which shows you aren't an old military hand. You prefer tea, don't you?'

'Yes, General.'

'You'll find it on the sideboard behind you – special order. Help yourself, then tell me what you know of this wretched business. My own people have already given me their version, but I've always had considerable respect for your people at SOE, you know that.'

Munro helped himself to the tea and sat in the window seat and gave Eisenhower a brief resume of the night's events.

'But surely the naval escorts should have been able to prevent such a thing happening,' the general said. 'On the other hand, I hear the weather wasn't too good. It's past belief. I visited Slapton myself only three days ago to see how the exercises were going. Went down by special train with Tedder and Omar Bradley.'

'Most of the crews of your LSTs are new to those waters, and the English Channel at the best of times can be difficult.' Munro shrugged. 'We've had torpedo boats from the Royal Navy hanging around off Cherbourg regularly during these exercises because Cherbourg, as the General knows, is the most important E-boat base on the French coast. There was a sea mist and the Germans obviously slipped out with their silencers on and probably with their radar sets switched off. They do more than forty knots, those things. Nothing afloat that's faster and they boxed rather cleverly on their approach. Fired off parachute flares so the people in the convoy assumed they were ours.'

'Goddammit, you never assume anything in this game. I'm tired of telling people that.' Eisenhower poured another coffee, stood up and went to the fire. 'Bodies coming ashore by the hundred, so they tell me.'

'I'm afraid so.'

'Needless to say, this whole thing stays under wraps. We're going to arrange for some kind of mass grave down there in Devon for the time being. At least it's a defense area under military rule, which should help. If this got out, so close to the invasion, it could have a terrible effect on morale.'

'I agree.' Munro hesitated and said carefully, 'There is the question of the Bigots, General.'

'Who should never have been there in the first place. No one knows the regulations on Bigots better than you.'

'It could be worse, sir. There were three in all. Two of the bodies have already been recovered. The third, this man.' Munro took a file from his briefcase and pushed it across. 'Is still missing.'

Eisenhower read the file quickly. 'Colonel Hugh Kelso.' His face darkened. 'But I know Kelso personally. He checked out two beaches in Normandy only weeks ago.'

'Utah and Sword. On those occasions he had commandos nursing him and he also had an L pill with him, just in case he was caught. As the General knows, the cyanide in those things kills instantaneously.'

Eisenhower pushed the file across. 'He knows, Brigadier, both when we're going and where. The implications are past belief.'

'We've men on the beaches around Slapton looking for him now, General. I've little reason to doubt that his body will turn up with the rest of them.'

'Don't try to make me feel good,' Eisenhower told him sharply. 'Some of those bodies will never come in on the tide. I know that and so do you, and if Kelso is one of them, we can never be certain that he wasn't picked up by the enemy.'

'That's true, General,' Munro admitted because there wasn't really anything else he could say.

Eisenhower walked to the window. Rain dashed against the pane. 'What a day,' he said morosely. 'One thing's for sure. I can only think of one man who'll have a smile on his face this morning.'

At that very moment Adolf Hitler was reading a report on the Slapton Sands affair in the map room of his underground headquarters known as Wolf's Lair, near Rastenburg, deep in the forests of East Prussia.

Most of those important in the Nazi hierarchy were present. Heinrich Himmler, Reichsführer of the SS and Chief of both State and Secret Police, Josef Goebbels, Reichsminister for Propaganda, Reichsleiter Martin Bormann, Secretary to the Führer among other things, and Oberführer Rattenhuber, Himmler's Chief of Security and Commander of the SS guard at Rastenburg.

Hitler almost danced with delight and crumpled the thin paper of the message in one hand. 'So, our Navy can still strike, and hard, right in the enemy's own backyard! Three ships sunk, and hundreds of casualties.' His eyes sparked. 'A bad morning for General Eisenhower, gentlemen.'

There was general enthusiasm. 'Good news indeed, my Führer,' Goebbels said and delivered his usual high laugh.

Bormann, who had been the first to see the message, said quietly, 'If we can do this to them off the coast of Devon, my Führer, all things are possible off the coast of France.'

'They won't even get ashore,' Himmler put in.

'Probably not,' Hitler said, in high good humor. 'But now, gentlemen, to the purpose of our meeting.' They grouped around the circular table and he tapped the large-scale map of France. 'The Westwall proceeds, I think.' He turned to Bormann. 'The report on Army Group B which I asked for? Has it arrived?'

Bormann turned inquiringly to Rattenhuber who said, 'I've just had a report from the airfield. The courier, a Captain Koenig, landed five minutes ago. He's on his way.'

'Good.' Hitler seemed abstracted now, as if somehow alone as he stared down at the map. 'So, gentlemen, where do we start?'

On December 26, 1943, a remarkable and gifted young German officer, Colonel Klaus von Stauffenberg, reported for a meeting at Rastenburg with a time bomb in his briefcase. Unfortunately, the meeting did not take place, as the Führer had already departed for Bavaria for the Christmas holiday. In spite of having lost his left eye and right hand in action, von Stauffenberg was Chief of Staff to General Olbricht of the General Army Office and the center of a conspiracy of army generals whose aim was to assassinate the Führer and save Germany from disaster.

His own abortive attempt at Christmas 1943 was only one of many that had failed. Yet there was no shortage of volunteers to the cause, as witness Captain Karl Koenig traveling in the rear of the military car from the airfield to Wolf's Lair on that gray April morning with the papers from Berlin that Hitler had requested. He was in a highly nervous state, which was hardly surprising when one considered the time bomb carefully placed in the false bottom of the briefcase. He had told the pilot at Rastenburg airfield to be ready for a quick turnaround and his fingers trembled as he lit a cigarette.

The SS driver and guard in front stared woodenly ahead, and as time passed, Koenig's nervousness increased. There were minefields on either side in the gloomy woods, electric fences, guards patrolling everywhere with savage dogs and three gates to pass through to reach the inner compound. Still, time to arm the bomb. Once done, it would give him exactly thirty minutes, they had told him.

He reached for the lock on the left-hand strap of the briefcase and depressed it. There was an immediate and very powerful explosion which killed Koenig and the two guards instantly and blew the car apart.

Hitler was beside himself with rage, pacing up and down in the map room. 'Again and yet again they try.' He turned on Rattenhuber. 'And you, Oberführer? What about you? Sworn to protect my personal safety.'

'My Führer,' Rattenhuber stammered. 'What can I say?'

'Nothing!' Hitler stormed and turned on the rest of them. 'You say nothing of use to me – not any of you.'

In the shocked silence, it was Himmler who spoke, his voice dry and precise. 'That there has been negligence here is true, my Führer, but surely we see further proof, in the failure of this dastardly attempt, of the certainty of your own destiny. Further proof of Germany's inevitable victory under your inspired guidance.'

Hitler's eyes blazed, his head went back. 'As always, Reichsführer, you see. The only one who does.' He turned on the others. 'Get out, all of you. I wish to talk to the Reichsführer alone.'

They went without a murmur, Goebbels the last one to leave. Hitler stood staring down at the map desk, hands clasped behind him. 'In what way may I serve my Führer?' Himmler asked.

'There is a plot, am I not right?' Hitler said. 'A general conspiracy to destroy me, and this Captain Koenig was simply an agent?'

'Not so much a general conspiracy as a conspiracy of generals, my Führer.'

Hitler turned sharply. 'Are you certain?'

'Oh, yes, but proof – that is something else.'

Hitler nodded. 'Koenig was an aide of General Olbricht. Is Olbricht one of those you suspect?' Himmler nodded. 'And the others?'

'Generals Stieff, Wagner, von Hase, Lindemann. Several more, all being closely watched.'

Hitler stayed remarkably cool. 'Traitors each and every one. No firing squad. A noose each when the time comes. No one higher, though? It would seem our field marshals are loyal at least.'

'I wish I could confirm that, my Führer, but there is one who is heavily suspect. I would be failing in my duty not to tell you.'

'Then tell me.'

'Rommel.'

Hitler smiled a ghastly smile that was almost one of triumph, turned and walked away and turned again, still smiling. 'I think I expected it. Yes, I'm sure I did. So, the Desert Fox wishes to play games.'

'I'm almost certain of it.'

'The people's hero,' Hitler said. 'We must handle him carefully, wouldn't you say?'

'Or outfox him, my Führer,' Himmler said softly.

'Outfox him. Outfox the Desert Fox.' Hitler smiled delightedly. 'Yes, I like that, Reichsführer. I like that very much indeed.'

Hugh Kelso slept until noon and when he awakened, he was sick. He turned over in the violently pitching life raft and pulled down the zip of the entrance flap. His heart sank. There was nothing but sea, the life raft twisting and turning on the angry waves. The sky was black, heavy with rain and the wind was gusting 5 or 6, he could tell that. Worst of all, there wasn't a hint of land anywhere. He was well out in the English Channel, so much was obvious. If he drifted straight across, wasn't picked up at all, he'd hit the coast of France, possibly the Cherbourg Peninsula. Below that, in the Gulf of St. Malo, were the Channel Islands. Alderney, Guernsey and Jersey. He didn't know much about them except that they were British and occupied by the enemy. He was not likely to be carried as far south as that, though.

He got the Verey light out, and fired an orange distress flare. There was seldom any German naval traffic in the Channel during daylight. They tended to keep to the inshore run behind their minefields. He fired another flare and then water cascaded in through the flap and he hurriedly zipped it up. There were some field rations in the emergency kit. He tried to eat one of the dried fruit blocks and was violently sick and his leg was on fire again. Hurriedly, he got another morphine ampule and injected himself. After a while, he pillowed his head on his hands and slept again.

Outside, the sea lifted as the afternoon wore on. It started to get dark soon after five o'clock. By that time the wind was blowing sou'westerly, turning him away from the French coast and the Cherbourg Peninsula so that by six o'clock he was ten miles to the west of the Casquets Light off the island of Alderney. And then the wind veered again, pushing him down along the outer edge of the Gulf of St. Malo toward Guernsey.

Kelso was aware of none of these things. He awakened around seven o'clock with a high temperature, washed his face with a little water to cool it, was sick again and dropped into something approaching a coma.

In London, Dougal Munro was working at his desk, the slight scratching of his pen the only sound in the quiet of the room. There was a knock at the door and Jack Carter limped in with a folder in one hand. He put it down in front of Munro.

'Latest list from Slapton, sir.'

'Anything on Kelso?'

'Not a thing, sir, but they've got every available ship out there in the bay looking for the missing bodies.'

Dougal Munro got up and moved to the window. The wind moaned outside, hurling rain against the pane. He shook his head and said softly, 'God help sailors at sea on a night like this.'

3

As commander of Army Group B, Field Marshal Erwin Rommel was responsible for the Atlantic Wall defenses, his sole task to defeat any Allied attempt to land in northern France. Since taking command in January of 1944 he had strengthened the coastal defenses to an incredible degree, tramping the beaches, visiting every strongpoint, impressing his own energetic presence on everyone from divisional commanders to the lowliest private.

His headquarters seemed permanently on the move so that no one could be sure where he was from one day to the next. He had an uncomfortable habit of turning up in his familiar black Mercedes accompanied only by his driver and his most trusted aide from Afrika Korps days, Major Konrad Hofer.

On the evening of that fateful day at about the time Hugh Kelso was somewhere in the general area of the Casquets Light, west of Alderney, the field marshal was sitting down to an early dinner with the officers of the 21st

Parachute Regiment in a chateau at Campeaux some ten miles from St. Lo in Normandy.

His primary reason for being there was sound enough. The High Command, and the Führer himself, believed that the invasion, when it came, would take place in the area of the Pas de Calais. Rommel disagreed and had made it clear that if he were Eisenhower, he would strike for Normandy. None of this had done anything for his popularity among the people who counted at OKW, High Command of the Armed Forces, in Berlin. Rommel didn't give a damn about that anymore. The war was lost. The only thing that was uncertain was how long it would take.

Which brought him to the second reason for being in Normandy. He was involved in a dangerous game and it paid to keep on the move, for since taking command of Army Group B he had renewed old friendships with General von Stulpnagel, military governor of France, and General Alexander von Falkenhausen. Both were involved, with von Stauffenberg, in the conspiracy against Hitler. It had not taken them long to bring Rommel around to their point of view.

They had all been aware of the projected assassination attempt at Rastenburg that morning. Rommel had sent Konrad Hofer by air to Berlin the previous day to await events at General Olbricht's headquarters, but there had been no news at all. Not a hint of anything untoward on the radio.

Now, in the mess, Colonel Halder, commanding the regiment, stood to offer the loyal toast. 'Gentlemen – to our Führer and total victory.'

'So many young men,' Rommel thought to himself, 'and what for?' But he raised his glass and drank with them.

'And now, Field Marshal Erwin Rommel, the Desert Fox himself, who does our mess so much honor tonight.'

They drained their glasses, then applauded him, cheering wildly, and Rommel was immensely touched. Colonel Halder said, 'The men have arranged a little entertainment in your honor, Field Marshal. We were hoping you might be willing to attend.'

'But of course.' Rommel held out his glass for more champagne. 'Delighted.'

The door opened at the back of the mess and Konrad Hofer entered. He looked tired and badly needed a shave, his field gray greatcoat buttoned up to his neck.

'Ah, Konrad, there you are,' Rommel called. 'Come and have a glass of champagne. You look as if you could do with it.'

'I've just flown in from Berlin, Field Marshal. Landed at St. Lo.'

'Good flight?'

'Terrible, actually.' Hofer swallowed the champagne gratefully.

'My dear boy, come and have a shower and we'll see if they can manage you a sandwich.' Rommel turned to Colonel Halder. 'See if you can delay this little show the men are putting on for half an hour.'

'No problem, Field Marshal.'

'Good – we'll see you later then.' Rommel picked up a fresh bottle of champagne and two glasses and walked out followed by Hofer.

As soon as the bedroom door was closed, Hofer turned in agitation. 'It was the worst kind of mess. All that fool Koenig managed to do was blow himself up outside the main gate.'

'That seems rather careless of him,' Rommel said dryly. 'Now calm yourself, Konrad. Have another glass of champagne and get under the shower and just take it slowly.'

Hofer went into the bathroom and Rommel straightened his uniform, examining himself in the mirror. He was fifty-three at that time, of medium height, stocky and thick-set with strong features, and there was a power to the man, a force, that was almost electric. His uniform was simple enough, his only decorations the Pour le Mérite, the famous Blue Max, won as a young infantry officer in the First World War, and the Knight's Cross with Oak Leaves, Swords and Diamonds, both of which hung around his neck. On the other hand, one hardly needed anything else if one had those.

Hofer emerged in a bathrobe toweling his hair. 'Olbricht and a few more up there are in a blue funk and I don't blame them. I mean the Gestapo or the SD could be on to this at any time.'

'Yes,' Rommel conceded. 'Himmler may have started life as a chicken farmer, but whatever else you may say about him he's no fool. How was von Stauffenberg?'

'As determined as ever. He suggests you meet with Generals von Stulpnagel and Falkenhausen within the next few days.'

'I'll see what I can do.'

Hofer was back in the bathroom pulling on his uniform again. 'I'm not so sure it's a good idea. If Himmler does have his suspicions about you, you could be under close surveillance already.'

'Oh, I'll think of something,' Rommel said. 'Now hurry up. The men are laying on a little show for me and I don't want to disappoint them.'

The show was presented in the main hall of the chateau. A small stage had been rigged at one end with some makeshift curtains. Rommel, Hofer and the regimental officers sat down in chairs provided at the front; the men stood in the hall behind them or sat on the grand staircase.

A young corporal came on, bowed and sat down at the grand piano and played a selection of light music. There was polite applause. Then he moved into the song of the Fallschirmjäger, the paratroopers' own song, sung everywhere from Stalingrad to North Africa. The curtains parted to reveal the regimental choir singing lustily. There was a cheer from the back of the hall and everyone started to join in, including the officers. Without pause, the choir moved straight into several choruses of *We March Against England*, an unfortunate choice, Rommel told himself. It was interesting to note that no one tried singing the *Horst Wessel*. The curtain came down to a storm of cheering and several instrumentalists came on, grouped themselves around the pianist and played two or three jazz numbers. When they were finished, the lights went down and there was a pause.

'What's happening?' Rommel demanded.

'Wait and see, Herr Field Marshal. Something special, I assure you.'

The pianist started to play the song that was most popular of all with the German forces, *Lili Marlene*. The curtains parted to reveal only a pool of light on a stool in the center of the stage from a crude spotlight. Suddenly, Marlene Dietrich stepped into the light straight out of *Blue Angel*, or so it seemed. Top hat, black stockings and suspenders. She sat on the stool to a chorus of wolf whistles from the men and then she started to sing *Lili Marlene*, and that haunting, bittersweet melody reduced the audience to total silence.

A man, of course, Rommel could see that, but a brilliant impersonation and he joined in the applause enthusiastically. 'Who on earth is that?' he asked Colonel Halder.

'Our orderly room corporal, Berger. Apparently he used to be some sort of cabaret performer.'

'Brilliant,' Rommel said. 'Is there more?'

'Oh, yes, Herr Field Marshal. Something very special.'

The instrumentalists returned and the choir joined them in a few more numbers. There was another pause when they departed and then a steady, muted drum roll. The curtain rose to reveal subdued lighting. As the choir started to sing the song of the Afrika Korps from the side of the stage, Rommel walked on. And it was quite unmistakably he. The cap with the desert goggles, the white scarf carelessly knotted at the neck, the old leather greatcoat, the field marshal's baton in one gloved hand, the other arrogantly on the hip. The voice, when he spoke, was perfect as he delivered a few lines of his famous battlefield speech before El Alamein.

'I know I haven't offered you much. Sand, heat and scorpions, but we've shared them together. One more push and it's Cairo, and if we fail . . . well, we tried – together.'

There was total silence from the body of the hall as Colonel Halder glanced anxiously at Rommel. 'Field Marshal, I hope you're not offended.'

'Offended? I think he's marvelous,' Rommel said and jumped to his feet. 'Bravo!' he called and started to clap and behind him, the entire audience joined in with the chorus of the Afrika Korps song, cheering wildly.

In the makeshift dressing room next to the kitchen, Erich Berger slumped into a chair and stared at himself in the mirror. His heart was beating and he was sweating. A hell of a thing for any actor to perform in front of the man he was taking off, and such a man. A name to conjure with. The most popular soldier in Germany.

'Not bad, Heini,' he said softly. 'Mazel tov.' He took a bottle of schnapps from the drawer, drew the cork and swallowed some.

A Yiddish phrase on the lips of a corporal in a German Fallschirmjäger regiment might have seemed strange to anyone who had overheard. His secret was that he wasn't Erich Berger at all, but Heini Baum, Jewish actor and cabaret performer from Berlin and proud of it.

His story was surprisingly simple. He had performed with success in cabaret all over Europe. He had never married. To be frank, his inclinations ran more toward men than women. He had persisted in living in Berlin, even as the Nazis came to power, because his aging parents had always lived there and would not believe that anything terrible could ever happen. Which it did, of course, though not for a long time. As an entertainer, Baum was of use to the Reich. He still had to wear his Star of David on his coat, but a series of special permits kept him afloat and his parents with him, while all around them their friends were taken away.

And then there was the fateful night in 1940 when he had arrived at the end of his street, coming home from cabaret, in time to see the Gestapo taking his mother and father from their house. He had turned and run, like the coward he was, pausing only in a side street to tear the Star of David from his coat. He was forty-four years of age and looked ten years younger on a good day. Nowhere to go, for his papers told the world he was a Jew.

So, he'd caught a train to Kiel with the wild idea that he might be able to get a ship from there to somewhere – anywhere. He'd arrived just after one of the first of the devastating RAF raids on that city, had stumbled through the chaos and flames of the city center, searching for shelter as the RAF came back for a second go. Lurching down into a cellar, he'd found a man and a woman and a twelve-year-old girl dead, all from the same family he learned when he examined their identity cards. Erich Berger, his wife and daughter. And one thing more. In Berger's pocket were his call-up papers, ordering him to report the following week.

What better hiding place could a Jew who was afraid to be a Jew find? Sure, he was ten years older than Berger, but it wouldn't show. To change the photos on the two identity cards was simple enough so that the body he dragged out to leave in the rubble of the street to be found later was that of Heini Baum, Jew of Berlin. It had been necessary to obliterate most of the dead man's face with a brick, just to help things along, but after what he'd been through that part was easy.

How ironic that it was the paratroops he'd been inducted into. He'd been everywhere. Crete, Stalingrad, North Africa, a nice flashy hero in his Luftwaffe blouse and baggy paratroopers' pants and jump boots, with the Iron Cross Second and First Class to prove it. He took another pull at the schnapps bottle, and behind him the door opened and Rommel, Colonel Halder and Hofer entered.

It was midnight and Hugh Kelso had never been happier, up at Cape Cod at the summer bungalow, sitting on the veranda in the swing seat, reading a book, a cool glass to his hand and Jane, his wife, was calling, on her way up from the beach, her face shaded by a sun hat, the good legs tanned under the old cotton dress, and the girls in swimming suits and carrying buckets and spades, voices faint on the warm afternoon air. Everyone so happy. So very happy. He didn't feel cold anymore, didn't really feel anything. He reached out to take Jane's hand as she came up the steps to the veranda and the voices faded and he came awake, shaking all over.

It was pitch dark and the sea wasn't as rough, and yet he seemed to be moving very fast. He pulled down the zip on the flap with stiff fingers and peered out. Only a slight phosphorescence as the water turned over and a vast darkness. His eyes were weary, sore from the salt water. For a wild moment he thought he saw a light out there. He shook his head, closed then opened his eyes again. A mistake, of course. Only the never-ending night. He zipped up the flap, lay back and closed his eyes, trying to think of Jane and his two daughters. Perhaps they would come back again?

Although he didn't know it, he had already drifted something like seventy miles since leaving Lyme Bay on the Devon coast and his eyes had not deceived him. What he had just seen through the darkness was a momentary flash of light as a sentry at the German guard post on Pleinmont Point on the southwest corner of the island of Guernsey had opened a door to go out on duty. To the southeast, perhaps thirty miles away, was Jersey, the largest of the Channel Islands. It was in this general direction that the freshening wind bore him as he slept on.

* * *

Rommel leaned on the mantelpiece and stirred the fire with his boot. 'So, the others would like me to talk with von Stulpnagel and Falkenhausen?'

'Yes, Herr Field Marshal,' Hofer said. 'But as you point out, one must take things very carefully at the moment. For such a meeting, secrecy would be essential.'

'And opportunity,' Rommel said. 'Secrecy and opportunity.' The clock on the mantelpiece chimed twice and he laughed. 'Two o'clock in the morning. The best time for crazy ideas.'

'What are you suggesting, Herr Field Marshal?'

'Quite simple, really. What is it now, Saturday? What if we arranged a meeting next week at some agreed rendezvous with von Stulpnagel and Falkenhausen while I was actually supposed to be somewhere else? Jersey, for example?'

'The Channel Islands?' Hofer looked bewildered.

'The Führer himself suggested not two months ago that I inspect the fortifications there. You know my feelings about the military importance of the islands. The Allies will never attempt a landing. It would cause too many civilian casualties. British civilian casualties, I might add.'

'And yet they tie up the 319 Infantry Division,' Hofer said. 'Six thousand troops in Jersey alone. Ten thousand service personnel in all, if you include Luftwaffe and Navy people.'

'And yet we've poured so much into them, Konrad, because the Führer wants to hang onto the only piece of British territory we've ever occupied. The strongest fortifications in the world. The same number of strongpoints and batteries as we have to defend the entire European coast from Dieppe to St. Nazaire.' He turned and smiled. 'The Führer is right. As commander of the Atlantic Wall, I should certainly inspect such an important part of it.'

Hofer nodded. 'I see that, Herr Field Marshal, but what I don't see is how you can be in two places at once. Meeting with Falkenhausen and Stulpnagel in France and inspecting fortifications in Jersey.'

'But you saw me in two places earlier this evening,' Rommel said calmly, 'both in the audience and on stage at the same time.'

The room was so quiet that Hofer could hear the clock ticking. 'My God,' he whispered. 'Are you serious?'

'Why not? Friend Berger even fooled me when he came on stage. The voice, the appearance.'

'But would he be intelligent enough to carry it off? There are so many things he wouldn't know how to handle. I mean, being a Field Marshal is rather different from being an orderly room clerk,' Hofer said.

'He seems intelligent enough to me,' Rommel told him. 'He's

obviously talented and a brave soldier to boot. Iron Cross First and Second Class. And you mustn't forget one important thing.'

'What's that, Herr Field Marshal?'

'He'd have you at his shoulder every step of the way to keep him straight.' Suddenly Rommel sounded impatient. 'Where's your enthusiasm, Konrad? If you're that worried, I'll give you a few days to prepare him. Let's see, it's Saturday now. How about descending on Jersey next Friday. I'm only thinking of thirty-six hours or so. Back in France on Saturday night or Sunday at the latest. If Berger can't carry it off for that length of time, I'll eat my hat.'

'Very well, Herr Field Marshal. I'll notify the Channel Islands that you'll be arriving next Friday.'

'No, you won't,' Rommel said. 'We box more cleverly than that. Who's the commander-in-chief?'

'Major General Count von Schmettow. His headquarters are in Guernsey.'

'I've met him,' Rommel said. 'Good officer.'

'With a reputation for being pro-English, which didn't do him any good in some quarters,' Hofer said.

'On the other hand, the fact that he's Field Marshal von Rundstedt's nephew certainly helped there. Who's military commander in Jersey?'

'I'll check.' Hofer took a file from his briefcase and worked his way down a unit situation list. 'Yes, here we are. Colonel Heine is military commander.'

'And civil administration?'

'The important people there are Colonel Baron von Aufsess and Captain Heider.'

'And the inhabitants themselves? Who are their representatives?'

'There's an organization called the Superior Council of the States of Jersey. The president is the bailiff of the island. A man called Alexander Coutanche.'

'Good,' said Rommel. 'This is what we do. Send General von Schmettow a signal ordering him to hold a coordinating meeting in Guernsey to consider the implications for the islands of the invasion of France threatened this summer.'

'And you want them all there?'

'Oh, yes. Military commander Jersey, the civil affairs people, the bailiff and his lot, and whoever's in charge of the Navy and Luftwaffe contingents in the islands.'

'Which will leave only junior officers in command.'

'Exactly.'

'There's not too much flying in and out of the Channel Islands these days. The RAF are far too active in that area. It's usual to travel between the islands by sea and at night.'

'I know,' Rommel said. 'I've taken advice on that point from Naval Headquarters in Cherbourg. Tell von Schmettow to call his meeting for next Saturday. In the circumstances they must travel either Thursday night or in the early hours of Friday to make sure they get there. I'll fly in on Friday morning in the Storch.'

'A risky flight, Herr Field Marshal.'

'For you, Konrad, and Berger, of course, not for me.' Rommel smiled with a kind of ruthless charm. 'The first thing they'll know about my arrival is when you ask the tower for permission to land at the airfield.'

'And what will von Schmettow think?'

'That the whole thing has been a deliberate ploy so that I can make a snap inspection of the military situation in the island and its defenses.'

'That's really rather clever,' Hofer said.

'Yes, I think it is.' Rommel started to unbutton his tunic. 'In the meantime, I'll meet with Falkenhausen and Stulpnagel at some quiet spot and get on with it.' He yawned. 'I think I'll go to bed. See that signal goes to von Schmettow in Guernsey tomorrow. Oh, and speak to Colonel Halder first thing in the morning. Tell him I'm much taken with Corporal Berger and want to borrow him for a while. I don't think he'll make any difficulties.'

'I doubt it, Herr Field Marshal,' Hofer said. 'Sleep well,' and he went out.

Dougal Munro slept on a small military bed in the corner of his office at Baker Street that night. It was about three o'clock in the morning when Jack Carter shook him gently awake. Munro opened his eyes instantly and sat up. 'What is it?'

'Latest lists from Slapton, sir. You asked to see them. Still over a hundred bodies missing.'

'And no sign of Kelso?'

'I'm afraid not. General Montgomery isn't too happy, but he has had an assurance from the Navy that the E-boats couldn't have picked survivors up. They were too far away.'

'The trouble with life, Jack, is that the moment someone tells you something is impossible, someone else promptly proves that it isn't. What time is first light?'

'Just before six. That should make a big difference to the final search.'

'Order a car for eight o'clock. We'll take a run down to Slapton and see for ourselves.'

'Very well, sir. Are you going back to sleep?'

'No, I don't think so.' Munro stood up and stretched. 'Think I'll catch up on some paperwork. No peace for the wicked in this life, Jack.'

At six o'clock on that same morning, Kelso came awake from a strange dream in which some primeval creature was calling to him from a great distance. He was very, very cold, feet and hands numb, and yet his face burned and there was sweat on his forehead.

He unzipped the flap and peered out into the gray light of dawn, not that there was anything much to see for he was shrouded in a sea fog of considerable density. Somewhere in the distance, the beast called again, only now he recognized it for what it was – a foghorn. Although he didn't know it, it was the Corbiere Light on the tip of the southernmost coast of Jersey, already behind him as the current swept him along. He sensed land, could almost smell it and, for a little while, came back to life again.

He could hear waves breaking on an unseen shore, and then the wind tore a hole in the curtain and he glimpsed cliffs, concrete gun emplacements on top. The place, although it meant nothing to Kelso, was Noirmont Point, and as the sea fog dropped back into place, the current carried him into St. Aubin's Bay, close inshore.

There were waves taking him in, strange, twisting currents carrying him round. At one side, a wave broke sending spray high in the air, and all around him was white foam, rocks showing through. And then there was a voice, high and clear, and the fog rolled away to reveal a small beach, rocks climbing steeply to a pine wood above. There was someone there, a man running along the shore, in woolen cap, heavy reefer coat and rubber boots.

The life raft slewed broadside in the surf, lifted high and smashed against rocks, pitching Kelso headfirst through the flap into the water. He tried to stand up, his scream as his right leg collapsed under him drowned by the roaring of the surf, and then the man was knee-deep in water, holding him. It was only then that he realized it was a woman.

'All right, I've got you. Just hang on.'

'Leg,' he mumbled. 'Leg broken.'

He wasn't sure what happened after that, and he came to in the shelter of some rocks. The woman was dragging the life raft out of the water. When he tried to sit up, she turned and came toward him. Kelso said as she knelt down, 'Where am I, France?'

'No,' she said. 'Jersey.'

He closed his eyes for a moment and shivered. 'You're British, then?'

'I should hope so. The last I heard of my husband, he was a major in the Tanks Corps serving in the Western Desert. My name's Helen de Ville.'

'Colonel Hugh Kelso.'

'American Air Force, I suppose? Where did your plane come down?'

'It didn't. I'm an army officer.'

'An army officer? But that doesn't make sense. Where on earth have you come from?'

'England. I'm a survivor of a ship that was torpedoed in Lyme Bay.' He groaned suddenly as pain knifed through his leg and almost lost his senses.

She opened his torn trouser leg and frowned. 'That's terrible. You'll have to go to hospital.'

'Will that mean Germans?'

'I'm afraid so.'

He clutched at the front of her reefer coat. 'No – no Germans.'

She eased him back down. 'Just lie still. I'm going to leave you for a little while. I'm going to need a cart.'

'Okay,' he said. 'But no Germans. They mustn't get their hands on me. You must promise. If you can't do that, then you must kill me. See, there's a Browning pistol here.'

He plucked at it and she leaned over him, face set, and took the pistol from its holster on his left thigh. 'You're not going to die and the Jerries aren't going to have you either – that's the only promise I'm prepared to give. Now wait for me.'

She slipped the pistol into her pocket, turned and hurried away. He lay there on that fog-shrouded shore, trying to get his bearings, and then the leg started to hurt again and he remembered the morphine in the emergency kit. He began to crawl toward the life raft. That, of course, was very definitely the final straw, and he plunged into darkness.

4

Helen de Ville left the cart track which was the usual way down to the beach and took a shortcut, scrambling up the steep hillside through the pine trees. She was strong and wiry, not surprising after four years of enemy occupation and the food restrictions that had caused her to lose nearly thirty pounds in weight. She often joked that it had given her back the figure she'd enjoyed at eighteen, an unlooked-for bonus at forty-two. And like most people, the lack of a car and a public transport system meant she was used to walking many miles each week.

She stood at the edge of the trees and looked across at the house. De Ville Place was not one of the largest manors on the island. It had been once in days of family glory, but a disastrous fire at the end of the nineteenth century had destroyed one entire wing. It was very old, constructed of Jersey granite weathered by the years. There were rows of French windows at the front on either side of the entrance, a granite wall dividing the house from a courtyard at one side.

She paused, taking her time, for there was an old Morris sedan parked in the courtyard, one of those requisitioned by the enemy. For two years now she'd had German naval officers billeted on her. They came and went, of course, sometimes staying only a night or two when E-boats of the 5th Schnellboote Flotilla came over from Guernsey.

Mostly they were regulars, young officers serving with various naval units based in Jersey. The war took its toll. There were often engagements with British MTBs in the area of the Channel Islands, and the RAF frequently attacked convoys to Granville, St. Malo and Cherbourg, even when they made a night run. Men died, but some survived. As she started across the lawn, the door opened and one of them came out.

He wore a white sweater, old reefer coat and seaboots and carried a duffel bag in one hand. The face beneath the salt-stained naval cap was good-humored and recklessly handsome. A bravo, this one, straight out of the sixteenth century, who wore a white top to his cap, usually an affectation of German U-boat commanders, but then Lieutenant Guido Orsini was a law unto himself, an Italian on secondment to the German Navy, trapped in the wrong place at entirely the wrong time when the Italian government had capitulated. Helen de Ville had long since given up pretending that she felt anything but considerable affection for him.

'Morning, Guido.'

'Helen, cara mia.' He blew her a kiss. 'I'm the last, as usual.'

'Where to today?'

'Granville. Should be fun in this fog. On the other hand, it keeps the Tommies at home. Back tomorrow. Do you want to go into St. Helier? Can I give you a lift?'

'No thanks. I'm looking for Sean.'

'I saw the good General not ten minutes ago coming out of the south barn with a felling axe and walking down toward his cottage. See you tomorrow. I must fly. Ciao, cara.'

He went through the small gate to the courtyard. A moment later, she heard the Morris start up and drive away. She crossed the courtyard herself, went through a field gate and ran along the track through trees. Sean

Gallagher's cottage stood by a stream in a hollow. She could see him now in old corduroy pants and riding boots, the sleeves of the checked shirt rolled up above muscular arms as he split logs.

'Sean!' she called and stumbled almost falling.

He lowered the axe and turned, pushing a lock of reddish brown hair from his eyes as he looked toward her. He dropped the axe and reached out to catch her as she almost fell again.

Sean Martin Gallagher was fifty-two and, as an Irish citizen, officially neutral in this war. He had been born in Dublin in 1892, his father a professor of surgery at Trinity College, a man who had taken no interest in women until, in his fiftieth year during a professional visit to Jersey, he had met a young nurse called Ruth le Brocq. He'd married her within a month and taken her back to Dublin.

She'd died in childbirth the following year and the boy Sean grew up spending the long summers each year in Jersey with his grandparents, the rest of the time in Dublin with his father. Sean's ambition was to be a writer, and he'd taken a degree in literature at his father's university, Trinity College. The exigencies of life made him a soldier, for as he finished college the First World War started.

He'd joined the Irish Fusiliers, a regiment that many Jerseymen served in, and by 1918 was a very old twenty-six. A major, twice wounded, and with an MC for gallantry on the Somme. As he used to say, any real experience of war came after that, fighting with the IRA in Ireland under Michael Collins' leadership, as commander of a flying column in County Mayo.

The treaty with the British government which had ended the conflict in 1922 had only proved a prelude to a bloody and vicious civil war between those elements of the IRA who refused to accept the treaty and those who chose to fight for the Irish Free State government under Collins. Sean Gallagher had chosen the Free State and found himself a general at the age of thirty, sweeping through the west of Ireland, ruthlessly hunting down old comrades.

Afterward, sick of killing, he'd traveled the world, living on money left to him by his father, writing the odd novel when he had a mind, finally settling in Jersey in 1930. Ralph de Ville had been a boyhood friend, and Helen he had loved desperately and hopelessly from the first moment they had met. His home in St. Lawrence, deep in the country, had been requisitioned by the Germans in 1940. Helen, with Ralph away serving with the British Army, needed a strong right arm, which explained his presence at the dower cottage on the estate. And he still loved her, of course, and still quite hopelessly.

★ ★ ★

The old cart had seen better days and the horse was considerably leaner than it should have been as they negotiated the track down to the beach, Sean Gallagher leading the horse, Helen at his side.

'If this goes wrong,' he said gravely. 'If they find out you're helping this man, it won't just be a prison sentence. It could mean a firing squad or one of those concentration camps they're talking about.'

'And what about you?'

'Jesus, woman, I'm a neutral, don't I keep telling you that?' He smiled mischievously, the gray eyes full of humor. 'If they want to keep that old bastard, de Valera, sweet back in Dublin, they've got to handle me with dress gloves. Mind you, after the way I chased the arse off him all over Ireland in the Civil War, he might welcome the news that they want to shoot me.'

She burst out laughing. 'I love you, Sean Gallagher. You always make me feel good at the worst times.' She put an arm around the small, lean man's shoulders and kissed him on the cheek.

'As a brother,' he said. 'You love me as a brother, as you often remind me, so keep your mad passion in your pocket, woman, and concentrate. Colonel Hugh Kelso, he said, an American army officer torpedoed off Devon?'

'That's right.'

'And what was all that about how the Germans mustn't get their hands on him?'

'I don't know. He was half out of his mind and his leg's in a terrible state, but at the suggestion he might have to go to hospital he went crazy. Said it would be better if I shot him.'

'A fine old mess from the sound of it,' Gallagher said, and led the horse down onto the fog-shrouded beach.

It was very quiet, the sea calm, so quiet that they could hear the whistle of the German military train from across the bay as it ran along the front from St. Helier to Millbrook.

Hugh Kelso lay face-down on the sand unconscious. Sean Gallagher turned him over gently and examined the leg. He gave a low whistle. 'He needs a surgeon, this lad. I'll get him in the cart while he's still out. You gather as much driftwood as you can and hurry.'

She ran along the beach and he lifted Kelso up, taking his weight easily, for he was surprisingly strong for a small man. Kelso groaned but stayed out, and the Irishman eased him onto the sacks in the cart and draped a few across him.

He turned as Helen came back with an armful of wood.

'Cover him with that while I see to the life raft.'

It was still bumping around in the shallows, and he waded into the water and pulled it up on the sand. He looked inside, removed the emergency kit, then took out a spring-blade gutting knife and slashed at the skin of the life raft fiercely. As air rushed out, it crumpled and he rolled it up and carried it to the cart, shoving it onto the rack underneath.

Helen arrived with another armful of wood which she put in the back with the rest. 'Will that do?'

'I think so. I'll stop by the paddock and we'll put the life raft down the old well shaft. But let's get moving.'

They started up the track, Helen sitting on the shaft of the cart, Sean leading the horse. Suddenly there was laughter up ahead and a dog barked. The Irishman paused and took his time over lighting one of the vile French cigarettes that he smoked. 'Nothing to worry about, I'll handle it,' he told her.

The Alsatian arrived first, a splendid animal which barked once, then recognized Gallagher as an old friend, and licked his hand. Two German soldiers in field gray and helmets, rifles over their shoulders, came next. 'Guten morgen, Herr General,' they both called eagerly.

'And good morning to you two daft buggers.' Gallagher's smile was his friendliest as he led the horse on.

'Sean, you're quite mad,' she hissed.

'Not at all. Neither of those two lads speak a word of English. It might have been fun if they'd looked under the cart though.'

'Where are we going?' she demanded. 'There's no one at the Place at the moment.'

It was always referred to in that way, never as a house.

'Isn't Mrs. Vibert in?'

'I gave her the day off. Remember that niece of hers had a new baby last week.'

'Naughty girl,' Gallagher said. 'And her man away serving in the British Army. I wonder what he'll think when he comes home and finds a bouncing boy with blue eyes and blond hair called Fritz.'

'Don't be cruel, Sean. She's not a bad girl. A little weak perhaps. People get lonely.'

'Do you tell me?' Gallagher laughed. 'I haven't exactly noticed you chasing me around the barn this week.'

'Be sensible,' she said. 'Now where do we take him? There's the Chamber.'

During the English Civil War, Charles de Ville, the Seigneur of the manor at that time, had espoused the Royalist cause. He'd had a room constructed in the roof with a secret staircase from the master bedroom known to the family over the years as the Chamber. It had saved his life during the time of Cromwell's rule when he was sought as a traitor.

'No, too awkward at the moment. He needs help and quickly. We'll take him to my cottage first.'

'And what about a doctor?'

'George Hamilton. Who else could you trust? Now hang on while I get this life raft down the well.'

He tugged it out and moved into the trees. She sat there, aware of her uneven breathing in the silence of the wood. Behind her, under the sacking and the driftwood, Hugh Kelso groaned and stirred.

At Slapton Sands just before noon, the tide turned and a few more bodies came in. Dougal Munro and Carter sat in the lee of a sand dune and had an early lunch of sandwiches and shared a bottle of beer. Soldiers tramped along the shoreline, occasionally venturing into the water at some officer's command to pull in another body. There were already about thirty laid out on the beach.

Munro said, 'Someone once said the first casualty when war comes is truth.'

'I know exactly what you mean, sir,' Carter said.

A young American officer approached and saluted. 'The beach is cleared of new arrivals at the moment, sir. Thirty-three since dawn. No sign of Colonel Kelso.' He hesitated. 'Does the Brigadier wish to view the burial arrangements? It's not too far.'

'No thank you,' Munro told him. 'I think I can manage without that.'

The officer saluted and walked away. Munro got up and helped Carter to his feet. 'Come on, Jack. Nothing we can do here.'

'All right, sir.'

Carter balanced on his walking stick and Munro stood, hands in pockets, and looked out to sea. He shivered suddenly. 'Anything wrong, sir?' Carter asked.

'Someone just walked over my grave, Jack. To be honest, I've got a bad feeling about this. A very bad feeling. Come on, let's get back to London,' and he turned and walked away along the beach.

'So, Berger, you understand what I am saying to you?' Konrad Hofer demanded.

Heini Baum stood rigidly at attention in front of the desk in the office which the CO had been happy to lend to the field marshal at Campeaux. He tried to ignore the fact that Rommel stood at the window looking out into the garden.

'I'm not sure, Herr Major. I think so.'

Rommel turned. 'Don't be stupid, Berger. You're an intelligent man, I can see that, and a brave one.' He tapped the Iron Cross First Class with the tip of his crop and the band around the left sleeve with the Gothic lettering. 'The Afrika Korps cuff-title, I see. So, we are old comrades. Were you at Alamein?'

'No, Field Marshal. Wounded at Tobruk.'

'Good. I'm a plain man so listen carefully. You did a wonderful impersonation of me last night, in both appearance and voice. Very professional.'

'Thank you.'

'Now I require a second performance. On Friday, you will fly to Jersey for the weekend accompanied by Major Hofer. You think you could fool them in Jersey for that long, Berger? King for a day? Would you like that?'

Baum smiled. 'Actually, I think I would, sir.'

Rommel said to Hofer. 'There you are. Sensible and intelligent, just as I told you. Now make the arrangements, Konrad, and let's get out of here.'

The cottage was built in the same kind of granite as the house. There was one large living room with a beamed ceiling and a dining table and half-a-dozen chairs in a window alcove. The kitchen was on the other side of the hall. Upstairs, there was one large bedroom, a storeroom and a bathroom.

Rather than negotiate the stairs, Gallagher had laid Kelso out on a long comfortable sofa in the living room. The American was still unconscious, and Gallagher found his wallet and opened it. There was his security card with photo, some snaps of a woman and two young girls, obviously his family, and a couple of letters which were so immediately personal that Gallagher folded them up again. He could hear Helen's voice from the kitchen as she spoke on the telephone. Kelso opened his eyes, stared blankly at him and then noticed the wallet in Gallagher's hand.

'Who are you?' He grabbed at it weakly. 'Give it back to me.'

Helen came in and sat on the sofa and put a hand on his forehead. 'It's all right. Just be still. You're burning up with fever. Remember me, Helen de Ville?'

He nodded slowly. 'The woman on the beach.'

'This is a friend, General Sean Gallagher.'

'I was just checking his papers,' Gallagher told her. 'The identity card is a little damp. I'll leave it out to dry.'

She said to Kelso. 'Do you remember where you are?'

'Jersey.' He managed a ghastly smile. 'Don't worry. I'm not quite out of my mind yet. I can think straight if I concentrate.'

'All right, then, listen to me,' Sean Gallagher said. 'Your leg is very bad indeed. You need hospital and a good surgeon.'

Kelso shook his head. 'Not possible. As I told this lady earlier, no Germans. It would be better to shoot me than let them get their hands on me.'

'Why?' Sean Gallagher demanded bluntly.

'She called you General. Is that true?'

'I was once in the Irish Army and I served with the Brits in the last war. Does that make a difference?'

'Perhaps.'

'All right, what's your unit?'

'Engineers – assault engineers, to be precise. We lead the way in beach landings.'

Sean Gallagher saw it all. 'Is this something to do with the invasion?'

Kelso nodded. 'It's coming soon.'

'Sure and we all know that,' Gallagher said.

'Yes, but I know where and I know when. If the Germans could squeeze that out of me, can you imagine what it would mean? All their troops concentrated in the right place. We'd never get off the beach.'

He was extremely agitated, sweat on his forehead. Helen soothed him, easing him down. 'It's all right, I promise you.'

'Is George Hamilton coming?' Gallagher asked.

'He was out. I left a message with his housekeeper that you wanted to see him urgently. I said you'd cut your leg and thought it needed a stitch or two.'

'Who's Hamilton?' Kelso demanded.

'A doctor,' Helen said. 'And a good friend. He'll be here soon to see to that leg of yours.'

Kelso was shaking again as the fever took hold. 'More important things to think of at the moment. You must speak to your resistance people here. Tell them to get on the radio as soon as possible and notify Intelligence in London that I'm here. They'll have to try to get me out.'

'But there is no resistance movement in Jersey,' Helen said. 'I mean, there's a hell of a lot of people who don't care to be occupied and make life as awkward for the enemy as they can, but we don't have anything like the French Resistance, if that's what you mean.'

Kelso stared at her in astonishment and Gallagher said, 'This island is approximately ten miles by five. There are something like forty-five thousand civilians. A good-size market town, that's all. How long do you think a resistance movement would last here? No mountains to run to, nowhere to take refuge. Nowhere to go, in fact.'

Kelso seemed to have difficulty in taking it in. 'So, there's no resistance movement. No radio?'

'No links with London at all,' Gallagher told him.

'Then what about France?' Kelso asked desperately. 'Granville, St. Malo. They're only a few hours away across the water, aren't they? There must be a local unit of the French Resistance in those places.'

There was a significant pause, then Helen turned to Gallagher. 'Savary could speak to the right people in Granville. He knows who they are and so do you.'

'True.'

'Guido was leaving as I came up from the beach,' she said. 'He told me they were trying for Granville this afternoon. Taking advantage of the fog.' She glanced at her watch. 'They won't have the tide until noon. You could take the van. There are those sacks of potatoes to go into St. Helier for the troops' supply depot and the market.'

'All right, you've convinced me,' Gallagher said. 'But if I know Savary, he won't want any of this, not in his head. That means writing it down, which is taking one hell of a chance.'

'We don't have any choice, Sean,' she said simply.

'No, I suppose you're right.' Gallagher laughed. 'The things I do for England. Look after our friend here. I'll be back as soon as I can.'

As he reached the door she called, 'And Sean?'

He turned. 'Yes?'

'Don't forget to drive on the right-hand side of the road.'

It was an old joke, but not without a certain amount of truth. One of the first things the German forces had done on occupying Jersey was to change the traffic flow from the left- to the right-hand side of the road. After four years, Gallagher still couldn't get used to it, not that he drove very often. They only had the old Ford van as a special dispensation because the de Ville farmlands supplied various crops for the use of the German forces. The size of the petrol ration meant the van could be used only two or three times a week anyway. Gallagher stretched it by coasting down the hills with the engine off, and there was always a little black-market petrol available if you knew the right people.

He drove down through the tiny picturesque town of St. Aubin and followed the curve of the bay to Bel Royal, St. Helier in the distance. He passed a number of gun emplacements with a few troops in evidence, but Victoria Avenue was deserted on the run into town. One of the French trains the Germans had brought over passed him on its way to Millbrook, the only sign of activity until he reached the Grand Hotel. He checked his watch. It was just before eleven. Plenty of time to catch

Savary before the *Victor Hugo* left for Granville, so he turned left into Gloucester Street and made his way to the market.

There weren't too many people about, mainly because of the weather. The scarlet and black Nazi flag with its swastika on the pole above the Town Hall entrance hung limply in the damp air. The German for Town Hall is Rathaus. It was, therefore, understandable that the place was now known as the Rat House by the local inhabitants.

He parked outside the market in Beresford Street. It was almost deserted, just a handful of shoppers and a sprinkling of German soldiers. The market itself was officially closed, open for only two hours on a Saturday afternoon. There would be enough people in evidence then, desperately hoping for fresh produce.

Gallagher got two sacks of potatoes from the van, kicked open the gate and went inside. Most of the stalls in the old Victorian Market were empty, but there were one or two people about. He made straight for a stall on the far side where a large genial man in heavy sweater and cloth cap was arranging turnips in neat rows under a sign *D. Chevalier*.

'So, it's swedes today?' Gallagher said as he arrived.

'Good for you, General,' Chevalier said.

'Do you tell me? Mrs. Vibert gave me swede jam for breakfast the other day.' Gallagher shuddered. 'I can still taste it. Two sacks of spuds for you here.'

Chevalier's eyes lit up. 'I knew you wouldn't let me down, General. Let's have them in the back.'

Gallagher dragged them into the room at the rear, and Chevalier opened a cupboard and took out an old canvas duffel bag. 'Four loaves of white bread.'

'Jesus,' Gallagher said. 'Who did you kill to get those?'

'A quarter pound of China tea and a leg of pork. Okay?'

'Nice to do business with you,' Gallagher told him. 'See you next week.'

His next stop was at the troop supply depot in Wesley Street. It had originally been a garage and there were half-a-dozen trucks parked in there. There wasn't much happening, but a burly Feldwebel called Klinger was sitting in the glass office eating a sandwich. He waved, opened the door and came down the steps.

'Herr General,' he said genially.

'God, Hans, but you do well for yourself.' Gallagher said in excellent German and prodded the ample stomach.

Klinger smiled. 'A man must live. We are both old soldiers, Herr General. We understand each other. You have something for me?'

'Two sacks of potatoes for the official list.'

'And?'

'Another sack for you, if you're interested.'

'And in exchange?'

'Petrol.'

The German nodded. 'One five-gallon can.'

'Two five-gallon cans,' Gallagher said.

'General.' Klinger turned to a row of British Army issue petrol cans, picked two up and brought them to the van. 'What if I turned you in? You're so unreasonable.'

'Prison for me and a holiday for you,' Gallagher said. 'They say the Russian Front's lovely at this time of the year.'

'As always, a practical man.' Klinger pulled the three sacks of potatoes out of the van. 'One of these days a patrol is going to stop you for a fuel check, and they'll discover your petrol is the wrong color.'

'Ah, but I'm a magician, my friend, didn't I tell you that?' and Gallagher drove away.

Military petrol was dyed red, the ration for agricultural use was green, and doctors enjoyed a pink variety. What Klinger hadn't discovered was that it was a simple matter to remove the dye by straining the petrol through the filter of the gas mask issued to the general public at the beginning of the war. A little green dye added afterward turned military petrol to the agricultural variety very quickly indeed.

Survival was what it was all about. This was an old island, and the Le Brocq half of him was fiercely proud of that. Over the centuries, the island had endured many things. As he passed the Pomme d'Or Hotel, German Naval Headquarters, he looked up at the Nazi flag hanging above the entrance and said softly, 'And we'll still be here when you bastards are long gone.'

5

Gallagher parked the van at the weighbridge and walked along the Albert Pier, going up the steps to the top section. He paused to light one of his French cigarettes and looked out across the bay. The fog had thinned just a little and Elizabeth Castle, on its island, looked strange and mysterious, like something out of a fairy story. Walter Raleigh had once ruled there as governor. Now Germans with concrete fortifications and gun emplacements up on top.

He looked down into the harbor. As always it was a hive of activity. The Germans used Rhine barges, among other vessels, to carry supplies to the Channel Islands. There were several moored on the far side at the New North Quay. There were a number of craft of various kinds from the 2 Vorpostenbootsflotille and two M40 Klasse minesweepers from the 24th Minesweeper Flotilla. Several cargo vessels, mostly coasters, among them the SS *Victor Hugo*, were moored against the Albert Pier.

Built in 1920 by Ferguson Brothers in Glasgow for a French firm engaged in the coastal trade, she had definitely seen better days. Her single smokestack was punctured in several places by cannon shell from RAF Beaufighters in an attack on one of the night convoys from Granville two weeks previously. Savary was the master with a crew of ten Frenchmen. The antiaircraft defenses consisted of two machine guns and a Bofors gun, manned by seven German naval ratings commanded by Guido Orsini.

Gallagher could see him now on the bridge, leaning on the rail, and called in English, 'Heh, Guido? Is Savary about?'

Guido cupped his hands. 'In the café.'

The hut farther along the pier which served as a café was not busy, four French seamen playing cards at one table, three German sailors at another. Robert Savary, a large, bearded man in a reefer coat and cloth cap, a greasy scarf knotted at his neck, sat on his own at a table next to the window, smoking a cigarette, a bowl of coffee in front of him.

'Robert, how goes it?' Gallagher demanded in French and sat down.

'Unusual to see you down here, Mon General, which means you want something.'

'Ah, you cunning old peasant.' Gallagher passed an envelope under the table. 'There, have you got that?'

'What is it?'

'Just put it in your pocket and don't ask questions. When you get to Granville, there's a café in the walled city called Sophie's. You know it?'

Savary was already beginning to turn pale. 'Yes, of course I do.'

'You know the good Sophie Cresson well and her husband Gerard?'

'I've met them.' Savary tried to give him the envelope back under the table.

'Then you'll know that their business is terrorism carried to as extreme a degree as possible. They not only shoot the Boche, they also like to make an example of collaborators, isn't that the colorful phrase? So if I were you, I'd be sensible. Take the letter. Needless to say, don't read it. If you do, you'll probably never sleep again. Just give it to Sophie with my love. I'm sure she'll have a message for me, which you'll let me have as soon as you're back.'

'Damn you, General,' Savary muttered and put the envelope in his pocket.

'The Devil took care of that long ago. Don't worry. You've nothing to worry about. Guido Orsini's a good lad.'

'The Count?' Savary shrugged. 'Flashy Italian pimp. I hate aristocrats.'

'No Fascist, that one, and he's probably got less time for Hitler than you have. Have you any decent cigarettes in your bag? I'm going crazy smoking that filthy tobacco they've been importing for the official ration lately.'

Savary looked cunning. 'Not really. Only a few Gitanes.'

'Only, the man says.' Gallagher groaned aloud. 'All right, I'll take two hundred.'

'And what do I get?'

Gallagher opened the bag Chevalier had given him. 'Leg of pork?'

Savary's jaw dropped. 'My God, my tongue's hanging out already. Give me.'

Gallagher passed it under the table and took the carton of cigarettes in return. 'You know my telephone number at the cottage. Ring me as soon as you get back.'

'All right.'

Savary got up and they went outside. Gallagher, unwilling to wait, got a packet of Gitanes out, opened it and lit one. 'Jesus, that's wonderful.'

'I'll be off then.' Savary made a move to walk toward the gangway of the *Victor Hugo*.

Gallagher said softly, 'Let me down on this one and I'll kill you, my friend. Understand?'

Savary turned, mouth open in astonishment as Gallagher smiled cheerfully and walked away along the pier.

George Hamilton was a tall, angular man whose old Harris tweed suit looked a size too large. A distinguished physician in his day, at one time professor of pharmacology at the University of London and a consultant of Guy's Hospital, he had retired to a cottage in Jersey just before the outbreak of war. In 1940, with the Germans expected at any day, many people had left the island, a number of doctors among them, which explained why Hamilton, an MD and Fellow of the Royal College of Physicians, was working as a general practitioner at the age of seventy.

He pushed a shock of white hair back from his forehead and stood up, looking down at Kelso on the couch. 'Not good. He should be in hospital. I really need an x-ray to be sure, but I'd say at least two fractures of the tibia. Possibly three.'

'No hospital,' Kelso said faintly.

Hamilton made a sign to Helen and Gallagher, and they followed him into the kitchen. 'If the fractures were compound – in other words, if there was any kind of open wound, bone sticking through, then we wouldn't have any choice. The possibility of infection, especially after all he's been through, would be very great. The only way of saving the leg would be a hospital bed and traction.'

'What exactly are you saying, George?' Gallagher asked.

'Well, as you can see, the skin isn't broken. The fractures are what we term comminuted. It might be possible to set the leg and plaster it.'

'Can you handle that?' Helen demanded.

'I could try, but I need the right conditions. I certainly wouldn't dream of proceeding without an x-ray.' He hesitated. 'There is one possibility.'

'What's that?' Gallagher asked.

'Pine Trees. It's a little nursing home in St. Lawrence run by Catholic Sisters of Mercy. Irish and French mostly. They have x-ray facilities there and a decent operating theater. Sister Maria Teresa, who's in charge, is a good friend. I could give her a ring.'

'Do the Germans use it?' Helen asked.

'Now and then. Usually young women with prenatal problems, which is a polite way of saying they're in for an abortion. The nuns, as you may imagine, don't like that one little bit, but there isn't anything they can do about it.'

'Would he be able to stay there?'

'I doubt it. They've very few beds and surely it would be too dangerous. The most we could do is patch him up and bring him back here.'

Gallagher said, 'You're taking a hell of a risk helping us like this, George.'

'I'd say we all are,' Hamilton told him dryly.

'It's vitally important that Colonel Kelso stay out of the hands of the enemy,' Helen began.

Hamilton shook his head. 'I don't want to know, Helen, so don't try to tell me, and I don't want the nuns to be involved either. As far as Sister Maria Teresa is concerned, our friend must be a local man who's had a suitable accident. It would help if we had an identity card for him, just in case.'

Helen turned on Gallagher. 'Can you do anything? You managed a card for that Spanish Communist last year when he escaped from the working party at those tunnels they've been constructing in St. Peter.'

Gallagher went to the old eighteenth-century pine desk in the corner of the kitchen, pulled out the front drawer, then reached inside and produced a small box drawer of the kind people had once used to hide valuables. There were several blank identity cards in there, signed and stamped with the Nazi eagle.

'Where on earth did you get those?' Hamilton asked in astonishment.

'An Irishman I know, barman in one of the town hotels, has a German boyfriend, if you follow me. A clerk at the Feldkommandatur. I did him a big favor last year. He gave me these in exchange. I'll fill in Kelso's details and we'll give him a good Jersey name. How about Le Marquand?' He took out pen and ink and sat at the kitchen table. 'Henry Ralph Le Marquand. Residence?'

He looked up at Helen. 'Home Farm, de Ville Place,' she said.

'Fair enough. I'll go and get the color of his eyes, hair and so on while you phone Pine Trees.' He paused at the door. 'I'll enter his occupation as fisherman. That way we can say it was a boating accident. And one more thing, George.'

'What's that?' Hamilton asked as he lifted the phone.

'I'm going with you. We'll take him up in the van. No arguments. We must all hang together, or all hang separately.' He smiled wryly and went out.

Pine Trees was an ugly house, obviously late Victorian in origin. At some time, the walls had been faced in cement which had cracked in many places, here and there, large pieces having flaked away altogether. Gallagher drove the van into the front courtyard, Hamilton sitting beside him. As they got out, the front door opened and Sister Maria Teresa came down the sloping concrete ramp to meet them. She wore a simple black habit, a small woman with calm eyes and not a wrinkle to be seen on her face though she was in her sixties.

'Dr. Hamilton.' Her English was good, but with a pronounced French accent.

'This is General Gallagher. He manages de Ville Place where the patient is employed.'

'We'll need a trolley,' Gallagher said.

'There's one just inside the door.'

He got it and brought it to the back of the van. He opened the doors, revealing Kelso lying on an old mattress, and they eased him out onto the trolley.

Sister Maria Teresa led the way inside, and as he pushed the trolley up the ramp, Gallagher whispered to Kelso, 'Don't forget, keep your trap shut, and if you have to moan in pain, try not to sound American.'

Hamilton stood in the operating theater examining the x-ray plates which young Sister Bernadette had brought in. 'Three fractures,' Sister Maria Teresa said. 'Not good. He should be in hospital, Doctor, but I don't need to tell you that.'

'All right, Sister. I'll tell you the truth,' Hamilton said. 'If he goes down to St. Helier they'll want to know how it happened. Our German friends insist on it. You know what sticklers for detail they are. Le Marquand was fishing illegally when the accident took place.'

Gallagher cut in smoothly, 'Which could earn him three months in jail.'

'I see.' She shook her head. 'I wish I had a bed to offer, but we're quite full.'

'Any Germans about?'

'Two of their girlfriends,' she said calmly. 'The usual thing. One of the army doctors handled that yesterday. Major Speer. Do you know him?'

'I've worked with him on occasion at the hospital,' Hamilton said. 'I've known worse. Anyway, Sister, if you'd care to assist me, you and Sister Bernadette, we'll get started.'

She eased him into a robe and he went to scrub up at the sink in the corner. As Sister Bernadette helped him on with rubber gloves, he said to Maria Teresa, 'A short-term anesthetic only. Chloroform on the pad will do.' He moved to the operating table and looked down at Kelso. 'All right?'

Kelso, gritting his teeth, nodded and Hamilton said to Gallagher. 'You'd better wait outside.'

Gallagher turned to leave, and at that moment, the door opened and a German officer walked in.

'Ah, there you are, Sister,' he said in French, then smiled and changed to English. 'Professor Hamilton, you here?'

'Major Speer,' Hamilton said, gloved hands raised.

'I've just looked in on my patients, Sister. Both are doing well.'

Speer was a tall, handsome man with a good-humored, rather fleshy face. His greatcoat hung open, and Gallagher noticed an Iron Cross First Class on the left breast and the ribbon for the Russian Winter War. A man who had seen action.

'Anything interesting, Doctor?'

'Fractures of the tibia. An employee of General Gallagher here. Have you met?'

'No, but I've heard of you many times, General.' Speer clicked his heels and saluted. 'A pleasure.' He moved to the x-rays and examined them. 'Not good. Not good at all. Comminuted fracture of the tibia in three places.'

'I know hospitalization and traction should be the norm,' Hamilton said. 'But a bed isn't available.'

'Oh, I should think it perfectly acceptable to set the bones and then plaster.' Speer smiled with great charm and took off his greatcoat. 'But, Herr Professor, this is hardly your field. It would be a pleasure to take care of this small matter for you.'

He was already taking a gown down from a peg on the wall and moved to the sink to scrub up. 'If you insist,' Hamilton said calmly. 'There's little doubt this is more your sort of thing than mine.'

A few minutes later, Speer was ready, leaning down to examine the leg. He looked up at Sister Maria Teresa. 'Right, Sister, chloroform now, I think. Not too much and we'll work very quickly.'

From the corner, Gallagher watched, fascinated.

Savary wasn't feeling too pleased with life as he walked along the cobbled streets of the walled city in Granville. For one thing, the trip from Jersey in the fog had been lousy, and he was distinctly unhappy at the situation Gallagher had placed him in. He turned into a quiet square. Sophie's Bar was on the far side, a chink of light showing here and there through the shutters. He walked across, slowly and reluctantly, and went in.

Gerard Cresson sat in his wheelchair playing the piano, a small man with the white intense face of the invalid, black hair hanging almost to his shoulders. He'd broken his back in an accident on the docks two years before the war. Would never walk again, not even with crutches.

There were a dozen or so customers scattered around the bar, some of them seamen whom Savary knew. Sophie sat on a high stool behind the marble counter, bottles ranged behind her against an ornate mirror, and read the local newspaper. She was in her late thirties, dark hair piled high on her head, black eyes, the face sallow like a gypsy's, the mouth wide and painted bright red. She had good breasts, the best Savary had ever seen. Not that it would have done any good. With a knife or a bottle she was dynamite, and there were men in Granville with scars to prove it.

'Ah, Robert, it's been a long time. How goes it?'

'It could be worse, it could be better.'

As she poured him a cognac, he slipped the letter across. 'What's this?' she demanded.

'Your friend Gallagher in Jersey uses me as a postman now. I don't know what's in it and I don't want to, but he expects an answer when I return. We sail tomorrow at noon. I'll be back.' He swallowed his cognac and left.

She came round the counter and called to one of the customers, 'Heh, Marcel, look after the bar for me.'

She approached her husband who had stopped playing and was lighting a cigarette. 'What was that all about?'

'Let's go in the back and find out.'

She pulled his wheelchair from the piano, turned and pushed him along the bar to the sitting room at the rear. Gerard Cresson sat at the table and read Gallagher's letter, then pushed it across to her, face grave.

She read it quickly, then got a bottle of red wine and filled two glasses. 'He's in a real mess this time, our friend the General.'

'And then some.'

Between them they had controlled the Resistance movement from Granville to Avranches and St. Malo for three years now. Gerard provided the organizing ability and Sophie was his good right arm. They were a very successful team. Had to be to have survived so long.

'You'll radio London?'

'Of course.'

'What do you think?' she said. 'Maybe they'll ask us to try to get this Yank out of Jersey.'

'Difficult at the best of times,' he said. 'Not possible with the state he's in.' He held out his glass for more wine. 'Of course, there is a rather obvious solution. Much better for everyone in the circumstances, I should have thought.'

'And what's that?'

'Send someone across to cut his throat.'

There was silence between them. She said, 'It's been a long war.'

'Too long,' he said. 'Now take me to the storeroom and I'll radio London.'

Major Speer turned from the sink, toweling his hands. Sister Bernadette was already mixing the plaster of Paris, and he crossed to the operating table and looked down at Kelso who was still unconscious.

'An excellent piece of work,' George Hamilton said.

'Yes, I must say I'm rather pleased with it myself.' Speer reached for his greatcoat. 'I'm sure you can handle the rest. I'm already late for dinner at the officers' club. Don't forget to let me know how he progresses, Herr Professor. General.' He saluted and went out.

Hamilton stood, looked down at Kelso, suddenly drained as he stripped off his gloves and gown. Kelso moaned a little as he started to come round and said softly, 'Janet, I love you.'

The American accent was unmistakable. Sister Bernadette appeared not to have noticed, but the older woman glanced sharply at Hamilton and then at Gallagher.

'He seems to be coming around,' Hamilton said lamely.

'So it would appear,' she said. 'Why don't you and General Gallagher go to my office. One of the nuns will get you some coffee. We have some of the real stuff thanks to Major Speer. Sister Bernadette and I will put the cast on for you.'

'That's very kind of you, Sister.'

The two men went out and along the corridor, past the kitchen where two nuns worked, to the office at the end. Hamilton sat behind the desk and Gallagher gave him one of his Gitanes and sat in the window seat.

'The moment he came through that door will stay with me forever,' the Irishman said.

'As I told you, he's not a bad sort,' Hamilton commented. 'And a damn fine doctor.'

'You think Kelso will be all right?'

'I don't see why not. We should be able to move him in an hour or so. We'll have to watch him closely for the next few days. The possibility of infection mustn't be discounted, but there were some ampules of this new wonder drug, penicillin, in that emergency kit from his life raft. I'll start him on that if he gets the wrong sort of reaction.'

'Sister Maria Teresa – she knows things aren't what they seem.'

'Yes, I feel rather bad about that,' George Hamilton said. 'As if I've used her. She won't tell, of course. It would be contrary to every belief she holds dear.'

'She reminds me of my old aunt in Dublin when I was a lad,' Gallagher said. 'Incense, candles and the Holy Water.'

'Do you still believe, Sean?' Hamilton asked.

'Not since the first of July, nineteen sixteen, on the Somme,' Gallagher said. 'I was attached to a Yorkshire Regiment, the Leeds Pals. The idiots at headquarters sent those lads over the top, packs on their backs, into heavy machine-gun fire. By noon, there were around forty or so survivors out of eight hundred. I decided then that if God existed, he was having a bad joke at my expense.'

'I take your point,' Hamilton said gravely.

Gallagher stood up. 'I think I'll sample the night air for a while,' and he opened the door and went out.

George Hamilton rested his head on his arms on the desk and yawned. It had been a long day. He closed his eyes and was asleep within a couple of minutes.

It was just after ten and Dougal Munro was still working away at his desk in his office at Baker Street when the door opened and Jack Carter limped in, his face grim. He placed a signal flimsy on the brigadier's desk. 'Brace yourself, sir.'

'What is this?' Munro demanded.

'Message just in from our Resistance contact in Granville. That's in Normandy.'

'I know where it is, for God's sake.' Munro started to read and suddenly sat up straight. 'I don't believe it.'

Munro read the signal through again. 'It couldn't be worse. There isn't a resistance movement in Jersey. No one to call on. I mean, this de Ville woman and the Gallagher man, how long can they manage, especially if he's ill? And how long can he get by on a small island like that? It doesn't bear thinking of, Jack.'

For the first time since Carter had known him he sounded close to despair, uncertain which way to go. 'You'll think of something, sir, you always do,' Carter said gently.

'Thanks for the vote of confidence.' Munro stood up and reached for his coat. 'Now you'd better phone through to Hayes Lodge and get me an immediate appointment with General Eisenhower. Tell them I'm on my way.'

Helen de Ville had been waiting anxiously for the sound of the van returning, and when it drove into the courtyard, at the side of de Ville Place, she ran out. As Gallagher and Hamilton got out of the van, she cried, 'Is he all right?'

'Still doped up, but the leg's doing fine,' Gallagher told her.

'There's no one in at the moment. They're either in Granville or at sea or at the officers' club, so let's get him upstairs.'

Gallagher and Hamilton got Kelso out of the van, joined hands and lifted him between them. They followed Helen through the front door, across the wide paneled hall and up the great staircase. She opened the door of the master bedroom and led the way in. The furniture was seventeenth-century Breton, including the four-poster bed. There was a bathroom through a door on the right side of the bed, on the left, carved library shelving from wall to ceiling crammed with books. Her fingers found a hidden spring and a section swung back to disclose a stairway. She led the way up and Gallagher and Hamilton followed with some difficulty, but finally made it to a room under the roof. The walls were paneled in oak, and there was a single window in the gable end. It was comfortable enough with carpet on the floor and a single bed.

They got Kelso onto the bed and Helen said, 'There's everything you need, and the only entrance is from my room, so you should be quite safe. An ancestor of mine hid here from Cromwell's people for years. I'm afraid the convenience hasn't improved since his day. It's that oak commode over there.'

'Thanks, but all I want to do is sleep,' Kelso said, his face tired and strained.

She nodded to Gallagher and the old doctor and they went out and downstairs. Hamilton said, 'I'll get off myself. Tell Helen I'll look in tomorrow.'

Sean Gallagher took his hand for a moment. 'George, you're quite a man.'

'All in a doctor's day, Sean.' Hamilton smiled. 'See you tomorrow.' And he went out.

Gallagher went through the hall and along the rear passage to the kitchen. He put the kettle on the stove, and was pushing a few pieces of wood in among the dying embers when Helen came in.

'Is he all right?' he asked.

'Fast asleep already.' She sat on the edge of the table. 'Now what do we do?'

'Nothing we can do until Savary gets back from Granville with some sort of message.'

'And what if there isn't any message?'

'Oh, I'll think of something. Now sit down and have a nice cup of tea.'

She shook her head. 'We've got a choice of either bramble or beet tea and, tonight, I just can't face either.'

'Oh, ye of little faith.' Gallagher produced the packet of China tea which Chevalier had given him that morning at the market.

She started to laugh helplessly and put her arms around his neck. 'Sean Gallagher, what would I do without you?'

Eisenhower was in full uniform for he'd been attending a dinner party with the prime minister when he'd received Munro's message. He paced up and down the library at Hayes Lodge, extremely agitated. 'Is there no way we can put someone in?'

'If you mean a commando unit, I don't think so, sir. The most heavily defended coast in Europe.'

Eisenhower nodded. 'What you're really saying is that it's impossible to get him out.'

'No, sir, but very, very difficult. It's a small island, General. It's not like hiding someone on the back of a truck and driving three hundred miles overnight to the Pyrenees or arranging for one of our Lysanders to fly in to pick him up.'

'Right, then get him across to France where you can fix those things.'

'Our information is that he's not capable of traveling.'

'For God's sake, Munro, everything could hang on this. The whole invasion. Months of planning.'

Munro cleared his throat and nervously for him. 'If worse came to worst, General, would you be willing to consider Colonel Kelso as expendable?'

Eisenhower stopped pacing. 'You mean have him executed?'

'Something like that.'

'God help me, but if there's nothing else for it, then so be it.' Eisenhower walked up to the huge wall map of western Europe. 'Six thousand ships, thousands of planes, two million men and the war in balance. If they find out our exact points of landing, they'll mass everything they've got.' He turned. 'Intelligence reported a Rommel speech of a few weeks ago in which he said just that. That the war would be won or lost on those beaches.'

'I know, General.'

'And you ask is Kelso expendable?' Eisenhower sighed heavily. 'If you can save him, do. If you can't . . .' He shrugged. 'In any case, considering what you've already said about the Jersey situation, how would you go about getting an agent in? I should think a new face would stick out like a sore thumb.'

'That's true, General. We'll have to think about it.'

Jack Carter, standing respectfully quiet by the fire, coughed. 'There is one way, General.'

'What's that, Captain?' Eisenhower inquired.

'The best place to hide a tree is in a wood. It seems to me the people who are most free to come and go are the Germans themselves. I mean, new personnel must be posted there all the time.'

Eisenhower turned sharply to Munro. 'He's got a point. Have you got any people capable of that kind of work?'

Munro nodded. 'Here and there, sir. It's a rare skill. Not just a question of speaking fluent German, but thinking like a German and that isn't easy.'

Eisenhower said, 'I'll give you a week, Brigadier. One week and I expect you to have this matter resolved.'

'My word on it, sir.'

Munro walked out briskly, Carter limping along behind. 'Radio Cresson in Granville to relay a message to Gallagher in Jersey saying someone will be with him by Thursday.'

'Are you sure, sir?'

'Of course I am,' Munro said cheerfully. 'That was a masterly suggestion of yours in there, Jack. Best place to hide a tree is in a wood. I like that.'

'Thank you very much, sir.'

'German personnel moving in and out all the time. What would one new arrival be among many, especially if provided with the right kind of credentials?'

'It would take a very special man, sir.'

'Come off it, Jack,' Munro said as they reached the street and the car. 'There's only one man for this job. You know it and I know it. Only one man capable of playing a Nazi to the hilt and ruthless enough to put a bullet between Kelso's eyes if necessary. Harry Martineau.'

'I must remind you, sir, that Colonel Martineau was given a definite promise after that business in Lyons that his services wouldn't be required again. His health alone should make it impossible.'

'Nonsense, Jack. Harry could never resist a challenge. Find him. And another thing, Jack. Check SOE files. See if we've got anyone with a Jersey background.'

'Men only, sir?'

'Good God, Jack, of course not. Since when have we been interested in men only in our business.'

He tapped on the partition and the driver took them away from the curb.

6

The cottage in Dorset, not far from Lulworth Cove, had been loaned to Martineau by an old friend from Oxford days. It stood in a tiny valley above the cliffs, and the way to the beach was blocked by rusting barbed wire. There had once been a notice warning of mines, not that there were any. That had been the first thing the landlord at the village pub had told Martineau when he'd moved into the area, which explained why he was walking along the shoreline, occasionally throwing stones into the incoming waves, the morning after Dougal Munro's meeting with Eisenhower at Hayes Lodge.

Harry Martineau was forty-four, of medium height, with good shoulders under the old paratrooper's camouflaged jump jacket which he wore against the cold. His face was very pale, with the kind of skin that never seemed to tan, and wedge-shaped, the eyes so dark that it was impossible to say what their true color was. The mouth was mobile, with a slight ironic smile permanently in place. The look of a man who had found life more disappointing than he had hoped.

He'd been out of hospital for three months now and things were better than they'd been for a while. He didn't get the chest pain anymore, except when he overdid things, but the insomnia pattern was terrible. He could seldom sleep at night. The moment he went to bed, his brain seemed to become hyperactive. Still, that was only to be expected. Too many years on the run, of living by night, danger constantly at hand.

He was no use to Munro anymore, the doctors had made that clear. He could have returned to Oxford, but that was no answer. Neither was trying to pick up the threads of the book he'd been working on in 1939. The war had taught him that if nothing else. So, he'd dropped out as thoroughly as a man could. The cottage in Dorset by the sea, books to read, space to find himself in.

'And where the hell have you gone, Harry?' he asked morosely as he started up the cliff path. 'Because I'm damned if I can find you.'

The living room of the old cottage was comfortable enough. A Persian carpet on the flagged floor, a dining table and several rush-backed chairs and books everywhere, not only on the shelves but piled in the corner. None of them were his. Nothing in this place was his except for a few clothes.

There was a sofa on each side of the stone fireplace. He put a couple of logs on the embers, poured himself a scotch, drank it quickly and poured another. Then he sat down and picked up the notepad he'd left on the coffee table. There were several lines of poetry written on it and he read them aloud.

The station is ominous at midnight. Hope is a dead letter. He dropped the notepad back on the table with a wry smile. 'Admit it, Harry,' he said softly. 'You're a lousy poet.'

Suddenly, he was tired, the feeling coming in a kind of rush, the lack of sleep catching up with him. His chest began to ache a little, the left lung, and that took him back to Lyons, of course, on that final and fatal day. If he'd been a little bit more on the ball it wouldn't have happened. A case of taking the pitcher to the well too often or perhaps, quite simply, his luck had run out. As he drifted into sleep, it all came back so clearly.

Standartenführer Jurgen Kaufmann, the head of the Gestapo in Lyons, was in civilian clothes that day as he came down the steps of the Town Hall and got into the back of the black Citroën. His driver was also in civilian clothes, for on Thursday afternoons Kaufmann visited his mistress and liked to be discreet about it.

'Take your time, Karl,' he said to his driver, an SS sergeant who'd served with him for two years now. 'We're a little early. I said I wouldn't be there till three and you know how she hates surprises.'

'As you say, Standartenführer.' Karl smiled as he drove away.

Kaufmann opened a copy of a Berlin newspaper which he had received in the post that morning and settled back to enjoy it. They moved through the outskirts of town into the country. It was really quite beautiful, orchards of apples on either side of the road, and the air was heavy with the smell of them. For some time Karl had noticed a motorcycle behind them, and when they turned into the side road leading to the village of Chaumont, it followed.

He said, 'There's a motorcyclist been on our tail for quite some time, Standartenführer.' He took a Luger from his pocket and laid it on the seat beside him.

Kaufmann turned to look through the rear window and laughed. 'You're losing your touch, Karl. He's one of ours.'

The motorcyclist drew alongside and waved. He was SS Feldgendarmerie in helmet, heavy uniform raincoat, a Schmeisser machine pistol slung across his chest just below the SS Field Police metal gorget that was only worn when officially on duty. The face was anonymous behind the goggles. He waved a gloved hand again.

'He must have a message for me,' Kaufmann said. 'Pull up.'

Karl turned in at the side of the road and braked to a halt and the motorcyclist pulled up in front. He shoved his machine up on the stand and Karl got out. 'What can we do for you?'

A hand came out of the raincoat pocket holding a Mauser semiautomatic pistol. He shot Karl once in the heart, hurling him back against the Citroën. He slid down into the road. The SS man turned him over with his boot and shot him again very deliberately between the eyes. Then he opened the rear door.

Kaufmann always went armed, but he'd taken off his overcoat and folded it neatly in the corner. As he got his hand to the Luger in the right pocket and turned, the SS man shot him in the arm. Kaufmann clutched at his sleeve, blood oozing between his fingers.

'Who are you?' he cried wildly. The other man pushed up his goggles and Kaufmann stared into the darkest, coldest eyes he had ever seen in his life.

'My name is Martineau. I'm a major in the British Army serving with SOE.'

'So, you are Martineau.' Kaufmann grimaced with pain. 'Your German is excellent. Quite perfect.'

'So it should be. My mother was German,' Martineau told him.

Kaufmann said, 'I'd hoped to meet you before long, but under different circumstances.'

'I'm sure you did. I've wanted to meet you for quite some time. Since nineteen thirty-eight, in fact. You were a captain at Gestapo Headquarters in Berlin in May of that year. You arrested a young woman called Rosa Bernstein. You probably don't even remember the name.'

'But I recall her very well,' Kaufmann told him. 'She was Jewish and worked for the Socialist Underground.'

'I was told that by the time you'd finished with her she couldn't even walk to the firing squad.'

'That's not true. The firing squad never came into it. She was hanged in cellar number three. Standard procedure. What was she to you?'

'I loved her.' Martineau raised his pistol.

Kaufmann cried, 'Don't be a fool. We can do a deal. I can save your life, Martineau, believe me.'

'Is that so?' Harry Martineau said, and shot him between the eyes, killing him instantly.

He pushed the heavy motorcycle off its stand and rode away. He was perfectly in control in spite of what he had just done. No emotion – nothing. The trouble was, it hadn't brought Rosa Bernstein back, but then, nothing ever could.

He rode through a maze of country lanes for over an hour, working his way steadily westward. Finally, he turned along a narrow country lane, grass growing so tall on either side that it almost touched. The farmhouse in the courtyard at the end of the lane had seen better days, a window broken here and there, a few slates missing. Martineau got off the bike, pushed it up on the stand and crossed to the front door.

'Heh, Pierre, open up!' He tried the latch and hammered with his fist and then the door opened so suddenly that he fell on his knees.

The muzzle of a Walther touched him between the eyes. The man holding it was about forty and dressed like a French farm laborer in beret, corduroy jacket and denim trousers, but his German was impeccable. 'Please stand, Major Martineau, and walk inside very slowly.'

He followed Martineau along the corridor into the kitchen. Pierre Duval sat at the table, tied to a chair, a handkerchief in his mouth, eyes wild, blood on his face.

'Hands on the wall and spread,' the German said, and ran his hands expertly over Martineau, relieving him of the Schmeisser and the Mauser.

He moved to the old-fashioned telephone on the wall and gave the operator a number. After a while he said, 'Schmidt? He turned up. Yes, Martineau.' He nodded. 'All right, fifteen minutes.'

'Friend of yours?' Martineau inquired.

'Not really. I'm Abwehr. Kramer's the name. That was the Gestapo. I don't like those swine any more than you do, but we all have a job to do. Take your helmet and raincoat off. Make yourself comfortable.'

Martineau did as he was told. Evening was falling fast outside, the room was getting quite dark. He put the helmet and coat down and stood there in the SS uniform, aware of Pierre on the other side of the table, eyes glaring wildly, leaning back in his chair, his feet coming up.

'What about a drink?' Martineau asked.

'My God, they told me you were a cool one,' Kramer said admiringly.

Pierre lunged with his feet at the edge of the table ramming it into the German's back. Martineau's left hand deflected the pistol and he closed, raising his knee. But Kramer turned a thigh, raising stiffened fingers under Martineau's chin, jerking back his head. Martineau hooked Kramer's left leg, sending the German crashing to the ground, going down with him, reaching for the wrist of the hand that held the pistol, smashing his fist into the side of Kramer's neck, aware of the pistol exploding between them.

There was the distinct sound of bone cracking and the German lay still, alive, but moaning softly. Martineau got to his feet feeling suddenly weak and faint, opened the table drawer, spilling its contents on the floor, and picked up a breadknife. He moved behind Pierre and sliced the ropes that bound him to the chair. The old Frenchman jumped up, pulling the gag from his mouth.

'My God, Harry, I've never seen so much blood.'

Martineau glanced down. The front of the SS blouse was soaked in blood. His own blood and there were three bullet holes that he could see, one of them smoldering slightly from powder burns.

He slumped into the chair. 'Never mind that.'

'Did you get him, Harry? Did you get Kaufmann?'

'I got him, Pierre,' *Martineau said wearily.* 'When's the pickup?'

'The old aero club at Fleurie at seven, just before dark.'

Martineau looked at his watch. 'That only gives me half an hour. You'll have to come too. Nowhere else for you to go now.'

He got to his feet and started for the door, swaying a little, and the Frenchman put an arm around him. 'You'll never make it, Harry.'

'I'd better because about five minutes from now the Gestapo are going to be coming up that road,' *Martineau told him and went outside.*

He got the bike off the stand and threw a leg across the saddle, then he kicked it into life, feeling curiously as if everything was happening in slow motion. Pierre climbed up behind and put his arms around him and they rode away, out of the yard and along the lane.

As they turned into the road at the end, Martineau was aware of two dark sedans coming up fast on his left. One of them skidded to a halt, almost driving him into the ditch. He swung the motorcycle to the right, wheels spinning as he gunned the motor, was aware of shots, a sudden cry from Pierre, hands loosening their hold as the old Frenchman went backward over the rear wheel.

Martineau roared down the road toward the canal at the far end, swerved onto the towpath, one of the Gestapo cars following close. Two hundred yards away there was a lock, a narrow footbridge for pedestrians crossing to the other side. He rode across with no difficulty. Behind him, the car braked to a halt. The two Gestapo operatives inside jumped out and began to fire wildly, but by then he was long gone.

He could never remember clearly afterward any details of that cross-country ride to Fleurie. In the end, it was all something of an anticlimax anyway. The field had been headquarters of an aero club before the war. Now it lay derelict and forlorn and long disused.

He was aware of the roaring of the Lysander's engine in the distance as he rode up to the airfield himself. He paused, waiting, and the Lysander came in out of the darkness for a perfect touchdown, turned and taxied toward him. He got off the bike, allowing it to fall to one side. He promptly fell down himself, got up again and lurched forward. The door swung open and the pilot leaned across and shouted, 'I wasn't too sure when I saw the uniform.'

Martineau hauled himself inside. The pilot reached over and closed and locked the door. Martineau coughed suddenly, his mouth and chin red.

The pilot said, 'My God, you're choking on your own blood.'

'I've been doing that for at least four years now,' Martineau said.

The pilot had other things on his mind, several vehicles converging on the other end of the runway by the old buildings. Whoever they were, they were too late. The Bristol Perseus engine responded magnificently when fully boosted. The Westland Lysander was capable of taking off from rough ground, fully loaded, in two hundred and forty yards. At Fleurie, that night, they managed it in two hundred, clearing the cars at the end of the runway and climbing up into the gathering darkness.

'Very nice,' Martineau said. 'I liked that.' And then he fainted.

'So, he's in Dorset, is he?' Munro said. 'Doing what?'

'Not very much from what I can make out.' Carter hesitated. 'He did take two bullets in the left lung, sir, and . . .'

'No sad songs, Jack, I've other things on my mind. You've had a look at my ideas on a way of getting him into Jersey? What do you think?'

'Excellent, sir. I would have thought it all pretty foolproof, at least for a few days.'

'And that's all we need. Now, what else have you got for me?'

'As I understand it from your preliminary plan, sir, what you're seeking is someone to go in with him to establish his credentials. Someone who knows the island and the people and so on?'

'That's right.'

'There's an obvious flaw, of course. How on earth would you explain their presence? You can't just pop up in the island after four years of occupation without some sort of an explanation.'

'Very true.' Munro nodded. 'However, I can tell by the throb in your voice that you've already come up with a solution, so let's get on with it, Jack. What have you got?'

'Sarah Anne Drayton, sir, age nineteen. Born in Jersey. Left the island just before the war to go out to Malaya where her father was a rubber planter. He was a widower apparently. Sent her home a month before the fall of Singapore.'

'Which means she hasn't been back in Jersey since when?' Munro looked at the file. 'Nineteen thirty-eight. Six years. That's a long time at that age, Jack. Girls change out of all recognition.'

'Yes, sir.'

'Mind you, she's young.'

'We've used them as young as this before, sir.'

'Yes, but rarely and only in extremes. Where did you find her?'

'She was put forward for SOE consideration two years ago, mainly because she speaks fluent French with a Breton accent. Her maternal grandmother was Breton. Naturally, she was turned down because of her youth.'

'Where is she now?'

'Probationer nurse here in London at Cromwell Hospital.'

'Excellent, Jack.' Munro stood up and reached for his jacket. 'We'll go and see her. I'm sure she'll prove to be intensely patriotic.'

That the Luftwaffe had been chased from British skies, the Blitz had long gone, was a tale for the front pages of newspapers only. In the spring of 1944 night attacks were renewed on London, using the JU88S with devastating results. That Sunday was no exception. By eight o'clock the casualty department at Cromwell Hospital was working flat out.

Sarah Drayton had been supposed to come off shift at six. She had now been on duty fourteen hours without a break, but there were simply not enough nurses or doctors available. She worked on, helping with casualties laid out in the corridors, trying to ignore the crump of bombs falling in the middle distance, the sound of fire engines.

She was a small, intense girl, dark hair pushed up under her cap, her face very determined, the hazel eyes serious. Her gown was filthy, stained with blood, her stockings torn. She knelt to help the matron sedate a panic-stricken young girl who was bleeding badly from shrapnel wounds. They stood up to allow porters to carry the girl away on a stretcher.

Sarah said, 'I thought night raids were supposed to be a thing of the past.'

'Tell that to the casualties,' the matron said. 'Almost a thousand of them in March. Right, you clear off, Drayton. You'll be falling down soon from sheer fatigue. No arguments.'

She walked wearily along the corridor, aware that the sound of the bombing now seemed to have moved south of the river. Someone was sweeping up broken glass, and she stepped around them and moved to the reception desk to book out.

The night clerk was talking to two men. She said, 'Actually, this is Nurse Drayton coming now.'

Jack Carter said, 'Miss Drayton, this is Brigadier Munro and I'm Captain Carter.'

'What can I do for you?' Her voice was rather low and very pleasant.

Munro was much taken with her at once, and Carter said, 'Do you recall an interview you had two years ago? An intelligence matter?'

'With SOE?' She looked surprised. 'I was turned down.'

'Yes, well, if you could spare us some time we'd like a word with you.'

Carter drew her over to a bench beside the wall, and he and Munro sat on either side of her. 'You were born in Jersey, Miss Drayton?'

'That's right.'

He took out his notebook and opened it. 'Your mother's name was Margaret de Ville. That has a particular interest for us. Do you by any chance know a Mrs. Helen de Ville?'

'I do. My mother's cousin, although she was always Aunty Helen to me. She was so much older than I was.'

'And Sean Gallagher?'

'The General? Since I was a child.' She looked puzzled. 'What's going on here?'

'In good time, Miss Drayton,' Munro told her. 'When did you last see your aunt or General Gallagher?'

'Nineteen thirty-eight. My mother died that year and my father took a job in Malaya. I went out to join him.'

'Yes, we know that,' Carter said.

She frowned at him for a moment, then turned on Munro. 'All right, what's this about?'

'It's quite simple really,' Dougal Munro said. 'I'd like to offer you a job with SOE. I'd like you to go to Jersey for me.'

She stared at him in astonishment, but only for a moment, and then she started to laugh helplessly and the sound of it was close to hysteria. It had, after all, been a long day.

'But, Brigadier,' she said. 'I hardly know you.'

'Strange chap, Harry Martineau,' Munro said. 'I've never known anybody quite like him.'

'From what you tell me, neither have I,' Sarah said.

The car taking them down to Lulworth Cove was a huge Austin, a glass partition separating them from the driver. Munro and Jack Carter were in the rear, side by side, and Sarah Drayton sat on the jump seat opposite. She wore a tweed suit with pleated skirt, tan stockings and black brogues with half-heels, blouse in cream satin with a black string tie at her neck. She looked very attractive, cheeks flushed, eyes flickering everywhere. She also looked extremely young.

'It was his birthday the week before last,' Carter told her.

She was immediately interested. 'How old was he?'

'Forty-four.'

'What they call a child of the century, my dear,' Munro told her. 'Born on the seventh of April, nineteen hundred. That must seem terribly old to you.'

'Aries,' she said.

Munro smiled. 'That's right. Before the advent of our so called enlight-
ened times astrology was a science. Did you know that?'

'Not really.'

'The ancient Egyptians always chose their generals from Leos, for
example.'

'I'm a Leo,' she said. 'July twenty-seventh.'

'Then you *are* in for a complicated life. Something of a hobby of mine.
Take Harry, for instance. Very gifted, brilliant analytical mind. A professor
in the greatest university in the world at thirty-eight. Then look at what he
became in middle life.'

'How do you explain that?' she demanded.

'Astrology explains it for us. Aries is a warrior sign, but very commonly
those born around the same time as Harry are one thing on the surface,
something else underneath. Mars decanate in Gemini, you see, and Gemini
is the sign of the twins.'

'So?'

'People like that can be very schizophrenic. On one level, you're Harry
Martineau, scholar, philosopher, poet, full of sweet reason, but on the dark
side . . .' He shrugged. 'A cold and ruthless killer. Yes, there's a curious
lack of emotion to him, wouldn't you agree, Jack? Of course, all this has
been extremely useful in the job he's been doing for the past four years.
Suppose that's what's kept him alive when most of the others have died.'

Carter said, 'Just in case you're getting a rather bad impression of Harry
Martineau, two things, Sarah. Although his mother was born in the States,
she was of German parentage, and Harry spent a lot of time with them in
Dresden and Heidelberg as he grew up. His grandfather, a professor of
surgery, was an active Socialist. He died in a fall from the balcony of his
apartment. A nasty accident.'

'Aided by two Gestapo thugs taking an arm and a leg each to help him on
his way,' Munro put in.

'And then there was a Jewish girl named Rosa Bernstein.'

'Yes,' Sarah put in. 'I was beginning to wonder whether females had ever
entered into his life. No mention of marriage.'

'He met Rosa Bernstein when she did a year at an Oxford College, St.
Hugh's, in nineteen thirty-two. He was spending increasing time in Europe
by then. Both his parents were dead. His father had left him reasonably well
off, and as an only child, he had no close relatives.'

'But he and Rosa never married?'

'No,' Munro said, and added bluntly: 'You'll often find prejudice on both
sides of the fence, my dear. Rosa's parents were Orthodox Jews, and they
didn't like the idea of their daughter marrying a Gentile. She and Harry

pursued what you might term a vigorous affair for some years. I knew them both well. I was at Oxford myself in those days.'

'What happened?'

It was Carter who answered her. 'She was active in the Socialist underground. Went backward and forward from England to Germany as a courier. In May, nineteen thirty-eight, she was apprehended, taken to Gestapo Headquarters at Prince Albrechtstrasse in Berlin. A good address for a very bad place. There, she was interrogated with extreme brutality and, according to our information, executed.'

There was a long silence. She seemed abstracted, staring out of the window into the distance. Munro said, 'You don't seem shocked? I find that strange in one so young.'

She shook her head. 'I've been nursing for two years now. I deal with death every day of my life. So Harry Martineau doesn't particularly care for Germans?'

'No,' Carter said. 'He doesn't like Nazis. There's a difference.'

'Yes, I can see that.'

She stared out of the window again, feeling restless, on edge, and it was all to do with Martineau, this man she had never met. He filled her mind. Would not go away.

Carter said, 'One thing we didn't ask. I hope you don't mind my being personal, but is there anyone in your life at the moment? Anyone who would miss you?'

'A man?' She laughed harshly. 'Good heavens, no! I never work less than a twelve-hour daily shift at the Cromwell. That leaves one just about enough time to have a bath and a meal before falling into bed.' She shook her head. 'No time for men. My father's in a Japanese prison camp. I've an old aunt in Sussex, his elder sister, and that's about it. No one to miss me at all. I'm all yours, gentlemen.'

She delivered the speech with an air of bravado and an illusion of calm sophistication that in one so young was strangely moving.

Munro, unusually for him, felt uncomfortable. 'This is important, believe me.' He leaned forward, put a hand on her arm. 'We wouldn't ask you if it wasn't.'

She nodded. 'I know, Brigadier, I know.' She turned and stared out of the window again at the passing scenery, thinking about Martineau.

He awoke with a dull ache just behind the right eye and his mouth tasted foul. Only one answer to that. He pulled on an old tracksuit and grabbed a towel, left by the front door and ran down to the sea.

He stripped and ran out through the shallows, plunging through the waves. It wasn't even a nice morning, the sky the color of slate gray, and there was rain on the wind. Yet quite suddenly, he experienced one of those special moments. Sea and sky seemed to become one. For a little while all sounds faded as he battled his way through the waves. Nothing mattered. Not the past or the future. Only this present moment. As he turned on his back, a herring gull fled overhead and it started to rain.

A voice called out, 'Enjoying yourself, Harry?'

Martineau turned toward the shore and found Munro standing there in old tweed coat and battered hat, holding an umbrella over his head. 'My God,' he said. 'Not you, Dougal?'

'As ever was, Harry. Come on up to the cottage. There's someone I'd like you to meet.'

He turned and walked back across the beach without another word. Martineau floated there for a while, thinking about it. Dougal Munro wasn't just paying a social call, that was for sure, not all the way from London. Excitement surged through him and he waded out of the water, toweled himself briskly, pulled on the old tracksuit and ran across the beach and up the cliff path. Jack Carter was standing on the porch, watching the rain and smoking a cigarette.

'What, you too, Jack?' Martineau smiled with real pleasure and took the other man's hand. 'Does the old sod want me to go back to work?'

'Something like that.' Carter hesitated, then said, 'Harry, I think you've done enough.'

'No such word in the vocabulary, Jack, not until they nail down the lid and put you six feet under.' Martineau brushed past Carter and went inside.

Munro was sitting by the fire, reading the notepad he'd found on the table. 'Still writing bad poetry?'

'Always did.' Martineau took the pad from him, tore off the top sheet, crumpled it up and tossed it into the fireplace. It was then that he became aware of Sarah Drayton standing in the kitchen doorway.

'I'm making tea for everyone. I hope that's all right, Colonel Martineau. I'm Sarah Drayton.'

She didn't bother holding out her hand, for it would have trembled too much. She was aware that she was close to tears and her stomach was hollow with excitement, throat dry. *Coup de foudre*, the French called it. The thunderclap. The best kind of love of all. Instant and quite irrevocable.

And at first, he responded, brushing a lock of black hair back from the white forehead, his face illuminated by a smile of great natural charm, and then the smile faded and he turned on Munro, anger in his voice, as if seeing everything.

'My God, what a bastard you are, Dougal. So now we're using schoolgirls?'

★ ★ ★

Hugh Kelso's adventures did not take long in the telling, but when he was finished, Munro carried on.

'The other month we knocked off a man called Braun in Paris. Jack has the details. I think you'll find it interesting.'

'What was he, Gestapo?' Martineau asked.

'No, SD.' Carter turned to Sarah Drayton sitting on the other side of the fire. 'That's the Secret Intelligence Department of the SS, responsible only to Himmler himself. More powerful than any other organization in Germany today.'

'Go on about Braun,' Martineau said.

'Well, according to his papers, he was RFSS.' Carter turned again to Sarah. 'That means Reichsführer SS. It's a cuff title that members of Himmler's personal staff wear on their uniform sleeve.' He took a paper from the file he was holding and offered it to Martineau. 'It seems Braun was a kind of roving ambassador, empowered to make his own investigations wherever he pleased.'

'With supreme authority over everyone he came into contact with,' Munro said. 'Read that letter.'

Martineau took it from its envelope and unfolded it.

It was on excellent paper, the heading embossed in black.

DER REICHSFÜHRER – SS   Berlin, 9 November 1943

SS – STURMBANNFÜHRER
BRAUN ERWIN, SS-NR 107863

This officer acts under my personal orders on business of the utmost importance to the Reich. All personnel, military and civil, without distinction of rank, must assist him in any way he sees fit.

                            H. HIMMLER

A remarkable document in itself. Even more astonishing was that it was countersigned across the bottom: *Adolf Hitler, Führer und Reichskanzler.*

'He obviously had a certain amount of influence,' Martineau said dryly, handing it back to Carter.

Munro said, 'Well the bastard's dead now, but our Paris people got some useful information out of him before he left.'

'I bet they did,' Martineau said, and lit a cigarette.

'He has a dozen or so of these special envoys floating around Europe, putting the fear of God into everyone wherever they turn up. All highly secret. Nobody knows who they are. I've got our forgery department preparing a complete set of papers for you. SD identity card and a copy of that letter and whatever else you need. Name of Max Vogel. We thought we'd give you a little rank, just to help the ship along, so it's Standartenführer.' He turned to Sarah, 'Colonel to you.'

'I get the picture,' Martineau said. 'I arrive on Jersey's fair shore and frighten the hell out of everyone.'

'You know as well as I, dear boy, that there's nothing more frightening than a schoolmaster in a leather overcoat turned revolutionary. Lenin for a start. And you must admit, you do a very good Nazi, Harry.'

'And the child?' Martineau inquired. 'Where does she fit in?'

'You need someone with you to establish your credentials with Mrs. de Ville and this chap Gallagher. Sarah is related to one and knows the other. Another thing, she was last in Jersey six years ago, aged thirteen – all plaits and ankle socks, I shouldn't wonder. Still herself enough for Helen de Ville and Gallagher to recognize, but different enough to pass as a stranger with other people, especially when we've finished with her.'

'And what's that supposed to mean?'

'Well, there's a fair trade in ladies of the night between France and Jersey.'

'You mean whores? You're not suggesting she play one of those?'

'Most senior German officers in France have French girlfriends. Why should you be any different? To start off, Sarah speaks excellent French with a Breton accent because that's what her grandmother was. By the time our people at Berkley Hall have finished with her, changed her hair color, got her into the right clothes – '

'You mean, turned her into a little French tart?' Martineau interrupted.

'Something like that. Perfect cover for her.'

'And when are we supposed to go in?'

'Day after tomorrow. A Lysander drop near Granville. Two-hour flight, Harry. Piece of cake. Sophie Cresson will meet you. Afterward, you use your authority to cross to Jersey on one of the night boats from Granville. Once over there, you make it up as you go along. You've got till Sunday at the outside.'

'And what if it's impossible to get him out? What then?'

'Up to you.'

'I see. I play executioner for you again?' He turned on Sarah. 'What do you think about all this?'

He was angry, the face whiter than ever, the eyes very dark. 'Oh, I don't know,' she said. 'It sounds as if it could be rather interesting.'

In a sense, the flippancy of her remarks was an attempt to control her feelings, and when she turned and moved to the table to pour more tea into her cup, her hand shook slightly. The death of her mother had sent her to live with her father on a plantation deep in the Malayan jungle. A life of discomfort and considerable danger, an extraordinary upbringing for a girl of thirteen, and yet she'd loved every minute of it. In moments of the greatest danger, she seemed to come alive. The hospital by night, the bombing, the casualties who needed her. Once again, she'd loved every minute of it.

And now this. It was not just sexual desire, although she was enough of a woman to know that she wanted Martineau. But that was only part of it. It was what this strange, intense, tortured man offered. The promise of danger, excitement of a kind she had never even dreamed of before.

'Rather interesting? Dear God!' Martineau poured himself a scotch. 'Have you read any of the works of Heidegger, Jack?'

'I'm familiar with them.'

'An interesting man. He believed that for authentic living what was necessary was the resolute confrontation of death.'

'That sounds fine by me,' Munro said.

'Really?' Martineau laughed harshly. 'As far as I'm concerned, it's idiots like that who made me give up on philosophy.' He raised his glass and toasted them all. 'Here we go then. Berkley Hall next stop.'

7

The firing range at Berkley Hall was in the basement. The armorer was an Irish Guards staff sergeant named Kelly, long past retirement and back in harness only because of the war. The place was brightly lit at the target end where cutout replicas of charging Germans stood against sandbags. Kelly and Sarah Drayton were the only people on the firing line. They'd given her battle dress to wear, slacks and blouse of blue serge, the kind issued to girls in the Women's Auxiliary Air Force. She'd tied her hair up and tucked it inside the peaked cap, leaving her neck bare. It somehow made her look very vulnerable.

Kelly had various weapons laid out on the table. 'Have you ever fired a handgun before, miss?'

'Yes,' she said, 'in Malaya. My father was a rubber planter. He used to be away a great deal so he made sure I knew how to use a revolver. And I've fired a shotgun a few times.'

'Anything here that looks familiar?'

'That revolver.' She pointed. 'It looks like the Smith and Wesson my father owned.'

'That's exactly what it is, miss,' Kelly said. 'Obviously in more normal circumstances you'd be given a thorough grounding in weaponry as part of your course, but in your case, there just isn't time. What I'll do is show you a few things, just to familiarize you with some basic weapons you're likely to come across. Then you can fire a few rounds and that will have to do.'

'Fair enough,' she said.

'Rifles are simple,' he said. 'I won't waste your time with those. Here we've got two basic submachine guns. The British Sten in standard use with our own forces. This is a Mark 11S. Silenced version, developed for use with the French Resistance groups. Thirty-two rounds in that magazine. Automatic fire burns out the silencer, so use it semiautomatic or single burst. Like to have a go?'

It was surprisingly light and gave her no problems at all when she fired it from the shoulder, the only sound being the bolt reciprocating. She tore a sandbag apart to one side of the target she aimed at.

'Not much good,' she said.

'Few people are with these things. They're good at close quarters when you're up against several people and that's all,' Kelly told her. 'The other submachine gun's German. An MP40. Popularly known as the Schmeisser. The Resistance use those a lot too.'

He went through the handguns with her then, both the revolvers and the automatics. When she tried with the Smith & Wesson, arm extended, she only managed to nick the shoulder of the target once out of six shots.

'I'm afraid you'd be dead, miss.'

As he reloaded, she said, 'What about Colonel Martineau? Is he any good?'

'You could say that, miss. I don't think I've ever known anyone better with a handgun. Now, try this way.' He crouched, feet apart, holding the gun two-handed. 'See what I mean?'

'I think so.' She copied him, the gun out in front of her in both hands.

'Now squeeze with a half breath of a pause between each shot.'

This time, she did better, hitting the target once in the shoulder and once in the left hand.

'Terrific,' Kelly said.

'Not if you consider she was probably aiming for the heart.'

Martineau had come in quietly behind them. He wore a dark polo neck sweater and black corduroy pants and he came to the table and examined the guns. 'As I'm going to have to look after this infant and as time is limited, do you mind if I take a hand?'

'Be my guest, sir.'

Martineau picked up a pistol from the table. 'Walther PPK, semiautomatic. Seven-round magazine goes in the butt, like so. Pull the slider back and you're in business. It's not too large. You wouldn't notice it in your handbag, but it will do the job and that's what matters. Now come down the range.'

'All right.'

They moved so close that the targets were no more than ten or twelve yards away. 'If he's close enough for you to hold it against him when you pull the trigger, do it that way, but you should never be farther away than you are now. Simply throw up your arm and point the gun at him. Keep both eyes open and fire very fast.'

She hit the target six times in the general area of the chest and belly. 'Oh, my word,' she said, very excited. 'That wasn't bad, was it?'

As they walked back to the firing line he said, 'Yes, but could you do it for real?'

'I'll only know when the time comes, won't I?' she said. 'Anyway, what about you? I hear a lot of talk, but not much to justify it.'

There was another Walther on the table with a round cylinder of polished black steel screwed on to the end of the barrel. 'This is what's called a Carswell silencer,' Martineau told her. 'Specially developed for use by SOE agents.'

His arm swung up. He didn't appear to take aim, firing twice, shooting out the heart of the target. The only sound had been two dull thuds, and the effect was quite terrifying.

He laid the gun down and turned, eyes blank in the white face. 'I've got things to do. Dougal wants us in the library in half an hour. I'll see you then.'

He walked out. There was an awkward silence. Sarah said, 'He seemed angry.'

'The colonel gets like that, miss. I don't think he likes what he sees in himself sometimes. Last November he killed the head of the Gestapo at Lyons. Man called Kaufmann. A real butcher. They brought him back from over there in a puddle of blood in a Lysander. Two bullets in his left lung for starters. He's been different since then.'

'In what way?'

'I don't know, miss.' Kelly frowned. 'Here, don't you go getting silly ideas about him. I know what you young girls can be like. I've got a daughter your age on an antiaircraft battery in London. Just remember he's got twenty-five years on you.'

'You mean he's too old?' Sarah said. 'Isn't that like saying you can't love someone because they're Catholic or Jewish or American or something? What's the difference?'

'Too clever for me, that kind of talk.' Kelly opened a drawer and took out a cloth bundle which he unwrapped. 'A little present for you, miss, in spite of what the colonel says.' It was a small black automatic pistol, very light, almost swallowed up by her hand. 'Belgian. Only .25, but it'll do the trick when you need it and, at that size, very easy to hide.' He looked awkward. 'I've known ladies to tuck them in the top of their stocking, not intending to be disrespectful, miss.'

She reached up and kissed him on the cheek. 'I think you're wonderful.'

'You can't do that, miss, you being an officer. Against regulations.'

'But I'm not an officer, Sergeant.'

'I think you'll find you are, miss. Probably one of the things the brigadier wants to tell you. I'd cut off and go to the library now if I were you.'

'All right and thank you.'

She went out and Kelly sighed and started to clear away the weapons. Munro, Carter and Martineau were already in the library when she went in, sitting by the fire having afternoon tea. 'Ah, there you are,' Munro said. 'Do join us. The crumpets are delicious.'

Carter poured her a cup of tea. She said, 'Sergeant Kelly said something about my being an officer now. What was he talking about?'

'Yes, well, we do prefer our women operatives to hold some sort of commissioned rank. In theory it's supposed to help you if you fall into enemy hands,' Munro told her.

'In practice, it doesn't do you any good at all,' Martineau interrupted.

'However, for good or ill, you are now a flight officer in the WAAF,' Munro said. 'I trust that is satisfactory. Now, let's look at the map.'

They all got up and went to the table where there were several large-scale maps, together making a patchwork that included the south of England, the Channel, and the general area of the Channel Islands and Normandy and Brittany.

'All those jolly films they make at Elstree showing you our gallant secret agents at work usually have them parachuting into France. In fact, we prefer to take people in by plane wherever possible.'

'I see,' she said.

'Our popular choice is the Lysander. These days the pilot usually manages on his own. That way we can take up to three passengers. They're operated by a Special Duties Squadron at Hornley Field. It's not too far from here.'

'How long will the flight take?'

'No more than an hour and a half, perhaps less depending on wind conditions. You'll land not far from Granville. The local Resistance people will be on hand to take care of you. We find the early hours of the morning best. Say four or five.'

'Then what?'

'The evening of the same day you'll leave Granville by ship for Jersey. Most convoys go by night now. We have air superiority during daylight hours.' He turned to Martineau. 'Naturally, the question of passage is a matter for Standartenführer Max Vogel, but I doubt whether anyone is likely to do anything other than run round in circles when they see your credentials.'

Martineau nodded. 'We'll be in trouble if they don't.'

'As regards your dealings with Mrs. de Ville and General Gallagher. Well, you have Sarah to vouch for you.'

'And Kelso?'

'Entirely in your hands, dear boy. You're the officer in the field. I'll back whatever you decide to do. You know how critical the situation is.'

'Fair enough.'

Munro picked up the phone at his side. 'Send Mrs. Moon in now.' He put the phone down and said to Sarah. 'We're very lucky to have Mrs. Moon. We borrow her from Denham Studios by courtesy of Alexander Korda. There's nothing she doesn't know about makeup, dress and so on.'

Hilda Moon was a large fat woman with a cockney accent. Her own appearance inspired little confidence, for her hair was dyed red and it showed, and she wore too much lipstick. A cigarette dangled from the corner of her mouth, ash spilling down on her ample bosom.

'Yes.' She nodded, walking round Sarah. 'Very nice. Of course I'll have to do something with the hair.'

'Do you think so?' Sarah asked in alarm.

'Girls who get by the way you're supposed to in this part, dear, always carry it up front. They make a living from pleasing men, which means they have to make the best of what they've got. You trust me, I know what's best for you.'

She took Sarah by the arm and led her out. As the door closed, Martineau said, 'We probably won't even recognize her when we see her again.'

'Of course,' Munro said. 'But then, I should have thought that was the general idea.'

It was early evening when the phone rang at Gallagher's cottage. He was in the kitchen, working through farm accounts at the table, and answered it instantly.

'Savary here, General. The matter of the package we discussed.'

'Yes.'

'My contact in Granville was in touch with their head office. It seems someone will be with you by Thursday at the latest to give you the advice you need.'

'You're certain of that.'

'Absolutely.'

The phone went dead. Gallagher sat there thinking about it, then he put on his old corduroy jacket and went up to de Ville Place. He found Helen in the kitchen with Mrs. Vibert, preparing the evening meal. The old lady didn't live on the premises, but just down the road in another farm cottage with her niece and young daughter. She was a widow herself, a good-hearted woman of sixty-five, devoted to Helen.

She dried her hands and took a coat down from behind the door. 'If that's all, I'll be off now, Mrs. de Ville.'

'See you in the morning,' Helen told her.

As the door closed behind her, Gallagher said, 'She doesn't suspect anything, does she?'

'No, and I want it to stay that way, for her own good, as much as anyone else's.'

'I've just had Savary on the phone. They got through to London. Someone will be with us by Thursday.'

She turned quickly. 'Are you certain?'

'As much as I can be. How is the good colonel?'

'Still feverish. George saw him this afternoon. He seems satisfied. He's trying him on this penicillin stuff.'

'I'm surprised Savary was in so early. They must have made the run this afternoon.'

'They did,' she said. 'Taking advantage of the fog again. Most of the officers have turned up here within the past hour.'

'Most?'

'Two dead. Bohlen and Wendel. Two of the ships were attacked by Hurricanes.'

At that moment, the green baize door leading to the dining room opened and Guido Orsini came in. He was wearing his best uniform, his hair still damp from the shower, and looked rather dashing. He wore the Italian Medal for Military Valor in gold, a medal equivalent to the British Victoria Cross and very rarely awarded. On his left breast he also wore an Iron Cross First Class.

Gallagher said in English, 'Still in one piece are you? Hear you had a bad time.'

'It could have been worse,' Guido told him. 'They're all sitting in there doing their conspicuous mourning bit.' He put a bag he was carrying on the table. 'Dozen bottles of Sancerre there from Granville.'

'You're a good boy,' she said.

'So I believe. Don't you think I also look rather beautiful tonight?'

'Very possibly.' He was mocking her as usual, she knew that. 'Now move to one side while I dish up the food.'

Guido inched open the serving hatch to the dining room and whispered to Gallagher. 'Sean, come and look at this.'

The hall was paneled in oak, darkly magnificent, and the long oaken table down the center could accommodate twenty-five. There were only eight in there now, all naval officers, seated at various places. In each gap, where someone was missing, a lighted candle stood at the plate. There were six such candles, each representing a member of the mess who had died in action. The atmosphere was funereal to say the least.

'They have to make everything into a Shakespearean tragedy,' Orsini said. 'It's really very boring. If it wasn't for Helen's cooking I'd go elsewhere. I discovered a remarkably good black-market restaurant in St. Aubin's Bay the other night. Amazing what one got and without coupons.'

'Now that *is* interesting,' Gallagher said. 'Tell me more.'

As Mrs. Moon and her two assistants worked on Sarah, the fat woman talked incessantly. 'I've been everywhere. Denham, Elstree, Pinewood. I do all Miss Margaret Lockwood's makeup and Mr. James Mason. Oh, and I've worked with Mr. Coward. Now he *was* a gentleman.'

When Sarah came out from under the dryer, she couldn't believe what she saw. Her dark hair was now a golden blonde, and they'd marcelled it tight against her face. Now, Mrs. Moon started with the makeup, plucking hairs from the eyebrows painfully then lining them into two thin streaks.

'Plenty of rouge, dear. A little too much, if you know what I mean, and lots of lipstick. Everything just a little overdone, that's what we want. Now, what do you think?'

Sarah sat looking into the mirror. It was the face of a stranger. Who am I? she thought. Did Sarah Drayton ever exist at all?

'We'll try one of the dresses. Of course, the underwear and every individual item will be of French origin, but you only need the dress at the moment, just for the effect.'

It was black satin, very tight and rather short. She helped Sarah into it and zipped it at the back. 'It certainly helps your breasts along, dear. They look very good.'

'I don't know about that, I can't breathe.' Sarah pulled on a pair of high-heeled shoes and looked at herself in the mirror. She giggled. 'I look the most awful tart.'

'Well, that *is* the idea, love. Now go and see what the brigadier thinks.'

Munro and Carter were still sitting by the fire when she went in, talking in low tones. Sarah said, 'No one told me my name.'

'Anne-Marie Latour,' Carter said automatically and then looked up. 'Good God!' he said.

Munro was far more positive. 'I like it. Like it very much indeed.' Sarah pirouetted. 'Yes, they'll go for you in the German officers' club in St. Helier.'

'Or in the Army and Navy in London, I should have thought,' Carter said dryly.

The door opened and Martineau entered. She turned to face him, hands on hips in a deliberate challenge. 'Well?' she demanded.

'Well, what?'

'Oh, damn you.' She was cross enough to stamp a foot. 'You're the most infuriating man I've ever met. Is there a village near here with a pub?'

'Yes.'

'Will you take me for a drink?'

'Like that?'

'You mean I don't look nice enough?'

'Actually, you transcend all Mrs. Moon's efforts. You couldn't be a tart if you tried, brat. I'll see you in the hall in fifteen minutes,' and he turned and went out.

There was a spring fete on in the village in aid of war charities. Stalls and sideshows on the village green and a couple of old-fashioned roundabouts. Sarah wore a coat over the dress and hung onto his arm. She was obviously enjoying herself as they moved through the noisy and good-humored crowd.

There was a tent marked *Fortunes – Gypsy Sara.* 'Sara without the H,' she said. 'Let's give it a try.'

'All right,' he said, humoring her.

Surprisingly, the woman inside had dispensed with the usual gypsy trappings, the headscarf and the earrings. She was about forty with a sallow face, neat black hair and wore a smart gabardine suit. She took the girl's hand. 'Just you, lady, or your gentleman as well?'

'But he isn't my gentleman,' she protested.

'He'll never belong to anyone else, never know another woman.'

She took a deep breath as if trying to clear her head, and Martineau said, 'Now let's hear the good news.'

She handed a tarot pack to Sarah, folded her own hands over Sarah's, then shuffled the pack several times and extracted three cards.

The first was Fortitude, a young woman grasping the jaws of a lion. 'There is an opportunity to put an important plan into action if one will take risks,' Gypsy Sara said.

The next card was the Star, a naked girl kneeling by a pool. 'I see fire and water, mingling at the same time. A contradiction and yet you come through both unscathed.'

Sarah turned to Martineau. 'I had that last month at the Cromwell.

Incendiary bombs on the nurses' quarters and water everywhere from the fire hoses.'

The third card was the Hanged Man. The woman said, 'He will not change however long he hangs in the tree. He cannot alter the mirror image, however much he fears it. You must journey on alone. Adversity will always be your strength. You will find love only by not seeking it, that is the lesson you must learn.'

Sarah said to Martineau, 'Now you.'

Gypsy Sara gathered up the cards. 'There is nothing I can tell the gentleman that he does not know already.'

'Best thing I've heard since the Brothers Grimm.' Martineau pushed a pound across the table and stood up. 'Let's go.'

'Are you angry?' Sarah demanded as they pushed through the crowd to the village pub.

'Why should I be?'

'It was only a bit of fun. Nothing to be taken seriously.'

'Oh, but I take everything seriously,' he assured her.

The bar was crowded but they managed to find a couple of seats in the corner by the fire, and he ordered her a shandy and had a scotch for himself. 'Well, what do you think of it so far?' he asked.

'Rather more interesting than the wards at the Cromwell.'

'In other circumstances you'd be trained for about six weeks,' he said. 'The Scottish Highlands to toughen you up. Courses in unarmed combat and so on. Twelve ways of killing someone with your bare hands.'

'That sounds very gruesome.'

'But effective. I remember one of our agents, a journalist in civilian life, who stopped going into pubs when he was home. He was afraid to get into an argument because of what he might do.'

'Can you do that sort of thing?' she asked him.

'Anybody can be taught to do it. It's brains that's important in this game.'

There were three soldiers in khaki battle dress at the bar, an older man who was a sergeant and a couple of privates. Hard young men who kept laughing, heads together, as they looked across at Martineau. When he went to replenish the drinks, one of them deliberately jogged his arm as he turned from the bar, spilling a little scotch.

'You want to be more careful, mate,' the youth told him.

'If you say so.' Martineau smiled cheerfully, and the sergeant put a hand on the youth's sleeve and muttered something.

When he sat down Sarah said, 'Jack Carter tells me you knew Freud.'

'Yes, I last saw him in London in nineteen thirty-nine just before he died.'

'Do you agree with psychoanalysis?'

'Everything coming down to sex? God knows, old Sigmund had enough problems in that direction himself. He was once doing a lecture tour in the States with Jung and told him one day that he kept dreaming of prostitutes. Jung simply asked him why he didn't do something about it. Freud was terribly shocked. "But I'm a married man," he said.'

She laughed helplessly. 'That's marvelous.'

'Talking of great minds, I used to have dealings with Bertrand Russell, who liked the ladies more than somewhat, which he justified by his strongly held personal belief that you couldn't get to know a woman properly until you'd slept with her.'

'That doesn't sound very philosophical to me,' she said.

'On the contrary.'

She got up and excused herself. 'I'll be back in a minute.'

As she went out to the cloakroom the three soldiers watched her go, then glanced at Martineau, and there was a burst of laughter. As she returned, the young soldier who had bumped Martineau at the bar grabbed her arm. She struggled to pull away and Martineau was on his feet and pushing through the crowd to her side.

'That's enough.'

'Who the hell are you, her father?' the boy demanded.

Martineau took him by the wrist, applying leverage in the way the instructor had shown him on the silent killing course at Arisaig in Scotland in the early days. The boy grimaced in pain. The sergeant said, 'Leave off. He didn't mean any harm. Just a bit of fun.'

'Yes, I can see that.'

As he took her back to the table she said, 'That was quick.'

'When I feel, I act. I'm a very existentialist person.'

'Existentialist?' She frowned. 'I don't understand.'

'Oh, a new perspective to things a friend of mine's come up with. A French writer called Jean-Paul Sartre. When I was on the run in Paris three years ago I holed up at his apartment for a couple of weeks. He's involved with the Resistance.'

'But what does it mean?'

'Oh, lots of things. The bit I like is the suggestion that you should create values for yourself through action and by living each moment to the full.'

'Is that how you've got yourself through the last four years?'

'Something like that. Sartre just put it into words for me.' He helped her into her coat. 'Let's go.'

It was dark outside, music and merriment drifting from the direction of the fair, although most of the stands were already closed because of the blackout regulations. They started across the deserted car park to where Martineau had left the car, and there was a sound of running footsteps. He turned as the two young soldiers ran up. The sergeant emerged on the porch at the rear of the pub and stood watching.

'Now then,' the young soldier who'd caused the scene at the bar said. 'You and me aren't finished yet. You need to be taught a lesson.'

'Is that a fact?' Martineau demanded, and as the youth moved in, swinging a punch, he caught the wrist, twisted it up and around, locking the shoulder. The soldier cried out as the muscle tore. The other soldier gave a cry of alarm and recoiled as Martineau dropped his friend on the ground and the sergeant ran forward angrily.

'You bastard!' he said.

'Not me, you for letting it happen.' Martineau had his identity card out. 'I think you'd better look at that.'

The sergeant's face dropped. 'Colonel, sir!' He sprang to attention.

'That's better. You're going to need a doctor. Tell chummy here when he's capable of listening that I hope he's learned something. Next time it could be the death of him.'

As they drove away, Sarah said, 'You don't hesitate at all, do you?'

'What's the point?'

'I think I understand what Jack Carter meant. You have an aptitude for killing, I think.'

'Words,' he said. 'Games in the head. That's all I had for years. Nothing but talk, nothing but ideas. Let's have some facts. Let's stop playing games in black satin dresses with our hair blonded. You know what the first technique is that the Gestapo employ in breaking down any woman agent who falls into their hands?'

'You're obviously going to tell me.'

'Multiple rape. If that doesn't do the trick, the electric shock treatment comes next. I used to have a girlfriend in Berlin. She was Jewish.'

'I know. Carter told me about her as well.'

'How they tortured, then murdered her in the Gestapo cellars at Prince Albrechtstrasse?' Martineau shook his head. 'He doesn't know everything. He doesn't know that Kaufmann, the head of the Gestapo in Lyons who I killed last November, was the man responsible for Rosa's death in Berlin in nineteen thirty-eight.'

'I see now,' she said softly. 'Sergeant Kelly said you were different and he was right. You hated Kaufmann for years and when you finally took your revenge, you found it meant nothing.'

'All this wisdom.' He laughed coldly. 'Going over there and taking on the Gestapo isn't like one of those movies they make at Elstree Studios. There are fifty million people in France. You know how many we estimate are active members of the Resistance?'

'No.'

'Two thousand, Sarah. Two lousy thousand.' He was disgusted. 'I don't know why we bother.'

'Then why do you? Not just for Rosa or your grandfather.' He turned briefly and she said, 'Oh, yes, I know about that too.'

There was a silence. He opened his cigarette case one-handed. 'Do you want one of these things? A bad habit, but a great comfort in the clinches.'

'All right,' she said and took one.

He gave her a light. 'Something I've never talked about. I was due to go to Harvard in nineteen seventeen. Then America joined in the war. I was seventeen, officially under age. Joined up on sheer impulse and ended up in the trenches in Flanders.' He shook his head. 'Whatever you mean by hell on earth, that was the trenches. So many dead you lost count.'

'It must have been terrible,' she said.

'And I loved every minute of it. Can you understand that? I lived more in one day, felt more, than in a year of ordinary living. Life became real, bloody, exciting. I couldn't get enough.'

'Like a drug?'

'Exactly. I was like the man in the poem, constantly seeking Death on the battlefield. That was what I ran away from, back to Harvard and Oxford cloisters and the safe world of classrooms and books, everything in the head.'

'And then the war came round again.'

'And Dougal Munro yanked me out into the real world . . . And the rest, as they say, you know.'

Later, lying in bed smoking a cigarette, listening to the rain tapping at the window, he heard the door open. She said softly through the darkness, 'It's only me.'

'Really?' Martineau said.

She took off her robe and got into bed beside him. She was wearing a cotton nightdress and he put an arm around her automatically. 'Harry,' she whispered. 'Can I make a confession?'

'You obviously intend to.'

'I know you probably imagine, along with everyone else, that I'm a delicate little middle-class virgin, but I'm afraid I'm not.'

'Is that a fact?'

'Yes, I met a Spitfire pilot at the hospital last year. He used to come in for treatment for a broken ankle.'

'And true love blossomed?'

'Not really. More like mutual lust, but he was a nice chap and I don't regret it. He was shot down over the Channel three months ago.'

She started to cry, for no reason that made any kind of sense, and Martineau held her tight, wordless in the dark.

8

The following day just after noon at Fermanville on the Cherbourg Peninsula, Karl Hagan, the duty sergeant at the central strongpoint of the 15th Coastal Artillery Battery, was leaning on a concrete parapet idly enjoying a cigarette in the pale afternoon sunshine when he observed a black Mercedes coming up the track. No escort so it couldn't be anyone important – and then he noticed the pennant fluttering on the bonnet. Too far away to see what it was, but to an old soldier it was enough. He was inside the operations room in a flash, where Captain Reimann, the battery commander, sprawled at his desk, tunic buttons undone, reading a book.

'Someone coming, sir. Looks like top brass to me. Shock inspection perhaps.'

'Right. Klaxon alarm. Get the men to fall in, just in case.'

Reimann buttoned his tunic, buckled his belt and adjusted his cap to a satisfactory angle. As he went out on the redoubt, the Mercedes pulled in below. The driver got out. The first person out was an army major with staff stripes on his pants. The second was Field Marshal Erwin Rommel in leather trenchcoat, white scarf knotted carelessly at his neck, desert goggles pulled up above the peak of his cap.

Reimann had never been so shocked in his life and he grabbed at the parapet. At the same moment he heard Sergeant Hagan's voice and the battery personnel doubled out in the courtyard below. As Reimann hurried down the steps the two battery lieutenants, Scheel and Planck, took up their positions.

Reimann moved forward and remembering what he'd heard of Rommel's preferences chose the military rather than the Nazi salute. 'Herr Field Marshal. You do us a great honor.'

Rommel tapped the end of his field marshal's baton against the peak of his cap. 'Your name?'

'Reimann, Herr Field Marshal.'

'Major Hofer, my aide.'

Hofer said, 'The Field Marshal will see everything, including the subsidiary strongpoints. Please lead the way.'

'First, Major, I'll inspect the troops,' Rommel told him. 'An army is only as strong as its weakest point, always remember that.'

'Of course, Herr Field Marshal,' Hofer said.

Rommel moved down the line, stopping here and there to talk to an individual who took his fancy. Finally he turned. 'Good turnout. Highly satisfactory. Now we go.'

For the next hour he tramped the clifftop from one strongpoint to another as Reimann led the way. Radio rooms, men's quarters, ammunition stores, even the urinals. Nothing escaped his attention.

'Excellent, Reimann,' he told the young artillery officer. 'First-rate performance. I'll endorse your field unit report personally.'

Reimann almost fainted with pleasure. 'Herr Field Marshal – what can I say?'

He called the honor guard to attention. Rommel tapped the baton against his cap again and got into the Mercedes. Hofer joined him on the other side, and as the driver drove away, the major checked that the glass partition was closed tight.

'Excellent,' Hofer said. 'Have a cigarette. I think you carried that off very well, Berger.'

'Really, Herr Major?' Heini Baum said. 'I get the booking then?'

'One more test, I think. Something a little bit more ambitious. Dinner at some officers' mess, perhaps. Yes, that would be good. Then you'll be ready for Jersey.'

'Anything you say.' Baum leaned back, inhaling deeply on the cigarette.

'So, back to the field marshal to report,' Konrad Hofer said.

When Sarah and Harry Martineau went into the library at Berkley Hall, Jack Carter was sitting at the table, the maps spread before him.

'Ah, there you are,' he said. 'Brigadier Munro has gone up to London to report to General Eisenhower, but he'll be back tonight. We'll both see you off from Hornley Field. Any problems?'

'None that I can think of.' Martineau turned to Sarah. 'What about you?'

'I don't think so.'

'Your clothes have all been double-checked for Frenchness,' Carter said. 'So that's taken care of. Here are your papers, Sarah. French identity card with photo. German Ausweis, with different photo. Now you know why they asked you to change clothes at the photography session. Ration cards. Oh, and a tobacco ration card.'

'You're supposed to have one of those even if you don't smoke,' Martineau told her.

'These documents are one hundred percent,' Carter said. 'Right paper, same watermarks. Typewriters, ink – everything perfect. I can assure you that there is no way that even the most skilled Abwehr or Gestapo operative could find them anything but genuine.' He handed her a slip of paper. 'There are your personal details. Anne-Marie Latour. We've kept to your own age and birthdate. Born in Brittany naturally, to explain your accent. We've made your place of birth Paimpol on the coast. I believe you know it well?'

'Yes, my grandmother lived there. I spent many holidays with her.'

'Normally you'd have some considerable length of time to get used to your new identity. In this case that just isn't possible. However, you will have Harry with you and it should be for no more than three days. Four at the most.'

'I understand.'

'One more thing. Your relationship with Standartenführer Vogel must at all times seem convincing. You do appreciate what that could entail?'

'Sharing a room?' The smile when she turned to Martineau was mischievous. 'Is that all right with you, Colonel?'

For once, Martineau was put out and he frowned. 'You little bitch!'

It was as if they were alone for a moment and she touched his face gently with her fingertips. 'Oh, Harry Martineau, you are lovely when you're angry.' She turned to Carter. 'I think you can take it there'll be no problem, Captain.'

Carter, hugely embarrassed, said hurriedly, 'All right. Then read this, both of you. Regulations, Sarah.'

It was a typical SOE operations order, cold, flat, precise, no-nonsense language. It laid out the task ahead of them, procedure, communication channel via the Cressons in Granville. Everything was covered, even down to a code name for the operation, JERSEYMAN. At the end of the flimsy it said: NOW DESTROY NOW DESTROY.

'All right?' Martineau asked her.

She nodded and he struck a match and touched it to the paper, dropping it into the ashtray. 'That's it then,' he said. 'I'll go and do my packing. See you two later.'

On the bed in his room, the wardrobe people had laid out a three-piece suit in light-gray tweed, shoes, some white shirts, two black ties. There was also a military overcoat in soft black leather of a kind worn by many SS officers.

The gray-green SS uniform hung behind the door. He checked it carefully. On the left sleeve was the RFSS cuff title of Himmler's personal staff, an SD patch above it. The Waffenfarben, the colored piping on the uniform and cap, was toxic green, indicating that he belonged to the SS

Security Service. The oak leaves of his collar patches indicating his rank were in silver thread. There was an Iron Cross First Class on the left side of the tunic. His only other decoration was the Order of Blood, a medal struck specially for old comrades of the Führer who had served prison sentences for political crimes during the twenties.

He decided to try the uniform on and undressed quickly. Everything fit to perfection. He buttoned the tunic and fastened the belt, a rare specimen that had an eagle on the buckle with a swastika in one claw and SS runes in the other. He picked up the cap and examined the silver death's-head badge, running his sleeve across it, then reached inside, scratched a slight tear in the silk lining and withdrew the rigid spring so that the cap crumpled. It was an affectation of many oldtimers, although against regulations.

He put it on his head at a slight angle. From behind, Sarah said quietly, 'You look as if you're enjoying yourself. I get the feeling you like uniforms.'

'I like getting it right,' he said. 'I often think I missed my vocation. I should have been an actor. Getting it right is important, Sarah. You don't get second chances.'

There was a kind of distress on her face and she moved close and gripped his arm. 'I'm not sure if it's you anymore, Harry.'

'It isn't, not in this uniform. Standartenführer Max Vogel, of the SD. Feared by his own side as much as the French. You'll see. This isn't a game anymore.'

She shivered and put her arms around him. 'I know, Harry, I know.'

'Are you frightened?'

'Good God, no.' She smiled up at him. 'Not with Gypsy Sara in my corner.'

Eisenhower sat at his desk in the study at Hayes Lodge, reading glasses perched on his nose as he worked his way through the file. He sat back, removed the glasses and looked across at Dougal Munro.

'Quite a man, Martineau. Extraordinary record, and an American.'

'Yes, sir. He told me once that his great-grandmother had immigrated to Virginia in the eighteen-fifties from England. Small town in Lancashire, I believe.'

'It sounds a kind of exotic name for Lancashire.'

'Not unknown, General. I believe it goes back to Norman times.'

He realized that Eisenhower was simply stalling for time while he thought about things. He got up and peered out the window, then turned. 'Flight Officer Drayton. She's very young.'

'I'm aware of that, General. However, she is in a unique position to help us.'

'Of course. You really think this could work?'

'I believe we can put Colonel Martineau and Flight Officer Drayton into France with no trouble. I can't see any problem with their continuing onward to Jersey by boat. Martineau has unique authority. No one would dare question it. If you want to query the Reichsführer's personal representative, the only way you can do it is to ring the Reichsführer himself in Berlin.'

'Yes, I see that,' Eisenhower said.

'However, once they're in Jersey, the game is really wide open. There is no way I can give you any assurance about what happens. We'll be entirely in Martineau's hands.' There was silence for a while, and then Munro added, 'They should be in Jersey by Thursday. Martineau has until Sunday. That's his deadline. It's only a few days.'

'And a hell of a lot of lives depending on it.' Eisenhower sat down behind the desk. 'Okay, Brigadier. Carry on and keep me informed at all times.'

Hornley Field had been an aero club before the war. It had also been used as a temporary fighter station during the Battle of Britain. It was now used for clandestine flights to the continent only, mainly Lysanders and the occasional Liberator. The runway was grass, but long enough. There was a tower, several huts and two hangars.

The commanding officer was a Squadron Leader Barnes, an ex-fighter pilot who'd lost his left arm in the summer of 1940. The pilot of the Lysander was a flight lieutenant named Peter Green. Sarah, standing at the window, saw him now, bulky in his flying jacket and helmet, standing by the plane.

It was two-thirty in the morning, but warm enough, the stove roaring away. 'Can I offer you some more coffee, Flight Officer?' Barnes asked Sarah.

She turned and smiled. 'No thanks. I shouldn't imagine Westland included a toilet facility in their Lysander.'

He smiled. 'No, I'm afraid there wasn't the room.'

Martineau stood by the stove, hands in the pockets of his leather trenchcoat. He wore the tweed suit and a dark slouch hat and smoked a cigarette. Carter sat by the stove, tapping his stick restlessly on the floor.

'We're really going to have to get moving, I'm afraid,' Barnes said. 'Just the right conditions at the other end if you go now. Too light if we wait.'

'I can't imagine what's happened to the brigadier,' Carter said.

'It doesn't matter.' Martineau turned to Sarah. 'Ready to go?'

She nodded and very carefully pulled on her fashionable leather gloves. She was wearing a black coat over her dress, nipped in at the waist with large shoulders, all very fashionable.

Barnes put a very large fur-lined flying jacket over her shoulders. 'It might be cold up there.'

'Thank you.'

Martineau picked up their two suitcases and they went out and crossed to the Lysander where Green waited. 'Any problems?' Martineau asked.

'Coastal fog, but only in patches. Slight headwind.' He glanced at his watch. 'We'll be there by four-thirty at the outside.'

Sarah went first and strapped herself in. Martineau passed up the suitcases then turned and shook hands with Carter. 'See you soon, Jack.'

'You've got the call sign,' Carter said. 'All Cresson has to do is send that. No message needed. We'll have a Lysander out to the same field at ten o'clock at night of the same day to pick you up.'

Martineau climbed in next to Sarah and fastened his seat belt. He didn't look at her or say anything, but he took her hand as Green climbed into the pilot's seat. The sound of the engines shattered the night. They started to taxi to the far end of the runway and turned. As they started to roll between the two lines of lights, gradually increasing speed, the Austin Princess turned in through the main gate, hesitated for the sentry's inspection then bumped across the grass to the huts. As Dougal Munro got out, the Lysander lifted over the trees at the far end of the field and was swallowed by darkness.

'Damnation!' he said. 'Held up at Baker Street, Jack. Something came up. Thought I'd just make it.'

'They couldn't wait, sir,' Barnes told him. 'Might have made things difficult at the other end.'

'Of course,' Munro said.

Barnes walked away and Carter said, 'What did General Eisenhower have to say, sir?'

'What could he say, Jack? What can any of us say?' Munro shrugged. 'The ball's in Harry Martineau's court now. All up to him.'

'And Sarah Drayton, sir.'

'Yes, I liked that young woman.' Aware suddenly that he had spoken in the past tense, Munro shivered as if at an omen. 'Come on, Jack, let's go home,' he said, and he turned and got back into the Austin.

Sophie Cresson waited on the edge of a wood beside the field seven miles northwest of Granville which was the designated landing strip. She was on her own and stood beside an old Renault van smoking a cigarette in her cupped hands. The door of the van was open, and a Sten gun lay ready to hand on the passenger seat. There was also the homing beacon. She'd waited at the bar until Gerard had received the message that they had actually left Hornley. Timing was critical in these things.

She wore a woolen cap pulled down over her ears against the cold, an old fur-lined hunting coat of Gerard's, belted at the waist, and slacks. She wasn't worried about problems with any security patrol she might run across. She knew all the soldiers in the Granville area and they knew her. As for the police, they did as they were told. There wasn't one she didn't know too much about. In the back of the van were several dead chickens and a few pheasants. Out on another black-market trip, that was her cover.

She checked her watch and switched on the homing beacon. Then she took three torches from the van and ran forward into the broad meadow and arranged them in an inverted L-shape with the crossbar at the upwind end. Then she moved back to the van and waited.

The flight had been completely uneventful, mainly because Green was an old hand, with more than forty such sorties under his belt. He had never belonged to the school of thought that recommended approaching the French coast below the radar screen. The one time he had tried this tactic the Royal Navy had fired at him. So, it was at 8,000 feet that the Lysander crossed over the Cherbourg Peninsula and turned slightly south.

He spoke over the intercom. 'Fifteen minutes, so be ready.'

'Any chance of running into a night fighter?' Martineau asked.

'Unlikely. Maximum effort strike by Bomber Command on various towns in the Ruhr. Jerry will have scrambled every night fighter in France to go and protect the Fatherland.'

'Look!' Sarah cut in. 'I can see lights.'

The L-shape was clearly visible below as they descended rapidly. 'That's it,' Green told them. 'I've landed here twice before so I know my stuff. In and out very fast. You know the drill, Colonel.'

And then they were drifting down over the trees into the meadow, rolling forward across the lights. Sophie Cresson ran forward, waving, the Sten gun in one hand. Martineau got the door open, threw out the suitcases and followed them. He turned to help Sarah. Behind her, Green reached for the door and slammed it shut, locking the handle. The engine note deepened to a full-throated roar as the Lysander raced across the meadow and took off.

Sophie Cresson said, 'Come on, let's get out of here. Bring your suitcases while I get my lamps.' They followed her to the van and she opened the rear door. 'There's just enough room for both of you to sit behind the two barrels. Don't worry, I know every flic in the district. If they stop me, all they'll do is take a chicken and go home.'

'Some things never change,' Sarah said.

'Heh, a Breton girl?' Sophie flashed her torch on Sarah's face and grunted. 'My God, now they send little girls.' She shrugged. 'In you get and let's be out of here.'

Sarah crouched behind the barrels, her knees touching Martineau as Sophie drove away. So, this was it, she thought, the real thing. No more games now. She opened her handbag and felt for the butt of the Walther PPK inside. The little Belgian automatic Kelly had given her was in her case. Would she be able to use them if necessary? Only time would tell. Martineau lit a cigarette and passed it to her. When she inhaled, nothing had ever felt better, and she leaned back against the side of the van feeling wonderfully, marvelously alive.

It was noon before she awoke, yawning and stretching her arms. The small bedroom under the roof was plainly furnished but comfortable. She threw back the sheets and crossed to the window. The view across the walls down to the harbor was really quite special. Behind her the door opened and Sophie came in with a bowl of coffee on a tray.

'So, you're up.'

'It's good to be back.' Sarah took the bowl from her and sat on the window seat.

Sophie lit a cigarette. 'You've been here before?'

'Many times. My mother was a de Ville. Half-Jersey, half-Breton. My grandmother was born at Paimpol. I used to come over to Granville from the island when I was a little girl. There was a fishermen's café on the quay that had the finest hot rolls in the world. The best coffee.'

'Not anymore,' Sophie said. 'The war has changed everything. Look down there.'

The harbor was crammed with shipping. Rhine barges, three coasters and a number of German naval craft. It was a scene of considerable activity as dockers unloaded the contents of a line of trucks on the quay into the barges.

'They're definitely sailing for the islands tonight?' Sarah asked.

'Oh yes. Some for Jersey, the rest on to Guernsey.'

'How do you find them?'

'The Boche?' Sophie shrugged. 'I'm a reasonable woman. I don't want to hate anybody. I just want them out of France.'

'It's just that we hear such bad things about them in England.'

'True,' Sophie said. 'SS and Gestapo are devils, but they frighten the hell out of the ordinary German soldier as much as they do anyone else. In any case, we've got those among our own people who are as bad as the Gestapo. Darnan's *milice*. Frenchmen who work with the Nazis to betray Frenchmen.'

'That's terrible,' Sarah said.

'It's life, child, and what it means is you can never really trust anyone. Now get dressed and come downstairs and we'll have some lunch.'

★   ★   ★

At Gavray in what had once been the country home of the count of that name, Heini Baum sat at one end of the table in the officers' mess of the 41st Panzer Grenadiers and smilingly acknowledged the cheers as the officers toasted him then applauded. When they were finished, he nodded his thanks.

The young colonel of the regiment, a veteran of the Russian Front, his black panzer uniform scattered with decorations, said, 'If you could manage a few words, Herr Field Marshal. It would mean so much to my officers.'

There was a worried look in Hofer's eye when Baum glanced at him, but he disregarded it and stood up, straightening his tunic. 'Gentlemen, the Führer has given us a simple task. To keep the enemy off our beaches. Yes, I say our beaches. Europe, one and indivisible, is our goal. The battle will be won on those beaches. There is no possibility of our losing. The destiny of the Führer is Godgiven. So much is obvious to anyone with a grain of sense.' His irony was lost on them as they gazed up, enraptured, drinking in every word. He raised his glass. 'So, gentlemen, join me. To our beloved Führer, Adolf Hitler.'

'Adolf Hitler!' they chorused.

Baum tossed his glass into the fire, and with a stirring of excitement, they all followed him. Then they applauded again, forming two lines as he walked out, followed by Hofer.

'Rather heavy on the glasses, I should have thought,' Hofer said as they drove back to Cressy where Rommel had established temporary headquarters at the old castle there.

'You didn't approve?' Baum said.

'I didn't say that. Actually, the speech was rather good.'

'If the Herr Major will excuse my saying so, it was heavily over the top, to use theatrical vernacular,' Baum told him.

'I take your point,' Hofer said. 'On the other hand, it's exactly what they wanted to hear.'

Crazy, Baum thought. *Am I the only sane man left alive?* But by then, they were drawing into the courtyard of the castle. He went up the steps fast, acknowledging the salutes, Hofer trailing him, all the way up to the suite on the second floor.

Rommel had locked himself in the study and only came out on Hofer's knock. 'How did it go?'

'Perfect,' Hofer said. 'Passed with flying colors. You should have heard the speech you made.'

'Excellent.' Rommel nodded. 'Everything progresses in the Channel Islands? You spoke to von Schmettow in Guernsey?'

'Personally, Herr Field Marshal. He's also had his orders in writing. As you were told by Naval HQ at Cherbourg, they do most of their traveling between the islands by night these days because of the enemy air superiority in the area. So they will travel from Jersey to Guernsey on Thursday night for the conference, returning on Sunday night.'

'Good,' Rommel said. 'Which still leaves you and Berger flying in out of the dawn in a Fiesler Storch with all that RAF superiority in the area that you speak of.' He turned to Baum. 'What do you think about that, Berger?'

'I think it could be interesting if the Herr Major and I went down in flames into the sea. The Desert Fox is dead.' He shrugged. 'That could lead to some strange possibilities, you must admit, Herr Field Marshal.'

Gerard Cresson sat in his wheelchair at the table in the sitting room and refilled the glasses with red wine. 'No, I hate to dispel your illusions,' he said to Sarah, 'But out in Jersey, just as in France and every other occupied country in Europe, the real enemy is the informer. Without them the Gestapo couldn't operate.'

'But I was told there weren't any Gestapo in Jersey,' Sarah said.

'Officially they have a Geheime Feldpolizei setup there. That's Secret Field Police, and they're supposed to be controlled by the Abwehr. Military Intelligence. The whole thing is part of the ruling-by-kindness policy, a cosmetic exercise aimed at fooling the people. The implication is that because you're British we won't sick the Gestapo onto you.'

'Which is shit,' Sophie said as she came in from the kitchen with fresh coffee, 'because several of the men working for the GFP in Jersey are Gestapo operatives on loan.'

'Do you know where they are?' Sarah asked.

'A hotel at Havre des Pas called Silvertide. You know it?'

She nodded. 'Oh yes. I used to go swimming at Havre des Pas when I was a child.'

'Gestapo, Secret Field Police, SD, Abwehr. Wherever you go, whoever the man is who knocks on the door, it's the Gestapo to the poor devil being arrested.'

'Exactly the same in Jersey,' Gerard told him. 'To the locals, they're Gestapo and that's it. Mind you, it's a Mickey Mouse operation compared to what goes on in Lyons or Paris, but watch out for a Captain Muller. He's temporarily in command, and his chief aide, an inspector called Kleist.'

'Are they SS?'

'I don't know. Probably not. They've never been seen in uniform. Probably seconded from the police in some big city. Full of themselves, like all flics. Out to prove something.' He shrugged. 'You don't have to be in the SS to be in the Gestapo. You don't even have to be a member of the Nazi Party.'

'True,' Martineau said. 'Anyway, how do you rate our chances of bringing Kelso over from Jersey?'

'Very difficult indeed. That's one item they are very tight on, civilian traffic. It would be impossible in a small boat at the moment.'

'And if he isn't able to walk . . .' Sophie shrugged expressively.

'They'll be standing by at SOE for a call from you at any time this weekend,' Martineau said. 'The Lysander can pick up on Sunday night.'

Gerard laughed suddenly. 'I've just had a brilliant thought. You could always arrest Kelso. Find him and arrest him, if you follow me. Bring him over here officially, then cut out.'

'That's all very well,' Sarah put in, 'but where would that leave Aunt Helen and the General? Wouldn't they have to be arrested too?'

Martineau nodded. 'It's one of those ideas that sounds good until you think about it. Never mind. We'll think of something when we get there.'

'Like a bullet in the head maybe?' Cresson suggested. 'I mean, if this man is as important as they say . . .'

'He's entitled to a chance,' Martineau said. 'If there's any way I can pull him out I will, if not . . .' He shrugged. 'Now, what's the procedure for booking passage to the island tonight?'

'There's a movement officer in the office in the green hut on the quay. He issues the passes. No difficulty in your case.'

'Good,' Martineau said. 'That seems to be about it then.'

Sophie filled four glasses with red wine. 'I'm not going to wish you luck, I'm just going to tell you something.'

'What's that?' Martineau inquired.

She put an arm around Sarah's shoulders. 'I like the kid here very much. Whatever happens over there, you bring her back in one piece, because if you don't, and you show your face here again, I'll put a bullet in you myself.'

She smiled genially and toasted him.

9

The 5th Schnellboote Flotilla, as was common with all German Navy E-boat units, was used to living on the move. On returning to their Cherbourg base after the Slapton Sands affair, three boats had been ordered to Guernsey for temporary duty as convoy escorts. One of them, S92, was tied up at the quay at Granville now.

Darkness was already falling and the harbor was a scene of frenzied activity as the convoy got ready to leave. Chief Petty Officer Hans Richter, checking the 40-mm Bofors gun in the stern, paused to watch dockers working on the *Victor Hugo* which was moored next to them. Now that her holds were crammed full, they were dumping sacks of coal and bales of hay on her decks so that there was hardly room to move.

The *Hugo's* antiaircraft defenses were 7.92-mm machine guns and a Bofors gun – not too much use when the Tommies swept in from the darkness in those damned Beaufighters with their searchlights on, but that's the way things were these days, and the Luftwaffe didn't seem to be able to do much about it. Richter could see the master of the *Hugo*, Savary, on the bridge talking to the officer in command of the gun crew, the Italian lieutenant, Orsini. Flamboyant as usual with the white top to his cap and the scarf at his neck. A good seaman for all that. They said he'd sunk a British destroyer off Taranto before being seconded to the 5th Schnellboote as an E-boat commander. They were only using him on secondary duties these days because nobody trusted the Italians anymore. After all, most of them were fighting for the Allies now.

As Richter watched, Guido Orsini went down the ladder and then the gangway to the quay and walked toward the port officer's hut. Richter turned back to the gun and a voice called 'Petty Officer!'

Richter looked over the rail. Standing a few feet away was an SS officer, a black leather trenchcoat over his uniform, the silver death's-head on the cap gleaming dully in the evening light. When Richter saw the oak leaf collar patches of a full colonel his heart sank.

He got his heels together quickly. 'Standartenführer. What can I do for you?'

The young woman standing at the colonel's shoulder was pretty in her little black beret and belted raincoat, the hair very fair, just like his daughter's back home in Hamburg. Too young for an SS bastard like this, Richter thought.

'Your commanding officer, Kapitanleutnant Dietrich, commands the convoy, I understand?' Martineau said. 'Is he on board?'

'Not at the moment.'

'Where is he?'

'Port officer's hut. The green one over there, Standartenführer.'

'Good. I'll have a word with him.' Martineau gestured to the two suitcases. 'See these go on board. We'll be traveling with you as far as Jersey.'

Which was a turnup for the book. Richter watched them walk away, then nodded to a young seaman who'd been listening with interest. 'You heard the man. Get those cases.'

'He was SD,' the sailor said. 'Did you notice?'

'Yes,' Richter said. 'As it happens I did. Now get on with it.'

Erich Dietrich was thirty years of age, a young architect in Hamburg before the war who had discovered his true vocation. He had never been happier than when he was at sea and in command, especially in E-boats. He did not want the war to end. It had taken its toll, of course, on him as much as anyone. Just now, leaning over the chart table with the port officer, Lieutenant Schroeder, and Guido Orsini, he was in the best of humors.

'Winds three to four at the most with rain squalls. Could be worse.'

Schroeder said, 'Intelligence is expecting big raids on the Ruhr again tonight, so things should be reasonably clear for us down here as regards the RAF.'

'If you believe that, you'll believe anything,' Orsini said.

'You're a pessimist, Guido,' Erich Dietrich told him. 'Expect good things and they'll always fall into your lap. That's what my old mother used to say.'

The door opened behind him, Schroeder's face dropped and Guido stopped smiling. Dietrich turned and found Martineau standing there, Sarah at his shoulder.

'Kapitanleutnant Dietrich? My name is Vogel.' Martineau produced his SD identity card and passed it across, then he took Himmler's letter from its envelope. 'If you would be kind enough to read this also.'

Sarah couldn't understand a word. He sounded like someone else, held himself like another person, the voice cold and dry. Dietrich read the letter, and Guido and Schroeder peered over his shoulder. The Italian made a face and Dietrich handed the document back.

'You noticed, of course, that the Führer himself was kind enough to countersign my orders?'

'Your credentials are without doubt the most remarkable I've ever seen, Standartenführer,' Dietrich said. 'In what way can we serve you?'

'I need passage for myself and Mademoiselle Latour to Jersey. As you are convoy commander I shall naturally travel with you. I've already told your petty officer to take our cases on board.'

Which would have been enough to reduce Erich Dietrich to speechless rage at the best of times, but there was another factor here. The Kriegsmarine had always been notoriously the least Nazi of all the German armed forces. Dietrich personally had never cared for the Party one little bit, which hardly disposed him in Standartenführer Max Vogel's favor. There were limits, of course, to what he could do, but he still had one possible objection on his side.

'Happy to oblige, Standartenführer,' he said smoothly. 'There is one problem, however. Naval regulations forbid the carrying of civilians on a fighting ship at sea. I can accommodate you, but not, alas, this charming young lady.'

It was difficult to argue with him because he was right. Martineau tried to handle it as a man like Vogel would have done, arrogant, demanding, determined not to be put down. 'What would you suggest?'

'One of the convoy ships, perhaps. Lieutenant Orsini here is in command of the gun crew on the SS *Victor Hugo*, whose cargo is destined for the port of St. Helier on Jersey. You could go with him.'

But Vogel would not have allowed himself to lose face completely. 'No,' he said calmly. 'It is good that I should see something of your work, Kapitanleutnant. I shall travel with you. Mademoiselle Latour, on the other hand, can proceed on the *Victor Hugo* if Lieutenant Orsini has no objections.'

'Certainly not,' said Guido who had hardly been able to take his eyes off her. 'A distinct pleasure.'

'Unfortunately Mademoiselle Latour speaks no German.' Martineau turned to her and carried on in French. 'We must separate for the journey across, my dear. A matter of regulations. I'll keep your luggage with me, so don't worry about that. This young officer will take care of you.'

'Guido Orsini, at your service, signorina,' he said gallantly and saluted. 'If you come with me I'll see you safely on board. We sail in thirty minutes.'

She turned to Martineau. 'I'll see you later then, Max.'

'In Jersey.' He nodded calmly.

She went out, Orsini holding the door open for her. Dietrich said, 'A charming girl.'

'I think so.' Martineau leaned over the chart table. 'Are we to enjoy an uneventful run tonight? I understand your convoys are often attacked by RAF night fighters.'

'Frequently, Standartenführer,' Schroeder told him. 'But the RAF will be busy elsewhere tonight.'

'Terror bombing the civilian population of our major cities as usual,' Martineau said because it was the kind of thing they would expect a Party fanatic like him to say. 'And the British Royal Navy?'

'Yes, their MTBs are often active in the area,' Dietrich admitted and tapped the map. 'From bases at Falmouth and Devonport.'

'And this doesn't worry you?'

'Standartenführer, there are more of them these days, but our E-boats are still the fastest thing of their kind afloat, as I will certainly have the chance to show you tonight.' He gathered up his charts. 'Now, if you will follow me, we'll go on board.'

★ ★ ★

The convoy left just after ten o'clock, eleven ships in all, including the barges. S92 led the way out of harbor, then swung hard to port. There was a light rain falling, and Dietrich stood on the bridge, probing into the darkness with his Zeiss night glasses. Martineau was at his right shoulder. Below them the wheelhouse was even more cramped with the helmsman and engine room telegraphist in there and the navigating officer at his small table behind. The wireless room was down a passage farther on.

'Not much room on these things,' Martineau commented.

'All engines, that's what we say,' Dietrich told him.

'And armaments?'

'The torpedoes. Bofors gun aft, twenty-millimeter cannon in the forward well deck. Eight machine guns. We manage.'

'And radar, of course?'

'Yes, but that's a difficult one in these waters. Lots of reefs, rocks, small islands. It makes for a lot of clutter on the screen. When the Tommies come down here they do exactly what I do when I'm operating out of Cherbourg and hitting their convoys.'

'What's that?'

'Turn off our radar so they can't find us with their location equipment and maintain radio silence.'

Martineau nodded and looked astern at the other ships bulking in the dark. 'What speed will the convoy maintain?'

'Six knots.'

'You must feel like a racing horse pulling a cart sometimes.'

Dietrich laughed. 'Yes, but I've got two thousand horses under me.' He slapped the rail. 'Nice to know just how fast they can get up and go when I ask them to.'

On the bridge of the *Victor Hugo* it was like being in a safe and enclosed world, rain and spray drifting against the glass. Savary stood beside the helmsman, and Sarah and Guido Orsini leaned over the chart table.

'This is the convoy route, what the Navy call Weg Ida, from Granville, east of the Chausey Isles.'

She liked him a lot, had from the moment he'd turned to look at her in the hut on the quay. He was certainly good-looking. Too handsome, really, in a way that Latins could be sometimes, but there was strength there too, and when he smiled . . .

His shoulder was touching hers. He said, 'Come to the saloon. I'll get you a coffee and you can use my cabin if you'd like to lie down.'

Savary turned. 'Not just now, Count. I want to check the engine room. You'll have to take the bridge.'

He went out. Sarah said, 'Count?'

'Lots of counts in Italy. Don't let it worry you.'

He offered her a cigarette and they smoked in companionable silence, looking out into the night, the noise of the engines a muted throbbing. 'I thought Italy capitulated last year?' she said.

'Oh, it did, except for those Fascist fanatics who decided to fight on under the Germans, especially when Otto Skorzeny hoisted Mussolini off that mountaintop and flew him to Berlin to continue the holy struggle.'

'Are you a Fascist?'

He looked down into that appealing young face, aware of a tenderness that he had never experienced with any woman in his life before. It was perhaps because of that fact that he found himself speaking so frankly.

'To be honest, I'm not anything. I loathe politics. It reminds me of the senator in Rome who's supposed to have said: "Don't tell my mother I'm in politics. She thinks I play the piano in a brothel."'

She laughed. 'I like that.'

'Most of my former comrades are now working with the British and American Navies. I, on the other hand, was seconded on special duties to serve with the Fifth Schnellboote Flotilla in Cherbourg. When Italy decided to sue for peace, there wasn't a great deal I could do about it, and I didn't fancy a prison camp. Of course, they don't trust me enough to allow me to command an E-boat anymore. I suppose they think I might roar across to England.'

'Would you?'

Savary returned to the bridge at that moment, and the Italian said, 'Right, let's go below now and get that coffee.'

She moved ahead of him. As he watched her descend the companionway he was conscious of a curious excitement. He'd known many women, and many who were more beautiful than Anne-Marie Latour with her ridiculous dyed hair. Certainly more sophisticated. And there was something about her that was not quite right. The image was one thing, but the girl herself, when he spoke to her, was something else again.

'Mother of God, Guido, what's happening to you?' he asked softly as he went down the companionway after her.

Captain Karl Muller, the officer in command of the Secret Field Police in Jersey, sat at his desk in the Silvertide Hotel at Havre des Pas and worked his way though a bulky file. It was wholly devoted to anonymous letters, the tip-offs that led to whatever success his unit enjoyed. The crimes were varied. Anything from possession of an illegal radio to helping a Russian slave worker on the run or involvement in the black market. Muller always insisted on his men tracking down the writers of anonymous letters. Once uncovered, they could be used in many ways because of his threat to expose them to friends and neighbors.

It was all very small beer, of course. Nothing like it had been at Gestapo Headquarters at Rue des Saussaies in Paris. Muller was not SS, but he was a Party member, a onetime Chief Inspector of Police in the Hamburg Criminal Investigation Department. Unfortunately, a young Frenchwoman in his hands for interrogation had died without disclosing the names of her associates. As she had been involved with the principal Resistance circuit in Paris, it had been a matter of some importance. To his superiors he'd botched things badly by being too eager. The posting to this island backwater had followed. So now, he was a man in a hurry, seeking any way he could to get back into the mainstream of things.

He stood up, a shade under six feet, with hair that was still dark brown in spite of the fact that he was in his fiftieth year. He stretched, started to the window to look out at the weather, and the phone rang.

He picked it up. 'Yes.'

It wasn't a local call, he could tell by the crackling. 'Captain Muller? This is Schroeder, port officer at Granville.'

Ten minutes later he was standing at the window, staring out into the dark, when there was a knock at the door. He turned and went to his desk and sat down.

The two men who entered were, like Muller, in civilian clothes. The GFP never wore uniform if they could help it. The one who led the way was broad and squat with a Slavic face and hard gray eyes. This was Inspector Willi Kleist, Muller's second-in-command, also seconded from the Gestapo and, like Muller, a former detective with the Hamburg police. They had known each other for years. The man with him was much younger with fair hair, blue eyes and a weak mouth. A suggestion of perverse cruelty there, but when confronted with Muller, so eager to please that it showed. This was Sergeant Ernst Greiser, who had been transferred from the Army's Field Police to the GFP six months earlier.

'An interesting development,' Muller told them. 'I've had Schroeder on the phone from Granville. Apparently an SD Standartenführer Vogel presented himself on the quay with a young French woman and demanded passage to Jersey. They put the woman on the *Victor Hugo*. He comes on the S92 with Dietrich.'

'But why, Herr Captain?' Kleist asked. 'We've had no notification. Why would he be coming?'

'The bad news,' Muller said, 'is that he's traveling under a special warrant from Reichsführer Himmler. According to Schroeder it's countersigned by the Führer.'

'My God!' Greiser said.

'So, my friends, we must be ready for him. You were going to take care of the passenger checks when the convoy ships get into St. Helier, isn't that so, Ernst?' he inquired of Greiser.

'Yes, Herr Captain.'

'Inspector Kleist and I will join you. Whatever his reason for being here, I want to be in on the action. I'll see you later.'

They went out. He lit a cigarette and went to the window, more excited than he had been in months.

It was just after eleven when Helen de Ville took the tray to her room, using the back stairs that led straight up from the kitchen. None of the officers ever used it, keeping strictly to their own end of the house. In any case, she was careful. Only one cup on the tray. Everything for one. If she chose to have late supper in her room, that was her affair.

She went into the bedroom, locking the door behind her, crossed to the bookshelves, opened the secret entrance and moved inside, closing it before going up the narrow stairway. Kelso was sitting up in bed, propped against pillows, reading by the light of an oil lamp. The wooden shutters in the gable window were closed, a heavy curtain drawn across.

He looked up and smiled. 'What have we got here?'

'Not much. Tea, but at least it's the real stuff, and a cheese sandwich. I make my own cheese these days, so you'd better like it. What are you reading?'

'One of the books you brought up. Eliot. *The Four Quartets*.'

'Poetry and you an engineer?' She sat on the end of the bed and lit one of the Gitanes Gallagher had given her.

'I certainly wasn't interested in that kind of thing in the old days, but this war.' He shrugged. 'Like a lot of people I want answers, I suppose. In my end is my beginning, that's what the man says. But what comes in between? What's it all mean?'

'Well, if you find out, don't forget to let me know.' She noticed the snap of his wife and daughters on the bedside locker and picked it up. 'Do you think of them often?'

'All the time. They mean everything. My marriage really worked. It was as simple as that. I never wanted anything else, and then the war came along and messed things up.'

'Yes, it has a bad habit of doing that.'

'Still, I can't complain. Comfortable bed, decent cooking, and the oil lamp gives things a nicely old-fashioned atmosphere.'

'They cut off the electricity to this part of the island at nine o'clock sharp,' she said. 'I know people who would be glad of that oil lamp.'

'Are things really as bad as that?'

'Of course they are.' There was a trace of anger in her voice. 'What on earth would you expect? You're lucky to have that cup of tea. Elsewhere in the island it could be a rather inferior substitute made from parsnips or blackberry leaves. Or you could try acorn coffee. Not one of life's great experiences.'

'And food?'

'You just have to get used to getting by with a lot less of it, that's all. The same with tobacco.' She held up her cigarette. 'This is real and very black market, but you can get anything if you have the right connections or plenty of cash. The rich here still do very well. The banks just operate in reichsmarks instead of pounds.' She smiled. 'Do you want to know what it's really like being occupied in Jersey?'

'It would be interesting.'

'Boring.' She plumped up his pillows. 'I'm going to bed now.'

'The big day tomorrow,' he said.

'If we're to believe the message Savary brought.' She picked up the tray. 'Try and get some sleep.'

Orsini had given Sarah his cabin. It was very small indeed, with a cupboard and washstand and a single bunk. It was hot and stuffy, the porthole blacked over, and the noise of the engine churning below gave her a headache. She lay on the bunk and closed her eyes and tried to relax. The ship seemed to stagger. An illusion, of course. She sat up and there was an explosion.

Things seemed to happen in slow motion after that. The ship fell perfectly still, as if everything waited, and then there was another violent shock. The explosion this time caused the walls to tremble. She cried out and tried to stand up, and then the floor tilted and she fell against the door. Her handbag, thrown from the locker top, was on the floor beside her. She picked it up automatically and tried the door handle, but the door stuck fast. She shook the handle desperately and then the door opened so unexpectedly that she was hurled back against the opposite wall.

Orsini stood in the entrance, his face wild. 'Move!' he ordered. 'Now! No time to lose.'

'What is it?' she demanded as he grabbed her hand and pulled her after him.

'Torpedo attack. We've been hit twice. We've only got minutes. This old tub will go down like a stone.'

They went up the companionway to the saloon which was deserted. He took off his reefer coat and held it out to her. 'Get this on.' She hesitated, aware suddenly that she was still clutching her handbag, then did as she was told, stuffing the bag into one of the reefer coat's ample pockets. He pulled her arms roughly through a life jacket and laced it up. Then he put one on himself as he led the way out onto the boat deck.

There was a scene of indescribable confusion as the crew tried to launch the boats and, above them, the machine-gun crews fired into the night. Fire arced toward them in return, raking the bridge above, where Savary shouted orders. He cried out in fear and jumped over the rail, bouncing off some bales of hay below. Cannon shell ripped into one of the lifeboats a few yards away, tearing great holes in it.

Orsini pushed Sarah down behind some sacks of coal. At the same moment there was another explosion, inside the ship this time, and a portion of the deck in the stern disintegrated, flames billowing into the night. The entire ship tilted sharply to port, and the deck cargo started to break free, sacks of coal, bales of hay, sliding down against the rail.

It had not been possible to launch a single boat, so rapidly had disaster struck, and men were already going over the rail, Savary leading the way. Orsini lost his balance and Sarah fell on her back, felt herself slide down the slippery deck, and then the rail dipped under and she was in the water.

The E-boat surged forward at speed within seconds of the first explosion, Dietrich scanning the darkness with his night glasses. Martineau almost lost his balance at the sudden burst of speed and hung on grimly.

'What is it?'

'I'm not sure,' Dietrich said, and then flames blossomed in the night five hundred yards away and he focused on the *Victor Hugo*. A dark shape flashed across that patch of light like a shadow and then another. 'British MTBs. They've hit the *Hugo*.'

He pressed the button on the battle stations alarm, and the ugly sound of the klaxon rose above the roaring of the Mercedes Benz engines winding up to top speed. Already the crew were moving to their stations. The Bofors gun and the well-deck cannon started to fire, lines of tracer curving into the night.

The only thing Martineau could think of was Sarah, and he grabbed Dietrich by the sleeve. 'But the people on that ship. We must help them.'

'Later!' Dietrich shrugged him aside. 'This is business. Now keep out of the way.'

Sarah kicked desperately to get as far from the ship as possible as the *Victor Hugo* continued to tilt. There was burning oil on the water toward the stern, men swimming hard to get away from it as it advanced relentlessly. One man was overtaken. She heard his screams as he disappeared.

She moved awkwardly because of the life jacket and the reefer coat was bulky, already saturated with water. She realized now why Orsini had given it to her as the cold started to eat at her legs. Where was he? She turned trying to make sense of the oil-stained faces. An MTB spun around the stern of the *Victor Hugo*, the violence of its wash hurling some of those in the sea up out of the water. There was a burst of machine-gun fire.

A hand grabbed at her life jacket from behind, and she turned and Orsini was there. 'Over here, cara. Just do as I say.'

There was wreckage floating everywhere, the bales of hay from the deck cargo buoyant in the water. He towed her toward one of these and they hung onto its binding ropes.

'Who were they?' she gasped.

'MTBs.'

'British?'

'Or French or Dutch. They all operate out of Falmouth.'

There was another mighty rushing sound in the night and machine-gun bullets churned the water as an MTB again carved its way through men and wreckage. A tracer flashed through the darkness in a great arc and a starshell burst. A moment later, a parachute flare illuminated the scene.

Some distance away two MTBs ran for cover, and the E-boat roared after them. 'Go get the bastards, Erich!' Orsini shouted.

She almost joined in. My God, she thought, what a way to go. My own people trying to kill me. She hung onto the rope and said, gasping, 'Did they have to do that? Machine-gun men in the water?'

'War, cara, is a nasty business. It makes everyone crazy. Are you managing?'

'My arms are tired.'

A hatch drifted by and he swam to it and towed it toward her. 'Let's get you onto this.'

It was a struggle, but she finally managed it. 'What about you?'

'I'll be fine hanging on.' He laughed. 'Don't worry, I've been in the water before. My luck is good, so stick with me.'

And then she remembered the spring fete and Gypsy Sara and her fire and water and she started to laugh shakily. 'Are you all right?' he demanded.

'Lovely. Nothing like the Channel Islands for a holiday at this time of the year. Perfect for sea bathing,' and then she realized, to her horror, that she'd spoken in English.

He floated there, staring up at her, and then said in excellent English, 'Did I tell you I went to Winchester? My father felt that only an English public school could give me the backbone I needed.' He laughed. 'Oh, I do so like to be right, and I knew there was something different about you from the first moment, cara.' He laughed again, excitedly this time. 'Which means there's something unusual about the good Standartenführer Vogel.'

'Please,' she said desperately.

'Don't worry, cara, I fell in love with you the moment you came through the door of that hut on the quay. I like you, I don't like them – whoever they are. We Italians are a very simple people.'

He coughed, rubbing oil from his face, and she reached for his hand. 'You saved my life, Guido.'

There was the sound of a throttled-down engine approaching. He glanced over his shoulder and saw an armed trawler, one of the escorts, approaching. 'Yes,' he said. 'I'm pleased to say I probably did.'

A moment later, the trawler was looming above them, a net over the side. Two or three German sailors clambered down, reaching for Sarah, and pulled her up. Guido followed and collapsed on the deck beside her.

A young lieutenant came down the ladder from the bridge and hurried forward. 'Guido, is that you?' he said in German.

'As ever, Bruno,' Guido answered in the same language.

'And you, fraulein, are you all right? We must get you to my cabin.'

'Mademoiselle Latour, Bruno, and she speaks no German,' Guido told him in French. He smiled at Sarah and helped her to her feet. 'Now let's take you below.'

10

As Sarah pulled the heavy white sweater over her head there was a knock on the door of Bruno's cabin. She opened it and a young rating said in poor French, 'Lieutenant Feldt's compliments. We're entering St. Helier Harbor.'

He closed the door and she went to the basin and tried to do something with her hair, which was impossible. The effects of salt water had proved disastrous, and it was now a tangled straw-colored mess. She gave up and rolled the Kriegsmarine dungarees up at her ankles.

The contents of her handbag, which she had stuffed into a pocket of Orsini's reefer before leaving the *Victor Hugo*, had survived surprisingly well. Her identity card and other papers were soaked, of course. She had laid them out now on the hot-water pipes to dry with her handbag. She replaced them all and retrieved the Walther PPK from under the pillow. The Belgian pistol Sergeant Kelly had given her was in her suitcase on board the E-boat. She sat on the edge of the bunk and pulled on a pair of old tennis shoes one of the young ratings had given her.

There was a knock and Guido came in. 'How are you?' he asked in French.

'Fine,' she said, 'except for the hair. I look like a scarecrow.'

He was carrying a Kriegsmarine reefer coat. 'Put this on. A damp morning out there.'

As she stood her handbag fell to the floor, spilling some of the contents, including the Walther. Guido picked it up and said softly, 'What a lot of gun for a little girl. Mystery piles on mystery with you.'

She took it from him and returned it to her handbag. 'All part of my fatal attraction.'

'Very fatal if an item like that is involved.'

His eyes were serious now, but she smiled lightly and, on impulse, kissed him on the cheek. Then she went out and he followed her.

A scene so familiar from her childhood. The harbor, Elizabeth Castle on her left in the bay, the Albert Pier, the sprawl of St. Helier, Fort Regent on the hill above. The same and yet not the same. Military strongpoints everywhere and the harbor more crammed with vessels than she had ever known it. The Rhine barges from the convoy were already safely in, but there was no sign of S92.

'Where's the E-boat?' Sarah asked Guido as she leaned on the bridge rail beside him and Lieutenant Feldt.

'Probably having a last look for survivors,' he said as they nosed in toward the Albert Pier.

Dockers were already starting to unload the barges, and there seemed to be soldiers everywhere. Below, half-a-dozen French seamen, survivors of the crew of the *Victor Hugo* picked up by the trawler after Guido and Sarah, waited at the rail in borrowed clothes. Two had sustained facial burns and were heavily bandaged. Another man who had swallowed oil lay on a stretcher.

'No sign of Savary,' Orsini said.

'Someone else may have picked him up,' Bruno Feldt said. 'I see the GFP are ready and waiting. Why is it that policemen always look like policemen?'

'GFP?' Sarah asked in a deliberate display of ignorance. 'What's that?'

'Geheime Feldpolizei,' Guido told her. 'As a matter of interest, the tall one, Captain Muller, is on loan from the Gestapo. So is the thug next to him, the one built like a brick wall. That's Inspector Willi Kleist. The young one with the fair hair is Sergeant Ernst Greiser. Now he *isn't* ex-Gestapo.'

'But wishes he were,' Bruno Feldt put in.

The three were the first up the gangway when it went over. Greiser paused among the French seamen, and Muller came on up the ladder to the ridge followed by Kleist. Sarah was aware of Guido's hand going into the pocket of her reefer coat and fumbling inside her handbag. She turned to glance briefly at him. As she realized it was the Walther he was seeking, it was already too late, as Muller reached the bridge.

'Herr Leutnant.' He nodded to Feldt and said to Orsini, 'You had quite a night of it, I hear?' He wore an old Burberry raincoat and felt hat and there was something curiously gentle about him as he turned to Sarah and said in French, 'You were a passenger on the *Hugo*, mademoiselle . . .?'

'Latour,' Orsini put in. 'We were in the water together.'

'A remarkable escape,' Muller nodded. 'You lost your papers?'

'No,' she said. 'I have them here.' She took the handbag from her pocket and started to open it. Muller held out his hand. 'The bag, if you please, mademoiselle.'

There was a moment only as if everyone waited, then Sarah handed it to him. 'Of course.'

He turned to Bruno Feldt. 'We'll use your cabin for a few minutes, if we may.'

He seemed so reasonable, Sarah thought, so polite, when very obviously most of those standing around were frightened to death of him. Not Guido, of course, who smiled and squeezed her arm. 'I'll wait for you, cara, and if the colonel doesn't arrive you can come up to my billet at de Ville Place. I have a very superior landlady. She'll look after you, I promise. All very high class. Only naval officers.'

She went down the companionway and back into Lieutenant Feldt's cabin. Muller followed her in and Kleist leaned against the open door.

'So, mademoiselle.' Muller sat on the bed, turned the handbag upside down and emptied it. Her papers fell out, her makeup case, powder compact and comb, and also the Walther. He made no comment. He opened her French identity card, examined it, the German Ausweis and the ration cards. He replaced them carefully in the bag and lit a cigarette. Only then did he pick up the Walther, a finger through the trigger guard. 'You are, I'm sure, aware that there is only one penalty for a civilian caught in possession of any kind of firearm?'

'Yes,' Sarah said.

'This is yours, I take it?'

'Certainly. It was a gift from a friend. He was concerned for my safety. These are troubled times, Captain.'

'And what kind of friend would encourage you to break the law so flagrantly? Would it not make him as guilty as you?'

From behind, a cold voice said in German, 'Then perhaps you should address that question to me?'

Harry Martineau stood in the doorway, Guido just behind him in the corridor. He presented a supremely menacing figure in the SS uniform and black leather trenchcoat, the silver death's-head in the crumpled cap.

Karl Muller knew the devil when he met him face-to-face and got to his feet very fast indeed. 'Standartenführer.'

'You are?'

'Captain Karl Muller, in charge of Geheime Feldpolizei here in Jersey. This is my second in command, Inspector Kleist.'

'My name is Vogel.' Martineau took out his SD pass and handed it over. Muller examined it and passed it back. Martineau produced the Himmler warrant. 'Read that – both of you.'

Muller did as he was told. Kleist, peering over his shoulder, was awestruck and gazed at Martineau in astonishment. Muller took it much more calmly, folded the letter and handed it back. 'In what way can I serve you, Standartenführer?'

'Mademoiselle Latour travels under my protection.' Martineau picked up the Walther and put it back in her handbag. 'She has done me the honor of choosing my friendship. There are those among her countrymen who do not approve. I prefer that she should be in a position to defend herself should any unfortunate situation arise.'

'Of course, Standartenführer.'

'Good, then kindly wait for me on deck.'

Muller didn't even hesitate. 'Certainly, Standartenführer.' He nodded to Kleist and they went out.

Martineau closed the door and turned. He smiled suddenly, turning Vogel into Harry. 'You look awful. Are you all right?'

'Yes,' she said. 'Thanks to Guido.'

'Guido is it?'

'He saved my life, Harry. It wasn't good when we went down. Burning oil, men dying.' She shuddered. 'And the MTBs machine-gunned us in the water. I thought it was only the Germans who were supposed to do that?'

'Only at the cinema, sweetheart.' He gave her a cigarette. 'In real life everybody does it.'

'We've got a problem,' she said. 'At one point when we were in the water I spoke to Guido in English.'

'Good God!'

She put up a hand defensively. 'It was pretty confusing out there to put it mildly. Anyway, he speaks good English himself. It seems he went to Winchester.'

'Stop!' Martineau said. 'It gets worse.'

'Not really. After we were saved he told the officer commanding the ship that I only spoke French. And he knows about the Walther and kept quiet about that.'

'You *have* been careless.'

'He's no Fascist, Harry. He's an Italian aristocrat who doesn't give a damn about politics, stuck here because he happened to be in the wrong place when the Italian government capitulated.'

'I see. So why should he go to all this trouble to lay himself on the line for you?'

'He likes me?'

'Likes you? He only met you last night.'

'You know what these Latins are like.'

She smiled mischievously and Martineau shook his head. 'Nineteen they told me. More like a hundred and nineteen.'

'Another thing, Harry, Guido's billeted on Aunt Helen at de Ville Place. Apparently a number of naval officers are. He was going to take me up there if you hadn't arrived.'

'Perfect,' Martineau said. 'As for the other business, we'll tell him your mother was English. You've kept quiet about this during the Occupation years in case it caused you problems.'

'Will he believe it?'

'I don't see why not. Are you going to be all right for clothes?'

'Yes. I've got a coat, shoes, hat, everything I need in the large case. A good job it traveled with you on the E-boat.'

They went up the companionway. Muller was standing on the bridge talking to Feldt and Orsini. Below, Kleist and Greiser were shepherding the French seamen ashore.

Martineau said to Orsini in French, 'Anne-Marie tells me you are billeted in most congenial circumstances. Some country house called de Ville Place?'

'That's right, Colonel.'

Martineau turned to Muller. 'It sounds as if it would suit my needs exactly. Would there be any objection?'

Muller, eager to please, said, 'None at all, Standartenführer. It has, by tradition, been allocated to officers of the Kriegsmarine, but Mrs. de Ville, the owner, is seven or eight below her complement.'

'That's settled then.'

Orsini said, 'I'll take you up there now, if you like. I have a car parked at the end of the pier.'

'Good,' Martineau said. 'I suggest we get moving then.'

They went down the gangway to the pier, and a Kriegsmarine rating, standing by the E-boat waiting, picked up the two suitcases and followed. Orsini and Sarah walked in front, Martineau followed with Muller at his side.

'Naturally once I'm settled in, I'll return to town to pay my respects to the military commandant. Colonel Heine, isn't it?'

'That's correct, Standartenführer. I understand he's leaving for Guernsey first thing in the morning for a weekend meeting with General von Schmettow.'

'I need to see him only to present my compliments,' Martineau told him. 'One thing I will need is a vehicle. A Kubelwagen would serve my purposes best in case I wish to use it over rough country.'

The Kubelwagen was the German Army's equivalent of the jeep, a general purpose vehicle that would go virtually anywhere.

'No problem, Standartenführer. I will also be happy to provide one of my men as a driver.'

'Not necessary,' Martineau said. 'I prefer to do things for myself, Muller. I'll find my way about this little island of yours, believe me.'

Muller said, 'If I could have some idea of the purpose of your visit.'

'I am here on special instruction from Reischführer Himmler himself, countersigned by the Führer. You have seen my orders,' Martineau told him. 'Are you querying them?'

'Certainly not.'

'Good.' They had reached Orsini's Morris sedan, and the sailor was stowing the suitcases. 'When the time comes, you will be informed, if and when necessary. I'll possibly call in on you later today. Where are your headquarters?'

'Silvertide Hotel. Havre des Pas.'

'I'll find it. In the meantime have the Kubelwagen delivered to me.'

Sarah was already in the back, Orsini behind the wheel. Martineau got into the front passenger seat beside him and the Italian moved away.

As they drove along Victoria Avenue, the military railway tracks between them and the bay, Martineau wound down the window and lit one of the Gitanes he'd got from the Cressons. 'You like it here?' he asked Orsini.

'There are worse places to wait out the end of a war. In the summer it's particularly beautiful.'

Martineau said, 'I believe there's a misunderstanding to be cleared up. Anne-Marie has a Breton father, but an English mother. She felt it sensible to keep quiet about this in case it caused problems with the occupying powers. In fact it was one of my own people who first made the discovery, a happy one for me as it brought us together. Isn't that so, my love?'

'An intriguing story, Colonel,' Orsini said. 'You may rely on my discretion in the matter. The last thing I would wish to do is embarrass Mademoiselle Latour in any way.'

'Good,' Martineau said. 'I felt sure you'd understand.'

Back in his office at the Silvertide, Muller sat behind his desk thinking about things. After a while, he flipped the intercom. 'Have Inspector Kleist and Sergeant Greiser come in.'

He went to the window and looked out. The sky was clear now, suddenly blue, and the tide, still advancing, blanketed the rocks on the shore with white foam. The door opened and the two policemen entered.

'You wanted us, Herr Captain?' Kleist asked.

'Yes, Willi.' Muller sat down, leaned back in his chair, lit a cigarette and blew smoke to the ceiling.

'What is it?' the Inspector asked.

'Remember old Dieckhoff, Chief of Detectives in Hamburg?'

'How could I forget him?'

'I always recall his number-one rule when I was a young detective. Dieckhoff's Law, he called it.'

'That it doesn't matter how good an egg looks. If it smells, there's something wrong,' Kleist said.

'Exactly.' Muller nodded. 'And this smells, Willi.' He got up and paced around the room. 'Nothing to do with evidence or appearance. Just every instinct I have as a detective tells me things aren't as they seem. I'd like to know more about Standartenführer Vogel.'

Kleist was obviously worried. 'But, Herr Captain, his background is impeccable. You can't very well ring up Reichsführer Himmler and ask him to fill you in on his personal envoy.'

'No, of course not.' Muller turned. 'But there is another possibility. Your brother used to work at Gestapo headquarters at Prince Albrecht-strasse in Berlin, Ernst?'

'Peter? Yes, Herr Captain, but now he's at Stuttgart Headquarters. Criminal records,' Greiser said.

'He must still have connections in Berlin. Book a call through to him. Ask about Vogel. I want to know how important he is.'

'Shall I telex? It would be quicker.'

'I want a judicious inquiry, you fool,' Muller told him wearily. 'Not a public one.'

'But I would remind you, sir, that calls for Germany are routed, as you know, via Cherbourg and Paris. They've been taking fifteen or sixteen hours recently, even at priority level.'

'Then book one now, Ernst.' The young man went out, and Muller

said to Kleist, 'See about a Kubelwagen. Have it delivered to de Ville
Place. Let's keep him happy for the time being.'

In the kitchen, Helen was rolling out the pastry made from potato flour
when Gallagher came in. 'Good, you can clean the fish for me,' she said.
    There were some plaice on the marble slab beside the sink. Gallagher
took a knife from his pocket. The handle was of yellowing ivory. When
he pressed one end, a razor-sharp double-edged blade sprang into view.
    'You know I loathe that thing,' she said.
    'When my old grandfather, Harvey Le Brocq, was twelve he made his
first trip in a schooner, all the way from Jersey to the Grand Banks of
Newfoundland for cod. This knife was his father's gift to him. He left it
to me in his will. Knives, guns – it's how they're used that's important,
Helen.'
    'What do you want me to do, applaud?' she asked as he started to
clean the fish. At that moment there was the sound of a car drawing up
outside. 'Probably Guido. I wonder what kind of a run they had?'
    There were steps in the passageway, a knock on the door, and Guido
came in carrying two suitcases. He put them down and straightened. 'A
good passage?' Helen asked.
    'No, the *Hugo* was torpedoed. Savary missing, three crew members
dead and four of my gun crew.' Sarah stepped in through the door
followed by Martineau, and Orsini carried on, 'This is Anne-Marie
Latour. She was a passenger on the *Hugo*. We were in the water
together.' He nodded to Martineau. 'Standartenführer Vogel.'
    Helen looked bewildered. 'What can I do for you?'
    'Put us up, Mrs. de Ville,' Martineau spoke in English. 'I'm in the
island for a few days. We need quarters.'
    'Impossible,' Helen told him. 'This is a billet for officers of the
Kriegsmarine only.'
    'And you are well short of your complement,' Martineau told her.
'However inconvenient, the matter is an accomplished fact. If you would
be kind enough therefore to show us to a suitable room.'
    Helen was angrier than she had been in years. The ice-cold assurance
of the man, the SS uniform and the silly little tart traveling with him,
with the tousled hair almost swallowed up by the huge reefer coat.
    Guido said hurriedly, 'Right, I'm going to have a bath and catch up
on a little sleep. I'll see you all later.'
    The door closed behind him. Gallagher still stood by the sink, the
knife in hand. Helen turned, pushing him out of the way angrily,
washing the potato flour from her hands under the tap. She was aware
of the SS officer still at the door with the girl.

Very softly, a voice said, 'Aunt Helen, don't you know me?' Helen went quite still. Gallagher was looking over her shoulder in astonishment. 'Uncle Sean?' And then, as Helen turned, 'It's me, Aunt Helen. It's Sarah.'

Helen dropped the cloth, moved forward and grabbed her by the shoulders, gazing at her searchingly. With recognition, there were sudden tears in her eyes. She laughed unsteadily and ran her fingers through the girl's hair.

'Oh, my God, Sarah, what have they done to you?' And then they were in each other's arms.

Hugh Kelso said, 'So what happens now? You two have obviously had one hell of a trip just getting to Jersey, so where do we go from here?'

'I know where Sarah goes. Straight into a hot bath,' Helen de Ville said. 'You three can carry on talking as long as you like.'

As she moved to the door, Gallagher said, 'I've been thinking. Mrs. Vibert's due this afternoon. It might be an idea to give her a few days off.'

'All right,' Helen told him. 'You can take care of it.'

They went out and Kelso said, 'What *does* happen now?' There was impatience in his voice.

Martineau said, 'I just got here, my friend, so give me time to catch my breath. When it's time to go, you'll be the first to know.'

'Does that include a bullet in the head, Colonel?' Kelso demanded. 'If that's the decision, do we get to talk about it or just do it?'

Martineau didn't bother to answer. He simply went downstairs and waited in the master bedroom for Gallagher. The Irishman closed the secret door and shrugged. 'He's had a hard time and that leg gives him a lot of pain.'

'We're all in pain one way or another,' Martineau said.

As he was about to open the door, Gallagher put a hand on his shoulder. 'Could he be right? About the bullet in the head, I mean?'

'Maybe,' Martineau said. 'We'll have to see, won't we? Now I think I'll have a bath as well.'

In London, Dougal Munro was just finishing breakfast at his flat when Jack Carter came in. 'Some mixed news, sir, about Jerseyman.'

'Tell me the worst, Jack.'

'We've heard from Cresson. Everything went according to plan, and Martineau and Sarah left Granville for Jersey last night.'

'And?'

'We've had another message from Cresson to say the word is the convoy ran into trouble. Attacked by MTBs. They don't have any hard facts.'

'Have you?'

'I've checked with Naval Intelligence. Apparently MTBs of the Royal Dutch Navy operating out of Falmouth last night did hit that convoy, and they claim one merchantman sunk. They were driven off by the escorts.'

'Good God, Jack, you're not seriously suggesting that Harry and the Drayton girl were on that boat?'

'We just don't know, sir, and what's more, there's no possible way we can find out.'

'Exactly, so sit down, stop worrying about it and have a cup of tea, Jack. You know what your trouble is.' Munro reached for the toast. 'You don't have enough faith.'

Sarah had washed her hair, using some homemade soft soap Helen had provided. She still looked a mess, and when Helen came into the bathroom she said, 'It's no good. You need a hairdresser.'

'Are there still such things?'

'Oh, yes, if you go into St. Helier. The general run of shops still function. The opening hours are shorter. Two hours in the mornings and two in the afternoon for most places.'

She tried combing the girl's hair into some semblance of a style and Sarah said, 'What's it been like?'

'Not good, but not too bad if you behave yourself. Plenty of people think the Germans are all right and a lot of the time they are, but step out of line and see what happens. You have to do as you're told, you see. They even made the Jersey States pass anti-Semitic laws. A lot of people try to excuse it by saying all the Jews had left, but I know two living in St. Brelade now.'

'What happens if the German authorities discover them?'

'God knows. We've had people sent off to those concentration camps we hear about for keeping Russian slave workers who were on the run. I have a friend, a teacher at Jersey College for Girls, whose father kept an illegal radio. She used to spread the BBC news around to her friends until an anonymous letter brought the Gestapo to the house. They sent her to prison in France for a year.'

'An anonymous letter? You mean from a local person? But that's terrible.'

'You get bad apples in every barrel, Sarah. Jersey is no different from anywhere else in that respect. And we've got the other kind as well. The postmen at the sorting office who try to lose as many of the letters addressed to Gestapo Headquarters as possible.' She finished combing. 'There, that's the best I can do.'

Sarah sat down, pulled on silk stockings and fastened them. 'My God!' Helen said. 'I haven't seen anything like that for four years. And that dress.' She helped Sarah pull it over her head and zipped it up. 'You and Martineau. What's the situation there? He's old enough to be your father.'

'My father he very definitely is not.' Sarah smiled as she pulled on her shoes. 'He's probably the most infuriating man I've ever met and the most fascinating.'

'And you sleep with him?'

'I *am* supposed to be Vogel's tart, Aunt Helen.'

'And to think that the last time I saw you, you had pigtails,' Helen said.

In the kitchen, she put two spoonfuls of her precious China tea into the pot, but Gallagher made his excuses. 'I'll go and put Mrs. Vibert off,' he said. 'It'll only complicate things having her around. Always the chance she might recognize you, Sarah. She knew you well enough, God knows.'

He went out and Helen, Sarah and Martineau sat around the table drinking tea and smoking. There was a knock at the door. When Helen opened it, Willi Kleist stood there.

Martineau got up. 'You want me?'

'We've brought your Kubelwagen, Standartenführer,' Kleist told him.

Martineau went out to have a look at it. The canvas top was up and the body was camouflaged. He looked inside and said, 'That seems satisfactory.'

Ernst Greiser was sitting behind the wheel of a black Citroën. Kleist said, 'If there's anything else we can do . . .'

'I don't think so.'

'By the way, Captain Muller wanted me to tell you he's spoken to Colonel Heine, the military commandant. Apparently he'll be at the Town Hall this afternoon if you'd care to call in and see him.'

'Thank you, I will.'

They drove away and Martineau went back inside. 'Transport problems taken care of. I'll go into town this afternoon, call on the military commandant, then Muller and his friends at this Silvertide place.'

'You'd better go in with him and get your hair done,' Helen told Sarah. 'There's a good hairdresser at Charing Cross. You can tell her I sent you.' She turned to Martineau. 'Very convenient. It's close to the Town Hall.'

'Fine,' he said, 'except for one thing. She mustn't say you sent her. In the circumstances that would be quite wrong.' He got up. 'I feel like a breath of air. How about showing me round the estate, Sarah?'

'A good idea,' Helen said. 'I've got things to do. I already had eight to cook for tonight so I've got my work cut out. I'll see you later.'

After leaving de Ville Place, Kleist and Greiser started down the road, but after about a quarter of a mile, the inspector touched the young man on the arm. 'Let's pull in here, Ernst. Stick the car in that track over there. We'll take a walk back through the woods.'

'Any particular reason?'

'I'd just like to have a look around, that's all.'

The cart track was heavily overgrown. Greiser drove along it until they were out of sight of the road, and they got out and left the Citroën there, taking a field path across the woods of the de Ville estate. It was very quiet and really rather pleasant, only the sound of the birds, and then a young woman carrying a basket appeared unexpectedly from beyond the high granite wall at the end of the field. It was impossible to see her face. For one thing, she was wearing a headscarf, but the old cotton frock was tight enough to reveal, even at a distance, a body that was full and ripe. She didn't notice them and followed the path into the wood.

Kleist said, 'Now that's interesting.' He turned to Greiser and smiled. 'Would you say we should investigate, Sergeant?'

'Very definitely, Herr Inspector,' the younger man said eagerly and they quickened their pace.

The young woman was in fact Mrs. Vibert's daughter, Mary. After Sean Gallagher's visit to tell her to take the weekend off, the old woman had remembered the eggs she had promised Helen de Ville for the evening meal. It was these that the girl was taking to the house now.

She was only sixteen and already blossoming into womanhood, but not very bright, with a simple, kindly face. She loved the countryside, the flowers, the birds, was never happier than when walking alone in the woods. Some little way in, there was an old granite barn long disused, the roof gaping, the doors hanging crazily. It always made her feel uneasy, and yet drawn to it by a strange fascination, she paused, then walked across the grass between crumbled walls to peer inside.

A harsh voice called, 'Now then. What do you think you're doing?'

She turned quickly and saw Kleist and Greiser advancing toward her.

* * *

After leaving Mrs. Vibert's, Sean Gallagher walked down to the south meadow where he had three cows grazing, tethered to long chains in the Jersey manner. They were a precious commodity in these hard times and he stayed with them there in the sunshine for a while then started back to his cottage.

When he was still two fields away he saw the Germans walking toward the wood, saw and recognized Mary. He paused, shading his eyes against the sun, saw the girl disappear into the trees, the Germans following. Suddenly uneasy, he started to hurry. It was when he was halfway across the field that he heard the first scream. He cursed softly and broke into a run.

The weather was the best of spring, delightfully warm as Sarah and Martineau followed the track from the house through the pine trees. There were daffodils everywhere, crocuses and snowdrops in profusion, camellias blooming. Beyond, through the trees, the waters of the bay were blue merging into green in places. Birds sang everywhere.

Sarah held his arm as they strolled along. 'God, that wonderful marvelous smell. Straight back to childhood and those long hot summers. Did they ever exist, I wonder, or was it all an impossible dream?'

'No,' he said. 'They were the only true reality. It's the past four years that have been the nightmare.'

'I love this place,' she said. 'It's an old race, the Norman stock here, and the de Villes are as old as any of them. We go back a long way. Robert de Ville fought at the Battle of Hastings with Duke William of Normandy.'

'Good old William the Conqueror?'

'That's right. He ruled Jersey before he became king of England, so it's we who colonized the English, if you like, not the other way about.'

'There's arrogance for you.'

'These are my roots,' she said. 'Here I belong. This is home. Where do you belong, Harry?'

'Stateless person, that's me,' he said lightly. 'For years an American living and working in Europe. No family left worth speaking of.'

'Citizen of the world?'

'Not really.' He was upset and it showed in a sudden angry unease. 'I just don't belong. Don't belong anywhere. Could be I should have died in those trenches back in nineteen eighteen. Maybe the man upstairs made a mistake. Perhaps I shouldn't be here at all.'

She pulled him around, angry. 'That's a terrible thing to say. I'm beginning to get rather tired of the cynical and sardonic bit, Harry Martineau. Can't you drop your guard just occasionally? Even with me?'

Before he could reply there was a sudden scream. They turned and looked down to the barn in the clearing through trees and saw Mary struggling in Kleist's arms, Greiser standing to one side laughing.

'For God's sake, Harry, do something,' Sarah said.

'I will, only you stay out of it.'

He started down the slope as Sean Gallagher ran out of the trees.

Kleist was excited, the supple young body squirming against him. 'Shut up!' he told her. 'Just be a good girl and I won't hurt you.'

Greiser's eyes were shining, the mouth loose. 'Don't forget, Inspector, fair shares for all, that's my motto.'

Gallagher arrived on the run, shouldering the sergeant out of the way like a rugby forward. As he reached Kleist, he stamped hard behind the German's left knee, causing the leg to buckle and punched him hard in the kidneys. Kleist grunted and went down, releasing the terrified girl.

Gallagher picked up Mary's basket and gave it to her and patted her face. 'It's all right now, love,' he said. 'You run on up to the house to Mrs. de Ville. Nobody's going to harm you this day.'

She ran like a frightened rabbit. As Gallagher turned, Greiser took a Mauser from his pocket, his eyes wild. Kleist called, 'No, Ernst, and that's an order. He's mine.' He got up, easing his back, and took off his raincoat. 'Like all the Irish you're cracked in the head. Now I shall teach you a lesson. I shall break both your arms.'

'Half-Irish, so only half-cracked, let's get it right.' Sean Gallagher took off his jacket and tossed it to one side. 'Didn't I ever tell you about my grandfather, old Harvey le Brocq? He was sailing in cod schooners at the age of twelve, bosun on windjammers on the grain run from Australia. Twelve times round the Horn by the age of twenty-three.'

'Talk away,' Kleist said circling him. 'It won't do you any good.'

He rushed in and swung a tremendous punch which Gallagher avoided with ease. 'In those days a bosun was only as good as his fists, and he was good. Very good.' He ducked in and landed a punch under the German's left eye. 'When I used to come over from Ireland as a kid to stay with him, the village lads would work me over because I talked funny. When I went home crying, he took me out in the orchard and gave me the first of many lessons. Science, timing, punching, that's what counts, not size. God, as he often reminded me, and he was a lay preacher, had never intended the brutes to rule on earth.'

Every punch the German threw was sidestepped, and in return, Gallagher seemed to be able to hit him wherever he wanted. On the hillside a few yards away, Sarah, Martineau and the Vibert girl watched as the Irishman drove the inspector back across the grass.

And then there was a sudden moment of disaster, for as Gallagher moved in, his right foot slipped on the grass and he went down. Kleist seized his chance, lifting a knee into his forehead and kicking him in the side as he went down. Gallagher rolled away with surprising speed and came up on one knee.

'God save us, you can't even kick straight.'

As he came up, Kleist rushed at him, arms reaching to destroy. Gallagher slipped to one side, tripping the German so that he went headfirst into the wall of the barn. The Irishman gave him a left and a right in the kidneys. Kleist cried out sharply and Gallagher swung him around. He grabbed him by the lapels and smashed his forehead against the bridge of the German's nose, breaking it. Then he stepped back. Kleist swayed and fell.

'Bastard!' Greiser called.

Gallagher swung around to find the sergeant confronting him with the Mauser, but in the same moment a shot rang out, kicking up dirt at Greiser's feet. They turned as Martineau walked down the slope, Walther in hand.

'Put it away!' he ordered.

Greiser stood there, staring at him, and it was Kleist, getting to his feet, who said hoarsely, 'Do as he says, Ernst.'

Greiser obeyed and Martineau said, 'Good. You are, of course, a disgrace to everything the Reich stands for. This I shall discuss with your commanding officer later. Now leave.'

Greiser tried to give Kleist his arm. The big man shoved him away and walked off through the trees. Gallagher turned and shouted to Mary Vibert, 'Go on girl, go up to the house.'

She turned and ran. Sarah took out a handkerchief and wiped blood from Gallagher's mouth. 'I never realized what a deadly combination Jersey was with the Irish.'

'A fine day for it, thanks be to God.' Gallagher squinted up at the sun through the trees. 'Better times coming.' He grinned and turned to Martineau. 'You wouldn't happen to have a cigarette on you? I seem to have left mine at home.'

Martineau and Sarah drove down through St. Aubin and along toward Bel Royal, passing a number of fortifications and gun positions on the way. The sky was very blue, the sun bright, and yet on the horizon, beyond Fort Elizabeth, there was a dark curtain.

'Rain,' she said. 'Typical Jersey spring weather. Wonderful sunshine and then the squalls sweep in across the bay, sometimes only for a few minutes.'

'It's warmer than I'd expected,' he said. 'Quite Mediterranean.' He nodded at the gardens as they passed. 'Especially with all those palm trees. I didn't expect those.'

She leaned back and closed her eyes. 'This island has a special smell to it in the spring. Nothing quite like it anywhere else in the world.' She opened her eyes again and smiled. 'That's the de Ville side of me speaking. Hopelessly prejudiced. Tell me something. Why have you taken off your uniform?'

He was wearing the leather military trenchcoat, but underneath was a gray tweed suit with a waistcoat and white shirt with a black tie. The slouch hat was also in black, the brim down at the front and back.

'Tactics,' he said. 'Everybody who is anybody will know I'm here, will know who I am, thanks to Muller. I don't need to appear in uniform if I don't want to. SD officers wear civilian clothes most of the time. It emphasizes our power. It's more frightening.'

'You said *our* power.'

'Did I?'

'Yes. You frighten me sometimes, Harry.'

He pulled the Kubelwagen in at the side of the road and switched off. 'Let's take a walk.'

He helped her out and they paused as one of the military trains approached and moved past, then they crossed the track to the seawall. There was a café there, all closed up, probably from before the war, a huge bunker not too far away.

A new unlooked-for delight was music, two young soldiers on the seawall, a portable radio between them. Below, on the sands, children played, their mothers sitting against the wall, faces turned to the sun. A number of German soldiers swam in the sea, two or three young women among them.

Martineau and Sarah leaned on the wall. 'Unexpectedly domestic, isn't it?' He gave her a cigarette.

The soldiers glanced at them, attracted by the girl, but turned from his dark stare. 'Yes,' she said. 'Not what I expected.'

'If you look closely you'll see that most of the soldiers on the beach are boys. Twenty at the most. Difficult to hate. When someone's a Nazi, then it's explicit. You know where you stand. But the average twenty-year-old German in uniform' – he shrugged – 'is just a twenty-year-old in uniform.'

'What do you believe in, Harry? Where are you going?' Her face was strained, intense.

'As I once told you, I'm a very existentialist person. "Action this day" – Churchill's favorite phrase. And that means defeating the Nazis because they must be destroyed totally. Hitler's personal philosophy is unacceptable in terms of any kind of common humanity.'

'And afterward, when it's all over? What happens to you?'

He stared out to sea, eyes very dark, leaning on the wall. 'When I was young I used to love railway stations, especially at night. The smell of the steam, the dying fall of a train whistle in the distance, the platforms in those great deserted Victorian palaces at night, waiting to go somewhere, any-where. I loved it and yet I also used to get a feeling of tremendous unease. Something to do with getting on the wrong train.' He turned to her. 'And once the train's on its way, you see, you can't get off.'

'The station is ominous at midnight,' she said softly. 'Hope is a dead letter.'

He stared at her. 'Where did you hear that?'

'One of your bad poems,' she said. 'That first day I met you at the cottage the brigadier was reading it. You took it from him, crumpled it up and threw it into the fireplace.'

'And you retrieved it?'

'Yes.'

For a moment she thought he would be angry. Instead he smiled. 'Wait here.' He left her and crossed the line to the Kubelwagen and opened the door. When he returned he was carrying a small Kodak camera. 'Helen gave me this. As the film is four years old she can't guarantee the results.'

He walked up to the soldiers. There was a brief exchange in which they put their heads together for a moment, standing stiffly to attention. Martineau gave one of them the camera and returned to her.

'Don't forget to smile.' He lit a cigarette and turned, hands in the pockets of the trenchcoat.

Sarah took his arm. 'What's this for?'

'Something to remember me by.'

It made her feel uneasy and she held his arm even more tightly. The young soldier took the photo. 'Another,' Martineau called in German, 'just to make sure.'

The boy returned the camera, smiling shyly, then saluted and walked away. 'Did you tell him who you were?' she asked.

'Of course I did.' He took her arm. 'Let's get going. I've got things to do.' They crossed the railway track and returned to the Kubelwagen.

Karl Muller prided himself on his control, his remarkable lack of emotion in all situations. He thought of it as his greatest asset, and yet, standing by the window in his office at the Silvertide Hotel, it almost deserted him for the first time.

'You what?' he demanded.

Kleist's face was in a dreadful state, flesh around the eyes purple and dark, the broken nose swollen. 'A misunderstanding, Herr Captain.'

Muller turned to Greiser. 'And that's your version also? A misunderstanding?'

'We were only questioning the girl, Herr Captain. She panicked, then Gallagher arrived. He placed entirely the wrong construction on the affair.'

'As your face proves, Willi,' Muller said. 'And Vogel was involved.'

'He arrived on the scene at an unfortunate moment,' Greiser told him.

'And *he* also placed entirely the wrong construction on things.' Muller was furious. 'Leaving me to get you off the hook when he turns up here this afternoon. Go on, get out of my sight!'

He turned to the window and slammed his palm against the wall.

Following Sarah's instructions, Martineau drove along Gloucester Street past the prison. 'One thing,' he said. 'When we're together in the town speak French. You never know who's listening, understand?'

'Of course.'

They could hear music now and turned into the Parade to find a German military band playing on the grass between the statue of General Don, a previous governor of the island, and the Cenotaph. There was quite a crowd standing listening, mainly civilians with a few soldiers.

'Just like *Workers' Playtime* on the BBC back in the UK.' Martineau said. 'Supposed to make people feel better about being occupied.'

'Pull in here,' she said. 'The Town Hall is just at the end.'

He parked at the curb and they got out, people turning to stare curiously, attracted by the sight of the military vehicle. Many seemed indifferent, but there were those unable to hide their anger when they looked at Sarah, especially the older women.

Someone muttered 'Gerrybag!' as they walked past. It was an ugly word meant to express the contempt most people felt for a girl who consorted with the enemy. Martineau swung around, Vogel to the life, and confronted the gray-haired woman who had spoken.

'You said something, madam?' he asked in English.

She was immediately terrified. 'No – not me. You're mistaken.' She turned and hurried away in a panic.

Sarah took his arm and said softly, 'There are times when I hate you myself, Harry Martineau.'

They passed the entrance of the Town Hall with the Nazi flag flying above and a Luftwaffe sentry on the steps with a rifle. They crossed to the other side of York Street and came to Charing Cross. Some of the shop windows were still taped to avoid flying glass, probably from the first year of the war. The Luftwaffe had bombed St. Helier once in 1940. It was obviously the last thing the RAF intended to do, which probably explained why a lot of shopkeepers had cleaned the tape off.

They paused at a doorway between two shops. The sign indicated that the hairdresser was upstairs. Sarah said, 'I remember this place.'

'Would you be recognized?'

'I shouldn't think so. The last time I was in here was to have my hair cut when I was ten years old.'

She led the way up the stairs, pushed open a door with a frosted glass pane and Martineau followed her in. It was only a small salon with two washbasins and a couple of hairdriers. The woman who sat in the corner reading a magazine was about forty with a round, pleasant face. She glanced up smiling, and then the smile was wiped clear away.

'Yes?' she said.

'I need my hair fixed rather badly,' Sarah said in French.

'I don't speak French,' the woman replied.

Martineau said in English, 'The young lady was a passenger on the *Victor Hugo* from Granville last night. As I am sure you are aware of the fate of that unhappy vessel, you will appreciate that she was in the water for some time. As she has no English I must speak for her. Her hair, as you can see, requires attention.'

'I can't help. I'm booked up.'

Martineau looked around the empty salon. 'So I see. Your identity card, if you please.'

'Why should I? I've done nothing.'

'Would you rather continue this conversation at Silvertide?'

There was fear in her eyes. Sarah had never felt so wretched in her life and waited as the unfortunate woman found her handbag and produced the identity card. It was in the name of Mrs. Emily Johnson. Martineau examined it and handed it back.

'My name is Vogel – Standartenführer Max Vogel. I have an appointment at the Town Hall with Colonel Heine, the commandant. I'll be gone for an hour, perhaps a little longer. While I am away you will do whatever is necessary to the young lady's hair. When I return, I am sure it will look quite delightful.' He opened the door. 'If it doesn't, I'll close this establishment so fast you won't know what's hit you.'

They listened to him descend the stairs. Mrs. Johnson took a robe down from behind the door and turned to Sarah with a delightful smile. 'All right, you dirty little French tart. Let's make you look pretty for that butcher,' she said in English. Her smile became even more charming. 'And I can only hope you get what you deserve.'

Sarah felt like cheering her out loud. Instead she stayed in control and replied in French, 'Ah, the coat.'

She took it off, handed it to her, put on the robe and went to the nearest chair.

As Martineau crossed to the Town Hall he saw a policeman in traditional British bobby's uniform and helmet standing on the steps talking to the sentry. They stopped talking, watching him warily as he approached.

'Standartenführer Vogel for the commandant.'

The sentry jumped to attention and the police constable faded away discreetly. 'The commandant arrived twenty minutes ago, Standartenführer.'

Martineau moved into the hall and found a table at the bottom of the stairs, an army sergeant sitting there. He glanced up and Martineau said, 'My name is Vogel. I believe Colonel Heine is expecting me.'

The sergeant leaped to his feet and picked up the phone. 'Standartenführer Vogel is here, Herr Major.' He replaced the receiver. 'Major Necker will be down directly, sir.'

'Thank you.' Martineau walked away and looked out through the open door. Within moments there was the sound of boots on the stairs. He turned to find a young man hurrying down, an infantry major, no more than thirty from the look of him.

He was all cordiality, but then he would be, pausing briefly to click his heels before putting out a hand. 'Felix Necker, Standartenführer.'

He'd seen action, that was plain enough from the shrapnel scar running into the right eye. As well as the Iron Cross First Class he wore the Wounded Badge in silver, which meant he'd been a casualty at least three times, the Infantry Assault Badge and a Close Combat Clasp in gilt. It was recognition and familiarity with such items that kept

Martineau alive. What they told him about people was important. What they said about this man was that he was a war hero.

'A pleasure to meet you, Herr Major,' he said. 'You've been in Jersey long?'

'Only a couple of months,' Necker told him. 'I'm not with the 319th Division normally. Only on loan.'

They went upstairs, he knocked and opened a door, stood to one side and Martineau went in first. It was a pleasant enough room, obviously originally the office of some official. The officer who stood up and came around the desk to meet him was a type he recognized instantly. A little stiff in manner, rather old-fashioned regular army and very definitely no Nazi. An officer and a gentleman.

'Standartenführer. A pleasure to see you.' The handshake was firm, friendly enough, but the eyes said something else. Only surface courtesy here.

'Colonel Heine.' Martineau opened his coat and produced his SD card.

Heine examined it and handed it back. 'Please sit down. In what way can we serve you? You've met Felix Necker, of course. He's only on loan from Paris. Temporarily my second in command. A holiday for him. Just out of hospital. He was on the Russian Front.'

'Indeed?' Martineau said. He took out the Himmler letter and passed it across.

Heine read it slowly, his face grave, then passed it to Necker. 'If I could know the purpose of your visit?'

'Not at this stage.' Martineau took the letter as Necker handed it back to him. 'All I need is assurance of total cooperation as and when required.'

'That goes without saying,' Heine hesitated. 'As for billeting arrangements, I understand you are staying at de Ville Place.'

'Yes, I spoke to Captain Muller of the GFP on the pier when we arrived. He was most cooperative. He has already supplied me with a suitable vehicle, so for the moment, there is really nothing else I require. It would be useful if you informed all unit commanders of my presence.'

'Of course. There is one thing,' Heine added. 'I have to go to Guernsey and so does the civil affairs commander. A weekend conference with General von Schmettow.'

Martineau turned to Necker. 'Presumably you will be in command?'

'That is correct.'

'Then I can see no problem.' He got to his feet and picked up his hat. Heine said, 'I'll see you when I get back then?'

'Possibly.' Martineau shook hands. 'A pleasure, Herr Colonel. I'll let you get on with it now. Don't bother to see me out, Major.'

The door closed behind him. Heine's whole demeanor changed. 'My flesh always crawls when these SS security people appear. What in the hell does he want, Felix?'

'God alone knows, Herr Colonel, but his credentials . . .' Necker shrugged. 'Not only signed by Himmler, but by the Führer himself.'

'I know.' Heine put up a hand defensively. 'Just watch him, that's all. I'll see what von Schmettow thinks when I get to Guernsey. But at all costs keep him sweet. Trouble with Himmler is the last thing we need.'

'Of course, Herr Colonel.'

'Good. Now show in these good citizens from the Food Control Committee and let's get on with it.'

Martineau had time in hand so he walked through the town. There were plenty of people about, more civilians than soldiers. Most people looked underweight, but that was to be expected, and clothes looked old and well-worn. There were few children about, they'd be at school. The ones he did see were in better shape than he had expected, but then, people always did put their children first.

So, people managed. He knew, because Helen de Ville had told them, of the communal kitchens and bakeries to conserve fuel. It occurred to him that people in the town obviously had a more difficult time of it than those in the country. At that moment, as he moved into Queen Street, he saw a crowd overflowing the pavement ahead, all staring into a shop window.

It contained an amazing display of food of every description. Canned goods, sacks of potatoes and flour, hams, bottles of red wine and champagne. People said nothing, just looked. A notice in the window said: *Black market goods. The enemy may be your own neighbor. Help defeat him.* It was signed by Muller. The pain in the faces of ordinary people deprived too long was unbearable. Martineau turned and went back to Charing Cross.

When he went upstairs to the salon, Sarah was just adjusting her hat in the mirror. Her hair looked excellent. He helped her on with her coat.

Emily Johnson said, 'Satisfied?'

'Very much so.' He opened his wallet and took out a ten-mark note.

'No!' Her anger overflowed. 'I don't want your money. You told me to do her hair and I've done it.' There were tears of frustration in her eyes. 'Just go.'

Martineau pushed Sarah out of the door. When he turned, his voice, to Emily Johnson's astonishment, was quite gentle. It was as if, for a moment, he had stepped out of the role of brutal SS officer that he had played so well. 'I salute you, Mrs. Johnson. You are a brave woman.'

The door closed behind him. She sat down, head in hands, and started to cry.

Martineau parked the Kubelwagen outside the Silvertide Hotel at Havre des Pas beside several other cars. 'I shan't be long.'

She smiled. 'Don't worry about me, I'll just take a walk along the seawall. I used to come to swim in the pool here when I was a kid.'

'As you please. Just try not to talk to any strange men.'

Muller had seen him arrive from the window of his office. When Martineau went inside, a young military policeman in plain clothes was waiting to greet him. 'Standartenführer Vogel? This way please.'

He ushered Martineau into Muller's office and closed the door. The captain stood up behind the desk. 'A great pleasure.'

'I wish I could say the same,' Martineau said. 'You've spoken to Kleist and Greiser?'

'About this misunderstanding at de Ville Place? Yes, they did explain . . .'

'Misunderstanding?' Martineau said coldly. 'You will have them in here now, Herr Captain, if you please, and quickly. My time is limited.'

He turned away and stood at the window, hands behind his back, as Muller asked for Kleist and Greiser over the intercom. They came in only a few moments. Martineau didn't bother to turn around, but looked out across the road to the seawall where Sarah was standing.

He said softly, 'Inspector Kleist, I understand you have put this morning's events at de Ville Place down to a misunderstanding?'

'Well, yes, Standartenführer.'

'Liar!' Martineau's voice was low and dangerous. 'Both of you liars.' He turned to face them. 'As I walked through the wood with Mademoiselle Latour we heard a girl scream. A child, Captain, barely sixteen, being dragged toward a barn by this animal here while the other stood and laughed. I was about to interfere when General Gallagher came on the scene and gave a bully the thrashing he deserved.'

'I see,' Muller said.

'Just to make things worse, I was obliged to draw my own pistol and fire a warning shot to prevent this idiot shooting Gallagher in the back. God in heaven, what kind of an imbecile are you, Greiser?' He spoke slowly as if to a child. 'The man is Irish, which means he is a neutral, and the Führer's declared policy is good relations with Ireland. On top of that he is a famous man back there in the old country. A hero of their revolution. A general. We don't shoot people like that in the back. Understand?'

'Yes, Standartenführer.'

Now he turned his attention to Kleist. 'And as the Führer's declared policy toward the inhabitants of Jersey has been one of reconciliation, we do not attempt to rape sixteen-year-old girls.' He turned to Muller. 'The actions of these men are an affront to every ideal the Reich holds dear and to German honor.'

He was thoroughly enjoying himself, especially when Kleist's anger overflowed. 'I'm not a child to be lectured like this.'

'Kleist!' Martineau said. 'As a member of the Gestapo you took an oath to our Führer. A holy oath. As I recall it runs: I vow to you and the superiors you appoint, obedience unto death. Is it not so?'

'Yes,' Kleist answered.

'Then remember from now on that you are here to obey orders. If I ask a question you answer, *"Jawohl, Standartenführer."* If I give you an order it's *"Zu befel, Standartenführer."* Do you follow?'

There was a pause before Kleist said in a low voice, *'Jawohl, Standartenführer.'*

Martineau turned on Muller. 'And you wonder why Reichsführer Himmler thought it worthwhile sending me here?'

He walked out without another word, went through the foyer and crossed the road to the Kubelwagen. Sarah was sitting on the bonnet. 'How did it go?' she asked.

'Oh, I think you could say I put the fear of God in them all rather satisfactorily.' He opened the door for her. 'Now you can take me on a Cook's tour of this island of yours.'

Muller started to laugh. 'I wish you could see yourself standing there in front of the desk, Willi. All you need is short pants.'

'I swear to God I'll . . .'

'You'll do nothing, Willi, just like the rest of us. You'll just do as you're told.' He went to a cupboard, opened it and found a glass and a bottle of cognac. 'I must say he sounded just like the Reichsführer on a bad day. All that German purity nonsense. All those platitudes.'

'Do you still want me to speak to my brother, Herr Captain?' Greiser asked. 'I've got a call booked through to Stuttgart for ten o'clock tonight.'

'Why not?' Muller poured some cognac into his glass and said impatiently, 'For God's sake, go down to the hospital and get that nose seen to, Willi. Go on, get out of my sight, both of you.'

* * *

Rommel was staying at a villa near Bayeux, in a place deep in the countryside and quite remote. It had been used as a weekend retreat by the commanding general of the area who had been happy to offer it to the field marshal when he'd expressed a desire for a quiet weekend. The Bernards, who ran the house, were extremely discreet. The wife was an excellent cook, the husband acted as butler.

Baum drove to the house ahead of the field marshal that afternoon in a Kubelwagen wearing his own Fallschirmjäger uniform. He also affected a heavy black patch over the right eye on Rommel's insistence. To Baum, he did not resemble the field marshal until he put on the clothes, changed his appearance with a few artful touches of makeup, the rubber cheekpads that made the face squarer. But the real change was in himself – the change that started inside. He thought Rommel, so he became Rommel. That was his unique talent as a performer.

Rommel and Hofer arrived later in the afternoon in the Mercedes driven by an engineer sergeant named Dreschler, an Afrika Korps veteran whom Hofer had specially selected. Madame Bernard provided the field marshal with a late luncheon in the drawing room. Afterward, Hofer brought Baum in to join them.

'Right, let's go over things,' Rommel said.

'According to my information the people from Jersey will leave for Guernsey at around two in the morning. Berger and I will leave here in the Kubelwagen at nine. There is an empty cottage on the estate a kilometer from here where we stop for him to change.'

'And afterward?'

'To a Luftwaffe reserve airstrip only ten kilometers from here. There is a pilot, an Oberleutnant Sorsa, waiting there under your personal order with a Fiesler Storch.'

'Sorsa? Isn't that a Finnish name?' Rommel asked.

'That's right.'

'Then what's he doing with the Luftwaffe? Why isn't he on the Eastern Front shooting down Russians with his own people?'

'Sorsa is hot stuff, a real ace. One of the greatest night fighter pilots in the business. These days he's of more use flying over the Reich knocking down Lancaster bombers. He's an excellent choice for this venture. He doesn't fit into the usual Luftwaffe command structure. An outsider.'

'They don't like us very much, the Finns,' Rommel said. 'I've never trusted them.' He lit a cigarette. 'Still, carry on.'

'Sorsa won't know his destination until we join the plane. I estimate we will land in Jersey around eleven o'clock. I've given orders for Headquarters of Army Group B to notify Berlin at noon that you've flown to Jersey. The reason for not letting them know earlier being the need to consider your safety when in flight.'

'And what happens here?'

'Generals Stulpnagel and Falkenhausen arrive later in the day. Stay overnight and leave on Saturday morning.'

'And you return in the evening?'

'Of course. This couple here at the house, the Bernards, will know you are here, but then they won't know you're also in Jersey. Neither will Sergeant Dreschler. He worships you anyway. An old desert hand. If there is any problem with him later, I can handle it.'

Rommel turned to Baum. 'And you, my friend, can you handle it?'

'Yes, Herr Field Marshal. I really think I can,' Baum told him.

'Good.' Rommel took the bottle of Dom Perignon from the ice bucket that Monsieur Bernard had brought in earlier and uncorked it. He filled three glasses and gave them one each. 'So, my friends, to the Jersey enterprise.'

Sarah and Martineau had spent an enlightening afternoon, driving to Gorey where she had intended to show him Mont Orgeuil, one of the most magnificent castles in Europe, only to find that it was now a heavily defended enemy strongpoint.

At Fliquet Bay, they had come across a party of slave workers cutting a new road through to a coastal artillery battery. They were the most ragged, filthy, undernourished creatures even Martineau had seen. He had made himself known to the sergeant in charge of the detail who told him they were Russians. It was particularly ironic, therefore, to discover a battalion of the Russian Liberation Army staffed mainly by Ukrainians, guarding the north coast around Bonne Nuit Bay.

They carried on to Grosnez with the few stones remaining of its medieval castle and spectacular views of Sark, Herm and Jethou, all reaching toward Guernsey. The interesting thing was that not once were they stopped or challenged, even when they drove along the Five Mile Road following the curve of St. Ouen's Bay, which looked to Martineau like the most heavily defended stretch they'd seen.

It was evening when they stopped at the church at the end of St. Brelade's Bay. Sarah got out and he followed her. They stood in the archway and peered inside. There was an entire section devoted to the military, rows of crosses, each one at the end of a neat grave.

'I don't know what Christ would have made of those crosses,' Martineau said. 'There's a swastika in the center of each one.'

She shivered. 'I used to attend this church. I had my first communion here.'

Martineau walked idly between the rows of German crosses. 'There're a couple of Italians here and a Russian.' He carried on, moving into the older section of the cemetery, passing between granite headstones and tombs. 'Strange,' he said. 'I feel quite at home.'

'That's a morbid thought,' Sarah told him.

'Not really. I just find it extraordinarily peaceful and the view of the bay is sensational. Still I suppose we should be getting back now.'

They got in the Kubelwagen and drove past the bay along Mont Sohier. Sarah said, 'So, now you've had the guided tour. What do you think?'

'A tight little island.'

'And how do we get Hugh Kelso off it?'

'To tell you the truth, I haven't the slightest idea, so if you can think of anything, let me know.'

He carried on driving, whistling tunelessly between his teeth.

Dinner was a strange affair. Martineau and Sarah joined the officers in the main dining room. Guido Orsini, Bruno Feldt, Kapitanleutnant Erich Dietrich and several others. There was a fresh lighted candle at each empty place which Sarah found rather macabre, but the young officers were polite and considerate, would obviously have put themselves out even more if it had not been for Martineau's presence. He was wearing his uniform in deference to the formality of the meal, and its effect on the others had been definitely depressing.

Helen de Ville passed in and out with the plates, and Sarah, bored with the stilted conversation, insisted on helping her to clear the table and joined her in the kitchen, where Sean Gallagher sat at the table eating the leftovers.

'Terrible in there. Harry's like a specter at the feast,' she said.

Helen had just prepared a tray for Kelso. 'I'll just take this up while they're all still in the dining room.'

She went up the back stairs and opened the door to the master bedroom at the same moment that Guido Orsini passed the end of the corridor. He saw her, noted the tray in astonishment and moved cautiously along the corridor. He hesitated, then tried the door of her bedroom. Helen, for once, had omitted to turn the key. He peered inside, saw the secret door ajar and tiptoed across. There was a murmur of voices from upstairs. He listened for a moment, then turned and went out again, closing the door.

Sarah and Gallagher were talking in low voices when Guido went into the kitchen. 'Ah, there you are,' he said. 'They're into politics now. Can I take you for a walk on the terrace?'

'Is he to be trusted?' she asked Gallagher.

'No more than most men I know, especially around a darling like you.'

'I'll have to take a chance then. If Colonel Vogel comes looking for me, tell him I'll be back soon,' she added formally.

There was a half-moon, the sky bright with stars, a luminosity to everything, palm trees etched against the sky. Everywhere there was the smell of flowers, drenched from the rain earlier.

'Azaleas.' She breathed deeply. 'One of my favorites.'

'You are a remarkable girl,' he said in English. 'You don't mind if we use English, do you? There's no one about and it helps me keep my hand in.'

'All right,' she said reluctantly, 'but not for long.'

'You've never been to Jersey before?'

'No. I was raised by grandmother in Paimpol after my mother died.'

'I see. And it was your mother who was English?'

'That's right.'

She was wary at this questioning and sat on a low granite wall, the moon behind her. He gave her a cigarette. 'You smoke Gitanes, don't you?'

She was used to cigarettes by now and nodded. 'On the other hand, one has to be content with whatever is available these days.'

He gave her a light. 'Yes, it's really quite remarkable. You speak French with a very Breton accent.'

'What's strange about that? My grandmother was Breton.'

'I know. It's your English that's so interesting. Very upper class. I went to Winchester, remember, so I can tell.'

'Really? I'm a lucky girl, then.' She stood up. 'I'd better get back now, Guido. Max can get rather restless if I'm out of his sight too long with another man.'

'Of course.' She took his arm and they strolled back through the azaleas. 'I like you, Anne-Marie Latour. I like you a lot. I want you to remember that.'

'Only like?' she said. 'I thought you said you loved me.' A dangerous game she was playing here. She knew that and yet could not resist taking it as far as it would go.

'All right,' he said. 'I love you,' and he pulled her into his arms and kissed her passionately. 'Now do you understand?'

'Yes, Guido,' she said softly. 'I think I do.'

Martineau appeared on the terrace in the moonlight. 'Anne-Marie, are you there?' he shouted in French.

326 *Night of the Fox*

'Coming!' she called back and reached to touch the Italian's face. 'I'll see you tomorrow, Guido,' and she ran up the steps to the terrace.

They were all in the private sitting room at the back of the house overlooking the terrace. Gallagher, Martineau, Helen and Sarah. Gallagher poured Burgundy into four glasses while Helen opened the French window a little. It was very close. She breathed in the perfumed air for a few moments, then drew the heavy curtains across.

'So, what happens now?' Sean Gallagher asked.

'He certainly can't walk at the moment,' Helen de Ville said. 'George Hamilton saw him this afternoon. A real chance he could lose the leg if he disturbs things.'

'At least he's safe for the time being upstairs,' Sarah said.

'He can't sit out the war there,' Martineau pointed out. 'We need to get him to Granville. Once there, Cresson can radio London and have a Lysander over any night we want.'

'But how to get him there, that's the thing,' Gallagher said. 'They've really got the small boat traffic closed up tight here. Observation posts all along the coast as you saw for yourself today. You wouldn't get far without being spotted. Any fishing boat that leaves harbor, even the lifeboat, has to have German guards on board when they put to sea.'

'So what *is* the solution?' Sarah demanded. 'We must do something.'

There was a movement at the window; the curtains parted. Martineau turned, drawing his Walther, and Guido Orsini stepped into the room. 'Perhaps I can help,' he said in English.

12

The following morning Martineau was on the upper level of the Albert Pier as Colonel Heine, the civil administration commander, and the bailiff and his party left for Guernsey on the E-boat with Dietrich. He watched them go as he leaned on the seawall, waiting for Orsini, who had gone to Kriegsmarine Headquarters at the Pomme d'Or Hotel.

The Italian's entry through the curtains the night before had certainly been as dramatic as it was unexpected. But his offer to throw in his lot with them made sense. Even if Orsini had been a thoroughgoing Fascist, it was reasonably certain who was going to win this war, and in Italy many of Mussolini's most fervent followers had transferred their allegiance to the winning side without a moment's hesitation. In any case, Orsini was not one of those. So Helen and Gallagher had assured him and so had Sarah, most fervently of all.

The young Italian came up the steps, saluted a couple of Kriegsmarine ratings and joined Martineau. 'Let's walk to the end of the pier.'

'What did you find out?' Martineau asked as they strolled along.

'A possible break. There's a small convoy due in from Guernsey early Sunday morning. The master of one of the ships, a Dutch coaster called the *Jan Kruger*, was taken ill yesterday. The bosun is handling her as far as Jersey.'

'And then?'

'Our old friend Robert Savary takes command for the run to Granville.'

'That certainly is interesting,' Martineau said. 'When can you speak to him?'

'There's the snag. He was picked up after the *Victor Hugo* went down by one of the search and rescue craft from St. Malo. He's due over from Granville early evening tomorrow on a fast patrol craft. What we call the dispatch boat.'

'And you think he might be willing to smuggle Kelso over?'

Orsini shrugged. 'From what you have told me of his part in this business already, I should imagine him an eminently suitable candidate for applied pressure. After what he's already done, I fail to see how he can say no.'

'True,' Martineau said. 'And he knows that if he puts a foot wrong the Cressons and their friends will arrange his funeral, priest included, free of charge.' He smiled. 'You know something, Count? I think you may well prove to be an asset to the corporation.'

'Fine,' said Guido. 'Only let us understand each other.'

'Go on.'

'I've had my bellyful of death and destruction. I'm tired of killing and sick of politics. The Allies are going to win this war, that is inevitable, so Jersey was the perfect billet for a sensible man to sit out the last few months in comfort. And don't let's pretend that anything that happens here will make the slightest difference. If the Germans got their hands on Kelso, Eisenhower's invasion plans would, at the most, be seriously inconvenienced. He'd still win in the end. We're engaged in a rather interesting game here. It's true that it's also a dangerous one, but still only a game.'

'Then why throw your hat in the ring?' Martineau asked.

'I think you know why,' Guido told him as they went down the steps to where his car was parked. He smiled amiably. 'Be warned, my friend. There is nothing more dangerous than the libertine who suddenly finds he has fallen in love with a good woman.'

* * *

When the phone rang in his office at command headquarters Felix Necker was just about to leave to go riding on the beach at St. Aubin. He picked up the receiver and listened and a look of horror appeared on his face. 'My God! What's his estimated time of arrival? All right. Arrange a guard of honor. I'll be there as soon as I can.'

He slammed down the receiver and sat there for a moment thinking about things, then he picked it up again and dialed GFP Headquarters at the Silvertide.

'Herr Major,' Muller said when he was put through. 'What can I do for you?'

'Rommel is due in at the airport in forty-five minutes.'

'Who did you say?' Muller demanded.

'Field Marshal Erwin Rommel, you idiot. He's arriving with his aide, a Major Hofer, from Normandy in a Fiesler Storch.'

'But why?' Muller demanded. 'I don't understand.'

'Well I do,' Necker told him. 'It all makes perfect sense. First of all his orders for Heine and the others to join General von Schmettow in Guernsey for the weekend, getting them all nicely out of the way so that he can fly in out of the blue and take the place apart. I know how Rommel operates, Muller. He'll go everywhere. Check every machine-gun post.'

'At least one mystery is solved,' Muller said.

'What's that?'

'The reason for Vogel being here. The whole thing ties in now.'

'Yes, I suppose you're right.' Necker said. 'Anyway, never mind that now. I'll see you at the airport.'

He put down the receiver, hesitated, then picked it up again and told the operator to connect him with de Ville Place. Martineau and Orsini had just returned, and it was Helen who answered the phone in the kitchen.

'It's for you,' she said to Martineau. 'Major Necker.'

He took the receiver from her. 'Vogel here.'

'Good morning,' Necker greeted him. 'I'm sure it will come as no surprise to you to know that Field Marshal Rommel arrives at the airport in just over half-an-hour.'

Martineau, concealing his astonishment, said, 'I see.'

'Naturally, you'll wish to greet him. I'll see you at the airport.'

Martineau put the phone down slowly as Sarah and Gallagher came in from the garden. 'What is it, Harry?' Sarah demanded. 'You look awful.'

'I should,' he said. 'I think the roof just fell in on me.'

At the Silvertide, Muller was hurriedly changing into uniform in the bathroom next to his office. He heard the outside door open and Kleist called, 'Are you there, Herr Captain? You wanted us.'

'Yes, come in,' Muller called.

He went into the office buttoning his tunic, picked up his belt with the holstered Mauser and fastened it quickly.

'Something up?' Kleist asked. He looked terrible. The bruising around the eyes had deepened, and the plaster they had taped across his nose at the hospital didn't improve things.

'You could say that. I've just heard Rommel's flying in on what looks like a snap inspection. I'll have to get up to the airport now. You can drive me, Ernst,' he told Greiser.

'What about me?' Kleist asked.

'With a face like that? I don't want you within a mile of Rommel. Better take a couple of days off, Willi. Just keep out of the way.' He turned to Greiser. 'Let's get moving.'

After they had gone, Kleist went to the cupboard where the captain kept his drink, took out a bottle of cognac and poured a large one into a glass. He swallowed it in one quick gulp and went into the bathroom and examined himself in the mirror. He looked awful and his face hurt. It was all that damned Irishman's fault.

He poured himself another cognac and said softly, 'My turn will come, you swine, and when it does . . .' He toasted himself in the mirror and emptied his glass.

As the Citroën moved past the harbor and turned along the esplanade, Greiser said, 'By the way, that call I had booked to my brother in Stuttgart last night.'

'What did he have to say?'

'He didn't. He was on leave. Due back today on the night shift. I'll speak to him then.'

'Not that it matters all that much now,' Muller said. 'Nothing very mysterious about friend Vogel any longer. He obviously came here in advance of the field marshal, that's all.'

'But what does Rommel want?' Greiser asked.

'If you consider the beach fortifications, strongpoints and batteries for the entire French coast south from Dieppe, exactly half are in these islands alone,' Muller told him. 'Perhaps, with the invasion coming, he thought it was time to see what he was getting for his money.' He glanced at his watch. 'But never mind that now. Just put your foot down hard. We've only got about ten minutes.'

At the airport, Martineau paused briefly to have his pass checked by the sentry. As he was in uniform, it was the merest formality. Several cars were parked outside the main entrance, drivers standing by them, obviously the official party. The big black Austin limousine in front carried the military commander's pennant.

Martineau parked the Kubelwagen behind Muller's Citroën. Greiser was at the wheel, the only driver in civilian clothes. Martineau ignored him and went inside the airport building. There were uniforms everywhere, mainly Luftwaffe. He felt a sense of detachment as he walked on through, no fear at all. He would have to do the best he could with the cards fate had dealt him.

Necker and a party of officers, Muller among them, were waiting on the apron outside, a Luftwaffe guard drawn up. The major came across, a slightly nervous smile on his face, followed by Muller. 'They'll be here in a few minutes.' He offered a cigarette from a silver case. 'A tremendous shock for us all, the field marshal coming in out of the blue like this, but not to you, I think.'

Martineau saw it all then. They thought there was some connection between his own unexplained presence in the island and Rommel's unexpected visit. 'Really? I can't imagine what you mean, my dear Necker.'

Necker glanced at Muller in exasperation. It was obvious that neither of them believed him, which was fine and suited his situation perfectly. He walked a few yards away and stood, hands behind his back, examining the airport. There were seven blister hangars, obviously constructed by the Luftwaffe. The doors to one of them stood open revealing the three engines and distinctive corrugated metal fuselage of a JU52, the Junkers transport plane that was the workhorse of the German Army. There was no sign of any other aircraft.

'He still persists in playing the man of mystery,' Necker said to Muller out of the side of his mouth.

Martineau rejoined them. 'The Luftwaffe doesn't seem to have much to offer.'

'Unfortunately not. The enemy has an overwhelming superiority in the air in this region.'

Martineau nodded toward the far blister hangar. 'What's the JU52 doing there?'

'That's the mail plane. He makes the run once a week, just the pilot and a crewman. Always under cover of darkness. They came in last night.'

'And fly out again?'

'Tomorrow night.'

There was the sound of an airplane engine in the distance. As they turned, the Storch came in across St. Ouen's Bay and made a perfect landing. Konrad Hofer put a hand on Baum's for a moment in reassurance as the pilot, Oberleutnant Sorsa, taxied toward the waiting officers. Baum turned to nod briefly at Hofer, then adjusted the brim of his cap and tightened his gloves. Showtime, Heini, he told himself, so let's give a performance.

Sorsa lifted the door and Hofer got out, then turned to help Baum, who unbuttoned his old leather coat revealing the Blue Max and the Knight's Cross at his throat. Felix Necker advanced to meet him and gave him a punctilious military salute, one soldier to another. 'Field Marshal. A great honor.'

Baum negligently touched the peak of his cap with his field marshal's baton. 'You are?'

'Felix Necker, sir. I'm temporarily in command. Colonel Heine has gone to Guernsey for the weekend. A conference with General von Schmettow.'

'Yes, I know about that.'

'If only we'd been aware that you were coming,' Necker went on.

'Well, you weren't. Konrad Hofer, my aide. Now then, who have we here?'

Necker introduced the offiers, starting with Martineau. 'Standartenführer Vogel, who I think you may know.'

'No,' Martineau said. 'I have never had the pleasure of meeting the field marshal before.'

Rommel's dislike was plain for everyone to see. He passed on, greeting Muller and the other officers and then inspecting the guard of honor. Afterward, he simply took off, walking toward the nearest flak gun, everyone trailing after him. He spoke to the gun crew, then cut across the grass to a hangar where Luftwaffe ground crew waited rigidly at attention.

Finally he turned and walked back toward the airport buildings, looking up at the sky. 'Fine weather. Will it stay like this?'

'The forecast is good, Herr Field Marshal,' Necker told him.

'Excellent. I want to see everything. You understand? I'll be returning tomorrow, probably in the evening, so we'll need a suitable billet for tonight. However, that can wait until later.'

'The officers of the Luftwaffe mess have had a light luncheon prepared, Herr Field Marshal. It would be a great honor if you would consent to join them.'

'Certainly, Major, but afterward, work. I've a lot to see. So, where do we go?'

The officers' mess was upstairs in what had been the restaurant before the war. There was a buffet of salad, roast chicken and tinned ham, served rather self-consciously by young Luftwaffe boys in white coats acting as waiters. The officers hung eagerly on the field marshal's every word, conscious of their proximity to greatness. Baum, a glass of champagne in his

332   Night of the Fox

hand, was more than enjoying himself. It was as if he were somewhere else looking in, observing. One thing was certain. He was good.

'We were surprised that you chose to fly in during daylight hours, Herr Field Marshal,' Necker said.

'And with no fighter escort,' Muller added.

'I've always believed in doing the unexpected thing,' Baum told them. 'And you must remember we had Oberleutnant Sorsa as pilot, one of our gallant Finnish comrades. He normally flies a JU88S night fighter and has thirty-eight Lancasters to his credit, which explains his Knight's Cross.' Sorsa, a small, vital man of twenty-five with very fair hair, looked suitably modest, and Baum carried on, 'I must also tell you that we flew across the sea so low that we were in more danger from the waves than anything the RAF might have come up with.'

There was a general laugh and he excused himself and went off to the toilet followed by Hofer.

Martineau had been standing against the wall, observing everything and drinking very little. Muller approached. 'A remarkable man.'

'Oh, yes.' Martineau nodded. 'One of the few real heroes of the war. And how is your Inspector Kleist?'

'A stupid man,' Muller observed. 'But then, I think you know that. More champagne?'

In the toilet, Baum checked himself in the mirror and said to Hofer, 'How am I doing?'

'Superbly.' Hofer was exhilarated. 'There are times when I really think it's the old man himself talking.'

'Good.' Baum combed his hair and adjusted the cheek pads. 'What about the SS colonel. I didn't expect that.'

'Vogel?' Hofer was serious for a moment. 'I was talking to Necker about him. He just turned up in the island yesterday, backed by a special pass signed by Himmler and the Führer himself. So far he's given no information as to why he's here.'

'I don't know,' Baum said. 'Those bastards always make me feel funny. You're certain his presence here has nothing to do with us?'

'How could it be? Army Group B Headquarters only released the news that you were in Jersey an hour ago. So, no need to panic, and back to the fray.'

Necker said, 'If you wouldn't mind coming into the CO's office, Field Marshal. General von Schmettow is on the line from Guernsey.'

Baum sat carelessly on the edge of the desk and took the receiver offered to him. 'My dear von Schmettow, it's been a long time.'

General von Schmettow said, 'An unexpected honor for my entire command. Heine is quite shocked and wishes to return at once.'

'Tell him if he does, it's the firing squad for him,' Baum said good-humoredly. 'Young Necker can show me around just as well. A fine officer. No, this suits me perfectly.'

'Do you intend to visit Guernsey?'

'Not this time. I return to France tomorrow.'

'May we expect you at some future date?' The line was crackling now.

'Of course, and before long, I promise you. Best wishes.'

Baum put down the receiver and turned to Necker. 'To work. Coastal defenses, that's what I wish to see, so let's get started.'

In the garden at de Ville Place Sarah sat on the wall looking out over the bay and Guido leaned beside her, smoking a cigarette. 'Sarah,' he said in English. 'It's as if I have to get to know you all over again.' He shook his head. 'Whoever told you that you could pass yourself off as a French tart was gravely mistaken. I knew there was something wrong with you from the start.'

'And Harry? Did you think there was something wrong about him?'

'No. He worries me, that one. He plays Vogel too well.'

'I know.' She shivered. 'I wonder how he's getting on?'

'He'll be fine. The last person I'd ever worry about. You like him, don't you?'

'Yes,' she said. 'You could put it that way.' Before they could take the conversation any further, Helen and Gallagher crossed the grass to join them.

'What are you two up to?' Helen demanded.

'Nothing much,' Sarah told her. 'We were wondering how Harry was getting on.'

'The devil looks after his own,' Gallagher said. 'He can take care of himself, that one. More important at the moment is a decision on what to do with Kelso. I think we should move him from the chamber to my cottage.'

Guido nodded. 'That makes sense. Much easier to take him from there down to the harbor once I get Savary sorted out.'

'Do you really think it has a chance of working?' Sarah demanded.

'Fake papers as a French seaman. The General and I can fix that up between us,' Guido told her.

'We'll bandage his face. Say he was in the water after the attack on the convoy and sustained burns,' Gallagher said. 'We'll move Kelso late tonight.' He smiled reassuringly and put an arm around Sarah. 'It's going to work. Believe me.'

* * *

Martineau joined on the end of the cavalcade of cars as it left the airport and took the road through St. Peter's. Rommel fascinated him, so did the idea of being so close to one of the greatest soldiers the war had produced, the commander of the Westwall himself. The man dedicated to smashing the Allies on the beaches where they landed.

He was certainly energetic. They visited Meadowbank in the Parish of St. Lawrence where for two years military engineers and slave workers had labored on tunnels designed to be an artillery depot. Now it was in process of being converted into a military hospital.

Afterward they saw the Russians in Defense Sector North and the strongpoints at Greve de Lecq, Plemont and Les Landes. It all took time. The field marshal seemed to want to look in every foxhole personally, visit every gun post.

He asked to see the war cemetery at St. Brelade and inspected the church while he was there. The Soldatenheim, the Soldiers' Home, was just along the road in a requisitioned hotel overlooking the bay. He insisted on calling in there, much to the delight of the matron in charge, and discovered a proxy wedding taking place. It was a system devised by the Nazi government to take care of the fact that it was increasingly difficult for soldiers on active duty to get married in the normal way any longer, as they seldom got furloughs back home in Germany. The groom was a burly sergeant and a Red Cross nursing sister stood in for his bride, who was in Berlin.

It was very much a Nazi marriage, totally without any religious significance at all. The insistence on the lack of Jewish blood in either the bride or bridegroom was something Baum found especially ironic, but he toasted the sergeant's good health with a glass of schnapps and moved on.

By the time they reached St. Aubin it was evening, and most of the party were beginning to flag. Baum, examining the map Necker had provided, noticed the artillery positions on Mont de la Rocque and asked to be taken up there.

Martineau followed, still on the tail of the line of cars climbing the steep hill of the Mont until they came to a narrow turning that led out on top where there were a number of flat-roofed houses.

'A gun platoon only now, Field Marshal,' Necker assured Baum as he got out.

The house at the very end with a courtyard behind a wall was called Septembertide. The one next to it had a French name, Hinguette. In its garden, a narrow entrance gave access to a series of underground bunkers and machine-gun posts which ran along the crest of the hill under the gardens. There were no civilians living in any of the houses, only troops, who were overwhelmed to have the Desert Fox in proximity to them, none more so than the commanding officer, a Captain Heider.

It transpired that his personal billet was Septembertide. When the field marshal expressed an interest in it, he eagerly led the way. They all trooped down into the garden. The views across the bay, St. Aubin on the right and St. Helier on the left, were breathtaking. The garden was edged with a low concrete wall, and the ground fell almost vertically down through trees and heavy undergrowth to the road far below.

Baum said, 'You'd need the Alpine Corps to get up here, gentlemen.' He looked up at the house. There was a large terrace in front of the sitting room and another above running the full length at bedroom level. 'Nice.' He turned to Heider. 'I need somewhere to lay my head tonight. Will you lend it to me?'

Heider was beside himself with joy. 'An honor, Herr Field Marshal. I can move into Hinguette for the night with my second in command.'

'I'm sure you can find us a decent cook among your men.'

'No problem, Field Marshal.'

Baum turned to Necker. 'You see, my dear Necker, all taken care of. This will suit me very well indeed. Impregnable on this side and Captain Heider and his boys guarding the front. What more could one ask for?'

'It was hoped you might join us for dinner at the officers' club at Bagatelle,' Necker said diffidently.

'Another time. It's been a long day and frankly, I'd welcome an early night. Call for me in the morning. Not too early. Let's say at ten, and we can do the other side of the island.'

'At your orders, Herr Field Marshal.'

They all went around to the front of the house where there was a general leavetaking. Heider took Baum and Hofer inside and showed them around. The living room was large and reasonably well furnished.

'It was like this when we moved in,' Heider said. 'If you'll excuse me, I'll get my things out of the bedroom, Field Marshal, then I'll arrange a cook.'

He went upstairs. Baum turned to Hofer. 'Did I do well?'

'Superb,' Hofer said. 'And this place is perfect. Just the right amount of isolation. You're a genius, Berger.'

The evening meal had already started at de Ville Place when Martineau got back. He peered in at the window and saw Sarah sitting with Guido and half-a-dozen other naval officers at the table. He decided not to go in and, instead, went round to the back door and let himself into the kitchen. Helen was washing dishes at the sink and Gallagher was drying for her.

'How did things go?' the Irishman demanded.

'Well enough. Absolutely no problems, if that's what you mean.'

'Did you see the great man?'

'As close as I am to you, but he made it clear the SS is not exactly his favorite organization.'

Helen poured him a cup of tea, and Gallagher said, 'We've been making decisions while you've been away.'

He told him how they'd decided to move Kelso. When he was finished, Martineau nodded. 'That makes sense to me. We'll make it later though. Say around eleven.'

'Should be safe enough then,' Gallagher said.

Martineau went upstairs and lay on the bed of the room he shared with Sarah. Although they slept in the same bed he had not made love to her again since that first night. There was no particular reason. There just didn't seem to be the need. But no. He wasn't being honest. It wasn't Sarah, it was him, something inside, some old wound of the spirit that made him afraid to give himself fully. A morose fear that it would all prove to be just another disappointment or perhaps simply the fear that this strange, enchanting, tough young woman was forcing him back into the real world again. Bringing him back to life.

He lay on the bed smoking a cigarette, staring at the ceiling, strangely restless, thinking of Rommel and the energy of the man – and what a target he was. He got up and put on his belt with the holstered PPK, then he opened his suitcase, found the Carswell silencer and put it in his pocket.

When he went downstairs, they were still eating in the great hall. He went back to the kitchen. Helen looked up in surprise. 'You're going out again?'

'Things to do.' He turned to Gallagher. 'Tell Sarah I'll be back soon.'

The Irishman frowned. 'Are you all right? Is something wrong?'

'Not in the whole wide world,' Martineau assured him. 'I'll see you later,' and he went out.

There was a half moon again and in its light, he saw the line of white houses high overhead on the ridge above the trees. He turned the Kubelwagen into La Haule Hill and parked in a track where it joined with Mont de la Rocque. For a while, he sat there thinking about it, and then he got out and started up through the trees.

It was nonsense, of course. Shoot Rommel and they'd have the island sewn up tight within an hour. Nowhere to go. On top of that they'd probably take hostages until the assassin gave himself up. They'd done that in other countries. No reason to think Jersey would be any different. But in spite of all reason and logic, the thought titillated, would not go away. He kept on climbing.

13

Muller was working in his office at the Silvertide, trying to catch up on his paperwork, when there was a knock on the door and Greiser looked in. 'Working late tonight, Herr Captain.'

'The field marshal accounted for most of my time today, and he's likely to take up more tomorrow,' Muller said. 'I've at least twelve case reports to work through for court appearances next week. I thought I'd try to get rid of them tonight.' He stretched and yawned. 'Anyway, what are you doing here?'

'The phone call I booked to my brother in Stuttgart. I've just been talking to him.'

Muller was immediately interested. 'What did he have to say about Vogel?'

'Well, he certainly never came across him at Gestapo Headquarters in Berlin. But he does point out that the SD are housed in a building at the other end of Prince Albrechtstrasse. He simply wasn't familiar with who was who, except for the big noises like Heydrich before they murdered him and Walter Schellenberg. However, it was an open secret during his time in Berlin, that the Reichsführer uses mystery men like Vogel with special powers and so on. He says nobody was all that sure who they were.'

'Which is exactly the point of the whole exercise,' Muller observed.

'Anyway, he says people like that operate out of the SD unit attached to the Reichsführer's office at the Reich Chancellery. As it happens, he knows someone on the staff there rather well.'

'Who?'

'An SS auxiliary named Lotte Neumann. She was his mistress during his Berlin period. She's secretary to one of the Reichsführer's aides.'

'And he's going to speak to her?'

'He has a call booked through to Berlin in the morning. He'll get back to me as soon as he can. At least it will tell us just how important Vogel is. She's bound to know something about him.'

'Excellent.' Muller nodded. 'Have you seen Willi tonight?'

'Yes,' Greiser admitted reluctantly. 'At the club. Then he insisted on going to a bar in some back street in St. Helier.'

'He's drinking?' Greiser hesitated and Muller said, 'Come on, man, tell me the worst.'

'Yes, Herr Captain, heavily. I couldn't keep up. As you know I drink very little. I stayed with him for a while, but then he grew morose and angry as he does. He told me to clear off. Became rather violent.'

'Damnation!' Muller sighed. 'Nothing to be done now. He's probably ended up with some woman. You'd better get off to bed. I'll need you again in the morning. Ten o'clock at Septembertide.'

'Very well, Herr Captain.'

He went out, and Muller opened another file and picked up his pen.

Kleist was at that moment parking his car on a track on the edge of the de Ville estate very close to Gallagher's cottage. He was dangerously drunk, way beyond any consideration of common sense. He had half a bottle of schnapps with him. He took a pull at it, put it in his pocket, got out of the car and walked unsteadily along the track toward the cottage.

There was a chink of light at the drawn curtains covering one of the sitting room windows. He kicked on the front door vigorously. There was no response. He kicked again, then tried the handle and the door opened. He peered into the sitting room. There was an oil lamp on the table, the embers of a fire on the hearth, but no other sign of life. The kitchen was also empty.

He stood at the bottom of the stairs. 'Gallagher, where are you?'

There was no reply. He got the oil lamp and went upstairs to see for himself, but both bedrooms were empty. He descended the stairs again, slowly and with some difficulty, went into the sitting room and put the lamp on the table.

He turned it down, leaving the room in darkness except for a dull glow from the embers of the fire. He pulled back the curtain at the window and sat there in a wing chair, looking at the yard outside, clear in the moonlight. 'Right, you bastard. You've got to come home sometime.'

He took a Mauser from his right-hand pocket and sat there nursing it in his lap as he waited.

At Septembertide, Baum and Hofer had enjoyed a surprisingly excellent meal. Cold roast chicken, Jersey new potatoes and a salad, washed down with a bottle of excellent Sancerre provided by Captain Heider. The half moon gave a wonderful view of St. Aubin's Bay, and they went out onto the terrace to finish their wine.

After a while, the corporal who had cooked the meal appeared. 'All is in order, Herr Major,' he told Hofer, 'the kitchen is clear again. I've left coffee and milk on the side. Will there be anything else?'

'Not tonight,' Hofer told him. 'We'll have breakfast at nine sharp in the morning. Eggs, ham, anything you can lay your hands on. You can return to your billet now.'

The corporal clicked his heels and withdrew. Baum said, 'What a night.'

'My dear Berger, what a day,' Hofer told him. 'The most remarkable of my life.'

'And the second act still to come.' Baum yawned. 'Speaking of tomorrow, I could do with some sleep,' and he went back inside.

Hofer said, 'You, of course, in deference to your superior rank, will take the large bedroom above this, which has its own bathroom. I'll take the small room at the end of the corridor. It overlooks the front of the house so I'll be more aware of what's going on there.'

They went upstairs, Baum still carrying his glass of wine. 'What time?' he said.

'If you're not already up I'll wake you at seven-thirty,' Hofer told him.

'Rommel would be up at five, but one can take play-acting too far.' Baum smiled. He closed the outer door to the bedroom suite, walked through the dressing area into the bedroom itself. It was plainly furnished with two wardrobes, a dressing table and a double bed, presumably left by the owners from whom the house had been requisitioned. The corporal had drawn the curtains at the windows. They were large and heavy, made of red velvet and touched the floor. When he parted them, he found a steel and glass door, which he opened and stepped out onto the upper terrace.

The view was even better at this height, and he could see down into St. Aubin's Harbor in the distance on his right. It was very still, the only sound a dog barking a couple of fields away. The blackout in St. Helier was anything but complete, lights dotted here and there. The sea was calm, a white line of surf down there on the beach, the sky luminous with stars in the moonlight. A night to thank God for.

He raised his glass. 'L'chayim,' he said softly and he turned, parted the curtains and went back inside, leaving the door open.

It took Martineau twenty minutes to make his way up through the trees. The undergrowth was thick in places and the going was rough, but he'd expected that and there was no barbed wire on the final approach to the garden, he'd noticed that earlier. He still had no idea what he intended and pulled himself up over the concrete block wall cautiously, aware of voices. He stood in the shadow of a palm tree, and looked up to see Hofer and Rommel on the terrace in the moonlight.

'What a night,' the field marshal said.

'My dear Berger, what a day,' Hofer told him.

'And the second act still to come.'

Martineau stayed in the shadow of the palm tree, astonished at this amazing exchange. It didn't make sense. After they had gone inside, he advanced cautiously across the lawn and paused by the covered way. A moment later, the field marshal appeared on the upper terrace and stood at the rail looking out over the bay.

He raised his glass. 'L'chayim,' he said softly, turned and went back inside.

L'chayim, which meant 'to life,' the most ancient of Hebrew toasts. It was enough. Martineau stood on the low wall, reached for the railings on the first terrace and pulled himself over.

Heini Baum took the Blue Max and the Knight's Cross with Oak Leaves, Swords and Diamonds from around his neck and laid them on the dressing table. He removed his cheek pads and examined his face in the mirror, running his fingers through his hair.

'Not bad, Heini. Not bad. I wonder what the great man would say if he knew he was being taken off by a Jew boy?'

He started to unbutton his tunic and Martineau, who had been standing on the other side of the curtain screwing the Carswell silencer on the barrel of the Walther, stepped inside. Baum saw him instantly in the mirror, and old soldier that he was, reached at once for the Mauser pistol in its holster on his belt which lay on the dressing table.

'I wouldn't,' Martineau told him. 'They've really done wonders with this new model silencer. If I fired it behind your back you wouldn't even know about it. Now, hands on head and sit on the stool.'

'Is this some plot of the SS to get rid of me?' Baum asked, playing his role to the hilt. 'I'm aware that Reichsführer Himmler never liked me, but I didn't realize how much.'

Martineau sat on the edge of the bed, took out a packet of Gitanes one-handed and shook one up. As he lit it he said, 'I heard you and Hofer talking on the terrace. He called you Berger.'

'You've been busy.'

'And I was outside a couple of minutes ago when you were talking to yourself, so let's get down to facts. Number one, you aren't Rommel.'

'If you say so.'

'All right,' Martineau said, 'let's try again. If I am part of an SS plot to kill you on Himmler's orders, there wouldn't be much point if you aren't really Rommel. Of course, if you are . . .'

He raised the PPK and Baum took a deep breath. 'Very clever.'

'So you aren't Rommel?'

'I should have thought that was sufficiently obvious by now.'

'What are you, an actor?'

'Turned soldier, turned actor again.'

'Marvelous,' Martineau said. 'I saw him in Paris last year and you fooled me. Does he know you're Jewish?'

'No.' Baum frowned. 'Listen, what kind of an SS man are you anyway?'

'I'm not,' Martineau laid the PPK down on the bed beside him. 'I'm a colonel in the British Army.'

'I don't believe you,' Baum said in astonishment.

'A pity you don't speak English and I could prove it,' Martineau said.

'But I do.' Baum broke into very good English indeed. 'I played the Moss Empire circuit in London, Leeds and Manchester in nineteen thirty-five and six.'

'And you went back to Germany?' Martineau said. 'You must have been crazy.'

'My parents.' Baum shrugged. 'Like most of the old folk, they didn't believe it would happen. I hid in the army using the identity of a man killed in an air raid in Kiel. My real name is Heini Baum. To Rommel, I'm Corporal Erich Berger, 21st Parachute Regiment.'

'Harry Martineau.'

Baum hesitated then shook hands. 'Your German is excellent.'

'My mother was German,' Martineau explained. 'Tell me, where is Rommel?'

'In Normandy.'

'And what's the purpose of the masquerade or don't you know?'

'I'm not supposed to, but I can listen at doors as well as anybody.' Baum took a cigarette from the field marshal's silver case, fitted it into the ivory holder Rommel had given him and lit it. 'He's having a quiet get-together with Generals von Stulpnagel and Falkenhausen. A highly illegal business as far as I can make out. Apparently they and a number of other generals, realizing they've lost the war, want to get rid of Hitler and salvage something from the mess while there's still a chance.'

'Possible,' Martineau said. 'There have been attempts on Hitler's life before.'

'Fools, all of them,' Baum told him.

'You don't approve? That surprises me.'

'They've lost the war anyway. It's only a question of time so there's no point in their scheming. By the time that mad bastard Himmler's finished with them, they'll be hanging on hooks, not that it would worry me. Most of them helped Hitler to power in the first place.'

'That's true.'

'On the other hand, I'm a German as well as a Jew. I've got to know Rommel pretty well in the past few days. He's a good man. He's on the wrong side, that's all. Now you know all about me. What about you? What are you doing here?'

Martineau told him briefly about Kelso, although omitting, for the moment, any mention of the Operation Overlord connection. When he was finished, Baum said, 'I wish you luck. From the sound of it, it's going to be tricky trying to get him out by boat. At least I fly out tomorrow night. A nice fast exit.'

Martineau saw it then, the perfect answer to the whole situation. Sheer genius. 'Tell me,' he said. 'Once back, you'll be returned to your regiment?'

'I should imagine so.'

'Which means you'll have every chance of having your head blown off during the next few months because the invasion's coming and your paratroopers will be in the thick of it.'

'I expect so.'

'How would you like to go to England instead?'

'You've got to be joking,' Baum said in astonishment. 'How could such a thing be?'

'Just think about it.' Martineau got up and paced around the room. 'What's the most useful thing about being Field Marshal Erwin Rommel?'

'You tell me.'

'The fact that everyone does what you tell them to do. For example, tomorrow evening you go to the airport to return to France in the little Storch you came in.'

'So what.'

'There's a JU52 transport up there, the mail plane, due to leave for France around the same time. What do you think would happen if Field Marshal Rommel turned up just before takeoff with an SS Standartenführer, a wounded man on a stretcher, a young Frenchwoman, and commandeered the plane? What do you think they'd say?'

Baum smiled. 'Not very much, I imagine.'

'Once in the air,' Martineau said, 'and the nearest point on the English coast would be no more than half an hour's flying time in that mail plane.'

'My God!' Baum said in awe. 'You really mean it.'

'Do you want to go to England or don't you?' Martineau asked. 'Make up your mind. Of course, if you hadn't met me you'd have gone back to France to rejoin the field marshal, and who knows what would happen. Another mad plot to kill the Führer fails, which would mean an unpleasant end for Erwin Rommel. I suspect that might also apply to anyone connected with him and, let's face it – the Gestapo and Himmler would find you very suspect indeed.'

'You really do have a way with the words,' Baum told him.

Martineau lit a cigarette. 'Even if you survive, my friend, Berlin will resemble a brickyard before long. The Russians want blood, and I think you'll find that the Allies will stand back and let them get on with it.' He peered out through the curtains. 'No, I really do think my alternative is the only option that would make sense to an intelligent man.'

'You could make an excellent living selling insurance,' Baum told him. 'As it happens, I used to have a cousin in Leeds which is in the north of England. Yorkshire, to be precise. My only relative, if he's still alive. I need someone to say kaddish for me. That's prayers for the dead, by the way.'

'I know what it is,' Martineau said patiently. 'Do we have a deal?'

'Berlin a brickyard.' Baum shook his head and smiled. 'I like that.'

'That's settled then.' Martineau unscrewed the silencer and put the PPK back in its holster.

'So what about Hofer?'

'What about him?'

'He's not so bad. No different from the rest of us. I wouldn't like to have to hurt him.'

'I'll think of something. I'll discuss it with my friends. I'll join your tour of the east of the island tomorrow morning. Be more friendly toward me. At a suitable point when Necker is there, ask me where I'm staying. I'll tell you de Ville Place – all about it. Its magical location, wonderful grounds, and so on. You tell Necker you like the sound of it. That you'd like to have lunch there. Insist on it. I'll finalize things with you then.'

'The third act, rewritten at so late a date we don't get any chance to rehearse,' Baum said wryly.

'You know what they say,' Martineau told him. 'That's show business,' and he slipped out through the curtain.

It was just after midnight when Sean Gallagher and Guido took Hugh Kelso down the narrow stairway to Helen's bedroom. Sarah waited by the partially open door for Helen's signal from the other end of the corridor. It came and she opened the door quickly.

'Now,' she said.

Gallagher and Guido linked arms again and hurried out, Hugh Kelso between them. The back stairs were wider and easier to negotiate, and they were in the kitchen within a couple of minutes. They sat Kelso down and Helen closed the door to the stairs, turning the key.

'So far so good,' Gallagher said. 'Are you all right, Colonel?'

The American looked strained, but nodded eagerly. 'I'm feeling great just to be moving again.'

'Fine. We'll take the path through the woods to my place. Ten minutes, that's all.'

Helen motioned him to silence. 'I think I hear a car.'

They waited and Sarah hurriedly turned down the lamp, went to the window and drew the curtains as a vehicle entered the yard outside. 'It's Harry,' she said.

Helen turned up the lamp again and Sarah unbolted the back door for him. He slipped in and closed the door behind him. After events at Mont de la Rocque he was on a high, full of energy, and the excitement was plain to see on the pale face shadowed by the SS cap.

'What is it, Harry?' Sarah demanded. 'Has something happened?'

'I think you could definitely say that, but it can wait until later. Ready to go, are we?'

'As ever was,' Kelso said.

'Let's get it done then.'

'Sarah and I will go on ahead to make sure everything's ready for you,' Helen said as she took a couple of old macs down from a peg, gave one to the girl and put the other one on herself.

She turned the lamp down again, opened the door and she and Sarah hurried across the yard. Gallagher and Guido linked hands and Kelso put his arms around their necks.

'Right,' Martineau said. 'Here we go. I'll lead the way. If anyone wants a rest, just say so.'

He stood to one side to let them go out, closed the door behind him and they started across the courtyard.

The pale moonlight filtered through the trees, and the track was clear before them, the night perfumed with the scent of flowers again. Sarah took Helen's arm. For a moment, there was an intimacy between them, and she was very aware of that warm, safe feeling she had known in the time following her mother's death when Helen had been not only a strong right arm but the breath of life to her.

'What happens afterward?' Helen said. 'When you get back?'

'Assuming that we do.'

'Don't be silly. It's going to work. If ever I met a man who knows what he's doing it's Harry Martineau. So, what happens on your return? Back to nursing?'

'God knows,' Sarah told her. 'Nursing was always only a stopgap. It was medicine I was interested in.'

'I remember.'

'But after this, who knows?' Sarah said. 'The whole thing's been like a mad dream. I've never known a man like Harry, never known such excitement.'

'Temporary madness, Sarah, just like the war. Not real life. Neither is Harry Martineau. He's not for you, Sarah. God help him, he's not even for himself.'

They paused on the edge of the clearing, the cottage a few yards away, bathed in the moonlight. 'It's nothing to do with me,' Sarah said. 'It never was. I had no control over what happened. It's beyond reason.'

In the cottage, sitting at the window, Kleist had seen them the moment they had emerged from the wood, and it was the intimacy that struck him at once. There was something wrong here, and he got up, moved to the door and opened it a little. It was then, of course, as they approached, that he realized they were speaking together in English.

Helen said, 'Loving someone is different from being in love, darling. Being in love is a state of heat and that passes, believe me. Still, let's get inside. The others will be here in a moment.' She put a hand to the door and it moved. 'It seems to be open.'

And then the door swung, a hand had her by the front of her coat, and Kleist tapped the muzzle of the Mauser against her cheek. 'Inside, Frau de Ville,' he said roughly. 'And let us discuss the curious fact that this little French bitch not only speaks the most excellent English, but would appear to be a friend of yours.'

For a moment, Helen was frozen, aware only of a terrible fear as the Mauser tapped again against her face. Kleist reached and got Sarah by the hair.

'And you are expecting others, I gather. I wonder who?' He walked backward, pulling Sarah by the hair, the gun still probing into Helen's flesh. 'No stupidities or I pull the trigger.' He released Sarah suddenly. 'Go and draw the curtains.' She did as she was told. 'Good, now turn up the lamp. Let's have everything as it should be.' She could see the sweat on his face, now, the terror and pain on Helen's. 'Now come back here.'

His fingers tightened in her hair again. The pain was dreadful. She wanted to cry a warning, but was aware of Helen's head back, the Mauser under her chin. Kleist stank of drink, was shaking with excitement as they waited, listening to the voices approaching across the yard. Only at the very last moment, as the door swung open and Gallagher and Guido backed in, Kelso between them, did he push the women away.

'Harry, look out!' Sarah cried as Martineau slipped in after them, but by then, her anguished cry was too late to help anyone.

Kelso lay on the floor and Helen, Sarah and the three men leaned against the wall in a row, arms outstretched. Kleist relieved Martineau of his PPK and slipped it into his pocket. 'The SS must be doing its recruiting in some strange places these days.'

Martineau said nothing, waiting, coldly, for his chance and Kleist moved on to Guido Orsini, running his hands over him expertly. 'I never liked you, pretty boy,' he said contemptuously. 'All you sodding Italians have ever done is give us trouble. The Führer should have sorted you lot out first.'

'Amazing.' Guido turned his head and said amiably to Gallagher, 'It can actually talk.'

Kleist kicked his feet from under him and put a boot in his side, then he turned to Gallagher, running a hand over him quickly, feeling for a gun. He found nothing and stood back. 'Now then, you bastard, I've been waiting for this.'

He smashed his right fist into the base of the Irishman's spine. Gallagher cried out and went down. Kleist booted him in the side and Helen screamed. 'Stop it!'

Kleist smiled at her. 'I haven't even started.' He stirred Gallagher with his boot. 'Get up and put your hands on your head.' Gallagher stayed on his hands and knees for a moment and Kleist prodded him with a toe. 'Come on, move it, you thick piece of Irish dung.'

Gallagher got to his feet and stood there, a half-smile on his face, arms at his sides. 'Half-Irish,' he said, 'and half-Jersey. As I told you before, a bad combination.'

Kleist struck him backhanded across the face. 'I told you to get your hands on your head.'

'Anything you say.'

The gutting knife was ready in Gallagher's left hand, had been for several minutes, skillfully palmed. His arm swung, there was a click as he pressed the button, the blade flickered in the lamplight, catching Kleist in the soft flesh under the chin. Kleist discharged the Mauser once into the wall, then dropped it and fell back against the table, wrenching the knife from Gallagher's grasp. He tried to get up, one hand tearing at the handle protruding from beneath his chin, then fell sideways to the floor, kicked convulsively and was still.

'Oh, my God!' Helen said and turned and stumbled into the kitchen, where she was immediately violently sick.

Martineau said to Sarah, 'Go and help her.'

The girl went out and he crouched down and took his Walther from the dead man's pocket. He looked up at Gallagher. 'They teach that trick in the SOE silent killing course. Where did you learn it?'

'Another legacy from my old grandfather,' Gallagher said.

'He must have been a remarkable man.'

He and Guido got Kelso onto the couch while Gallagher retrieved his knife. It took all his strength to pull it free. He wiped it on the dead man's coat. 'Do you think this was an official visit?'

'I shouldn't imagine so.' Martineau picked up the empty bottle of schnapps. 'He'd been drinking and he had blood in his eye. He wanted revenge, came up here looking for you, and when you weren't here, he waited.' He shook his head. 'Poor sod, he almost got lucky for once. It would have been the coup of his career.'

'But what happens now?' Kelso demanded. 'This could ruin everything. I mean, a Gestapo man doesn't turn up for work, they start looking.'

'No need to panic.' Martineau picked up a rug and covered Kleist. 'There's always a way out. First, we find his car. It's bound to be parked nearby.' He nodded to Guido and Gallagher and led the way out.

It was Guido who found the Renault within ten minutes and whistled up the others. Martineau and Gallagher joined him. 'Now what?' Guido asked.

'Kelso's right. If Kleist doesn't turn up for work in the morning, Muller will turn this island inside out,' Gallagher said. 'So what do we do?'

'Give him to them,' Martineau said crisply. 'He was drunk and ran off the road in his car, it's as simple as that.'

'Preferably over a cliff,' Guido put in.

'Exactly.' Martineau turned to Gallagher. 'Have you anywhere suitable to suggest? Not too far, but far enough for there to be no obvious connection with here.'

'Yes,' Gallagher said. 'I think I've got just the place.'

'Good. You lead the way in the Renault, and I'll follow in the Kubelwagen.'

'Shall I come?' Guido asked.

'No,' Martineau said. 'You hold the fort here. I'll go up to the house and get the Kubelwagen. You two take the Renault back to the cottage and put Kleist in the boot.'

He turned and hurried away through the wood.

*   *   *

When Martineau arrived back at the cottage they already had Kleist's body in the boot of the car, and Gallagher was ready to go. Martineau asked, 'How long will it take us to get to this place?'

'The far side of La Moye Point.' Gallagher unfolded an old pocket touring map of the island. 'About fifteen or twenty minutes at this time in the morning.'

'Are we likely to run into anybody?'

'We have an honorary police system out here in the parishes, and they don't turn out to work for the enemy unless they have to.'

'And the Germans?'

'The odd military police patrol, no more than that. We've every chance of driving to La Moye without seeing a soul.'

'Right, then let's get moving.' Martineau turned to Guido and the two women standing in the doorway. 'Wait for us here. There are things to discuss,' and he drove away.

Gallagher was right. Their run from Noirmont to Woodbine corner and along the main road to Red Houses passed without incident, no sign of another vehicle all the way along La Route Orange and moving toward Corbiere Point. Finally, Gallagher turned into a narrow lane. He stopped the Renault and got out.

'There's a strongpoint down there on our right at Corbiere, an artillery battery on the left toward La Moye Point. The area up ahead is clear, and the road turns along the edge of the cliffs about two hundred yards from here. It's always been a hazard. No protecting wall.'

'All right,' Martineau said. 'We'll leave the Kubelwagen here.'

He got a can of petrol and stood on the running board of the Renault as Gallagher drove along the bumpy road between high hedges. They came out on the edge of the cliffs, going down into a small valley, a defile on the left running down to rocks and surf below.

'This will do.' Martineau hammered on the roof.

Gallagher braked to a halt, got out and went around to the boot. He and Martineau got Kleist out between them, carried him to the front and put him behind the wheel. Gallagher had left the engine running. As he shut the door the dead man slumped forward.

'All right?' Gallagher demanded in a low voice.

'In a minute.' Martineau opened the can and poured petrol over the front seat and the dead man's clothes. 'Okay, let him go.'

Gallagher released the handbrake, leaving the engine in neutral, and turned the wheel. He started to push and the Renault left the track, moving across the grass.

'Watch yourself!' Martineau called and struck a match and dropped it through the open passenger window.

For a moment, he thought it had gone out and then, as the Renault bumped over the edge, orange and yellow flame blossomed. They turned and ran back along the lane, and behind them, there was a grinding crash and then a brief explosion.

When they reached the Kubelwagen, Martineau said, 'You get down in the back, just in case.'

It was too good to last, of course, and five minutes later, as he turned from the Corbiere Road into Route du Sud, he found two military police motorcycles parked at the side of the road. One of them stepped out, hand raised in the moonlight. Martineau slowed at once.

'Military police,' he whispered to Gallagher. 'Stay low.'

He opened the door and got out. 'Is there a problem?' At the sight of the uniform, the two policemen jumped to attention. One of them still had a lighted cigarette between the fingers of his left hand. 'Ah, now I see, what we might term a smoke break,' Martineau said.

'Standartenführer, what can I say?' the man replied.

'Personally, I always find it better to say nothing.' There was something supremely menacing in the way he delivered the words. 'Now, what did you want?'

'Nothing, Standartenführer. It's just that we don't often see a vehicle at this time in the morning in this sector.'

'And you were quite properly doing your duty.' Martineau produced his papers. 'My SD card. Come on, man, hurry up!' He raised his voice and it was harsh and ugly.

The policeman barely glanced at it, hands shaking as he handed it back. 'All is in order.'

'Good, you can return to your duties then.' Martineau got back in the car. 'As for smoking, be a little more discreet, that's my advice.'

He drove away. Gallagher said, voice slightly muffled, 'How in the hell do you manage to sound such a convincing Nazi?'

'Practice, Sean, that's what it takes. Lots of practice,' Martineau told him, and he turned into La Route Orange and moved toward Red Houses.

When they got back to the cottage, Sarah opened the door instantly to them. 'Everything all right?'

'Perfect,' Gallagher told her as he followed Martineau inside. 'We put the car over a cliff near La Moye and made sure it burned.'

'Was that necessary?' Helen shivered, clasping her arms around herself.

'We want him to be found,' Martineau said. 'And if the sentries at the coastal strongpoints in the area are even half-awake they'll have noticed the flames. On the other hand, we don't want him in too good a condition, because if he was, there would be that knife wound to explain.'

Kelso said, 'So, you had no trouble at all?'

'A military police patrol stopped us on the way back,' Gallagher said. 'I was well out of sight and Harry did his Nazi bit. No problem.'

'So, all that remains now is for Guido to contact Savary in the morning,' Sarah said.

'No,' Martineau said. 'Actually, there's been a rather significant change of plan.'

There was general astonishment. Gallagher said, 'Sweet Jesus, what have you been up to now?'

Martineau lit a cigarette, stood with his back to the fire and said calmly, 'If you'll all sit down, I'll tell you.'

14

At nine the following morning Gallagher drove down to St. Helier, two more sacks of potatoes in the van. He didn't call at the central market, but went straight to the troop supply depot in the old garage in Wesley Street. The first trucks went out with military supplies to various units around the island at eight-thirty, which was why he had chosen his time carefully. Feldwebel Klinger was up in his glass office eating his breakfast. Sausage, eggs, bacon, all very English. The coffee was real, Gallagher could smell that as he went up the stairs.

'Good morning, Herr General, what have you got for me today?'

'A couple of sacks of potatoes if you're interested. I'll take canned food in exchange, whatever you've got, and coffee.' He helped himself to a piece of bacon from Klinger's plate. 'Whenever I see you, you're eating.'

'And why not? The only pleasure left to me in this lousy life. Here, join me in a coffee.' Klinger poured it out. 'Why are human beings so stupid? I had a nice restaurant in Hamburg before the war. All the best people came. My wife does her best, but more bomb damage last week and no compensation.'

'And worse to come, Hans,' Gallagher told him. 'They'll be on the beaches soon, all those Tommies and Yanks, and heading for the Fatherland and the Russians coming the other way. You'll be lucky to have a business at all. Those Reichsmarks you keep hoarding won't be worth the paper they're printed on.'

Klinger wiped a hand across his mouth. 'Don't, you'll give me indigestion with talk like that so early in the morning.'

'Of course, this kind of money never loses its value.' Gallagher took a coin from his pocket, flicked it in the air, caught it and put it down on the table.

Klinger picked it up and there was awe on his face. 'An English sovereign.'

'Exactly,' Gallagher said. 'A gold sovereign.'

Klinger tried it with his teeth. 'The real thing.'

'Would I offer you anything less?' Gallagher took a small linen bag from his pocket and held it up tantalizingly. 'Another forty-nine in there.'

He placed the bag on the table and Klinger spilled the coins out and touched them with his fingers. 'All right, what do you want?'

'A sailor's uniform. Kriegsmarine,' Gallagher told him. 'No big deal, as our American friends say. You've got stacks of them in store here.'

'Impossible,' Klinger said. 'Absolutely.'

'I'd also expect boots, reefer coat and cap. We're doing a play at the Parish Hall at St. Brelade. Very good part for a German sailor in it. He falls in love with this Jersey girl and her parents . . .'

'Stop this nonsense,' Klinger said. 'Play? What play is this?'

'All right.' Gallagher shrugged. 'If you're not interested.'

He started to pick up the coins and Klinger put a hand on his arm. 'You know the GFP at Silvertide would be very interested to know what you wanted with a German uniform, Herr General.'

'Of course they would, only we're not going to tell them, are we? I mean, you don't want them nosing around in here, Hans. All that booze and cigarettes in the cellar and the canned goods. And then there's the coffee and the champagne.'

'Stop it!'

'I know it's spring now,' Gallagher carried on relentlessly. 'But it still can't be too healthy on the Russian Front serving with a penal battalion.'

The threat was plain in his voice and the prospect too horrible to contemplate. Klinger was trapped, angry that he'd ever got involved with the Irishman. Too late to cry about that now. Better to give him what he wanted and hope for the best.

'All right, I hear you.' Klinger scooped up the sovereigns, put them in one of his tunic pockets. 'I've always loved the theater. It would be a privilege to assist.'

'I knew I could rely on you,' Gallagher told him. 'Here are the sizes,' and he pushed a piece of paper across the desk.

★　★　★

At ten o'clock the cavalcade left Septembertide and drove to Beaumont and Bel Royal and then along Victoria Avenue to St. Helier. The first stop was Elizabeth Castle. The tide was out and they parked the cars opposite the Grand Hotel and clambered on board an armored personnel carrier which followed the line of the causeway across the beach, its half-tracks churning sand.

'When the tide is in, the causeway is under water, Herr Field Marshal,' Necker told him.

Baum was in his element, filled with excitement at the turn events had taken. He could see Martineau seated at the other end of the truck talking to a couple of young officers and Muller and for a wild moment wondered whether he might have dreamed the events of the previous night. Martineau certainly played a most convincing Nazi. On the other hand, he didn't do too bad a job on field marshals himself.

The carrier drove up from the causeway through the old castle gate and stopped. They all got out and Necker said, 'The English fortified this place to keep out the French in Napoleon's time. Some of the original guns are still here.'

'Now we fortify it further to keep out the English,' Baum said. 'There's irony for you.'

As he led the way along the road to the moat and the entrance to the inner court, Martineau moved to his shoulder. 'As a matter of interest, Herr Field Marshal, Sir Walter Raleigh was governor here in the time of Queen Elizabeth Tudor.'

'Really?' Baum said. 'An extraordinary man. Soldier, sailor, musician, poet, historian.'

'Who also found time to introduce tobacco to the Western world,' Martineau reminded him.

'For that alone he should have a statue in every major city,' Baum said. 'I remember the Italian campaign in nineteen seventeen. A terrible time. I think the only thing that got us through the trench warfare was the cigarettes.'

He strode on ahead, Martineau at his shoulder, talking animatedly, and Hofer trailed anxiously behind with Necker. An hour later, after a thorough inspection of every gun and strongpoint Baum could find, they returned to the personnel carrier and were taken back across the beach to the cars.

On the cliffs near La Moye Point a group of field engineers hauled on a line, helping the corporal on the other end walk up the steep slope. He came over the edge and unhooked himself. The sergeant in charge of the detail gave him a cigarette. 'You don't look too good.'

'Neither would you. He's like a piece of badly cooked meat, the driver down there.'

'Any papers?'

'Burned along with most of his clothes. The car is a Renault and I've got the number.'

The sergeant wrote it down. 'The police can handle it now.' He turned to the other men. 'All right, back to the post, you lot.'

Mont Orgeuil at Gorey on the east coast of Jersey is probably one of the most spectacular castles in Europe. The Germans had garrisoned it with coastal artillery batteries. In fact there were two regimental headquarters situated in the castle. Baum visited both of them, as well as conducting his usual energetic survey. In the observation post which had been constructed on the highest point of the castle, he stood with a pair of fieldglasses and looked across at the French coast, which was clearly visible. He was for the moment slightly apart from the others and Hofer moved to his shoulder.

'Is everything all right?' Baum asked, the glasses still to his eyes.

'Vogel seems to be pressing his attentions,' Hofer said softly.

'He wanted to talk, so I let him,' Baum replied. 'I'm keeping him happy, Major. I'm trying to keep them all happy. Isn't that what you want?'

'Of course,' Hofer told him. 'Don't take it the wrong way. You're doing fine. Just be careful, that's all.'

Necker moved up to join them, and Baum said, 'Fantastic, this place. Now I would like to see something in the country. The sort of strongpoint one might find in a village area.'

'Of course, Herr Field Marshal.'

'And then some lunch.'

'Arrangements have been made. The officers' mess at Battle HQ were hoping to entertain you.'

'No, Necker, something different, I think. I'd like to see the other side of island life. Vogel tells me he's billeted at some manor house called de Ville Place. You know it?'

'Yes, Herr Field Marshal. The owner, Mrs. Helen de Ville, is married to the Seigneur who is an officer in the British Army. A most charming woman.'

'And a delightful house according to Vogel. I think we'll have lunch there. I'm sure Mrs. de Ville won't object, especially if you provide the food and wine.' He looked up at the cloudless blue sky. 'A beautiful day for a picnic.'

'As you say, Herr Field Marshal. If you'll excuse me I'll go and give the orders.'

Ten minutes later, as the cavalcade of officers moved out through the main entrance to where the cars waited, a military police motorcyclist drove up. He pulled in beside Greiser, who sat behind the wheel of Muller's Citroën. Greiser read the message the man handed him, then got out of the car and hurried across to Muller, who was talking to a couple of officers. Martineau, standing nearby, heard everything.

'The bloody fool,' Muller said softly and crumpled the message up in his hand. 'All right, we'd better get moving.'

He went to Necker, spoke briefly to him and then got into the Citroën. It moved away quickly, and Martineau walked over to Necker. 'Muller seemed agitated.'

'Yes,' Necker said. 'It would seem one of his men has been killed in a car accident.'

'How unfortunate.' Martineau offered him a cigarette. 'Allow me to compliment you on the way you've handled things at such short notice.'

'We do what we can. It's not every day a Rommel comes visiting.'

'On the other hand, I expect you'll heave a sigh of relief when that Storch of his takes off tonight. Is he leaving before or after the mail plane?'

'In my opinion he should make the flight under cover of darkness. The mail plane usually leaves at eight for the same reason.'

'Don't worry, Major.' Martineau smiled. 'I'm sure he'll see sense. I'll speak to him personally about it.'

On a wooded slope in the parish of St. Peter with distant views of St. Ouen's Bay, the field marshal visited a complex of machine-gun nests, talking to gun crews, accepting a cigarette here and there. With the men, he was a sensational success, Necker had to admit that, although God alone knew where all the energy came from.

They had visited every part of the defense complex, were circling back through the wood, when an extraordinary incident took place. They came out of the trees, Baum in the lead. Below them, a gang of slave laborers worked on the track. They were the most wretched creatures Baum had ever seen in his life, dressed for the most part, in rags.

'What have we here?' he demanded.

'Russians, Herr Field Marshal, plus a few Poles and Spanish Reds.'

No one below was aware of their presence, especially the guard who sat on a tree trunk and smoked a cigarette, his rifle across his knees. A cart emerged from the lower wood pulled by a rather thin horse, a young woman in a headscarf and overalls leading it. There was a little girl of five or six in the back of the cart. As they passed the road gang, she tossed them several turnips.

The German guard shouted angrily and ran along the track after the cart. He grabbed the horse by the bridle and brought it to a halt. He said something to the woman and then walked to the back of the cart, reached up and pulled the child down roughly. He slapped her face and, when the young woman ran to help her, knocked the woman to the ground.

Baum did not say a word, but went down the hillside like a strong wind. As he reached the track, the guard's hand rose to strike the child again. Baum caught him by the wrist, twisting it up and around. The guard turned, the anger on his face quickly replaced by astonishment, and Baum punched him in the mouth. The guard bounced off the side of the cart and fell on his hands and knees.

'Major Necker,' the field marshal said. 'You will oblige me by arresting this animal.' He ignored them all, turning to the young woman and the child clutching her. 'Your name, Fraulein?' he asked in English.

'Jean le Couteur.'

'And this is?' Baum picked the child up.

'My sister Agnes.'

'So?' He nodded. 'You are a very brave girl, Agnes le Couteur.' He put her up in the cart again, turned and saluted the young woman courteously. 'My deepest regrets.'

She gazed at him, bewildered, then grabbed the bridle and led the horse away along the track. Just before they disappeared from view into the trees, the child raised an arm and waved.

There was general laughter from all the officers present. Baum turned and said to Necker, 'Honor being satisfied, I suggest we adjourn to the de Ville Place for lunch.'

Muller stood on the edge of the cliff with Greiser and looked down at the wreck of the Renault. 'There was a fire,' Greiser told him. 'From what the engineer sergeant I spoke to says, he's pretty unrecognizable.'

'I can imagine.' Muller nodded. 'All right, make arrangements with them to get the body up sometime this afternoon. We'll need a postmortem, but discreetly handled. We must keep the drunkenness factor out of it.'

He turned away and Greiser said, 'But what was he doing out here? That's what I can't understand.'

'So far the only thing we do know is that he was drinking heavily last night. Check with military police for this area, just in case someone saw his car,' Muller told him. 'I'll have to get back to the official party now so I'll take the Citroën. You'll have to commandeer something from the military police. The moment you have any information at all, let me know.'

The mess sergeant and his men who had descended on de Ville Place from the officers' club at Bagatelle brought ample supplies of food and wine. They simply took over, carrying tables and chairs from the house, covering them with the white linen tablecloths they had brought with them, working very fast. The mess sergeant was polite but made it clear to Helen that as the field marshal was due at any time, he would appreciate it if she did not get in the way.

She went up to her bedroom, searched through the wardrobe and found a summer dress in pale green organdy from happier days. As she was pulling it over her head, there was a tap on the door and Sarah came in.

'Getting ready to play hostess?'

'I don't have much choice, do I?' Helen told her. 'Even if he was the real thing.'

She brushed back her hair and fitted ivory side combs. Sarah said, 'You look very nice.'

'And so do you.' Sarah was wearing a dark coat and tiny black hat, the hair swept up.

'We do our best. I'll be glad when it's all over.'

'Not long now, love.' Helen put her arms around her and held her for a moment, then turned and smoothed her dress.

'You haven't changed your mind, you and Sean? You won't come with us?'

'Good heavens no. Can you imagine what would happen to de Ville Place if I wasn't here? Nothing for Ralph to come home to, and remember that Sean, as he keeps telling us, is a neutral.' She applied a little lipstick. 'I certainly have nothing to worry about. You and Standartenführer Vogel were uninvited guests here. Anyway, there's always Guido in the background to back me up.'

'You're really quite a remarkable woman,' Sarah said.

'All women are remarkable, my darling. They have to be to get by. It's a man's world.' She moved to the window. 'Yes, I thought so. They're here.' She turned, smiled. 'Don't forget that down there among all those officers you and I are formally polite. French only.'

'I'll remember.'

'Good. Into battle then. I'll go first. Give me a few minutes,' and she went out.

When Sarah went into the Great Hall she found Guido, Bruno Feldt and three other young naval officers, all hovering uncertainly around the front door, peering outside. 'Ah, Mademoiselle Latour,' Guido said in French. 'You look ravishing as usual. The field marshal has just arrived.'

They moved out onto the steps. Baum was being introduced to Helen by Necker, and Sarah saw Harry standing at the back of the group of officers. Someone took the field marshal's leather coat, baton and gloves. He turned back to Helen, smoothing his tunic, and spoke in English.

'This is most kind of you, Frau de Ville. A gross imposition, but I felt I wanted to see for myself one of your famous Jersey manor houses. De Ville Place comes highly recommended.'

'Quite modest compared to some, Herr Field Marshal. St. Ouen's Manor, for example, is much more spectacular.'

'But this is delightful. Truly delightful. The gardens, the flowers and palm trees and the sea down there. What a fantastic color.' He offered her his arm gallantly. 'And now, if you would do me the honor. A little lobster? Some champagne? Perhaps we can forget the war for a while?'

'Difficult, Herr Field Marshal, but I'll try.' She took his arm and they walked across the grass to the tables.

The afternoon started off well. Guido Orsini asked permission to take photos which the Field Marshal graciously agreed to, posing with the assembled officers, Martineau standing next to him. The whole affair was obviously a huge success.

Necker, on his fourth glass of champagne, was standing by the drinks table with Hofer and Martineau. 'I think he's enjoying himself.'

Hoffer nodded. 'Most definitely. A marvelous place and a most charming hostess.'

'However reluctant,' Martineau commented acidly. 'But too well bred to show it. The English upper classes are always the same.'

'Perhaps,' Necker said coldly. 'And understandably so. Her husband, after all, is a major in the British Army.'

'And therefore an enemy of the Reich, but then I hardly need remind you of that.'

Martineau picked up another glass of champagne and walked away. Sarah was surrounded by the naval officers and Guido was taking a photo. She waved and Martineau joined them.

'Please, Max,' she said. 'We must have a photo together.'

He laughed lightly and handed his glass to Bruno. 'Why not?'

The others moved to one side and he and Sarah stood there together in the sunshine. She felt strange, remembering what Helen had said, her hand tightening on his arm as if trying desperately to hold on.

Guido smiled. 'That's fine.'

'Good.' Martineau retrieved his champagne from Bruno. 'And now I must speak to the field marshal. You'll look after Anne-Marie for me, Lieutenant?' he said to Guido and walked away.

He'd noticed Muller arrive, rather later than everyone else. He was standing talking to Necker, and behind him, a military police motorcycle drove up with Greiser in the saddle. Martineau paused, watching. Greiser got off, pushed the motorcycle up on its stand and approached Muller, who made his excuses to Necker and moved away, listening to what the sergeant had to say. After a while, he looked around as if searching for someone. When he found Martineau, he crossed the grass toward him.

'I wonder if I might have a few words in private, Standartenführer?'

'Of course,' Martineau said, and they moved away from the others, walking toward the trees. 'What can I do for you?'

'My man Kleist was killed last night. A messy business. His car went over a cliff at La Moye.'

'Not good,' Martineau said. 'Had he been drinking?'

'Perhaps,' Muller replied cautiously. 'The thing is we can't think of any convincing reason for him having been there. It's a remote sort of place.'

'A woman perhaps?' Martineau suggested.

'No sign of another body.'

'A mystery then, but what has it to do with me?' Martineau knew, of course, what was to come.

'We ran a routine check with the military police patrols in that sector in case they'd noticed his car.'

'And had they?'

'No, but we have got a report that you were stopped in your Kubelwagen on Route du Sud at approximately two o'clock this morning.'

'Correct,' Martineau told him calmly. 'But what has that to do with the matter in hand?'

'To get to the area of La Moye where Kleist met with his unfortunate accident it would be necessary to drive along Route du Sud, then take the Corbiere road.'

'Do get to the point, Muller, the field marshal is expecting me.'

'Very well, Standartenführer. I was wondering what you were doing there at two o'clock in the morning.'

'It's quite simple,' Martineau said. 'I was about my business, under direct orders of the Reichsführer, as you well know. When I return to Berlin he will expect a report on what I found here in Jersey. I'm sorry to say it will not be favorable.'

Muller frowned. 'Perhaps you could explain, Standartenführer.'

'Security for one thing,' Martineau told him. 'Or the lack of it. Yes, Muller, I was stopped by a military police patrol on Route du Sud this morning. I left de Ville Place at midnight, drove through St. Peter's Valley, up to the village and along to Greve de Lecq. Just after one o'clock I reached L'Etacq at the north end of St. Ouen's Bay, having taken a back lane around Les Landes. A defense area, am I right?'

'Yes, Standartenführer.'

'And the places all have important military installations?'

'True.'

'I'm glad you agree. I then drove along the bay to Corbiere lighthouse and was eventually stopped in Route du Sud by two military policemen who appeared to be having a smoke at the side of the road. You do get the point, don't you, Muller?' His face was hard and dangerous. 'I drove around this island in the early hours of the morning close to some of our most sensitive installations and only got stopped once.' He allowed his voice to rise so that officers nearby turned curiously. 'Would you say that was satisfactory?'

'No, Standartenführer.'

'Then I suggest you do something about it.' Martineau put his glass down on a nearby table. 'And now I think I've kept the field marshal waiting long enough.'

As he walked away, Greiser joined Muller. 'What happened?'

'Nothing very much. He says he was on a tour of inspection. Says that in two hours of touring the west of the island, he was only stopped once – on Route du Sud.'

'Do you believe him, Herr Captain?'

'Oh, it fits well enough,' Muller said. 'Unfortunately we're back with that policeman's nose of mine. He was in the area, that's a fact, and I hate coincidences.'

'So what shall I do?'

'When they get poor old Willi's body up, get it straight in for a postmortem. If he was awash with schnapps when he died, at least it will show and we'll know where we are.'

'All right, Herr Captain, I'll see to it.' Greiser went back to his motorcycle, mounted and rode away quickly.

Baum, talking to Helen and a couple of officers, turned as Martineau approached. 'Ah, there you are, Vogel. I'm in your debt for suggesting my visit to such a delightful spot.'

'A pleasure, Herr Field Marshal.'

'Come, we'll walk a while and you can tell me how things are in Berlin these days.' He took Helen's hand and kissed it. 'You'll excuse us, Frau de Ville?'

'Of course, Herr Field Marshal.'

Martineau and Baum turned away and strolled across the grass toward the trees, taking the path that led to the rampart walk with its view of the bay. 'This whole thing becomes more like a bad play by the minute,' Baum said.

'Yes, well we don't have time right now to discuss what Brecht might have made of it. This is what happens. The mail plane leaves at eight. They expect you to fly out in the Storch at about the same time.'

'So?'

'I'll turn up at Septembertide at seven. I'll have Sarah with me, also Kelso in Kriegsmarine uniform and heavily bandaged.'

'And how does Hofer react?'

'He does exactly as he's told. I've got a syringe and a strong sedative, courtesy of the doctor who's been treating Kelso. An armful of that and he'll be out for hours. We'll lock him in his bedroom.'

'When does this happen?'

'I'd say the best time would be at the end of your tour when you return to Septembertide. Probably around five o'clock. Get rid of Necker and the others, but ask me to stay for a drink.'

'But how do I explain his absence at the airport?'

'Simple. Necker will be there with his staff to bid you a fond farewell. It's at that point you announce you intend to fly out in the mail plane. You can't arrange it earlier because Hofer would want to know what you were up to. You tell Necker that the chief medical officer at the hospital has made representations on behalf of this sailor, badly wounded in the convoy attack the other night and in urgent need of specialist treatment on the mainland. As you're using the bigger plane, you're giving me and Sarah a lift.'

'And Hofer?'

'Tell Necker that Hofer is following behind. That he's going to fly out in the Storch on his own.'

'And you think all this will work?'

'Yes,' Martineau said, 'because it's actually rather simple. I could have tried something like it without you, using my letter from the Reichsführer, but perhaps the Luftwaffe commanding officer here would have insisted on getting permission from Luftwaffe HQ in Normandy.' He smiled. 'But to Erwin Rommel, nobody says no.'

Baum sighed, took the cigarette Martineau offered and fitted it into the holder. 'I'll never get a role as good as this again. Never.'

15

On the slab in the postmortem room at the general hospital, Willi Kleist's corpse looked even more appalling. Major Speer stood waiting while the two medical corporals who were assisting him carefully cut away the burned clothing. Greiser, standing by the door, watched in fascinated horror.

Speer turned to look at him. 'If you feel like being sick, the bucket is over there. Nothing to be ashamed of.'

'Thank you, Herr Major. Captain Muller asked me to tell you how much he appreciates your attending to him personally.'

'I understand, Sergeant. Discretion, in a case like this, is of the utmost importance. So, we are ready?'

The last vestiges of clothing were stripped away, and one of the corporals washed the body down with a fine spray, while the other wheeled across a trolley on which a selection of surgical instruments had been laid out.

'I'd normally start with taking out the brain,' Speer said cheerfully. 'But in this case, speed being of the essence, or so you inform me, we'll have the organs out first so the lab technicians can get on with their side of things.'

The scalpel in his right hand didn't seem particularly large, but when he ran it down from just below the throat to the belly, the flesh parted instantly. The smell was terrible, but Greiser hung on, a handkerchief to his mouth. Speer worked at speed, removing the heart, the liver, the kidneys, all being taken away in enamel basins to the laboratory next door.

Speer seemed to have forgotten about Greiser. One of the corporals passed him a small electric saw which plugged into a floor socket. When he started on the skull, Greiser could take no more and removed himself hurriedly to the lavatory where he was violently sick.

Afterward, he sat outside in the corridor and smoked. A young nurse with an Irish accent came up and put a hand on his shoulder. 'You look awful.'

'I've just been watching them do a postmortem,' Greiser told her.

'Yes, well it gets you like that the first time. I'll bring you a coffee.'

She meant well, but it was not the real thing: acorn coffee, a taste Greiser found particularly loathsome. He lit another cigarette and walked down to the main entrance and phoned through to Muller at the Silvertide from the porter's desk.

'It's Greiser, Herr Captain.'

'How are things going?' Muller asked.

'Well, it's hardly one of life's great experiences, but Major Speer obviously knows his stuff. I'm waiting for his conclusions now. They're doing lab tests.'

'You might as well hang on until they're ready. An interesting development. I've had your brother on the phone from Stuttgart. He's heard from this Neumann woman in Berlin. The one who works in the Reichsführer's office at the Chancellery.'

'And?'

'She's never heard of Vogel. She's kept her inquiries discreet for the moment. Of course, as your brother points out, these special envoys of Himmler are mystery men to everyone else.'

'Yes, but you'd think someone like Lotte Neumann would have at least heard of him,' Greiser said. 'What are you going to do?'

'Think about it. As soon as Speer's ready with those results, give me a ring and I'll come around myself to see what he has to say.'

It was just before five when the cavalcade of cars returned to Septembertide. Baum and Hofer got out and Necker joined them with one or two officers. Martineau stood at the back of the group and waited. 'A memorable day, Major,' Baum said. 'I'm truly grateful.'

'I'm pleased everything has gone so well, Herr Field Marshal.'

'How long does it take to the airport from here?'

'No more than ten minutes.'

'Good. We'll see you up there sometime between seven-thirty and eight.'

Necker saluted, turned and got back into his car. As the officers dispersed, Baum and Hofer turned to the front door and Martineau stepped forward. 'Might I have a word, Herr Field Marshal?'

Hofer was immediately wary, but Baum said cheerfully, 'Of course, Standartenführer. Come in.'

At that moment Heider, the platoon commander, appeared in the gateway and saluted. 'Is there anything I can do for you, Herr Field Marshal?'

'What about the cook we had last night?'

'I'll send him over.'

'Not for half an hour, Heider.'

He went inside followed by Hofer and Martineau. They went into the living room. Baum took off his leather coat and his cap and opened the glass door to the terrace. 'A drink, Standartenführer?'

'That would be very acceptable.'

'Konrad.' Baum nodded to Hofer. 'Cognac, I think. You'll join us?'

He fitted a cigarette to his holder, and Martineau gave him a light as Hofer poured the drinks. 'What an extraordinary view,' Baum said, looking down at St. Aubin's Bay. 'In peacetime, with the lights on at night down there, it must resemble Monte Carlo. Wouldn't you think so, Konrad?'

'Perhaps, Herr Field Marshal.' Hofer was nervous and trying not to show it, wondering what Vogel wanted.

'To us, gentlemen.' Baum raised his glass. 'To soldiers everywhere who always bear the burden of man's stupidity.' He emptied his glass, smiled and said in English, 'All right, Harry, let's get on with it.'

Hofer looked totally bewildered and Martineau produced the Walther with the Carswell silencer from his trenchcoat pocket. 'It would be stupid to make me shoot you. Nobody would hear a thing.' He removed the Mauser from Hofer's holster. 'Sit down.'

'Who are you?' Hofer demanded.

'Well I'm certainly not Standartenführer Max Vogel any more than Heini here is the Desert Fox.'

'Heini?' Hofer looked even more bewildered.

'That's me,' Baum said. 'Heini Baum. Erich Berger was killed in an air raid on Kiel. I took his papers and joined the paratroops.'

'But why?'

'Well, you see, Herr Captain, I happen to be Jewish, and what better place for a Jew to hide?'

'My God!' Hofer said hoarsely.

'Yes, I thought you'd like that. A Jew impersonating Germany's greatest war hero. A nice touch of irony there.'

Hofer turned to Martineau. 'And you?'

'My name is Martineau. Lieutenant Colonel Harry Martineau. I work for SOE. I'm sure you've heard of us.'

'Yes.' Hofer reached for his glass and finished the rest of his brandy. 'I think you can say that.'

'Your boss is a lucky man. I was close to putting a bullet in him last night after you'd gone to bed. Happily for our friend here, he likes to talk to himself and I discovered all was not as it seemed.'

'So what do you intend to do?' Hofer asked.

'Simple. Field Marshal Rommel flies out in the mail plane tonight, not the Storch, which means I can leave with him, along with a couple of friends. Destination England.'

'The young lady?' Hofer managed a smile. 'I liked her. I presume she also is not what she seems.'

'One more thing,' Martineau said, 'but it's important. You might wonder why I don't shoot you. Well, Heini having a bad habit of listening at doors, I know where Rommel has been this weekend and what he's been up to. The assassination of Hitler at this stage of the war would suit the Allied cause very well. In the circumstances, when we get back to England and I tell my people about this business, I think you'll find they keep very quiet. We wouldn't want to make things too difficult for Field Marshal Rommel, if you follow me. More power to his arm. I want you to live so you can tell him that.'

'And how does he explain to the Führer what happened here?'

'I should have thought that rather simple. There's been more than one plot against Rommel's life already by French Resistance and Allied agents. The British nearly got him in North Africa, remember. To use Berger to impersonate him on occasion made good sense, and what happened here in Jersey proved it. If he'd come himself, he'd have died here. The fact that Berger has decided to change sides is regrettable, but hardly your fault.'

'Now you say Berger again.'

'I think he means you might overcomplicate things if you introduce the Jewish bit,' Heini told him.

'Something like that.' Martineau stood up. 'All right, let's have you upstairs.'

Hofer did as he was told, because he didn't have any choice in the matter, and they followed him up and along the corridor to the small bedroom he had been using.

Through the half-drawn curtains he could see into the courtyard and over the wall to where Heider stood beside one of the armored personnel carriers.

'Obviously you don't intend to kill me,' he said.

'Of course not. I need you to tell all to Rommel, don't I?' Martineau replied. 'Just keep still and don't make a fuss and you'll be fine.'

There was a burning pain in Hofer's right arm and almost instantaneous darkness. Baum emptied the contents of the syringe before pulling it out, and Martineau eased the major down onto the bed, arranged his limbs in a comfortable position and covered him with a blanket.

They went down to the hall. Martineau said, 'Seven o'clock.'

As he opened the front door, the cook corporal from the night before walked across the courtyard. Baum said, 'I'll see you later then, Standartenführer.'

He turned and walked back inside to the living room and the corporal followed. 'At your orders, Herr Field Marshal.'

'Something simple,' Baum said. 'Scrambled eggs, toast and coffee, I think. Just for me. Major Hofer isn't feeling too well. He's having a rest before we leave.'

In Gallagher's cottage, he and Martineau eased Kelso into the Kriegsmarine uniform while Sarah stayed discreetly out of the way in the kitchen. Gallagher cut the right trouser leg so that it would fit over the cast.

'How's that?' he asked.

'Not bad.' Kelso hesitated then said awkwardly, 'There's a lot of people putting themselves on the line because of me.'

'Oh, I see,' Martineau said. 'You mean you deliberately got yourself blown over the rail of that LST in Lyme Bay?'

'No, of course not.'

'Then stop agonizing,' Martineau told him and called to Sarah: 'You can come in now.'

She entered from the kitchen with two large bandage rolls and surgical tape. She went to work on Kelso's face and head, leaving only one eye and the mouth visible.

'That's really very professional,' Gallagher said.

'I am a professional, you fool,' she told him.

He grinned amiably. 'Jesus, girl, I bet you look great in that nurse's uniform.'

Martineau glanced at his watch. It was almost six o'clock. 'We'll go up to the house now, General. You keep an eye on him. I'll be back with the Kubelwagen in an hour.'

He and Sarah left, and Gallagher went into the hall and came back with a pair of crutches. 'Present for you.' He propped them against the table. 'See how you get on.'

Kelso pushed himself up on one leg, got first one crutch under an arm and then the other. He took one hesitant step forward, paused, then moved on with increasing confidence, until he reached the other side of the room.

'Brilliant!' Gallagher told him. 'Long John Silver to the life. Now try again.'

'Are you certain?' Muller asked.

'Oh, it's quite definite,' Speer said. 'I'll show you.' The brain slopped about in the enamel basin and he turned it over in gloved hands. 'See the pink discoloration at the base? That's blood, and that's what gave me the clue. Something sharp sheared right up through the roof of the mouth into the brain.'

'Is it likely such an injury would be explained by the kind of accident he was in?'

'Oh, no,' Speer said. 'Whatever did this was as razor sharp as a scalpel. The external flesh of the face and neck is badly burned and I can't be certain, but if you want my opinion, he was stabbed under the chin. Does that make any kind of sense?'

'Yes,' Muller said. 'I think it does. Thanks very much.' He nodded to Greiser. 'Let's go.'

As he reached the door and opened it, Speer said, 'Oh, one more thing.'

'What's that?'

'You were quite right. He had been drinking heavily. I'd say, from the tests, about a bottle and a half of spirits.'

On the steps outside the main entrance of the hospital, Muller paused to light a cigarette. 'What do you think, Herr Captain?' Greiser asked.

'That another word with Standartenführer Vogel is indicated, Ernst, so let's get moving.'

He got into the passenger seat of the Citroën. Greiser slid behind the wheel and drove away.

In the kitchen at de Ville Place, Sarah, Helen and Martineau sat round the table. The door opened and Guido came in with a bottle. 'Warm champagne,' he said. 'The best I can do.'

'Are you certain the place is empty?' Sarah asked.

'Oh, yes. Bruno was the last to leave. They're all on tonight's convoy to Granville. Kriegsmarine Headquarters haven't come up with a new assignment for me yet.'

He pulled the cork and poured champagne into the four kitchen glasses Helen provided. She raised hers. 'What shall we drink to?'

'Better days,' Sarah said.

'And life, liberty and the pursuit of happiness,' Guido added, 'not forgetting love.'

'You wouldn't.' Sarah kissed his cheek and turned to Martineau. 'And you, Harry, what do you wish?'

'One day at a time is all I can manage.' He finished the champagne. 'My God, that tastes awful.' He put down the glass. 'I'll go and get Kelso now. Be ready to leave when I get back, Sarah.'

He went out, got into the Kubelwagen and drove away, taking the track down through the wood. At the same time, two hundred yards to the right, the Citroën carrying Muller and Greiser moved along the road to de Ville Place and turned into the courtyard.

In the bedroom, Sarah put on her hat and coat, turning to check in the mirror that her stocking seams were straight. She freshened her mouth with lipstick and made a face at herself in the mirror. 'Goodbye, little French tart, it's been nice knowing you.'

At that moment she heard a car outside and glanced out of the window and saw Muller get out of the Citroën. It was trouble, she knew that instantly. She opened her handbag. The PPK was in there but also the little Belgian automatic Kelly had given her. She lifted her skirt and slipped the smaller gun into the top of her right stocking. It fit surprisingly snugly. She smoothed down her coat and left the room.

Muller was in the hall talking to Helen, Greiser over by the entrance. Guido was standing by the green baize door leading to the kitchen. As Sarah came down the stairs, Muller looked up and saw her.

'Ah, there you are, mademoiselle,' Helen said in French. 'Captain Muller was looking for the Standartenführer. Do you know where he is?'

'I've no idea,' Sarah said continuing on down. 'Is there a problem?'

'Perhaps.' Muller took her handbag from her quite gently, opened it and removed the PPK which he put in his pocket. He handed the bag back to her. 'You've no idea when he'll be back?'

'None at all,' Sarah said.

'But you are dressed to go out?'

'Mademoiselle Latour was going to take a walk in the grounds with me,' Guido put in.

Muller nodded. 'Very well, if the Standartenführer isn't available, I'll have to make do with you.' He said to Greiser. 'Take her out to the car.'

'But I protest,' Sarah started to say.

Greiser smiled, his fingers hooking painfully into her arm. 'You protest all you like, sweetheart. I like it,' and he hustled her through the door.

Muller turned to Helen who managed to stay calm with difficulty. 'Perhaps you would be good enough to tell Standartenführer Vogel on his return that if he wishes to see Mademoiselle Latour, he must come to the Silvertide,' and he turned and walked out.

Kelso was doing quite well with the crutches. He made it to the Kubelwagen under his own steam, and Gallagher helped him into the rear seat. 'Nice going, me old son.'

Martineau got behind the wheel and Guido emerged from the trees on the run. He leaned against the car, gasping.

'What is it, man?' Gallagher demanded.

'Muller and Greiser turned up. They were looking for you, Harry.'

'And?' Martineau's face was very pale.

'They've taken Sarah. Muller says if you want to see her, you'll have to go to the Silvertide. What are we going to do?'

'Get in!' Martineau said and drove away as the Italian and Gallagher scrambled aboard.

He braked to a halt in the courtyard where Helen waited anxiously on the steps. She hurried down and leaned in the Kubelwagen. 'What are we going to do, Harry?'

'I'll take Kelso up to Septembertide to connect with Baum. If worse comes to worst, they can fly off into the blue together. Baum knows what to do.'

'But we can't leave Sarah,' Kelso protested.

'I can't,' Martineau said, 'but you can, so don't give me a lot of false sentimentality. You're what brought us here in the first place. The reason for everything.'

Helen clutched his arm. 'Harry!'

'Don't worry. I'll think of something.'

'Such as?' Gallagher demanded.

'I don't know,' Martineau said. 'But you keep out of it, that's essential. We'll have to go.'

The Kubelwagen moved away across the yard, and the noise of the engine faded. Gallagher turned to Guido. 'Get the Morris out and you and I'll take a run down to the Silvertide.'

'What do you have in mind?' Guido asked.

'God knows. I never could stand just sitting around and waiting, that's all.'

Martineau drove into the courtyard at Septembertide and braked to a halt. He helped Kelso out and the American followed him, swinging between his crutches. The door was opened by the corporal. As they went in, Baum appeared from the sitting room.

'Ah, there you are, Vogel! And this is the young man you told me about?' He turned to the corporal. 'Dismissed. I'll call you when I want you.'

Baum stood back and Kelso moved past him into the sitting room. Martineau said, 'There's been a change of plan. Muller came looking for me at de Ville Place. As it happens, I wasn't around at the right moment, but Sarah was. They've taken her to the Silvertide.'

'Don't tell me, let me guess,' Baum said. 'You're going to go to the rescue.'

'Something like that.'

'And what about us?'

Martineau glanced at his watch. It was just after seven. 'You and Kelso keep to your schedule. Getting him out of here is what's important.'

'Now look here,' Kelso began, but Martineau had already walked out.

The Kubelwagen roared out of the courtyard. Kelso turned and found Baum pouring cognac into a glass. He drank it slowly. 'That's really very good.'

'What goes on here?' the American demanded.

'I was thinking of Martineau,' Baum said. 'I might have known that under all that surface cynicism he was the kind of man who'd go back for the girl. I was at Stalingrad, did you know that? I've had enough of heroes to last me for a lifetime.'

He pulled on his leather trenchcoat and gloves, twisted the white scarf around his neck, adjusted the angle of the cap and picked up his baton.

'What are you going to do?' Kelso demanded.

'Martineau told me that the important thing about being Field Marshal

Erwin Rommel was that everyone would do what I told them to do. Now we'll see if he's right. You stay here.'

He strode through the courtyard into the road and the men leaning beside the personnel carrier sprang to attention. 'One of you get Captain Heider.'

Baum took out a cigarette and fitted it in his holder. A sergeant sprang forward with a light. A second later Heider hurried out. 'Herr Field Marshal?'

'Get through to the airport. A message for Major Necker. I shall be a little later than I thought. Tell him also that I shall leave for France, not in my Storch, but in the mail plane. I expect it waiting and ready to go when I arrive, and I'd like my personal pilot to fly it.'

'Very well, Herr Field Marshal.'

'Excellent. I need them all, fully armed and ready to go in five minutes. You'll find a wounded sailor in Septembertide. Have a couple of men help him out and put him in the personnel carrier. And they can bring the corporal you loaned me with them, too. No sense in leaving him hanging around the kitchen.'

'But Herr Field Marshal, I don't understand,' the captain said.

'You will, Heider,' the field marshal told him. 'You will. Now send that message to the airport.'

Muller had drawn the curtains in his office and Sarah sat on a chair in front of his desk, hands folded in her lap, knees together. They'd made her take off her coat and Greiser was searching the lining while Muller went through the handbag.

He said, 'So you are from Paimpol?'

'That's right.'

'Sophisticated clothes for a Breton girl from a fishing village.'

'Oh, but she's been around this one, haven't you?' Greiser ran his fingers up and down her neck, making her flesh crawl.

Muller said, 'Where did you and Standartenführer Vogel meet?'

'Paris,' she said.

'But there is no visa for Paris among your papers.'

'I had one. It ran out.'

'Have you ever heard of the Cherche Midi or the women's prison at Troyes? Bad places for a young woman like you to be.'

'I don't know what you're talking about. I've done nothing,' she said.

Her stomach contracted with fear, her throat was dry. Oh, God, Harry, she thought, fly away. Just fly away. And then the door opened and Martineau walked into the office.

There were tears in her eyes and she had never known such emotion as Greiser stood back and Harry put an arm around her gently.

The emotion she felt was so overwhelming that she committed the greatest blunder of all then. 'Oh, you bloody fool,' she said in English. 'Why didn't you go?'

Muller smiled gently and picked up the Mauser that lay on his desk. 'So, you speak English also, mademoiselle. This whole business becomes even more intriguing. I think you'd better relieve the Standartenführer of his Walther, Ernst.'

Greiser did as he was told, and Martineau said in German, 'Do you know what you're doing, Muller? There's a perfectly good reason for Mademoiselle Latour to speak English. Her mother was English. The facts are on file at SD headquarters in Paris. You can check.'

'You have an answer for everything,' Muller said. 'What if I told you that a postmortem has indicated that Willi Kleist was murdered last night? The medical examiner indicates the time of death as being between midnight and two o'clock. I need hardly remind you that it was two o'clock when you were stopped on Route du Sud, no more than a mile from where the body was discovered. What do you have to say to that?'

'I can only imagine you've been grossly overworking. Your career's on the line here, Muller, you realize that. When the Reichsführer hears the full facts he'll . . .'

For the first time Muller almost lost his temper. 'Enough of this. I've been a policeman all my life – a good policeman and I detest violence. However, there are those with a different attitude. Greiser here, for instance. A strange thing about Greiser. He doesn't like women. He would actually find it pleasurable to discuss this whole affair in private with Mademoiselle Latour, but I doubt that she would.'

'Oh, I don't know.' Greiser put an arm around Sarah and slipped a hand inside her dress, fondling a breast. 'I think she might get to like it after I've taught her her manners.'

Sarah's left hand clawed down his face, drawing blood, only feeling rage now, more powerful than she had ever known. As Greiser staggered back, her hand went up her skirt, pulling the tiny automatic from her stocking. Her arm swung up and she fired at point-blank range, shooting Muller between the eyes. The Mauser dropped from his nerveless hand to the desk; he staggered back against the wall and fell to the floor. Greiser tried to get his own gun from his pocket, too late as Martineau picked up the Mauser from the desk.

★   ★   ★

Gallagher and Guido were sitting in the Morris on the other side of the road from the Silvertide when they heard the sound of approaching vehicles. They turned to see a military column approaching. The lead vehicle was a Kubelwagen with the top down and Field Marshal Erwin Rommel standing in the passenger seat for the whole world to see. The Kubelwagen braked to a halt, he got out as the soldiers, carried by the other vehicles in the column, jumped down and ran forward in obedience to Heider's shouted orders.

'Right, follow me!' Baum called and marched straight in through the entrance of the Silvertide. A moment after Sarah fired the shot that killed Muller, the door crashed open and Baum appeared. He advanced into the room, Heider and a dozen armed men behind him. He peered over the desk at Muller's body.

Greiser said, 'Herr Field Marshal, this woman has murdered Captain Muller.'

Baum ignored him and said to Heider, 'Put this man in a cell.'

'Yes, Herr Field Marshal.' Heider nodded and three of his men grabbed the protesting Greiser. Heider followed them out.

'Back in your vehicles,' Baum shouted to the others and held Sarah's coat for her. 'Can we go now?'

Gallagher and Guido saw them come out of the entrance to the hotel and get into the Kubelwagen, Martineau and Sarah in the back, Baum standing up in front. He waved his arm, the Kubelwagen led off, the whole column following.

'Now what do we do?' Guido asked.

'Jesus, is there no poetry in you at all?' Gallagher demanded. 'We follow them, of course. I wouldn't miss the last act for anything.'

At Septembertide, on the bed in the small room, Konrad Hofer groaned and moved restlessly. The sedative the doctor had given Martineau was, like most of his drugs, of prewar vintage, and Hofer was no longer completely unconscious. He opened his eyes, mouth dry, and stared at the ceiling, trying to work out where he was. It was like awaking from a bad dream, something you knew had been terrible and yet already forgotten. And then he remembered, tried to sit up and rolled off the bed to the floor.

He pulled himself up, head swimming, and reached for the door handle. It refused to budge and he turned and lurched across to the window. He fumbled with the catch and then gave up the struggle and slammed his elbow through the pane.

The sound of breaking glass brought the two soldiers Captain Heider had left on sentry duty at Hinguette next door running into the courtyard. They stared up, machine pistols at the ready, a young private and an older man, a corporal.

'Up here!' Hofer called. 'Get me out. I'm locked in.'

He sat on the bed, his head in his hands, and tried to breathe deeply, aware of the sound of their boots clattering up the stairs and along the corridor. He could hear voices, saw the handle turn.

'There's no key, Herr Hofer,' one of them called.

'Then break it down, you fool!' he replied.

A moment later, the door burst open, crashing against the wall, and they stood staring at him.

'Get Captain Heider,' Hofer said.

'He's gone, Herr Major.'

'Gone?' Hofer still had difficulty thinking clearly.

'With the field marshal, Herr Major. The whole unit went with them. We're the only two here.'

The effects of the drug made Hofer feel as if he were underwater and he shook his head vigorously. 'Did they leave any vehicles?'

'There's a Kubelwagen, Herr Major,' the corporal told him.

'Can you drive?'

'Of course, sir. Where does the Herr Major wish to go?'

'The airport,' Hofer said. 'And there's no time to lose, so help me downstairs and let's get moving.'

16

At the airport, the Luftwaffe honor guard waited patiently as darkness fell. The same group of officers who had greeted the field marshal on his arrival now presented themselves to say goodbye. The Storch was parked on the far side of the JU52, which awaited its illustrious passenger some fifty yards from the terminal building. Necker paced up and down anxiously, wondering what on earth was going on. First of all that extraordinary message from Heider at Mont de la Rocque about the mail plane and now this. Twenty minutes past eight and still no sign.

There was the sudden roar of engines, the rattle of a halftrack on concrete. He turned in time to witness the extraordinary sight of the armored column coming around the corner of the main airport building, the field marshal standing up in the Kubelwagen at the front, hands braced on the edge of the windshield.

The column made straight for the Junkers. Necker saw the field marshal wave to Sorsa in the cockpit, who was looking out of the side window. The center engine of the plane coughed into life, and Rommel was turning and waving, barking orders. Soldiers leaped from the trucks, rifles ready. Necker recognized Heider and then saw a bandaged sailor being taken from the personnel carrier by two soldiers who led him to the Junkers and helped him inside.

The whole thing had happened in seconds. As Necker started forward, the field marshal came to meet him. It was noisy now as the Junkers' wing engines also started to turn. To Necker's further astonishment he saw, beyond the field marshal, Standartenführer Vogel and the French girl dismount from the personnel carrier and go up the short ladder into the plane.

Baum was enjoying himself. The ride up from the Silvertide had been truly exhilarating, and he smiled and put a hand on Necker's shoulder. 'My deepest apologies, Necker, but I had things to do. Young Heider was good enough to assist me with his men. A promising officer.'

Necker was truly bewildered. 'But, Herr Field Marshal . . .' he began.

Baum carried on. 'The chief medical officer at the hospital told me of this young sailor wounded in some convoy attack the other night and badly in need of treatment at the burns unit in Rennes. He asked me if I'd take him with me. Of course, in the state he's in we'd never have got him into the Storch. That's why I need the mail plane.'

'And Standartenführer Vogel?'

'He was going back tomorrow anyway, so I might as well give him and the young woman a lift.' He clapped Necker on the shoulder again. 'But we must be off now. Again, my thanks for all you've done. I shall, of course, be in touch with General von Schmettow to express my entire satisfaction with the way things are in Jersey.'

He saluted and turned to go up the ladder into the plane. Necker called, 'But, Herr Field Marshal, what about Major Hofer?'

'He should be arriving any minute,' Baum told him. 'He'll leave in the Storch as arranged. The mail plane pilot can fly him across.'

He scrambled inside the plane; the crewman pulled up the ladder and closed the door. The Junkers taxied away to the east end of the runway and turned. There was a deepening roar from the three engines as it moved faster and faster, a silhouette only in the gathering gloom, and then it lifted, drifting out over St. Ouen's Bay, still climbing.

★   ★   ★

Guido had parked the Morris a couple of hundred yards along the airport road. Standing there beside it, they saw the Junkers lift into the evening sky and fly west to where the horizon was tipped with fire.

The noise of the engines faded into the distance and Guido said softly, 'My God, they actually pulled it off.'

Gallagher nodded. 'So now we can go home and get our stories straight for when all the questioning starts.'

'No problem,' Guido said. 'Not if we stick together. I am, after all, an authentic war hero, which always helps.'

'That's what I love about you, Guido. Your engaging modesty,' Gallagher told him. 'Now let's move. Helen will be getting worried.'

They got into the Morris and Guido drove away quickly, a Kubelwagen passing them a moment later coming the other way, driving so fast that they failed to see Hofer sitting in the rear seat.

At the airport, most of the officers had dispersed, but Necker was standing by his car talking to Captain Adler, the Luftwaffe duty control officer, when the Kubelwagen came around the corner of the main airport building and braked to a halt. They turned to see Hofer being helped out of the rear seat by the two soldiers.

Necker knew trouble when he saw it. 'Hofer? What is it?'

Hofer slumped against the Kubelwagen. 'Have they gone?'

'Less than five minutes ago. The field marshal took the mail plane. He said you'd follow in the Storch. He took his own pilot.'

'No!' Hofer said. 'Not the field marshal.'

Necker's stomach contracted. So many things that had worried him and yet . . . He took a deep breath. 'What are you saying?'

'That the man you thought was Field Marshal Rommel is his double, a damn traitor called Berger who's thrown in his lot with the enemy. You'll also be happy to know that Standartenführer Max Vogel is an agent of the British Special Operations Executive. So is the girl, by the way. The wounded sailor is an American colonel.'

But Necker, by now, was totally bewildered. 'I don't understand any of this.'

'It's really quite simple,' Hofer told him. 'They're flying to England in the mail plane.' His head was suddenly clearer and he stood up. 'Naturally, they must be stopped.' He turned to Adler. 'Get on the radio to Cherbourg. Scramble a night fighter squadron. Now let's get moving. There's no time to lose.' He turned and led the way to the operations building.

The Junkers was a workhorse and not built for comfort. Most of the interior was crammed with mail sacks and Kelso sat on the floor propped against them, legs outstretched. Sarah was on a bench on one side of the plane, Baum and Martineau on the other.

The crewman came out of the cockpit and joined them. 'My name is Braun, Herr Field Marshal. Sergeant observer. If there is anything I can get you. We have a Thermos flask of coffee and . . .'

'Nothing, thank you.' Baum took out his cigarette case and offered Martineau one.

'And Oberleutnant Sorsa would take it as an honor if you would care to come up front.'

'You don't have a full crew? Just the two of you?' Martineau inquired.

'All that's necessary on these mail runs, Standartenführer.'

'Tell Oberleutnant Sorsa I'll be happy to take him up on his offer a little later. I'll just finish my cigarette,' Baum said.

'Certainly, Herr Field Marshal.'

Braun opened the door and went back into the cockpit. Baum turned to Martineau and smiled. 'Five minutes?'

'That should be about right.' Martineau moved across to sit beside Sarah. He gave her his lighted cigarette. 'Are you all right?'

'Absolutely.'

'You're sure?'

'You mean am I going through hell because I just killed a man?' Her face was very calm. 'Not at all. My one regret is that it was Muller instead of Greiser. He was from under a stone. Muller was just a policeman on the wrong side.'

'From our point of view.'

'No, Harry,' she said. 'Most wars are a stupidity. This one isn't. We're right and the Nazis are wrong. They're wrong for Germany and they're wrong for everyone else. It's as simple as that.'

'Good for you,' Kelso said. 'A lady who stands up to be counted. I like that.'

'I know,' Martineau said. 'It's wonderful to be young.' He tapped Baum on the knee. 'Ready?'

'I think so.'

Martineau took his Walther from its holster and gave it to Sarah. 'Action stations. You'll need that to take care of the observer. Here we go.'

He opened the cabin door and he and Baum squeezed into the cockpit behind the pilot and the observer. Oberleutnant Sorsa turned. 'Everything to your satisfaction, Field Marshal?'

'I think you could say that,' Baum told him.

'If there is anything we can do for you?'

'There is actually. You can haul this thing round and fly forty miles due west until we are completely clear of all Channel Islands traffic.'

'But I don't understand.'

Baum took the Mauser from his holster and touched it against the back of Sorsa's neck. 'Perhaps this will help you.'

'Later on when I call you, you'll turn north,' Martineau said, 'and make for England.'

'England?' young Braun said in horror.

'Yes,' Martineau told him. 'As they say, for you, the war is over. Frankly, the way it's shaping up, you're well out of it.'

'This is crazy,' Sorsa said.

'If it helps you to believe that the field marshal is proceeding to England as a special envoy of the Führer, why not?' Martineau said. 'Now change course like a good boy.'

Sorsa did as he was told and the Junkers plowed on through the darkness. Martineau leaned over Braun. 'Right, now for the radio. Show me the frequency selection procedure.' Braun did as he was told. 'Good. Now go and sit down in the cabin and don't do anything stupid. The lady has a gun.'

The boy squeezed past him, and Martineau got into the copilot's seat and started to transmit on the frequency reserved by SOE for emergency procedure.

In the control room in the tower at Jersey Airport, Hofer and Necker waited anxiously while Adler spoke on the radio. A Luftwaffe corporal came up and spoke to him briefly.

Adler turned to the two officers. 'We've still got them on radar, but they appear to be moving due west out to sea.'

'My God!' Necker said.

Adler talked into the microphone for a moment, then turned to Hofer. 'All night fighters in the Brittany area were scrambled an hour ago for operations over the Reich. Heavy bombing raids expected over the Ruhr.'

'There must be something, for God's sake,' Hofer said.

Adler waved him to silence, listening, then put down the mike and turned, smiling. 'There is. One JU88S night fighter. Its port engine needed a check and it wasn't finished in time to leave with the rest of the squadron.'

'But is it now?' Necker demanded eagerly.

'Oh, yes.' Adler was enjoying himself. 'He's just taken off from Cherbourg.'

'But can he catch them?' Necker asked.

'Herr Major, that old crate they're flying in can do a hundred and eighty flat out. The JU88S with the new engine boosting system does better than four hundred. He'll be with them before they know it.'

Necker turned in triumph to Hofer. 'They'll have to turn back, otherwise he'll blow them out of the sky.'

But Hofer had been thinking about that, among other things. If the mail plane returned, it would mean only one thing. Martineau and the others would be flown to Berlin, and few people survived interrogation in the cellars of Gestapo Headquarters at Prince Albrechtstrasse. That couldn't be allowed to happen. Berger knew about Rommel's connection with the generals' plot against the Führer, and so did Martineau. Perhaps he'd even told the girl.

Hofer took a deep breath. 'No, we can't take a chance on their getting away.'

'Herr Major?' Adler turned inquiringly.

'Send an order to the pilot of that night fighter to shoot on sight. They mustn't reach England.'

'As you say, Herr Major.' Adler picked up the microphone.

Necker put a hand on Hofer's shoulder. 'You look terrible. Let's go down to the mess and get you a brandy. Adler will call us when things start to warm up.'

Hofer managed a weak smile. 'The best offer I've had tonight.' And they went out together.

Dougal Munro was at his Baker Street desk working late when Carter came in with the signal and passed it across. The brigadier read it quickly and smiled. 'Good God, this is extraordinary, even for Harry.'

'I know, sir. I've alerted Fighter Command about receiving them. Where do you want them to put down? I suppose Cornwall would be closest.'

'No, let's bring them all the way in. They can land where they started, Jack. Hornley Field. Let Fighter Command know. I want them down in one piece.'

'And General Eisenhower, sir?'

'We'll leave him until Kelso's actually on the ground.' Munro stood up and reached for his jacket. 'And we'll have the car round, Jack. We can get there in just over an hour. With any luck, we'll be able to greet them.'

In the mail plane the atmosphere was positively euphoric as Martineau left Heini Baum in the cockpit to keep an eye on Sorsa and joined the others.

'Everything okay?' Kelso asked.

'Couldn't be better. I've made contact with our people in England. They're going to provide an escort to take us in, courtesy of the RAF.' He turned and smiled at Sarah, taking her hand. She'd never seen him so excited. Suddenly he looked ten years younger. 'You all right?' he asked her.

'Fine, Harry. Just fine.'

'Dinner at the Ritz tomorrow night,' he said.

'By candlelight?'

'Even if I have to take my own.' He turned to Braun, the observer. 'You said something about coffee, didn't you?'

Braun started to get up and the plane bucked wildly as a great roaring filled the night, then dropped like a stone. Braun lost his balance and Kelso rolled on the floor with a cry of pain.

'Harry!' Sarah screamed. 'What is it?'

The plane regained some sort of stability and Martineau peered out one of the side windows. A hundred yards away on the port side flying parallel with them he saw a Junkers 88S, one of those deadly black twin-engined planes that had caused such catastrophic losses to RAF Bomber Command in the night skies of Europe.

'We've got trouble,' he said. 'Luftwaffe night fighter.' He turned and wrenched open the cabin door and leaned into the cockpit.

Sorsa glanced over his shoulder, face grim and pale in the cockpit lights. 'We've had it. He's come to take us back.'

'Has he said so?'

'No. No radio contact at all.'

'Why not? It doesn't make sense.'

The JU88S suddenly climbed steeply and disappeared, and it was Heini who gave the only possible answer to the question. 'Every kind of sense if they don't want us back, my friend.'

Martineau saw it all then. Something had gone wrong and it had to involve Hofer, and if that were so, the last thing he'd want was to have them back in Gestapo hands to bring down Erwin Rommel.

'What do I do?' Sorsa demanded. 'That thing can blow us out of the skies. I know. I've been flying one for two years now.'

At that moment, the roaring filled the night again, and the mail plane shuddered as cannon shell slammed into the fuselage. One came up through the floor of the cockpit, narrowly missing Sorsa, splinters shattering the windscreen. He pushed the column forward, going down in a steep dive into the cloud layer below, and the Junkers 88S roared overhead, passing like a dark shadow.

Martineau fell to one knee, but got the door open and scrambled out.

Several gaping holes had been punched into the fuselage of the plane and two windows were shattered. Kelso was on the floor, hanging onto a seat, and Sarah was crouched over Braun, who lay on his back, his uniform soaked with blood, eyes rolling. He jerked convulsively and lay still.

Sarah looked up, her face surprisingly calm. 'He's dead, Harry.'

There was nothing to say, couldn't be, and Martineau turned back to the cockpit, hanging on as the mail plane continued its steep dive down through the clouds. They rocked again in the turbulence as the Junkers 88S passed over them.

'Bastard!' Sorsa said, in a rage now. 'I'll show you.'

Baum, crouched on the floor, looked up at Harry with a ghastly smile. 'He's a Finn, remember? They don't really like us Germans very much.'

The mail plane burst out of the clouds at three thousand feet and kept on going down.

'What are you doing?' Martineau cried.

'Can't play hide and seek with him in that cloud. He'd get us for sure. Just one trick up my sleeve. He's very fast and I'm very slow and that makes it difficult for him.' Sorsa glanced over his shoulder again and smiled savagely. 'Let's see if he's any good.'

He kept on going down, was at seven or eight hundred feet when the Junkers 88S came in again on their tail, far too fast, banking to port to avoid a collision.

Sorsa took the mail plane down to five hundred and leveled off. 'Right, you swine, let's have you,' he said, hands steady as a rock.

In that moment Martineau saw genius at work, understood all those medals the Finn wore, the Knight's Cross, and a strange feeling of calm enveloped him. It was all so unreal, the lights from the instrument panel, the wind roaring in through the shattered windscreen.

And when it happened, it was over in seconds. The Junkers 88S swooped in on their tail again, and Sorsa hauled back the column and started to climb. The pilot of the Junkers 88S banked steeply to avoid what seemed like an inevitable collision, but at that height and speed had nowhere else to go but straight down into the waves below.

Sorsa's face was calm again. 'You lost, my friend,' he said softly and eased back the column. 'All right, let's get back upstairs.'

Martineau pushed back the door and glanced out. The inside of the plane was a shambles, wind blowing in through innumerable holes, Braun's blood-soaked body on the floor, Sarah crouched beside Kelso.

'You two all right?' he called.

'Fine. Don't worry about us. Is it over?' Sarah asked.

'You could say that.'

He turned back to the cockpit as Sorsa leveled out at six thousand feet. 'So, the old girl's leaking like a sieve, but everything appears to be functioning,' the Finn said.

'Let's try the radio.' Martineau squeezed into the co-pilot's seat. He twisted the dial experimentally but everything seemed to be in working order. 'I'll let them know what's happened,' he said and started to transmit on the SOE emergency frequency.

Heini Baum tried to light a cigarette but his hands shook so much he had to give up. 'My God!' he moaned. 'What a last act.'

Sorsa said cheerfully, 'Tell me, is the food good in British prisoner-of-war camps?'

Martineau smiled. 'Oh, I think you'll find we make very special arrangements for you, my friend.' And then, he made contact with SOE Headquarters.

At the control room at Jersey, Adler stood by the radio, an expression of disbelief on his face. He removed the earphones and turned slowly.

'What is it, for God's sake?' Necker demanded.

'That was Cherbourg Control. They've lost the JU88S.'

'What do you mean, lost it?'

'They had the pilot on radio. He'd attacked several times. They suddenly lost contact and he disappeared from the radar screen. They think he's gone into the drink.'

'I might have known,' Hofer said softly. 'A great pilot, Sorsa. An exceptional man. I should know. I chose him myself. And the mail plane?'

'Still on radar, moving up-Channel toward the English coast. No way on earth of stopping her.'

There was silence. A flurry of rain drifted against the window. Necker said, 'What happens now?'

'I'll leave in the Storch at dawn,' Hofer told him. 'The pilot of the mail plane can fly me. It's essential I get to Field Marshal Rommel as soon as possible.'

'And what then?' Necker asked. 'What happens when Berlin hears about this?'

'God knows, my friend.' Hofer smiled wearily. 'A bleak prospect — for all of us.'

About fifteen minutes after Sorsa had changed course for the second time, Martineau received a response to his message.

'Come in, Martineau.'

'Martineau here,' he answered.

'Your destination Hornley Field. Fly at five thousand feet and await further instructions. Escorts will assist. Should be with you in minutes.'

Martineau turned to Sorsa who had his headphones on. 'Did you get that?'

The Finn shook his head. 'I don't understand English.'

Martineau translated, then crouched down beside Baum. 'So far, so good.'

Baum sat up and pointed. 'Look out there.'

Martineau turned and saw, in the moonlight, a Spitfire take station to port. As he turned to check the starboard side, another appeared. He reached for the copilot's headphones.

A crisp voice said, 'Martineau, do you read me?'

'Martineau here.'

'You are now twenty miles east of the Isle of Wight. We're going to turn inland and descend to three thousand. I'll lead and my friend will bring up the rear. We'll shepherd you right in.'

'Our pleasure.' He translated quickly for Sorsa and sat back.

'Everything okay?' Baum asked.

'Fine. They're leading us in. Another fifteen minutes or so, that's all.'

Baum was excited. This time when he took a cigarette from his case his hand was steady. 'I really feel as if I'm breaking out of something.'

'I know,' Martineau said.

'Do you really? I wonder. I was at Stalingrad, did I tell you that? The greatest disaster in the history of the German Army. Three hundred thousand down the drain. The day before the airstrip closed I was wounded in the foot. I flew out in a good old JU52, just like this. Ninety-one thousand taken prisoner, twenty-four generals. Why them and not me?'

'I spent years trying to find answers to questions like that,' Martineau told him.

'And did you?'

'Not really. In the end, I decided there weren't any answers. Also no sense and precious little reason.'

He pulled down the earphones as the voice came over the air again, giving him new instructions and a fresh course. He passed them on to Sorsa. They descended steadily. A few minutes later, the voice sounded again. 'Hornley Field, right in front. In you go.'

The runway lights were plain to see, and this time Sorsa didn't need any translation. He reduced power and dropped his flaps to float in for a perfect landing. The escorting Spitfires peeled away to port and starboard and climbed into the night.

The Junkers started to slow, and Sorsa turned and taxied toward the control tower. He rolled to a halt, switched off the engines. Baum got up and laughed excitedly. 'We made it!'

Sarah was smiling. She reached for Martineau's hand and held on tight and Kelso, on the floor, was laughing out loud. The feeling of release was fantastic. Baum got the door open and he and Martineau peered outside.

A voice called over a bullhorn, 'Stay where you are.'

A line of airmen in RAF blue, each carrying a rifle, moved toward them. There were other people in the shadows behind them, but Martineau couldn't make out who.

Baum jumped down onto the runway. The voice called again, 'Stay where you are!'

Baum knotted the white scarf around his throat and grinned up at Harry, saluting him, touching the field marshal's baton to the rim of his cap. 'Will you join me, Standartenführer?' And then he turned and strode toward the line of men, the baton raised in his right hand. 'Put the rifles away, you idiots,' he called in English. 'All friends here.'

There was a single shot. He spun around, took a couple of steps back toward the Junkers, then sank on his knees and rolled over.

Harry ran forward, waving his arms. 'No more, you fools!' he shouted. 'It's me, Martineau.'

He was aware of the advancing line slowing and Squadron Leader Barnes was there, telling them to stay back. Martineau dropped to his knees. Baum reached up with his left hand and grabbed him by the front of the uniform.

'You were right, Harry,' he said hoarsely. 'No sense, no reason to anything.'

'Quiet, Heini. Don't talk. We'll get a doctor.'

Sarah was crouched beside him and Baum's grip tightened. 'Last act, Harry. Say kaddish for me. Promise.'

'I promise,' Martineau said.

Baum choked, there was blood on his mouth. His body seemed to shake and then the hand lost its grip on Martineau's tunic and he lay still. Martineau got up slowly and saw Dougal Munro and Jack Carter standing in front of the line of RAF men beside Barnes.

'An accident, Harry,' Munro said. 'One of the lads panicked.'

'An accident?' Martineau said. 'Is that what you call it? Sometimes I really wonder who the enemy is. If you're still interested, by the way, you'll find your American colonel in the plane.'

He went past them and through the line of airmen, walking aimlessly toward the old aero club buildings. Strange, but he had that pain in the chest again, and it hadn't bothered him once in Jersey. He sat down on the steps of the old clubhouse and lit a cigarette, suddenly cold. After a while, he became aware of Sarah sitting a few feet away.

'What did he mean, say kaddish for him?'

'It's a sort of mourning prayer. A Jewish thing. Usually relatives take care of it, but he didn't have any. All gone to the bloody ovens.' He took the half-smoked cigarette from his mouth and passed it to her. 'Anyway, now you know. Now your education's complete. No honor, no glory, only Heini Baum out there, lying on his back.'

He got to his feet and she stood up also. Someone had brought a stretcher and they were carrying Baum away, and Kelso was crossing the runway on his crutches, Munro and Carter on either side of him.

'Did I remember to tell you how well you did?' he asked.

'No.'

'You were good. So good that Dougal will probably try to use you again. Don't let him. Go back to that hospital of yours.'

'I don't think one should ever go back to anything.' They started to walk toward the waiting cars. 'And you?' she asked. 'What's going to happen to you?'

'I haven't the slightest idea.'

She took his arm and held on tight and as the runway lights were switched off, they moved on through the darkness together.

Jersey 1985

17

It was very quiet there in the library, Sarah Drayton standing at the window peering out. 'Dark soon. Sometimes I wonder whether the rain will ever stop. A bad winter this year.'

The door opened and the manservant, Vito, came in with a tray which he placed on a low table by the fire. 'Coffee, Contessa.'

'Thank you, Vito, I'll see to it.'

He went out and she sat down and reached for the coffeepot. 'And afterward?' I asked her.

'You mean what happened to everybody? Well, Konrad Hofer flew out in the Storch the following morning, got to Rommel and filled him in on what had happened.'

'And how did Rommel cover himself?'

'Very much as Harry had suggested. He flew to Rastenburg.'

'The Wolf's Lair?'

'That's right. He saw Hitler personally. Told him Intelligence sources had warned him of the possibility of plots against his life, which was why he'd used Berger to impersonate him. He stayed pretty much with the facts. If he'd gone to Jersey himself, Harry would have assassinated him. Berger was dismissed as a rat who'd deserted the sinking ship.'

'I'm sure he didn't put it to the Führer in quite those terms,' I said.

'Probably not. There was an official investigation. I read the Gestapo file on the case a few months after the war ended. They didn't come up with anything very much. They knew nothing about Hugh Kelso, remember, and what made the story so believable from Rommel's point of view was Harry himself.'

'I don't understand,' I said.

'Remember that Harry had gone to some pains to tell Hofer who he was, and that meant something concrete to the Gestapo. They had him on file, had been after him for a long time. Remember, they only just failed to get their hands on him after that business at Lyons when he shot Kaufmann.'

'So Rommel was believed?'

'Oh, I don't think Himmler was too happy, but the Führer seemed satisfied enough. They drew a veil over the whole thing. Hardly wanted it on the front page of national newspapers at that stage in the war. The same thing applied with our people, but for different reasons.'

'No publicity?'

'That's right.'

'In the circumstances,' I said, 'the accidental shot that killed Heini Baum was really rather convenient. He could have been a problem.'

'Too convenient,' Sarah said flatly. 'As Harry once said to me, Dougal Munro hated loose ends. Not that it gave anyone any problems. With D Day coming, Eisenhower was only too delighted to have got Kelso back in one piece, and our own Intelligence people didn't want to make things difficult for Rommel and the other generals who were plotting against Hitler.'

'And they almost succeeded,' I said.

'Yes, the bomb plot in July, later that year. Hitler was injured but survived.'

'And the conspirators?'

'Count von Stauffenberg and many others were executed, some of them in the most horrible of circumstances.'

'And Rommel?'

'Three days before the attempt on Hitler's life, Rommel's car was machine-gunned by low-flying Allied planes. He was terribly wounded. Although he was involved with the plot it kept him out of things in any practical sense.'

'But they caught up with him?'

'In time. Someone broke under Gestapo torture and implicated him. However, Hitler didn't want the scandal of having Germany's greatest war hero in the dock. He was given the chance of taking his own life on the promise that his family wouldn't be molested.'

I nodded. 'And what happened to Hofer?'

'He was killed in heavy fighting near Caen not long after D Day.'

'And Hugh Kelso?'

'He wasn't supposed to return to active duty. That leg never fully recovered, but they needed his engineering expertise for the Rhine crossings in March forty-five. He was killed in an explosion while supervising work on the damaged bridge at Remagen. A booby trap.'

I got up and walked to the window and stared out at the rain, thinking about it all. 'Amazing,' I said. 'And the most extraordinary thing is that it never came out, the whole story.'

'There was a special reason for that,' she said. 'The Jersey connection.

This island was liberated on the ninth of May, nineteen forty-five. The fortieth anniversary in a couple of months time. It's always been an important occasion here, Liberation Day.'

'I can imagine.'

'But after the war, it was a difficult time. Accusations and counteraccusations about those who were supposed to have consorted with the enemy. The Gestapo had actually hunted down some of the people who had sent them anonymous letters denouncing friends and neighbors. Those names were on file. Anyway, there was a government committee appointed to investigate.'

'And what did it find?'

'I don't know. It was put on hold with a special one-hundred-year security classification. You can't read that report until the year twenty forty-five.'

I went back and sat down again. 'What happened to Helen de Ville, Gallagher and Guido?'

'Nothing. They didn't come under any kind of suspicion. Guido was taken prisoner at the end of the war, but Dougal Munro secured his release almost at once. Helen's husband, Ralph, returned in bad shape. He'd been wounded in the desert campaign. He never really recovered and died three years after the war.'

'Did she and Gallagher marry?'

'No. It sounds silly, but I think they'd known each other too long. She died of lung cancer ten years ago. He followed her within a matter of months. He was eighty-three and still one hell of a man. I was with him at the end.'

'I was wondering,' I said, 'About de Ville Place and Septembertide. Would it be possible to take a look?'

'I'm not sure,' she said. 'Jersey has changed considerably since those war years. We're now one of the most important banking centers in the world. There's a great deal of money here and a considerable number of millionaires. One of them owns de Ville Place now, perhaps I could arrange something. I'm not certain.'

I'd been putting off the most important question, she knew that, of course. Would be expecting it. 'And you and Martineau? What happened there?'

'I was awarded the MBE, Military Division, the reason for the award unspecified, naturally. For some reason the Free French tossed in the Croix de Guerre.'

'And the Americans? Didn't they come up with anything?'

'Good God, no!' She laughed. 'From their point of view the whole episode had been far too uncomfortable. They preferred to forget it as quickly as possible. Dougal Munro gave me a job on the inside at Baker Street. I couldn't have said no even if I'd wanted to. He'd made me a serving officer in the WAAF, remember.'

'And Martineau?'

'His health deteriorated. That chest wound from the Lyons affair was always trouble, but he worked on the inside at Baker Street also. There was a lot on after D Day. We lived together. We had a flat within walking distance of the office at Jacobs Well Mansions.'

'Were you happy?'

'Oh, yes.' She nodded. 'The best few months of my life. I knew it couldn't last, mind you. He needed more, you see.'

'Action?'

'That's right. He needed it in the way some people need a drink, and in the end, it did for him. In January nineteen forty-five, certain German generals made contact with British Intelligence with a view to bringing the war to a speedier end. Dougal Munro concocted a scheme in which an Arado operated by the Enemy Aircraft Flight was flown to Germany by a volunteer pilot with Harry as passenger. As you know, the aircraft had German markings and they both wore Luftwaffe uniforms.'

'And they never got there?'

'Oh, but they did. Landed on the other side of the Rhine where he met the people concerned and flew back.'

'And disappeared?'

'There was a directive to Fighter Command to expect them. Apparently the message hadn't been forwarded to the pilots of one particular squadron. A blunder on the part of some clerk or other.'

'Dear God,' I said. 'How trivial the reasons for disaster can sometimes be.'

'Exactly.' She nodded. 'Records showed that an Arado was attacked by a Spitfire near Margate. Visibility was very bad that day, and the pilot lost contact with it in low clouds. It was assumed to have gone down in the sea. Now we know better.'

There was silence. She picked a couple of logs from the basket and put them on the fire. 'And you?' I said. 'How did you manage?'

'Well enough. I got a government grant to go to medical school. They were reasonably generous to ex-service personnel after the war. Once I was qualified I went to the old Cromwell for a year as a house physician. It seemed fitting somehow. For me, that's where it had all started.'

'And you never married.' It was a statement, not a question, and her answer surprised me, although I should have known, by then, if I'd had my wits about me.

'Good heavens, whatever gave you that idea? Guido visited London regularly. One thing he'd omitted to tell me was just how wealthy the Orsini family was. Each year I was at medical school he asked me to marry him. I always said no.'

'And he'd still come back and try again?'

'In between his other marriages. Three in all. I gave in at last on the strict understanding that I would still work as a doctor. The family estate was outside Florence. I was partner in a country practice there for years.'

'So you really are a Contessa?'

'I'm afraid so. Contessa Sarah Orsini. Guido died in a car crash three years ago. Can you imagine a man who still raced Ferraris at sixty-four years of age?'

'From what you've told me of him, I'd say it fits.'

'This house was my parents'. I'd always hung onto it so I decided to come back. As a doctor on an island like this it's easier to use my maiden name. The locals would find the other rather intimidating.'

'And you and Guido? Were you happy?'

'Why do you ask?'

'The fact that you came back here, I suppose, after so many years.'

'But this island is a strange place. It has that kind of effect. It pulls people back, sometimes after many years. I wasn't trying to find something I'd lost if that's what you mean. At least I don't think so.' She shook her head. 'I loved Guido dearly. I gave him a daughter and then a son, the present count, who rings me twice a week from Italy, begging me to return to Florence to live with him again.'

'I see.'

She stood up. 'Guido understood what he called the ghost in my machine. The fact of Harry that would not go away. Aunt Helen told me there was a difference between being in love and loving someone.'

'She also told you that Martineau wasn't for you.'

'She was right enough there. Whatever had gone wrong in Harry's psyche was more than I could cure.' She opened the desk drawer again, took out a yellowing piece of paper and unfolded it. 'This is the poem he threw away that first day at the cottage at Lulworth. The one I recovered.'

'May I see it?'

She passed it across and I read it quickly. *The station is ominous at midnight. Hope is a dead letter. Time to change trains for something better. No local train now, long since departed. No way of getting back to where you started.*

I felt inexpressibly saddened as I handed it back to her. 'He called it a rotten poem,' she said. 'But it says it all. *No way of getting back to where you started.* Maybe he was right after all. Perhaps he should have died at seventeen in that trench in Flanders.'

There didn't seem a great deal to say to that. I said, 'I've taken enough of your time. I think I'd better be getting back to my hotel.'

'You're staying at L'Horizon?'

'That's right.'

'They do you very well there,' she said. 'I'll run you down.'

'There's no need for that,' I protested. 'It isn't far.'

'That's all right. I want to take some flowers down to the grave anyway.'

It was raining heavily, darkness moving in from the horizon across the bay as we drove down the hill and parked outside the entrance to St. Brelade's Church. Sarah Drayton got out and put up her umbrella and I handed the flowers to her.

'I want to show you something,' she said. 'Over here.' She led the way to the older section of the cemetery and finally stopped before a moss-covered granite headstone. 'What do you think of that?'

It read: *Here lie the mortal remains of Captain Henry Martineau, late of the 5th Bengal Infantry, died July 7, 1859.*

'I only discovered it last year quite by chance. When I did, I got one of those ancestor-tracing agencies to check up for me. Captain Martineau retired here from the army in India. Apparently he died at the age of forty from the effects of some old wound or other. His wife and children moved to Lancashire and then emigrated to America.'

'How extraordinary.'

'When we visited this place he told me he had this strange feeling of being at home.'

As we walked back through the headstones I said, 'What happened to all those Germans who were buried here?'

'They were all moved after the war,' she said. 'Back to Germany, as far as I know.'

We reached the spot where he had been laid to rest earlier that afternoon. We stood there together, looking down at that fresh mound of earth. She laid the flowers on it and straightened and what she said then astonished me.

'Damn you, Harry Martineau,' she said softly. 'You did for yourself, but you did for me as well.'

There was no answer to that, could never be, and suddenly, I felt like an intruder. I turned and walked away and left her there in the rain in that ancient churchyard, alone with the past.